THE DARK SIDE OF DIXIE

D. R. BUCY

D1215908

THE DARK SIDE OF DIXIE

D. R. BUCY

Mockingbird Lane Press

The Dark Side of Dixie
Copyright © 2017 D. R. Bucy

Mockingbird Lane Press—Maynard, Arkansas

ISBN: 978-1-6353524-9-8

Library of Congress Control Number is in publication data

0 9 8 7 6 5 4 3 2 1

www.mockingbirdlanepress.com
Cover photo by: Jack Paschall
Graphic art cover: Jamie Johnson

This novel is dedicated to all my neighbors, the hard-working God-fearing people of the South.

First and foremost, I must thank my Lord and Savior for giving me the strength to stay the course and finish this novel. To my friend Pamba Hooten, a heartfelt *thank you,* for reading my work over and over and offering words of encouragement when I wanted to give up. I also must thank Donald Ivy for sharing his knowledge of correct "coon dog" lingo. And last, but not least, thank God for Google.

INTRODUCTION

The Bible says there's a time and season for every purpose under heaven. This is the way I think of my life growing up in the South, like the seasons of the year, each new phase important and necessary in order for me to grow and move on to the next one. Some people view the South as portrayed through the eyes of Margaret Mitchell, in what is in my opinion, one of the greatest novels ever written, *Gone with the Wind*. Perhaps the novel isn't totally realistic, but a beautiful story of a much simpler time when the hearts of men swelled with chivalry for their fair maidens pure and fragile as a Magnolia blossom in bloom. A time when family had meant everything and people willing to lay down their life for the land they loved. That time, if it ever did truly exist, is gone with the wind. Reality is rarely ever that beautiful or romantic, and along with it went the innocence of a people steeped in family traditions and a false sense of entitlement due to the color of their skin. The Civil War put an end to the atrocity of slavery, but what remained in its wake, was a dark side of Dixie many would like to forget. It heralded the beginning of reuniting the country, but for the people of the South, a precursor to years of devastating poverty, racism and illiteracy, and sparked the re-birth of something there all along, the making of "moonshine whiskey." The ancient art got its start in the mountains of Appalachia in the 1700s when the Scotch-Irish began pouring into America, the regions of Tennessee and

Kentucky, Virginia, and North Carolina well known for the practice. Making moonshine and being poor wasn't the only thing these mountain folks had in common. They despised anything to do with the federal government. A proud and a tough lot they never gave up or gave in, and when prohibition passed in 1919, these rugged mountaineers found, for once, they possessed something the rest of country wanted, alcohol. They dug in their heels and began making this illegal potion to sell for cash. They simply tried to survive the best way they knew how. I believe they may have drunk a lot of their product too. Alcohol is the most abused substance known to man and unfortunately, it seems to be passed down from one generation to the next. Not all the people involved in the illicit whiskey business were "good ol' boys" or poor farmers trying to provide for their families. Prohibition brought about a considerable increase in the price of alcohol, and anywhere lots of money was to be made, you're likely to get a large criminal element, and more often than not, that spells trouble.

Some people have said the South would never rise again, not after Lee surrendered that April day at the courthouse in Virginia. That's a matter of opinion also, and according to which side of the Mason-Dixon you reside. For the people who lived through it, and for those of us born into it, we cannot forget—nor should we, it's our heritage and in part, our legacy. We must change the things we can and learn from those things we cannot.

PROLOGUE

My story begins on a hot August day in 1941 in the upstairs bedroom of the family home. I would be the third generation of Carson's to be born in this house and the sixth to be born on this land in the Tennessee River Valley. My great-great-great paternal grandfather, Josiah Carson, came through the Cumberland Gap with his family when eleven years old. They traveled from North Carolina in a covered wagon and at times these early frontiersmen had to move their families and goods by flatboat and keelboats along the treacherous river. Up until the early 1800's only the upper and lower Tennessee valleys were open for settlement, this due in part to numerous navigational hazards and the presence of powerful Indian nations in the area. When the settlers did come they looked for the cheap, unclaimed fertile land they heard about. My ancestors and a few other families chose to stop in a spot where the river bends. They called their little settlement, Johnson's Bend, after the man who led them to the beautiful valley. It became one of many such little towns that would eventually spring up along the course of the river.

The first small dwellings had been crude and quickly thrown together and built near the river, in the unwise belief, closer is better. When the heavy spring rains came the families had to flee from their little homes. The Tennessee, once known as the "River of the Cherokees," would overflow its banks and wash away everything in its path. There were no dams to control its waters and those of its many tributaries along the miles of shore line from Knoxville, Tennessee all the way to Paducah, Kentucky where it flowed into the Ohio. The little group relocated their tiny settlement on a high bluff well away from the unbridled waters of the fickle river, and my father's family chose a small clearing surrounded by a grove of tall cedars. Here they would construct their one room log cabin from local timber and stones hauled from the river bank. Several years later, my great-grandfather, William Thomas Carson, built a two story frame house on the site. I have often said it resembles a huge wooden bread box. The front porch runs the entire length of the house and it has two main entrances. One leads into a small foyer while the other into what is now the master bedroom. The upper story is similar, an open balcony across the front but with only one door. It opens into a narrow hallway that goes to the lower level stairs and to the large bedrooms on both sides and a smaller room in the back used for storage. The house later passed to my grandpa, Jackson Carson, and my grandma, Clette Beth. This is the house of my birth and the house where I grew up. The original little log cabin remains and sits behind the new house and was converted into a smokehouse for curing the fresh meat when the hogs were butchered in the winter. The roof and the floor have been repaired, but the walls hewed from large red oaks, remains solid. Only a little new chinking has been applied from time to time.

My father, William Carson, and my mother, Jean, were of the mindset I would be a boy. They chose the name, Billy Gene for me, a combination of their names as I would be a combination of them. When I arrived and obviously not a boy, they were so set on the name, they gave it to me anyway, only changing the spelling to the feminine gender, Billie Jean. On December 7, 1941, a mere five months after my birth, the Japanese bombed Pearl Harbor, and my father was called to active duty and sent to the Pacific Theater, and I would be nearly four years old before I saw him again. Perhaps due to our brief time together or maybe because his heart had been set on a boy, for whatever the reason, the natural child-parent bond never seemed to form. Even after my father returned, for years I felt a distance existed between us. Now I in no way want to give you the impression he mistreated me, nothing could be further from the truth. We were more like casual acquaintances that happened to live under the same roof and eat at the same table, but never really got to know one another.

After my father left, my mother, only eighteen at the time, became sad and lonely. She began to go out on Friday and Saturday nights and leave me with my paternal grandparents. One Friday night she didn't come home. The following morning Grandpa Carson went into town and asked around for her. He asked everyone he could find, but no one would admit seeing her or knowing her whereabouts. He finally came across one of Mama's female acquaintances who had enough gumption to tell Grandpa the truth. Mama had run off with a married man. The fellow lived right down the road from us, and was a lot older than Mama, what with all the younger men off fighting in the war. He had left behind a wife and four little children, and her without any means to provide for them. A few weeks later my mama came back and wanted to take me with her, but my grandma told her: "It'll be over my dead body."

"She's my child ol' woman. You can't keep her from me!" Mama screamed.

"I'm not tryin' to keep her from you. You can see her any time you want. You're just not takin' her with you," Grandma calmly replied.

My mother left, threatening to come back with the law, but she never did. A few weeks later she and her lover were killed in a car crash outside of New Orleans. My poor grandparents who didn't have the heart to write and tell Daddy my mother had left, were now faced with the sad task of telling him she was dead.

They brought my mother's body back to the Valley along with her gentleman friend. By my father's request, my grandparents' made the funeral arrangements and paid for the burial. My mother's parents, Poppaw and Mamaw Chappell didn't have the money to bury Mama, so she was buried on the bluff behind our house in the Carson family cemetery. The man's wife claimed his body. A better woman than me. I would have let him rot in a ditch somewhere. I suppose she took into consideration the feelings of her children, he was their daddy after all. It was told she earned the money to pay for his burial by doing other folks washing and ironing and cleaning their houses. It took her several years of paying five dollars a month, but she paid every penny of the debt. Of course I learned all this second hand years later. Only a baby at the time I didn't have any idea of the pain and misery going on around me.

Poppaw and Mamaw Chappell never got over the shame of what Mama did—or the loss of her. Born in their later years they had adored Mama, and said I was so much like her, they often mistakenly called me by her name. I remained close to them throughout their life. They never tried to take me from my daddy, or more to the point, from my Grandma Carson. I believe if anyone had tried, Grandma would have fought them to the death. You have to understand, she was the one that walked the floor with me at night when I became colicky, and she was the one who sat by my bedside and nursed me through all the childhood illnesses, and she was the one to wipe away the tears when I fell and skinned my knee. In her mind, I belonged to her.

My father's older sister, Grace, one of the most wonderful and caring people I've ever known, lived with my Uncle Ted and my cousins, Ruth and Boase, yes, just like in the Bible, in the next town over from Johnson's Bend. Folks would refer to it as "Big Town," as opposed to Johnson's Bend, which is a small town. Going into Big Town, we would say. If my Aunt Grace was ever jealous of all the time and attention Grandma lavished on me, she never let it be known. In later years I would worry I took more than my share of Grandma's love. Troubled at the thought Ruth and Bo might have been pushed to the side, I asked Ruth about this.

"Mama always told us Grandma loves us just as much as she loves you," Ruth said, "but that you needed her more 'cause you didn't have a Mama." Ruth was always so sweet and good. I never lacked for love in my life. Aunt Grace might have added this to her declaration, and seems her daddy doesn't know how to be a father either. Yet she never appeared to feel she thought my daddy lacked in any way in his fatherly duties.

My Grandma Carson, a woman of small stature, wore her thick brown hair in a braid wrapped around her head. I think she thought it made her look taller, but what Grandma lacked in height, she made up for in fire and grit. Born Clette Beth Wilson, the youngest of four girls, her daddy was a circuit gospel preacher and gone from home much of the time. Her mama pretty much raised Grandma and her sisters on her own. Great-Grandpa Wilson would say: "I couldn't have spread the 'Good News', if I hadn't had a 'Good Woman' at home." Grandma Clette met my grandpa, Jackson Thomas Carson, at a church social. He and a friend heard there would be singing and dinner on the ground. Grandpa did love to sing, and had a pretty fair voice, but the idea of all that free food was likely what appealed to him. I think Grandpa did fancy himself to be a ladies man, and rather a dashing figure. I've seen pictures of him in his younger days, tall and lanky with broad shoulders and a dark mustache. The story goes he complemented Grandma on her pecan pie.

"Miss Clette, I reckon that's the best pie I've ever et," he said, and the rest is history. I suppose there have been better pick-up lines, but it must have worked, for they were together for over seventy years.

Grandpa Jack wasn't a religious man, but he was a good man, and loved to laugh and cut-up. Grandma would say she could see the devil in his blue eyes, but I think she was only teasing. It's not that Grandpa didn't believe in God. The worshipping of Him inside of four walls on a regular basis is what he didn't cotton to. "Ever preacher I ever met," he would say, "was more concerned with how much I dropped in the collection plate than he ever was with my soul." This was his favorite excuse when Grandma got on to him for not going to church with her. Grandpa liked to take a drink once in a while, on holidays and special occasions. I never saw him drink, but I knew he had a bottle hidden behind the barn and would sneak out there every so often and take a nip. And I'm pretty sure Grandma had known it was there too. She said that's just one of those things a woman had to abide. "A man's goin' to take a drink ever now and then, that's just the way it is." Grandma never made a big deal of it, even though she was about as straight-laced as they came.

Grandpa got a kick out of getting Grandma riled, and usually managed this by making some distasteful or disparaging remark about the little church where she attended faithfully. Grandma vowed she was going to get down on her knees and beg the Lord not to strike Grandpa dead, and Grandpa would howl with laughter. I don't think Grandpa had anything against the church, or the people there, so long as they left him alone. What he enjoyed most was pulling Grandma's chain. Grandma was never able to save Grandpa's soul, but never stopped trying. I truly believe she took this as a personal failure, and the greatest disappointment of her life. I can say this because I, too, know what it's like to fail to save someone you love so dearly. It is anguish like none other and a bitter pill to swallow, when you realize, sometimes, love just isn't enough.

After the war Daddy returned to farming with Grandpa and we continued to live in the house with my grandparents. People said to look at Daddy you wouldn't know he had seen all that awful "fightin' and killin'." I knew it had affected him in ways people couldn't see.

Months after he came home, I would be awakened late at night by the sound of someone sobbing. When I opened my eyes, Daddy would be kneeling beside my bed, his head in his hands, crying. About him was a strong, pungent odor, sweet yet sour. Sometimes it made my nose burn. When older, I learned that smell—alcohol, and from those early childhood memories, I first began to associate this smell with tears and sadness.

In 1933 the Tennessee Valley Authority brought generated electricity to the Tennessee River Valley. Even by depression standards the area remained in sad shape. Most folks of the day were naturally suspicious of any government agency, and placed electricity in the same category as education, a luxury they could ill afford. Numerous families tried to survive on as little as a hundred dollars a year—much of the land farmed too hard for too long and the soil depleted. I guess for many it was only logical to turn to what they knew how to do well, make moonshine. Well known, if not documented, much of the money given back then for support of the local churches came from the sale of bootleg whiskey. I think it had been one of those "don't ask don't tell" policies. I suppose the question one must ask—does the end justify the means?

Hard times coupled with the fact some fifteen thousand families were displaced when the TVA built the dams and created a natural wildlife refuge, it was no wonder there was great resentment against the agency in many rural areas. My grandparents' believed the TVA had done wonderful things for the people of Tennessee, especially the farmers. Our house was among the first in our community to be hooked up to electricity, but then again, Johnson's Bend wasn't affected by the relocation.

For several years after acquiring electricity, we didn't have running water, indoor bathroom, or modern home appliances. I can remember when Grandma cooked on an old wood stove and would heat the water for my bath in a big black kettle. In the winter months, the large metal tub sat by the stove, and in the summer time, it was placed on the back porch. Even after Grandma got a new gas stove, which she promptly blew up trying to light and singed off her eyebrows and the front of her hair, and we were afraid we might never have another hot biscuit or homemade pie, bath time had remained special. This is when Grandma and I would have some of our best talks and she would share with me some of her great words of wisdom.

SPRING

Oh, give us pleasure in the flowers today:
And give us not to think so far away
As the uncertain harvest; keep us here
All simply in the springing of the year.

From, "A Prayer in Spring," by Robert Frost

CHAPTER 1

"Grandma, what's a Camel Light?" The night was hot and humid. A typical midsummer's evening in the great state of Tennessee. The wood door was opened in the hopes a cool breeze might find its way through. I sat on the back steps and watched for shooting stars while I waited for my bath water to heat. In the kitchen behind me it had suddenly become deathly quiet, and I glanced over my shoulder through the screen door at Grandma. She paused in the middle of taking the big iron pot of boiling water off the stove and now stared at me over the top of her glasses. This was never a good sign.

"Where in the name of all that's holy, did you hear that?"

From the living room I heard a snort of laughter. That's where Grandpa sat listening to the radio. "Henry Lee Evans," I replied. "He said we thought we were better than other folks and gonna be the only ones in heaven, 'cause we were Camel Lights."

"Well, you have to consider the source darlin'. Them little kids haven't had much of a chance, what with their daddy bein' the way he is and all. Lord knows their sweet mama has tried. She shor' led her ducks to poor water there."

I heard the stories that circulated in the community about Ol' Man Evans. He was the personification of the *Boogey Man* to me. Never mind the fact he was a real flesh and blood person, and the father of some of my closest playmates. It was said he was mean and worked his older boys like mules. If they didn't do to suit him, he would whip them with the plow lines. If their mama tried to intervene, he would then turn on her. It seemed the entire neighborhood knew of the situation, but no one ever tried to do anything to help. Child abuse and domestic violence were not household words back then. What a man did in his home with his family was his business, and not many folks would interfere. There was a time in small isolated areas like Johnson's Bend, where a man such as Mr. Evans might have gotten a late night visit from a group of concerned citizens. The other men in town would come together and have a serious heart-to-heart with a man like him. People in these backwoods places liked to handle their own affairs. They didn't take kindly to strangers snooping around.

"I would bet if I were a bettin' woman," Grandma said, "course I'm not, that Henry Lee hasn't been to church a half dozen times in his life. He's probably heard someone else say that, and thought he could insult you by callin' you a 'Campbellite', and there is no such thing. Only mean spirited people who don't know any better use that word. When you're older, I'll explain it to you."

Another one of those, 'when you're older things,' I thought. Sure would be a lot of stuff I would learn when I got older. I figured I might end up as smart as Grandma. "Anyways, Bobby Ray told him to shut up," I said. From the living-room, I heard the Carter Family singing *Beautiful Home* on the radio, but the music didn't drown out the sound of Grandpa's laughter.

Grandma poured the last pot of hot water into the tub. "Shuck them dirty clothes and get in. Mind you test it first with your big toe."

I peeled off my clothes and climbed into the tub and sat down. "Here, lean back and let me wash your hair, then you can do the rest," Grandma said. "Where'd you get all this sand and mud in your hair? You been in that creek again?"

"Yes ma'am."

"You're gonna get snake bit child if you don't stay outta there."

"Yes ma'am. Grandma, what's it like to have a baby?"

Grandma stopped scrubbing my head. I looked up at her and she looked down at me over the top of her glasses. "Now what brought that on?" she asked.

"Henry Lee says havin' a baby is like a chicken shootin' an egg out its butt. That so?"

Grandpa continued to laugh loudly from the other room, and I wondered what was so funny on the radio. Grandma got off her knees and closed the door between the kitchen and the living room. I didn't understand why she did this. Grandpa never came in while I was taking a bath. He said I was a young lady now and it wouldn't be proper.

"It appears Henry Lee was an over-flowin' fount of information today," Grandma said dryly, and went back to washing my hair.

"Ow Grandma, too hard," I yelled.

"Sorry. You know, you may have to quit playin' with the Evans kids if Henry Lee can't keep all his worldly knowledge to himself."

"Yes ma'am. Well, is it?"

"Is it what?"

"Grandma!" I exclaimed in exasperation. "Is havin' a baby like a chicken shootin' an egg out its butt?"

Grandma thought for a moment. "I suppose there's a similarity of sorts, but you don't need to worry 'bout that now. When you're..."

"I know, I know, when I'm older." Down in the bottoms, a whippoorwill called. A few moments later from farther away, I heard another one. It seemed like a good time to change the subject.

"Grandma, why do the whippoorwills make that sound every night 'bout this time?" Finished with my hair, Grandma sat back in her chair to watch and make sure I washed everything else to her satisfaction.

"They're talkin' to one another," she said. "When they get home at night they like to sit on their tree branch and tell each other about their day. Like we set on the front porch and visit with neighbors sometimes."

I looked back at Grandma and thought she was only funning me, but she looked serious. "But they all sound alike," I replied.

"To us maybe, but not to the other whippoorwills." I guessed Grandma was right. She did know everything. Grandpa said so every day.

CHAPTER 2

By the late forties great strides made to improve the productivity of the land, and farming in Tennessee was on the up-swing. I can't remember a time when the rolling hills hadn't been lush and green, and the river, lying low, stretched out for miles and ran through the middle like a long flowing ribbon. But Daddy and my grandparents said they remembered very well when huge stretches of land lay brown and dead. By the time the TVA came along, fertile topsoil had all but disappeared from more than a million acres in the River Valley, the result of the three main cash crops grown in the region, cotton, corn and tobacco, draining the soil of its nutrients. The TVA realized Tennessee farmers wouldn't listen to anyone in a suit and tie, so they recruited leaders in rural communities and convinced them of the need to rotate their crops. They had to show these men the benefits of manufactured fertilizer and allowing the land to rest as grass and pastureland. Once they achieved this, other farmers in the area would follow their example. For the more reluctant to give up the old ways, the TVA helped set up thousands of demonstration farms across the state. My grandpa Jack, a very innovative thinker for his day and well respected in the farming arena became one of the leaders in our county. He said he could see the sense of it right off, and our farm became the perfect example of how this could work. We quickly saw the difference in the increased crop yields and the family's income.

At one time our farm grew all three of the big money crops, but after World War II, Daddy and Grandpa stopped growing cotton and stuck mainly to corn, tobacco, and soybeans. Daddy and Grandpa worked hard in the fields and Grandma took care of the house and for the most part, the yard. In the summer she would can the fresh garden vegetables and I would help. We were a happy and contented home. We didn't have a lot by some people's standards, but neither did anyone else in our little community. When I was small, Grandma made most of my pinafores from flour sacks. Back then the sacks were made of cloth and usually had some type of flowery design on them.

The farm kept Daddy and Grandpa busy and out of the house most of the day, normally only coming in at meal times. This left Grandma to entertain me and answer my endless stream of questions.

"Grandma, will there be cats and dogs in heaven?" I asked, sitting crossed-legged on the floor snapping green beans. A job I could do well. I only had to remember not to put the snapped off ends in with the beans Grandma would cook.

"I don't think so, honey. Animals don't have souls. Besides, they would poop all over the streets of gold. Mind where you're puttin' them ends."

"Well, I ain't goin' if Snowball and Ol' Blue can't go. Who would I play with all day?"

"You're not goin'," Grandma corrected. "Don't say ain't. And you won't think on them things in heaven. You'll just sit around and sing and be happy all the time."

"I won't be happy if there's no dogs and cats. And I'll get tired of just sittin' around singin' all the time." I was always dragging home every stray animal I could find. Grandpa said it got to the point he was afraid to crawl into bed at night, not knowing what might be in there with him.

"You'll understand it better when you're older."

"Another one of those when I'm older things," I mumbled, and shook my head.

"And I think there's probably a special place for dogs and cats," Grandma said.

"You mean like a cat and dog heaven?" I asked, and my eyes lit up.

"Kind of."

"Where is it? Is it up in the clouds too? How do you know 'bout it Grandma?"

"Well, I don't know exactly where it is—where you goin'? I ran from the kitchen to the table by Grandma's chair and grabbed her old Bible and ran back.

"Show me, Grandma. Show me where it's at in the Bible."

"Honey, it's not in the Bible. It's just somethin' people know."

"I thought you said everythin' a person needs to know is in the Bible. I want to know 'bout heaven for cats and dogs."

"Billie Jean, hon, why don't you run down to the barn and tell your daddy and grandpa dinner's ready." I looked at the antique grandfather clock that sat on the shelf on the wall. We never ate dinner until the big hand and little hand both pointed straight up.

"But it's not time," I said.

"That's okay, we're goin' to eat early today. Now you run along and tell them."

I grumbled to myself as I left the house, "How's a body to learn 'bout things like cat and dog heaven iffen it ain't in the Bible and Grandma don't know?" At the barn lot I found Grandpa bent over unhitching the mules, Jenny and Jack. I wrinkled my nose at the smell of fresh manure.

"Grandpa, when will Jenny and Jack have a baby?"

"Huh, they won't. Mules can't have babies' darlin'."

"Why?"

"They just can't, that's the way the Good Lord made 'em."

"Then how do you get baby mules?" Daddy walked up and seemed to be very interested in our conversation. I wondered if he didn't know where baby mules came from either.

"William, feel free to jump in here anytime," Grandpa said.

"Oh no, you're doin' just fine," Daddy said, a big grin on his face. "Besides, she asked you the question."

Grandpa looked flustered. "Well, you take a donkey and a mare and they get hitched and then have a baby mule."

"Oh." Why hadn't he said so in the first place? I reckoned Grandpa must be near as smart as Grandma. "Grandpa, do you know about dog and cat heaven?"

Before Grandpa could answer, Grandma yelled from the back steps, "Dinner's ready." It looked as though I would never get an answer to my question. I hung my head and drug my feet as I walked to the house. I thought about asking Daddy, but if he didn't know where baby mules came from, he probably didn't know about dog and cat heaven either. Although Daddy did read a lot and sat by the battery powered radio every night taking in every bit of the local and world news. After we settled at the table, Daddy said grace and then turned to me.

"You were wonderin' if there's a heaven for dogs and cats."

"Yes sir," I said. "Grandma says they can't go to people heaven 'cause they don't have souls. I'm real worried 'bout what's goin' to happen to Ol' Blue and Snowball when they die."

"When good dogs and cats, or any animal that's been loved by someone here on earth passes away, a part of that animal's spirit stays with that person. And the love they felt for one another remains forever in that person's heart. Ol' Blue and Snowball's bodies will give out, but the good times you've had with them will live forever in your memories, and that's heaven for animals."

I sat with my elbows propped on the table and my chin cupped in my hands and gazed at my father with admiration. I figured he was nigh as smart as Grandpa and Grandma put together, and I would bet he had known all along where baby mules came from.

Grandma dabbed at her eyes with her apron. "Take your elbows off the table, dear, and eat your dinner," she said.

After our noon meal Daddy and Grandpa went back to the field and I helped clear the table and wash the dishes. When not answering my numerous questions, Grandma taught me how to do many things around the house. She allowed me to dust the low places so she didn't have to bend over, and showed me how to handle with care the many antique glass bowls and vases she had sitting around, as well as the fine china cups and saucers and delicate figurines that once belonged to Grandma's mother and grandmother. She told me one day some of them would belong to me and Ruth and Bo. Grandma also taught me how to cook. She said any respectable Southern lady takes great pride in what comes out of her kitchen.

"It don't matter how pretty you are and how much he loves you, a man likes to eat," Grandma said. By the time I was ten years old, I could make a pan of biscuits and cornbread as well as any grown woman. Another dish I became very proficient at was mashed potatoes, and every time we made them, my pet cat, Snowball, would show up at the back door carrying on something awful until we opened the door and gave him a piece of raw potato. Darnedest thing you've ever seen.

I didn't spend all of my time in the house. In fact, most of it I spent outdoors. I had plenty of dolls and girl toys, but I was more of a tomboy. I preferred climbing trees and playing with the farm animals and the dogs. Besides Ol' Blue, Daddy and Grandpa usually had one or two more coon dogs that wandered around the yard getting fat and lazy, and part of this my fault.

"Billie Jean, quit feedin' them dogs," Grandpa said.

"Yes sir," I replied, and went back to feeding them whatever I was eating at the time. It only seemed natural to me the dogs would enjoy it too, but of course this was in addition to the feed they were already getting. And I loved to play dress-up with them.

"Billie Jean, didn't your Grandpa just tell you to quit feedin' them dogs?" Daddy said, trying to sound stern. "And get that baby bonnet off Ol' Blue's head. No self-respectin' coon dog worth his salt wants to be seen that way."

I knew Daddy wasn't really mad, I could see the grin twitching at the corners of his mouth. He said the dogs were not worth a durn to hunt anymore anyway, 'cause I petted them too much. Truth being, neither Daddy nor Grandpa were avid hunters like many of the men in the neighborhood.

Playing in the hayloft in the big barn was another one of my favorite things to do. We were never without a wealth of barn cats, in addition to my pet cat, Snowball, and usually one or more of them had a new litter. I loved the smell of the cuddly, newborn kittens, a mixture of their mother's milk and the sweet hay.

Ross Williams, the little boy from across the road was usually my partner in crime. We were best friends and nearly inseparable growing up. The Williams' were our closest neighbors and our houses literally faced one another. Ross's older sister died very young from complications related to polio. So basically he was an only child like me. We had that in common along with many other similarities. I could tell Ross things I wouldn't tell another living soul. I have wondered how many miles he must have pulled me in his little red wagon during those happy, carefree childhood years.

CHAPTER 3

Grandma Carson was not a woman who usually had a problem telling you what's on her mind. She labored in the Lord's vineyard under the misconception that she had the knack for helping people deal with their problems—those personal things they might be a little skittish talking to others about. She said with a little subtle encouragement most anything can be hashed out. Grandma was about as subtle as a red fox shut-up in a chicken house full of setting hens. Her version of encouragement—she gave you her opinion and expected you to act upon it accordingly. Where Daddy and I were concerned, she tried to approach the situation with a little more finesse.

"William, you still plannin' to take that load of corn to the mill this mornin'?" Grandma asked. The four of us sat at the kitchen table finishing our big country breakfast of fried sausage, eggs, milk gravy with biscuits, and fresh garden tomatoes and cantaloupe on the side.

"I was plannin' to. Why, you need me to do somethin' else?" Daddy replied.

"No. No. I just thought Billie Jean might enjoy ridin' along with you," Grandma said.

"To the mill?" Daddy looked skeptical. "I don't know. There'll be a bunch of rough talkin' men there." Grandpa and I looked back and forth between Daddy and Grandma. I hated it when they talked about me like I wasn't there.

"Well then, tell them to watch their mouth, your little girl is present." Grandma had an answer for everything.

Daddy looked at me. "Little Miss, do you want to go to mill with me? It's gonna be a scorcher today."

"Yes sir, I would." I tried to keep the excitement out of my voice. This would be the first time I went anywhere alone with my daddy.

"Okay, you get ready while I go hitch the mules to the wagon."

I was ready and waiting by the time Daddy pulled the wagon loaded with corn up to the back door. I wore my little straw hat, an exact replica of his and Grandpa's. My father climbed down and looked at me.

"You sure you want to do this, it's gonna be a rough, bumpy ride?"

"Yes sir, I'm sure."

Daddy lifted me up and placed me on the smooth wooden seat and climbed up beside me. The wagon groaned under its heavy burden as it labored over the ruts and holes in the gravel road. I could smell the sweat from the mules' and saw the fine sheen of lather on their flanks. Since I didn't have a lot of padding on my backside, the constant jarring and bouncing on the hard seat was nearly unbearable. It made my tailbone feel like it was being driven up my spine, but I would have died before I let on how badly it hurt. The wagon suddenly came to a stop, and I looked up questioningly at Daddy.

"C'mere," Daddy said, and held out his arms. I slid down from the seat and Daddy lifted me up onto his lap and tucked me under his arm. "That better?"

"Yes sir." When the wagon started again, I could hardly feel the bumps in the road. I felt so safe and secure sitting in Daddy's lap. Every once in a while I would glance up at him. He had a nice clean face with a strong jaw line and square chin. He'd shaved that morning, but I could still see the shadow of his beard. His was a kind face, but it gave nothing away in what the man behind it truly thought.

So many questions I wanted to ask Daddy that day. Like why he never talked about the war? I knew he had been stationed on islands in the South Pacific, the Philippines for one, and a few others I couldn't remember the names of. He brought back pictures, but I wasn't allowed to see them. He kept them in a shoe box on the highest shelf in his closet. The only story I ever heard him tell, was how he and the other GI's used to trade the island kids' bubble gum for fresh pineapples. I wanted to ask him about my mother. The only comments ever made about her—she was beautiful. I already knew that, I had several pictures of her. Daddy still had one of them taken on their wedding day sitting on the chest in his bedroom. There were many, many things, I wanted to ask and say to him, but I was just a little girl, and didn't know how to go about it, and Daddy was a man who definitely kept his own counsel.

The feed mill was located on the road into town and there was a hub of activity when we arrived. Daddy pulled the wagon onto a platform that dropped down in the back and this allowed the ears of corn to slide out. He then pulled the wagon to the side under the shade trees so the mules would be out of the hot sun. After this we went inside to wait for the corn to be ground into feed, and while we waited, a farmer I didn't known came up to us.

"You sure got a perty little helper there," he said to Daddy.

"Yep," Daddy said, and laid his hand on my shoulder. "She looks like her mama."

I enjoyed watching the process of the corn being turned into feed, but it was very dusty and loud inside the mill. My attention was soon drawn to the numerous calendars hanging on the walls, mostly of pretty ladies without many clothes on. Daddy noticed my interest in these, and asked why I didn't go outside in the fresh air. I knew this was more of a request than a question, so I did.

After we finished at the mill, we drove into Johnson's Bend to pick up weekly supplies from the store. Johnson's Bend wasn't a very big place, and only had one grocery store. The store also carried a fair amount of dry goods and a few hand tools. The proud owner and operator of this small rural establishment, Herbert Utley, was a fine Southern gentleman that would go out of his way to help anyone. If he knew you were in need of anything and short of money, he would try to get it for you. A payment plan could be worked out in a manner satisfactory to all. That's probably why there was always an abundance of the brown country eggs on hand, and salt pork, if you felt so inclined. In addition to the store, the little town featured a tiny post-office, a school, a couple of churches; a small funeral parlor that at one time was a dwelling house, and a doctor's office. Doctor Miller, a true country doctor would make house calls if necessary, but if anyone was really sick, they drove twenty miles down the road to the hospital in Big Town.

Inside the store was cool and quiet and Daddy bought me a Coca-Cola and a Baby Ruth candy bar.

"Don't tell your grandma I let you have this before your dinner," he grinned. Breakfast had been around six and it being close to noon, I was getting hungry.

"Okay," I said, between mouthfuls.

On the way home I sat on the bags of feed and finished my candy bar and my Coca-Cola. The hot midday sun blazed down on my little straw hat with a vengeance. The candy bar melted on my hands and chocolate smeared around my mouth, but I licked it off the best I could. I didn't want to waste a single morsel. At home Daddy pulled the wagon into the barn and tried to clean me up before I went inside. He dipped his handkerchief into the rain barrel kept out for the barn cats and the dogs. The wooden barrel was cut in half and it was likely at some time held whiskey.

"You be sure and wash your face and hands real good when you get in the house," Daddy told me. Not very hungry at dinner, I mostly pushed my food around on my plate.

"Why ain't you eaten', Billie Jean?" Grandma asked. "I hope you're not gettin' sick."

"Leave the child alone, Clette Beth," Grandpa said. "She'll eat when she's hungry."

"I'm just sayin', probably too hot for her ridin' in that wagon. I knew I shouldn't have let her go."

Daddy and Grandpa stopped eating and sat back in their chairs and stared at Grandma dumbfounded. It must have slipped her mind it her idea for me to go in the first place.

All at once my stomach began to feel funny. "May I be excused please?" I asked.

"But you haven't finished your dinner," Grandma complained. "It's your favorite, sugar, fried chicken."

Before I could stand up, undigested peanuts mixed with chocolate and Coca-Cola spewed from my mouth across the table.

"Oh my Lord," Grandma cried.

Daddy jumped up, but he wasn't quick enough. Grandma swooped down and grabbed me up and rushed to the back porch. That's where the well had been and the porch built around it, we still didn't have running water in the house. Grandma hurriedly dipped water from the wooden bucket and poured it into the porcelain wash basin that sat on the nearby washstand. She then cleaned the evidence of my morning's adventure from my face and hands and the front of my dress. With reluctance Grandma allowed Daddy to carry me upstairs to my room where he laid me on the bed. Grandpa, looking anxious, followed behind and hovered in the doorway. I don't imagine anyone had much of an appetite left.

"William, what did you feed this child?" Grandma asked.

"Just a candy bar and a soda, Mama." Poor Daddy looked stricken.

"You should have known better. Givin' her chocolate out in that hot sun," Grandma said, and clucked her tongue the way she did when unhappy with something or someone.

The whole time she scolded Daddy, she sponged me with a cool cloth, and it felt so good, but I didn't want her to be mad at Daddy. I thought to myself, I would do it all again, even the vomiting, if it meant being able to spend time with him.

"Clette Beth, it's just a sour stomach," Grandpa said. "William didn't mean the child no harm. Leave it be."

Grandma hadn't said any more, but you could feel the tension in the air. After the crisis appeared to be over, Daddy and Grandpa went back to work and Grandma sat with me until she thought I was asleep. She then tiptoed from the room, but I wasn't asleep.

After she left I allowed the hot tears I had fought back to slide down my cheeks. The tears weren't from the humiliation of being sick in front of everyone, but from being so afraid Daddy would never want to take me with him anywhere ever again.

CHAPTER 4

There no shortage of children for me to play with growing up. Besides Ross, the Evans family lived down the road and across the creek, eight of them to be exact. Cole and John Wesley were around Daddy's age. Margaret, Bennie and Lester came next about two years apart. After a lull of a few years, along came Henry Lee, Bobby Ray and Mary eighteen months apart. I guess Mr. Evans must have gotten his second wind. Mary and I were the same age and in the same grade in school and good friends. Bobby Ray was a year ahead of us, and Henry Lee a year ahead of him. Bobby Ray was nearly held back in third grade due to missing a lot of school. Supposedly he'd been sick, but he always looked as healthy as a horse to me; other than the bruises I noticed on him from time to time. Said he had gotten them rough housing with Henry Lee, at least that's the story he told. I remember Henry Lee coming to school once with an awful shiner, same story. He and Bobby Ray were scuffling and Henry Lee was accidentally hit in the eye by an elbow. When I was a kid, I believed this, but Grandma was right, when I got older, there would be a lot of things I would learn and question.

The Evans' family moved to Tennessee from eastern Kentucky looking for a better life. Cole and John Wesley were born in Kentucky and Cole got his name from the black, solid, combustible substance the Appalachia region became famous for. Their extended family remained in the mountains of eastern Kentucky and continued to work the coal mines.

Mary and Bobby Ray and I always got along really well together, but when we were kids, Henry Lee was a thorn in my flesh. I will never forget one afternoon Mary came to my house to play. She always came to mine because I wasn't permitted to go to hers. We didn't discuss the reason behind this and Mary never seemed to mind, but I'm sure she knew it had to do with her father. I think Mary enjoyed coming to my house and Grandma loved having her. She was well-mannered, polite, and smart as a whip. Grandma said she talked like a grown-up. When it came time for Mary to go home that day, I walked with her as far as the bridge. As we neared the creek we heard laughing and hollering and recognized the voices of Ross, Bobby Ray, and Henry Lee. Mary and I crept quietly up to the creek bank and peeked through the tall weeds.

The boys were skinny-dipping, and stood buck naked in water about knee high. Naturally the two of us couldn't keep from giggling. We might have been all of nine or ten. The boys heard us and stopped their fooling around and looked toward the tall grass where we were hiding, but they couldn't see us. Mary and I hunkered down, but they knew someone was there. Ross and Bobby Ray lit out for the creek bank for their clothes, but Henry Lee stood there grinning like a big doofus. I tried not to look, but the budding curiosity of early puberty repeatedly drew my young eyes to the dark patch between Henry Lee's legs. After he was sure we had a good look, he turned and sauntered over to his clothes. Mary didn't seem very impressed by any of this. I suppose when you have as many brothers as she did, you've seen it all already, but it was a whole lot more of Henry Lee than I ever expected to see, and to give the Devil his due, there was a lot of Henry Lee to see.

This wouldn't be the last encounter at the creek between the five of us. A couple of years later Mary and I waded in the creek, talking girl talk and daydreaming. We were just beginning to feel the first stirrings of the power of young womanhood. We spent the morning at my house practicing curling and teasing one another's hair. The finished products were sprayed so stiff it would have taken a good north wind to move a hair on either of our heads. Mary and I wore matching sundresses Grandma often made for us. We could wear a dab of makeup, but like most pre-teen girls, we had a tendency to get a little heavy-handed. Suddenly, from out of nowhere, three bodies cannonballed off the creek bank and landed in the water, drenching Mary and I from head to toe. Henry Lee, Ross, and Bobby Ray were the culprits.

"Look what you've done!" Mary and I yelled.

"What?" Henry Lee asked, and tried to look all innocent. "You're supposed to get wet. In case you forgot, it's a swimmin' hole."

"Not with your clothes on, you big dummy!" I said, and glared at the three of them. Ross and Bobby Ray didn't say a word, but both grinned from ear to ear.

"Well, take'em off then," Henry Lee said. "Y'all ain't got nothin' to hide anyway."

"Shut up, Henry Lee," Mary yelled at her brother.

"You've got a brassiere and panties on, don't ya? Ain't no different than one of them, 'bikinis'," Henry Lee came back with a smirk.

I glanced over at Bobby Ray, still with a grin on his face, and thought I saw a hint of hopeful anticipation in his eyes at the possibility I might strip down to my underclothes. Ross wouldn't look at me. I could tell he felt uncomfortable at Henry Lee's crude bantering. I looked back at Henry Lee.

"The day I take my clothes off in front of you, Henry Lee Evans, will be the day Hell freezes over," I said scathingly, and with as much dignity as we could muster, Mary and I turned and stomped off.

Our once coiffed hair-dos were now a drooped, wet, sticky mess. Our dab of makeup was streaked and smudged on our cheeks, and the tepid creek water took the starch out of our pretty little sundresses.

Behind us we heard Henry Lee laughing and yelling, "chicken, chicken," and making clucking sounds like an old hen.

I was so furious with Henry Lee at that moment, I truly believe I could have done him bodily harm, and I suspected there a circus somewhere missing a good clown.

From behind our retreating backs, Mary and I heard Ross and Bobby Ray yell, "Shut up, Henry Lee."

From that day on until we were grown, a verbal battle of words and will existed between me and Henry Lee. Everyone talked about how good-looking he and Bobby Ray were and how much they looked alike, but I couldn't see it. I'm sure it had something to do with the fact every time Henry Lee opened his mouth I wanted to smack him.

Actually, all the Evans kids were very nice looking, with dark wavy hair and dark eyes with thick lashes that curled up on the ends. Folks said they had gotten their good looks from their father. I couldn't say, at the time I had never seen the man close up. I thought Bobby Ray, "just plum perty", and truth be told, he and Henry Lee did look enough alike to have been twins, except Henry Lee was a little taller. But the funniest thing is, back then, I don't think Henry Lee ever realized I didn't like him.

CHAPTER 5

Daddy never said much about the way Grandma raised me. I guess he felt she did okay with him and Aunt Grace. The one thing he did insist on; that I made regular visits to my maternal grandparents. In the summer I would spend a week or two with them and I always looked forward to it. I'm pretty sure Grandma Carson hadn't been real keen on the idea, but this was one area where Daddy exerted his parental authority. My Poppaw and Mamaw Chappell were right out of the Louisiana bayous, dirt poor, "Coon-Ass Cajuns," and Catholic. To most folks in our small community that was as foreign as a Republican. My mother's family was direct descendants of the French-speaking Acadians that the English governor Charles Lawrence had expelled from Canada in 1755, and many of them relocated in southern Louisiana.

Poppaw and Mamaw spoke the true Cajun-French dialect, a mixture of French, German, Spanish, Native American and African American, and after moving to Tennessee, its version of the English language. It made for some real interesting conversations, but eventually I learned to understand them.

They lived in a little house back in the holler among the pin oaks and the cedars. The only thing that kept it from qualifying as a shack was the new front porch Daddy built for them. Poppaw and Mamaw didn't have electricity for years after everyone else did, but they didn't seem to mind. They would sit on their new front porch in their rocking chairs content as you please. When I was a child, it was never exactly clear to me how or why my grandparents had come to be in Tennessee. My Poppaw sure wasn't a farmer. All he knew how to do well was trap and fish, and had an uncanny knack for finding ginseng and other herbs. They tried to survive off of what little Poppaw made from selling the herbs, and the *poisson* (fish), they didn't eat, to the fish market on the river. Each time I went for a visit, Grandma Carson would send a ton of food with me. I think she was afraid I might go hungry, and I knew Daddy took food to them on occasion, Mamaw told me he did. At least she'd thought it was him. From time to time a box of groceries would appear mysteriously on their front porch.

Poppaw and Mamaw loved Daddy like one of their own. My uncles, Blanchard and Allain, several years my mother's senior, left Tennessee as soon as they were old enough. Uncle Blanchard traveled north to Chicago and took a job in a factory that made high quality bedroom furniture. I'm sure he sent money home to his parents when he could. Uncle Allain returned to Lafayette Parrish and ended up working on an oil rig out in the Gulf. I don't know if he could send my grandparents' any money or not, times remained hard in Louisiana, and he had a passel of young-uns. When Uncle Allain came home for a visit, he always brought fresh *d'écrevisses* (crawfish) and my favorite, *chevrette* (shrimp). Now that's some good eating.

My Poppaw Chappell was a *boire bougre* (drinking man), but I never remember a single time thinking him drunk. He was never mean and always had a smile, laughed and appeared happy. I didn't realize it then, but his mind was like that of a child. The doctors called it alcoholic dementia, brought on by a lifetime of heavy drinking, and it got worse as he grew older. What stayed in my mind the most from those early years, was how much he loved me. He called me his 'Tit Jean (Little Jean), because I looked so much like my mother. I knew I favored my mother, but in my estimation, I hadn't been nearly as beautiful. My grandparents had a hand-painted portrait of her that hung in their living room. She had the true coloring of her French-Cajun heritage, hair as dark as a raven's wing and her eyes that unusual shade of blue, like violets at dusk. Grandpa Carson likened my hair to the color of polished buckeyes, and my eyes are more of a gray-blue.

Through the years I heard many wild stories about my Cajun grandparents. My favorite was the one when they first came to Tennessee. Apparently Poppaw had made a little *shine* on the side, and buried the Mason jars under the watermelon and tomato vines in the garden. When the revenuer men came snooping around they couldn't find his stash, and when they left, Poppaw would give them a big ripe melon or a bag of fresh tomatoes and smile and wave and tell them to be sure and *vini encore* (come again). They had known Poppaw made shine and sold it, but they couldn't catch him with the proof.

It's probably a good thing I didn't live with my mama's parents all the time. If I did, I likely would have been so spoiled no one could have stood me. Poppaw thought anything I wanted, I should have. One incident in particular stands out in my mind. I came to spend a few days with them shortly after heavy rains fell in the area. The downpours occurred soon after the county dumped fresh gravel on many of the back roads and it was terribly muddy and nearly impassable in places.

"Tit Jean and me go to *boutique* for bon-bons," Poppaw told Mamaw. Two of the first Cajun words I learned, *bon-bons* and *le candi*. Any kid can figure those out.

"Claudell, you be careful with dat child, de roads very bad," Mamaw cautioned.

Mamaw never seemed to pay any attention to Poppaw's drinking except where I was concerned. She knew if anything happened to me on their watch, the "Wrath of God" would descend upon them in the form of five feet two inches Clette Beth Wilson Carson. After we were in the car, a beat-up old Studebaker with faded chipped paint and a hole in the floorboard, I got the idea I would like to drive. Bear in mind I was somewhere around eight or nine.

"Poppaw, can I drive?"

"You know how to drive de car?" Papaw asked with a big grin.

"I surely do. Daddy and Grandpa let me drive all the time," I assured him. It wasn't a complete untruth, Grandpa had been teaching me how to use the clutch and shift the gears in his old truck, and Daddy let me sit on his lap and steer the tractor all the time. Of course this happened only in the yard or the cow pasture.

"*Oui, 'tit jeunne,* I think you should drive," Papaw laughed.

I was able to get the car started, but I let off the clutch too fast and it died. On my second try I eased the clutch out slowly and gave it just enough gas to get us moving and we bucked and jumped onto the gravel road. I wasn't tall enough to see over the steering wheel, so I looked through it to see the windshield. All the while Poppaw's laughing and telling me what a fine job I was doing. Everything probably would have gone fine, if it hadn't been so muddy. The road grader had come down the road earlier that morning and pushed the new gravel to the sides. This created a barrier of sorts. If you have never been on a gravel road, you may not understand what happens when rock and sand and a little red clay gets wet. It sticks to your tires like super glue. Somehow I managed to get a little too close to the side of the road into the high gravel and it gave way. The car slid off the road into the ditch and the tires dropped down into the mud and refused to budge. Luckily the ditch was not very deep. Poppaw looked at me and I looked at him, and then he burst out laughing.

"*Maudit* (damned) car done slid in de ditch. Maybe we just leave it, somebody will bring it home later," Poppaw said. Not one word about it being my fault or maybe we should try and get it out. Poppaw and I exited the car on my side and left the keys in the ignition and walked to the store not far down the road. We purchased our candy and walked back home.

"Where de car, Claudell?" Mamaw asked.

Poppaw told her the truth, that we got stuck below the house. He left out the part where I was the one driving when it happened and he already told me maybe we should keep that between the two of us. I don't think Poppaw's mind was as bad all the time as people believed. About sundown, sure enough, two neighborhood men pulled the car in front of the house and Poppaw went out and thanked them. I think the folks in the community understood the situation.

Another thing I loved about visiting Poppaw and Mamaw was the music and the dancing. Mamaw would light the oil lamps and we would go out onto the porch and Poppaw would play the *le vioion* like you have never seen and Mamaw played the Cajun *l' accordéon*. They taught me all the songs and dances of the bayou people. Many times the neighbors would come and bring lawn chairs and sit out in the yard. Nearly every family had someone that could pick or play a musical instrument. When everyone came together this way, we would *laissez les bons temps rouler*, and that translates, let the good times roll.

These precious memories I carried with me for the rest of my life. Without Poppaw and Mamaw, I wouldn't have known anything about my mother's heritage and her upbringing. After each of these visits, I would feel the need to go to my mother's grave. I would stand and stare at the name carved into her headstone, Jean Marie Chappell Carson. I would wonder who this young woman had been that wore this name for such a short time and what would she have been like if she lived? Would she have liked me, and would we have been close? Most of all I wondered what made her leave her post as wife and mother and go off with a man old enough to be her father? I hoped someday to have the courage to talk to Daddy about her.

CHAPTER 6

In 1950, President Truman thought it high time to take a stand against communism, and he felt a little country in Northeast Asia called Korea, as good a place as any to start. When the war began on June 25, 1950, the Evans family had two boys of draft age, Bennie and Lester. The two older boys, Cole and John Wesley had fought in World War II same as my daddy. The local newspaper made a big to-do about one family having four sons to serve in their country's armed forces, and ran a full page story about the boys along with a picture of Mr. and Mrs. Evans sitting on their front porch. I'd been so glad it only showed the house from the front. In the back of this modest dwelling, sat numerous wrecked and rusted out cars, and behind the sad looking little outhouse, a broken down sofa lay at the edge of the woods.

One evening as my family and I sat at the supper table, a soft knock had come at the back door. Grandpa had gotten up to go and see who there. "Bobby Ray? Come on in—what's wrong, son?" I heard Grandpa ask.

"No thank you, sir. I was just wonderin' if I might speak to Billie Jean for a bit."

I took a swig of sweet tea and got up from the table and went to the door. Bobby Ray's eyes were red and puffy from crying. Grandpa later said he guessed his daddy had whipped him and he ran to our house. As I stepped out onto the porch, I heard Grandma say, "Tell him to come on in and have some supper." Her voice had faded away when Grandpa closed the door.

"What's wrong, Bobby Ray?"

"They killed him, Billie Jean. Those stinkin' commies killed Bennie," Bobby Ray said, and dropped to his knees as racking sobs took over his body. I knelt down beside him and cradled his head in my arms.

"I'm so, so sorry, Bobby Ray." I couldn't think of anything else to say. I had longed to be older and smarter, maybe then I would have known how to ease his pain. Bobby Ray cried a long time, and after he was all cried out, we sat down on the back steps between Grandma's pink azalea bushes. The sweet smell of honeysuckle lingered in the night air and the cicadas sang their song in the trees around us. Bobby Ray laid his head in my lap and I stroked his hair, much as a mother would soothe a sick child. I suppose the need to comfort and console is natural to most women, born into them, and it did seem to help.

Later we took Bobby Ray home and went inside to offer our condolences. This was my first time inside the Evans' house. Their furniture was well-worn and little of it, but the house was tidy and spotless, like the kids always were. When Bobby Ray, Mary and Henry Lee stepped onto the school bus of a morning, their hair was clean, shiny, and neatly combed and their clothes might be old and patched, especially the boys, probably hand-me-downs from the older ones, but they were clean and pressed. Grandma often said there's no shame in being poor, but that's no excuse for being dirty. When we first entered Mary sat on the couch with her mama and Henry Lee squatted in the corner by the door. He stood and spoke politely to me and Grandma. He then sat down again with his head down and didn't have much else to say. This was a side of Henry Lee I'd never seen before. Bobby Ray sat down beside him and Mary stood and gave me a hug.

"Thanks for comin'," Mary said.

"I'm so sorry about Bennie, Mary. He was always real nice to me."

"Bennie was nice to everybody. I'm sure goin' to miss him." Tears welled in Mary's eyes.

Daddy and Grandpa walked over to Mr. Evans and shook hands with him. I don't know what I expected; maybe for him to have two heads with horns, but certainly not this old wrinkled man with thick, steel gray hair and no teeth that sat before me. He looked harmless enough at the present. I then noticed his eyes, black and piercing, like they could see right through you, and I understood why people were afraid of him. There was something about the man that made you uneasy. Mr. Evans kept a lit cigarette in his hand at all times and waved it around while he talked, ashes flying where ever. On the small table beside him sat a pint fruit jar half full of a clear liquid, and it wasn't water. I could smell the alcohol from across the room—homemade shine. Not only had I seen the likes of it before, but I recognized that unmistakable odor. My Poppaw kept a jug of the brew under the cabinet at his house.

"They kilt my boy, Jackson." Harlan Evans' voice was coarse and raspy. "Them slant-eyed, commie bastards, kilt my boy." Hardly anyone other than Grandma called Grandpa by his given name. Folks usually referred to him as Jack or Mr. Carson.

"I know, Harlan, and I'm sure sorry," Grandpa said.

"Should've kilt 'em all in the last war, William, then we wouldn't had to gone a second time." Mr. Evans waved his cigarette toward Daddy and then erupted into a fit of coughing. He picked up the jar beside him and took a drink. I suppose it wasn't a good time to bring up political views, like the atom bomb and human rights.

I knew Mary was embarrassed and tried to pretend I didn't notice her dad was more than a little drunk. After all, nobody's at their best at a time like this. Grandma took Mary's place on the couch with Mrs. Evans and patted her hand.

"Minnie, I'm so sorry. Bennie was such a nice and polite young man—and such a good worker. It's just a cryin' shame."

"No mother should ever have to out live her children, Clette," Mrs. Evans said. "I don't know why the Lord couldn't have taken me and spared him."

Ms. Minnie Mae Evans was a frail thin woman with wispy gray hair and a voice so soft you had to strain your ears to hear her. She may have been a real pretty lady when younger, but now had what I referred to as the "beat-down-dog-look." She never completely raised her head and looked anyone square in the eye, and she didn't have any teeth either. I wondered if this was a family trait.

"I don't think that's for us to know, Minnie Mae. We'll understand it all better by and by," Grandma said softly.

"I shore 'preciate you bringin' Bobby Ray home. He run out of the house when we got the news and nobody could find him. I was startin' to worry when it got dark and he didn't come home."

We left a short time later. Only so much you can say at moments like this, when life has thrown you a curve you never saw coming. The next day Grandma prepared a huge box of food and Daddy and I took it to the Evans's house. A car with Kentucky plates sat in the yard. Some of their family came in during the night and the house was full of people. Daddy said he sure hoped the other neighbors brought food, they would need all they could get. I wondered where everybody would sleep, the house was so small. I then noticed an old army tent set up beside the house. Bobby Ray told me later that he and Henry Lee and some of their cousins slept in it.

As we left I glanced around the yard and saw Ms. Minnie's crape myrtles were about to bloom. Soon they would make a natural border of deep pink blossoms on each side of the house. In the back there was a pen with four or five coon dogs inside. All the Evans boys were big coon hunters, and it made me really sad to think Bennie would never hunt the hills and hollers again. He had been a crack shot with a rifle. I figured somebody must have snuck up behind Bennie when he wasn't looking. Mr. Evans followed us out of the house.

"William, you thank your maw for the food, we're much obliged." He walked bent to one side with a hand on his hip and gasped for every breath. He looked down at me with his piercing black eyes. "You've got a mighty perty girl there. Looks right smart like her mama did, don't she, best I recall?"

"Yep, she does indeed," Daddy said. As we backed out, Ross and his parents pulled in and he waved to me from the back seat.

The following morning the headlines in the local paper read: HOME TOWN BOY KILLED IN KOREA. It showed a picture of Bennie in his military uniform and the story of how he died.

> PFC. Benjamin Leroy Evans, A Company, 180th Infantry, 45th Division Regt., killed in battle at Baldy Ridge, Chowan, Korea, June 6, 1952.

The story told of how the hill earned its nickname "Baldy Ridge" after heavy artillery and mortar fire destroyed the trees on its crest.

It took a few days for Bennie's remains to arrive back in Tennessee. Lester, stationed elsewhere, was granted leave to come home for the funeral of his fallen brother. Daddy said he was thankful the military was able to bring Bennie home. That a lot of men killed and missing in action in World War II were never found. Probably would be the same in this war.

I had never been to a military funeral, but it was one of the saddest, yet in some ways, one of the most uplifting things I ever experienced. The family chose to have only a graveside service. The Evans males weren't much on church going. Ms. Minnie and the girls attended regularly at the tiny Primitive Baptist church in Johnson's Bend. They buried Bennie in a small secluded cemetery right below their house. It was located a short distance from the main road down a narrow dirt lane in a low wooded area. The cemetery didn't have a drive into it, so the cars and the hearse had to park on the side of the road. The dry pine needles made a silent spongy carpet for the large crowd of mourners that filed in. It looked as if the entire county had turned out for Bennie. Of course there several friends and relatives, and a few probably came out of curiosity, but many came out of respect for a local boy that had given his life in the service of his country.

After everyone settled down, the funeral director opened the back of the hearse and the military pallbearers slid Bennie's casket out. Immediately all military personnel, except the pallbearers, came to attention and saluted, and remained that way as Bennie's flag draped coffin, followed by the family, made its way to the gravesite. To the side of the grave stood three soldiers, one held a bugle, one the American flag, and the other the state flag of Tennessee. Lester stood at attention beside his brother's coffin with tears streaming down his face and made a striking figure in his full military dress.

Daddy stood beside me and leaned down and whispered in my ear, "The pallbearers are called the 'Honor Guard', and this is called to 'Present Arms'."

I'll always remember how quiet and peaceful it seemed. The only sound, the sharp, crisp, commands given by one of the soldiers. A military chaplain performed the service and said some really nice things about Bennie. After he finished, seven soldiers standing at the back of the cemetery fired their guns three times. Their shots pierced the stillness and echoed through the surrounding woods. I flinched at the sound of each one. After this the soldier with the bugle lifted it to his mouth and played.

Daddy leaned down once more and whispered in my ear, "This is called 'Taps'." I doubt there was a dry eye in that cemetery, except for Harlan Evans. I stood directly across from him and watched him throughout the proceedings. He sat like a man carved from stone and his black eyes stared into the distance—like he gazed into eternity.

After Taps the Honor Guard folded the American flag draped over Bennie's casket and handed it to the soldier in command. He walked to Bennie's parents and bent down in front of them and in a subdued voice said something I couldn't hear. He then presented the flag to Ms. Minnie. It absolutely broke your heart to see her sitting there with tears dripping down her face clutching that flag to her breast. I then saw something that made me take in a sharp breath, and Daddy glanced down at me. Mr. Evans reached over and patted his wife on the shoulder. Maybe he had a heart after all.

After the service was over, Mary, Bobby Ray and Henry Lee walked over to Ross and I. Ross and his family stood directly behind Daddy and me. Bobby Ray and Henry Lee wore black pants with white, short sleeved shirts and black ties. They were both fine looking young men, and yes, even Henry Lee. Mary wore a new white dress with pink eyelet trim and hand stitched pink roses across the front. She looked so pretty, and I thought she had a crush on Ross.

"Mary, you look so pretty," I said. "Doesn't she look pretty, Ross?"

"Oh, yeah. You look real pretty, Mary," Ross agreed, and looked embarrassed.

"Thank you." Mary replied, and blushed.

No matter what was thought about Harlan Evans, there no denying him and Ms. Minnie made beautiful babies. But I had other things on my mind, curious about something at the end of the funeral. "What did the man say when he bent down to give your mama and daddy the flag?" I asked the Evans' kids.

"I really couldn't hear him," Henry Lee said, and shook his head.

"Somethin' 'bout givin' them the flag 'cause they were proud of Bennie for fightin,'" Bobby Ray said.

"He said, 'this flag is presented on behalf of a grateful nation and the United States of America as a token of appreciation for your loved one's honorable and faithful service'." We stared at Mary in amazement.

"How can you remember all that?" I asked.

"I don't know. I can hear somethin' or read somethin', and it just sticks with me," Mary said, and made it sound like it was nothing. Mary was really smart in school and never had to study like I did.

As we left the cemetery I glanced back for one last look at Bennie's final resting place. I thought to myself, Bennie would like it here, among the trees surrounded by nature. Bobby Ray said of the four brothers to serve in the military, Bennie was the proudest to wear the uniform of his country. Korea was never officially declared a war, only a conflict. I don't understand the difference nor do I know who gets to make that determination, but I would bet to the families of the thirty-three thousand seven hundred and forty-one Americans killed between the years of 1950 and1953, it doesn't matter what it's called. Their loved ones are still gone, and no glorified title can ever change that.

CHAPTER 7

The fifties brought about many changes in my life, and for the most part, good changes. In fact, I think of these years as some of the happiest of my life, due in part to the booming post war economy. Farming in Tennessee entered into its heyday, and because of this Daddy and Grandpa were able to make great improvements to the family home. By the mid-fifties we had running water and an indoor bathroom, and that for me the greatest thing ever invented. No more having to go to the outhouse with the spiders and snakes. Grandma at last mastered the knack of lighting her new gas stove and didn't know how she ever lived without it. Our old hand cranked wooden telephone that hung on the wall, was replaced by a new black plastic rotary phone that sat on the oak table in the foyer. But in rural areas like ours, the party lines remained for several more years. This meant Mrs. Cooper could still listen in on everyone else's business. The old wooden phone continued to hang on the wall and eventually these relics from the past became hot commodities.

Daddy surprised us with a new twenty-one inch screen black and white TV he purchased for less than two hundred dollars. The color TV's were already out, but more expensive. As simple folks, we thought ourselves right up-town with our little black and white. To my grandparents' great delight, in 1951 their most favorite entertainer, Lawrence Welk, began broadcasting from the

Aragon Ballroom in Venice Beach, California. In 1955 one of our local TV stations picked up the program. They now could see the show where before they could only listen. They felt life couldn't get any better.

It's only natural for there to be a little bad mixed in with the good. Your only hope, the good outnumbered the bad. Somewhere around the early fifties I first remember hearing the name, "Preacher" that didn't have anything to do with a man of the cloth. Local gossip had it he was one of the biggest "bootleggers" on either side of the river, maybe in the entire state. Rumors circulated his operation was so large he did business in other states besides Tennessee.

The only reason his name stuck with me had to do with one of the older Evans boys. John Wesley had been incarcerated at that very time in Mississippi. He was caught red-handed transporting moonshine whiskey across state lines, supposedly for this guy called Preacher. John Wesley was a real nice fellow, and I could see where Henry Lee had gotten some of his foolishness, but he wasn't the sharpest tack in the box.

As the story goes, John Wesley stopped at a small roadside diner that had a big sign out front that read, "Best BBQ in Mississippi." It just so happened this was where all the local law enforcement liked to eat too. When the law pulled up and saw John Wesley's new Dodge Ram with the homemade camper on the back and Tennessee tags, they become suspicious. Nature of the job I guess. They went inside and asked who owned the truck and John Wesley raised his hand. They began to question him in regard to his business in their fair state. Apparently John Wesley couldn't improvise very well and come up with a plausible story they would buy, so they searched his truck. *Bingo!*

Perhaps a better lawyer might have gotten John Wesley off since there no real probable cause to search his truck. Cole and John Wesley's wife, Queenie, had gone to Mississippi and hired a local guy to represent him, and they went back for the trial hoping to bring him home, but John Wesley was found guilty. I guess if you have a Mississippi lawyer, a Mississippi judge, and a Mississippi jury, you're going to get Mississippi justice. They sentenced John Wesley to two years of hard labor on a farm in a little Mississippi town by the name of Parchman.

This was all the talk for months, but the man called Preacher remained invisible, like a ghost. No one could tell you with any certainty what he looked like or where lived. Small town rumor mill also had it that all the Evans' boys were well acquainted with him. I hoped that wasn't true. I remember hearing Daddy and Grandpa tell about young men being shot and killed for hauling moonshine. I believe a couple of them were from our own county. I asked Ross why a man who made illegal "Devil's Brew," (that's what Grandma called it) would go by the nickname of Preacher. It surely couldn't be his Christian name.

"It's said his shine is so good it will make you 'see the light'," Ross said, laughing and waving his arms over his head.

"Strike you blind would be more like it," I replied with more than a little sarcasm. How anybody could drink the mess I couldn't figure out, the smell alone made me sick. Mary told me while John Wesley was away Cole had taken care of his family. Cole was a very good person and well thought of in the community. He looked a lot like his daddy, but had a heart of gold, and helped several people in the area that were down on their luck. I'm sure being the oldest of the clan, he felt it his duty to see to his brother's family.

At the same time the gossip circulated about John Wesley and Preacher, Daddy created a little gossip of his own. He began courting a widow woman from Big Town that had a son about my age. This really didn't bother me. Like most kids, I was wrapped up in my own affairs—the big news at school or whatever scandal happen to be brewing in my new teen magazines. I didn't see any harm in Daddy having a lady friend if he wanted one, but Aunt Grace and Grandma were all in a titter over the new friendship.

"William, you ashamed of your family, or that woman you're seein'?" My grandma asked one Sunday morning out-of-the-blue while the four of us lingered at the breakfast table. It seemed this was where most of the best conversations from my childhood took place.

"No, I'm not. Why do you ask?" Daddy said. A grin tugged at the corners of his mouth.

"Well, you've been seein' this woman..."

"Her name is Dora," he said, and tried not to laugh outright in Grandma's face.

"You've been seein' Dora for over a month now, and you haven't brought her around once. I just thought you might be ashamed of us." Grandma tried to look innocent, but didn't fool anyone. She was a good Christian woman, but on occasion, she did love to meddle in other folk's business.

"It just so happens I was plannin' to bring her by this afternoon," Daddy said with a smug look on his face.

"This afternoon? William, why didn't you tell me? This house is a mess."

Grandma had immediately jumped up and began fussing and bustling around. Of course the house was fine. There'd never been a time you couldn't have eaten off of Grandma's floors. A faint scent of Pine-Sol and Linseed oil always lingered in the air. My grandpa had kept right on eating and drinking his coffee, like nothing out of the ordinary was taking place. He was accustomed by now to Grandma making a mountain out of every little mole hill and no longer got too excited about any of it.

Daddy then looked at me, "Billie Jean, I want you here this afternoon when I bring Dora and her son by. I want you to meet them."

"Sure. Okay, I don't have any plans that I can think of." I didn't mind meeting Daddy's lady friend and her son, and I couldn't figure out why everyone was acting so silly.

"Leave your Sunday dress on too. I want you to look real pretty."

Why did it matter what I looked like? I wondered. I wasn't courting her. Grandpa looked at me and raised his eyebrows and winked. Grinning like he knew something that I didn't and I wondered what that was all about.

My father had been back in church for some time before he began to see Dora. When he first returned from the war, it had taken him awhile to reconnect with the faith of his youth. I am so glad he didn't allow the whiskey to take over his life. The older I became, the more I realized and understood he had used the whiskey as a crutch to lean on. It became his companion to help him forget the war and mama. I think he could have very easily let it consume him and destroy everything he held dear. I hadn't forgotten those nights when he came into my room and sat by my bedside and cried. That was another one of those many things I had wanted to talk to him about someday, but it would be much later before I ever did.

On this Sunday morning when I strolled into church there had been nothing pressing on my mind, other than a little mild curiosity about the earlier conversation at the breakfast table. I did feel everyone knew something I didn't. I had no idea a year later, on a similar Sunday morning, I would make my public confession of faith.

I do remember thinking how long the aisle looked, and when I finally got the courage to step out and make my way toward the front, after only a few steps, I felt someone behind me. I glanced over my shoulder and Ross was there, and like so many other things we shared, from popsicles to the secrets of our soul, we would now make our professions of faith and be baptized together for the remission of our sins. As a rule we didn't shout in our church. You might hear an occasional, "amen," if the preacher got really fired up, but I'm pretty sure above the congregational singing I heard Grandma shout: "Halleluiah, praise the Lord." Later on that day Grandma would share with me probably some of her greatest words of wisdom.

"You'll never be perfect darlin', no one ever is. But if you keep strivin' for it, and keep your eyes on the cross, especially when you feel your faith startin' to waver, you'll be okay and you'll find the strength to stay the course and finish the race."

I know at the time I hadn't fully grasped the meaning of this advice, but I do remember that great feeling of exhilaration. When your faith is new you believe you can face any trial life throws at you. That's the way I felt that day, but this was the faith of youth. I had yet to be tested or, *tried by fire*, so to speak. The Bible says the Devil is our adversary, walking to and fro through the land seeking whom he may devour.

I would come to know he isn't always walking. Sometimes he's carried in bottles and cans and Mason jars, and there would come a time when my faith would not only waver, but all but disappear. I would lose sight of the cross and the prospect of staying the course and finishing the race, would be in grave doubt. But this waited for me years later down the road and in an entirely different season of my life. I suppose it is a good thing we can't see what lies ahead, for if we could, we would never make the journey.

After church that day Daddy dropped Grandma and me off at home and then drove into Big Town to have dinner with Dora and her son. Afterwards he brought them to our house for *the visit*. After my grandparents and I finished our dinner, we sat on the front porch and waited for our guests to arrive. I had contemplated how soon after the introduction before I could politely excuse myself and go change into my old jeans. I hated dresses and fidgeted around and pulled at the neck of my shirtwaist cotton garment, a navy blue with tiny, white polka dots. With this I had on white patent leather shoes and white anklets.

"Billie Jean, stop tuggin' on that dress before you tear it," Grandma said. She sat straight as a rod in her chair in her Sunday best, a stiff organdy floral print with little cap sleeves, and around her neck, a string of pearls. They had been a gift from my grandpa. Before Daddy arrived, Aunt Grace, Uncle Ted, Ruth, and Bo showed up. They too, wore their church clothes. My cousins looked as excited about this as me. Grandpa Jack, the most comfortable of us all in his best overalls with a white shirt. This was his concession to dressing up on Sunday. When Daddy's truck at last turned into our drive, I heaved a sigh of relief, more than ready to get this thing over with.

The woman and boy that exited the truck looked perfectly normal. From all the hoopla, I hadn't known what to expect. Dora, an attractive lady with brownish-blond hair and pale blue eyes, was a tad on the pudgy side. She looked to be somewhat older than Daddy, but I didn't claim to be the best judge of age. The boy, a good-looking enough kid with sandy blond hair and pale blue eyes, sported a baby face. We learned over time he didn't particularly care for that analogy. Daddy introduced them to the adults first, and then to my cousins, and then turned to me.

"Dora, Steve, this is my daughter, Billie Jean." Daddy pulled me close and placed his arm around my waist.

"How do you do, Billie Jean?" Dora said. She had a nice voice and gentle eyes. "It's so good to finally meet you—and you're even prettier than your daddy said."

This made me blush. "I'm fine, thank you, and it's nice to meet you too," I replied. If there was one thing Grandma had taught me, and she taught me many things, it's to have good manners.

"Hi," Steve said, and he seemed friendly too.

"Hi," I said in return.

"Well, now that everyone's acquainted, why don't we set down and visit," Grandma said. What she really meant was, so she and Aunt Grace could give Dora the third degree. "Billie Jean, why don't you kids show Steve around the farm?"

"Okay, sure," I said. "Then maybe he would like to go to the creek and see our swimmin' hole."

"Oh, I don't know about that," Dora spoke up. "Isn't there snakes and things in that water? Will, do you think that would be all right?"

Will? I bet no one had called Daddy that since he was a boy.

"I think so," Daddy answered. "They won't get in the water."

My cousins and I rolled our eyes at one another—a *mama's boy.*

"Mama, I'll be okay." Steve looked embarrassed.

First we took Steve to the barn. He loved the farm animals, especially the barn cats. Right off that made a lot of brownie points with me. Anyone who loved animals was okay in my book. "I've always wanted a cat or a dog," Steve said wistfully, "but we have always lived in town and never had a place to keep one. Mama won't let it stay in the house, she's afraid it might have germs."

I felt so sorry for Steve. I couldn't imagine never having a cat or dog. After the barn tour, we headed to the creek. Ross saw us and joined the group at the road and I introduced him to Steve. Ruth, Bo, and Steve had gone on ahead and I lagged behind with Ross.

"Well, what do you think?" Ross asked.

"About what?" I looked up at him completely unaware of the implications of his question.

"You're soon-to-be new step-mom and step-brother, of course, silly."

"What are you talkin' 'bout? I'm not gettin' a step anythin'."

"Billie Jean, when a man brings a woman home to meet his family that means he's goin' to ask her to marry him."

"And just how do you know that?"

"I guess I don't really, but that's what Mommy and Daddy said."

It hit me then. Oh, my gosh. How dense could I be? Of course, that's why Grandma and Aunt Grace were so anxious to meet Dora. They knew Daddy likely planned to ask her to marry him. How did I feel about this? I wasn't sure. I needed time to process it all.

At the swimming hole Steve removed his shoes and socks and rolled up his pants legs, wading into the water.

"You sure you should do that, Steve?" I asked.

"Oh, Mom worries too much," Steve said. "She's just afraid I'll die and leave her like my daddy did." Steve didn't seem a bit affected by this. Poor Dora, I thought, how awful to have to live everyday afraid you might lose everyone you loved the most.

The Evans family lived close enough that Henry Lee, Bobby Ray and Mary, heard us at the creek and came down.

"Hey, what y'all doin?" Henry Lee called.

I introduced them to Steve. He and Henry Lee hit it off right from the start, obvious they had a lot in common. They both loved to take chances and do the outrageous.

When Henry Lee pulled a pack of Lucky Strikes from his shirt pocket and passed it around, Steve had taken one. Henry Lee, nearly grown, could do pretty much what he liked. For the rest of us, still an innocent thrill, to think we'd snuck around doing the forbidden. Each of the guys accepted a cigarette, as did Mary, even though I knew she didn't like the taste. Actually, I did, but shook my head no when Henry Lee offered me one, and so did Ruth.

"Chicken," Henry Lee whispered under his breath, and made a clucking sound.

"Don't start with me, Henry Lee," I whispered back through clenched teeth. I knew if I smoked one, Grandma would smell it right off. She had a nose that could track a two day old scent better than any bloodhound.

Ross came back to the house with us to meet Dora. Out of the corner of my eye I saw Grandma sniffing the air. She shot me a look that I pretended not to see. Dora fussed over Steve and brushed imaginary dirt from his pants. She would have had a conniption fit if she saw his feet. Steve tried to wash the mud and sand off, but had given up and put his socks and shoes on anyway. From the first time we met, I felt sorry for Dora and Steve. It very evident Dora worshipped her only child and tried to please him in every way imaginable. But at the same time, she smothered him to the point when Steve was away from her, he went hog wild.

Steve never did anything mean or hurtful, but he took crazy chances. He did things knowing it would get him into trouble. But he wanted so badly for others to like him and to be accepted, to the point he could be a little obnoxious. There were times I was embarrassed for him. He always had to push the envelope just a little further.

CHAPTER 8

Ross's prediction was spot on. A few weeks after Daddy brought Dora and Steve to meet the family, he proposed, and Dora said yes. I was the first to hear the news. Daddy came to my room one evening and knocked lightly on my door, "May I talk to you in private for a minute?" he asked.

"Sure," I said, "come in." I suspected what was on his mind and had given the matter a lot of thought.

"What do you think about me and Dora gettin' married? Would you be real upset to get a new step-mother and step-brother all at the same time?"

"No, I wouldn't be upset at all, Daddy," I told him. "I think it's great. You deserve some happiness, and if Dora makes you happy, then you should do it."

"Dora's really taken with you, so is Steve. She's always wanted another child, a daughter perhaps, but things didn't work out that way. She was left a widow at a very young age. I can't see any reason why we couldn't be happy together as a family."

I could see it on his face and hear it in his voice— hope. I truly wanted this for him, but we all know the first bliss of new love rarely lasts long. The cold, hard, fact, where more than one person's feelings or opinions are involved, there's bound to be problems. Daddy didn't have long to wait for his first obstacle. It came even before the wedding.

When Daddy married my mother, both were very young, and lived in the house with my grandparents, planning to get a place of their own eventually. Then war came along, and you already know the rest of the story. Dora was no child and used to having her own home, and her own kitchen, refused to move in with my grandparents, and I didn't blame her. No house is big enough for two women, especially if one of them is my grandma. Dora said she and Daddy could live in her house in town and that she had plenty of room for me also. Only thing is, that would mean Daddy would have to drive back and forth from town to the farm every day. Daddy came up with the ideal solution—build a new house right there on the farm.

The small clearing on the far side of the apple orchard presented the perfect spot, and not all that far from our present house. At the beginning, it wasn't clear if Dora wanted to be this close to my grandparents', and I'm sure it wasn't my grandpa she was concerned about. Dora quickly figured out that Grandma could be a tiny bit on the controlling side, but Dora was a very good woman and truly loved my daddy and knew he needed to be close to his parents. Not only because of the farming, but because they were getting up in years. In the end she agreed to the little red brick house beside the apple orchard and was as proud of it as any eighteen room mansion.

When I first heard about the new house, it never dawned on me Daddy intended for me to live there with them. I had mixed emotions about this and I wasn't the only one. I don't think it had ever occurred to Grandma, if Daddy remarried, he might move out and expect me to go with him. Just how split the two of them were on the matter become quite clear one morning as I prepared to leave for school. I came downstairs and heard raised voices coming from the kitchen.

"I've been good enough to raise her all these years," Grandma said.

I heard the hurt in Grandma's voice, and I could tell she was on the verge of crying. This was not the pretend hurt she sometimes faked when not getting her way. No, this had the quality of the real thing.

"Mama, nobody's sayin' you haven't done a good job raisin' Billie Jean; me least of all. I don't know what I would have done without you and Daddy." My father pleaded with Grandma to try and see things from his point of view, but Grandma had a way of shutting out anything she didn't want to accept.

"I don't see why Billie Jean can't still live here just because you're gettin' married. This is the only home she's ever known," Grandma said, and I heard her sniff.

"Clette Beth! You've been after William for years to take the lead raisin' Billie Jean. Now that he's tryin' to, you gonna fight him tooth and nail?" I never heard Grandpa speak to Grandma in that tone of voice, and the first time I could remember him actually going up against her. I don't know who was more surprised, me or Grandma.

"I just don't understand why she can't still live here with us, Jackson," Grandma said and broke into a sob. I wanted to go in and comfort her, but they would know I was eavesdropping.

"Mama, please don't be like this. She'll only be across the yard from you. You'll still see her every day." Daddy begged for Grandma to give in, and I felt for him too.

"If you'd be honest with yourself, Clette, you never really wanted the boy to leave this house and take Billie Jean. More to the point, you don't want anyone to take your place in her life." Grandpa spoke the last words softly, and I heard a chair scrape across the floor as someone stood up from the table. The back door opened and closed.

From outside Ross hollered, "Billie Jean, bus," and I turned and hurried out the door. I would have loved to hear the rest of the conversation.

"I thought you weren't goin' to make it," Ross said, as I ran up right as the bus stopped in front of the house.

"I've got a problem, Ross, and I need to talk to you about it." I saw the Evans' kids sitting in the back of the bus and Bobby Ray motioned to me to sit with him.

"You can have my seat, Billie Jean," he called over the noise.

"That's okay, I'll just stand. Thanks anyway," I yelled back.

"I'm all ears, Miss Carson," Ross said, and grinned. "What's on your pretty mind?"

"Well, you know daddy's gettin' married and buildin' a new house on the other side of the apple orchard."

"Sure. Don't tell me you're havin' second thoughts about him gettin' married."

"No. It's nothin' like that. It's only Daddy's expectin' me to live with him and Dora, and Grandma's not takin' it very well."

"Oh, I bet she's not," Ross laughed. "Well, it's simple. Live with the both of them."

"What? How I'm supposed to do that?

"You stay with your daddy part of the time and with your grandparents' part of the time. Kids whose folks are divorced do it all the time, and besides, it's not like you can't stand on your grandparents' back steps and spit on your daddy's new house."

"Ross, you're a genius," I said, and reached up and laid my hand on his arm. Over his shoulder I saw Bobby Ray staring at me with a strange expression on his face. I couldn't put a name to it, but I guess a sardonic grin would come close. It made me feel like I'd been caught doing something I shouldn't. Bobby Ray continued to stare at me with his beautiful, dark eyes. A funny little quiver began in the pit of my stomach. His gaze never wavered from mine and I felt like I couldn't catch my breath, but I couldn't make myself look away.

"We're here," Ross said, and I tore my eyes away from Bobby Ray's, surprised to see we had pulled into the school parking lot. I had lost all track of time, and snuck one last look back at Bobby Ray before I turned to get off the bus. He had stood up, still staring at me, and there no mistaking the grin on his face this time, but it was different from the other. This grin reminded me of Henry Lee's when he tormented me. Surely Bobby Ray wasn't upset with me because I wouldn't sit with him. Boys!

I hadn't known it then, but matters were about to get much worse. Those life changing things called *hormones* kicked in full force. The easy comradery we shared as children would be no more and we were about to travel down a path that would change our lives forever. Things between us would never be the same again.

CHAPTER 9

Daddy and Dora married a few months before their new house was finished and stayed in Big Town in Dora's old house until then. I would go and spend the weekends with them. Dora and I got on real well together. Probably because I didn't have any preconceived notions about stepmothers. Surrogate mothers were all I'd ever known. After they moved into their new house I would stay at my grandparents' place the first part of the week and at Daddy's the latter part and through the weekend. This was due mainly to "Rock & Roll." I grew up on Hank Williams Sr., Kitty Wells, the Grand Ole Opry and the *Lawrence Welk Show*. But the music revolution that hit the world in the fifties was something else, and being led by a tall, lanky kid with long sideburns from right there in Tennessee, Elvis Presley. Grandma labeled it the devil's music and didn't want me to play it in the house. And she had better not catch me dancing. One Saturday afternoon while I'd been at my grandparents' house, Ross came over and we turned on *American Band Stand*. We were jumping and bumping around, trying to learn the new dance steps and accidentally knocked a picture off one of the small tables. It landed face down and shattered into a zillion tiny pieces and the small shards of glass skittered across Grandma's newly polished poplar wood floor. She had a fit. No more of that in her house, she said. This would be the catalyst for the second head butting session between her and Daddy in a span of a few months.

"Mama, they're just kids, and there's nothin' wrong with them playin' their music here in the house and dancin' around. It's not harmin' nobody."

"That music is trashy, I tell you, and I'm not goin' to have it in my house. Gyratin' around like a bunch of wild Indians."

"Didn't you and Daddy square dance in your younger days?" Daddy asked. "So what's so bad about these kids dancin' to their music?"

"It's not the same, William, and you know it." You could hear the finality in Grandma's voice. She had made up her mind and there no point in discussing it any further.

"That's fine," Daddy said. "Billie Jean and her friends can come to my house and have their little dance parties."

This was something Daddy could do for me and be on my side about that Grandma wouldn't be. I'm not saying it was entirely right to do Grandma that way. I knew Daddy wasn't all that crazy about rock and roll, although he did like Elvis, nor was he a big advocate of dance, but he was willing to pull out all the stops to make up for lost time. He desperately wanted me to feel at home in his house and to come to him with my problems, and I suspected we were likely in for numerous Sunday morning sermons on the perils of dancing.

This is why Daddy and Dora, and a few times, Ross's parents, began to host our get-togethers for the neighborhood kids on Friday nights. In the beginning the guests list consisted primarily of Bobby Ray and Mary, Ross, Steve, and usually Henry Lee who brought a date, never the same girl twice of course. Sometimes I would invite a few kids from school, and as the popularity of the small dance parties spread, the number of kids that showed up grew. Daddy said he didn't care how many came. For him it was well worth a few bags of chips and some soft drinks, and a worn spot in his grass, to see a bunch of kids having a great and safe time, and it meant so much to me for my daddy to be an active part of my life. If the weather permitted the parties were held in Daddy's backyard, but if it was cold or raining, we would shove the furniture in the family room against the wall and party inside. Ross's parents' had the best place. Their enclosed garage had a concrete floor, but they tended to lean more toward Grandma's way of thinking on the dancing. They tried to overcome their misgivings by rationalizing they would rather have Ross at home with his friends than parked on a dark back country road somewhere.

Henry Lee was a "dancin' fool," and he became our dance instructor. He had been around a whole lot more than the rest of us and knew all the latest steps. At the time Henry Lee drove an old green and white Ford that didn't have a reverse gear, and he had to be sure he aimed the car in the direction he wanted to leave before killing the motor, or at least have an area available wide enough to turn around in. I will never forget the first of our little parties Henry Lee came to. He brought Mary and Bobby Ray with him and he pulled into Daddy's drive, made a wide sweep through Daddy's new yard, and parked at the edge of the road facing back the way he had come.

"Henry Lee, when you gonna put a reverse in that thing?" Daddy asked.

"Aw, one of these days. It don't bother me none though. 'Course I got to lay off robbin' them convenience stores 'till I do," Henry Lee laughed.

Daddy and Dora stared at Henry Lee and I thought Ross would choke trying not to laugh. "Not that I would— rob a store," Henry Lee stammered.

Bobby Ray had that "dear in the head lights look" and kind of laughed a couple of times. "Huh. Huh," he said, and poor Mary looked mortified.

I knew Henry Lee was only kidding. Daddy burst out laughing. "Yeah, son, that would probably be a wise decision," and slapped Henry Lee good naturedly on the back. "Come on in, let's get this party started." Dora offered a weak grin, but I'm not sure she was fully convinced Henry Lee was only joking.

I led the way to the house, and from behind me I heard Bobby Ray exclaim under his breath, "Damn, Henry Lee!"

"What? They know I wasn't serious—don't they?"

"Henry Lee, maybe you shouldn't do a lot of talkin' tonight," Mary said.

God love him, no one could break the ice at a party better than Henry Lee, and when you had him and Steve together, they fed off of one another. They could keep the party going all by themselves and everyone laughing. I could tell Dora wasn't happy with the growing friendship, but I felt it harmless enough. For all my blustering I knew deep down Henry Lee wasn't a bad guy. I was still young and hadn't understood a lot of things, but I wasn't the only one to miss the warning signs where certain people were concerned.

A few guys from school came to the parties hoping to spend time with me, but soon realized that wouldn't happen. Ross and Bobby Ray pretty well monopolized most of my time. Everything was always a competition between them, and had been since they in diapers, and it now centered on me. Who would I dance with first and the most? Which one would I talk to the longest? But the competition didn't end there. Ross and Bobby Ray played basketball and each were very talented. You knew it would be a good show to see which one could outscore the other. I bet if they would admit to it, they even had contests to see which one could pee the furthest.

Ross played football as well, as defensive end and was quite good. So good in fact, he hoped to earn a free ride to college this way. Bobby Ray didn't play football, but was exceptional at baseball. In high school they were definitely a pair of jocks and had more girls after them than you could shake a stick at. Mary's crush on Ross had continued all through school, even though she denied it, and Ross chose to ignore it. Henry Lee on the other hand, hadn't tried to impress anyone. You could take him or leave him. It was all the same to Henry Lee. A natural at most sports and he sure didn't have to work at getting female company. I'm surprised he could keep all his women straight.

The heated rivalry between Ross and Bobby Ray intensified as we grew older, especially where I was concerned. Most of the guys that came to the parties to get close to me soon gave up and stopped coming, but not all of them.

"Henry Lee, don't hold me so tight, Daddy's watchin'." Henry Lee and I slow danced around the yard, and he did it so beautifully, and he smelled so good.

"I don't think its yore daddy you need to be worryin' 'bout." Henry Lee said, looking over my shoulder. I glanced back to see who he referring to. Ross and Bobby Ray stood on opposite sides of the yard, sulking with their arms crossed, staring at us.

"Which one do you think will cut in first? I'd put my money on little brother? Yep, here he comes."

"Henry Lee, let somebody else dance with Billie Jean. You've been hoggin' her all night," Bobby Ray whined.

"I'm just considerin' her feet little brother." Henry Lee handed me over to Bobby Ray.

"Well, go consider them somewhere else. You might try dancin' with your own date for a change." Bobby Ray turned his back on his brother.

Bobby Ray wasn't joking. Henry Lee had danced mainly with me. He brought a girl from his class at school named Susan. She seemed nice and I had seen her around, but we didn't hang out together.

"Ow!" I cried, before I could catch myself as Bobby Ray stepped on my foot.

"Sorry,"

"That's okay."

I liked dancing with Bobby Ray. He had gotten much better, as had Ross. I looked around and noticed Ross dancing with Mary. She looked so happy, but Ross reminded me of a thunder cloud about to erupt. He continued to glare at me and Bobby Ray. Now that I was close to Bobby Ray, I felt unsure of myself, but I didn't always feel that way around him. As kids we could talk and laugh and have a great time together. Then all of a sudden something changed. It was like we hardly knew one another. Bobby Ray smelled good, too. I think he and Henry Lee must have shared the same cologne. As we danced I could feel Bobby Ray's warm breath on my neck, and it sent shivers down my spine. The skin on the small of my back felt hot underneath his hand. By the end of the dance my face was flushed and my knees weak. Bobby Ray's dark eyes shone and he had that peculiar little grin on his face again. I think he knew exactly what kind of effect he had on me, and loved every minute of my discomfort.

CHAPTER 10

Henry Lee dropped out of high school between his junior and senior year. Now how dumb was that? Naturally I raked him over the coals about this. "Why in the world, Henry Lee, would you quit school with only one year to go?"

"I just got tired of goin'. Besides, I need to go to work. You know Daddy's down most of the time now with emphysema. He's on oxygen."

"No, I didn't. I'm sorry."

Henry Lee managed to land a good job at the grain elevators on the river. He had always been a really hard worker, as was all the Evans' kids, and before you knew it, he made foreman. Only Henry Lee could step in a cow pile and come out smelling like a rose.

"Can you believe it," he said, "they gave me the keys to the place."

Around this same time, the gossip about Preacher started up again, that Henry Lee might be running shine for him. I hoped that wasn't true. I was afraid Bobby Ray would get the idea in his head to quit school as well, but he didn't. I think the main reason he stayed was his love of playing ball, and the bus ride home after the away games.

I was a cheerleader my four years of high school, *paper shakers*, they called us. On the way to the games we had to sit in the front of the bus and the players in the back. The return trip we could sit wherever we wanted. I guess the coach didn't want the boys to get too excited until they were on the court. This would become another competition for Ross and Bobby Ray, to see who could get to the bus first and sit beside me and maybe sneak a kiss. I invariably wound up sandwiched in between them.

"Williams, why don't you sit in that empty seat in the back?" Bobby Ray got to the bus first, but that didn't deter Ross.

"Evans, why don't you sit in the empty seat in the back?" Ross shot back.

"If the two of you don't shut up, I'm goin' to sit in the empty seat in the back all by myself."

"Can I take you home, Billie Jean?" Bobby Ray had asked. It was his senior year and Ross couldn't wait for him to graduate and be out of his hair.

"She can ride home with me, Evans," Ross said. "I do live right across the road from her, remember?"

"Well, I'm goin' right past her house, remember?" Bobby Ray fired back. They were still going at it when we arrived at the school.

"I don't know why the two of you are arguin' 'bout this. You know Daddy will be waitin' for me." And he was, standing next to our car smoking a cigarette. He never missed a single game, home or away, but I couldn't understand why he insisted on coming to pick me up. He knew Ross and Bobby Ray had cars and were going my way. Daddy walked toward us when we excited the bus.

"You boys played a real fine game tonight," he said.

"Thank you sir," Ross and Bobby Ray replied.

I didn't see Dora and Steve in the car. Either Daddy already took them home, or they caught a ride with Ross's parents. Steve had been one of the team's managers until one of his hair-brained ideas backfired. He thought it would be funny to play a trick on the ballplayers. One afternoon after practice when the guys came out of the shower in their birthday suits they couldn't find any clean towels. Steve had hidden all of them. The boys hadn't seen the humor in this and Steve had been relieved of his duties.

"Bobby Ray, you got a ride home?" Daddy asked.

"Yes sir, I've got my car here," Bobby Ray replied, and Ross grunted.

Bobby Ray inherited Henry Lee's old Ford, still without a reverse, but it ran like a blue blaze. I felt sorry for Bobby Ray and Henry Lee. Neither had much family support for their sporting events, or any school activities for that matter. Not that their family didn't care about them, it more the circumstances of the situation. After Henry Lee quit school he tried to come to some of the games, but worked mostly at night, especially in the fall and early winter. Mary came to most of the home games and occasionally rode with my family to the away ones. Mr. and Mrs. Evans had come a few times when Bobby Ray and Henry Lee entered high school.

Ms. Minnie would sit on the bleachers and talk with folks. You could tell she really enjoyed being there. Mr. Evans would stand in the doorway to the gym sucking air. I guess it reached the point where he hadn't been able to come and couldn't be left alone. From time to time we'd see the older Evans' siblings at the games, except for Margaret. She had already married and moved out of state. Bobby Ray said her husband had wanderlust, he always thought the grass would be greener someplace else. Cole came to the games more often than any of the others. John Wesley tried to keep a low profile after his release from the penitentiary. Lester couldn't stand to be in a large crowd after he returned from Korea, but we still had the impression the Evans' brood was a very close knit bunch. They were most protective of their mama, and I never heard them utter one bad word about their daddy.

"How's your daddy doin', Bobby Ray?" Daddy asked.

"Okay, I guess, if he don't blow the house up. He still wants to smoke." Bobby Ray gave a short laugh. "We tried hidin' his cigarettes and matches from him, but he raised so much cane, we gave 'em back. He takes his oxygen off and hobbles out to the porch and smokes, then comes back in and puts it back on."

"I know it must be a very hard time for all of you. If there's anythin' I can ever do, please don't hesitate to ask," Daddy said.

"Thank you, Sir."

"Well, we'll say goodnight then." Daddy turned and started for the car, and I knew this was my cue to follow.

Ross went to his car, but didn't leave, and wouldn't until Daddy and I did. There was no way he would have wanted Bobby Ray to have a second with me he didn't. I waved to Ross as he opened his car door and got in. I then turned and waved at Bobby Ray. I thought he looked a little hurt. It was obvious to anyone, mine and Ross's family were all for any relationship that might develop between the two of us. And Bobby Ray was no fool, he knew it too.

I'm glad I never had to make the decision which one to ride home with. I had feelings for the both of them, and I think Daddy realized this. Until I became old enough to date, Daddy took me to and from the games. When I reached the age to make my own choices, he let me, but I knew deep down in his heart who he wanted me to choose. This was very evident when Bobby Ray asked me to his Senior Prom.

"Billie Jean, don't you think Ross will get his feelin's hurt if you go with Bobby Ray to his prom?" Daddy asked.

"Why? Ross doesn't own me, Daddy."

"No, he doesn't, but he's always there when you want him. If you want to go to a picture show, he's ready to take you. You want to go into Big Town for ice cream, he's there. You can't just use him and then put him away until the next time you need him to do somethin'. It doesn't work that way, sweetheart."

"I know, but he does the asking most of the time. Sometimes he acts like I shouldn't go anywhere unless it's with him." And that was true. Ross wanted all of my free time.

"I want you home by eleven."

"Eleven? Daddy, its prom night."

"Eleven-thirty at the very latest—after that time of night, there's nothin' goin' on little girls like you need to be involved in."

I wasn't a little girl anymore, I was nearly seventeen. Well I would be that August, but I could see there no need to argue the point any further.

Aunt Grace and Grandma created a magnificent dress for me to wear. A dark coral pink satin and chiffon, tea-length, with only one strap over the shoulder, and Dora dyed my shoes the exact same shade to match. It took my cousin Ruth, with help from everyone else, the entire afternoon to put my mound of hair up in curls. She left a few loose strands to fall down my back in long chestnut waves. I looked pretty good if I do say so, and was not the only one of that opinion.

"Wow, double wow," Steve exclaimed, when I came down the stairs at my grandparents. I had gotten ready in my room there. It still felt more like home to me. "You'll knock Bobby Ray's socks off," he said.

"Just as long as his socks are all that comes off," Grandma remarked dryly.

"You look beautiful, darlin'," Grandpa said, and bent down and kissed me on my cheek.

Ruth and Dora stood back like two mother hens surveying their handiwork. Daddy placed his hands on my shoulders, "You look lovely, sweetheart, you'll be the prettiest girl there," he said softly, and kissed me on the forehead. "I love you. You do know that, don't you?" His eyes filled with tears and I wondered what he truly thought as he gazed down at me.

"I love you too, Daddy," I said, fighting back tears of my own.

"William, don't make her cry and ruin her makeup," Aunt Grace warned. She had been snapping pictures like crazy from the moment I appeared at the top of the stairs. And then Bobby Ray arrived.

"Wow, you look like a million bucks," he said, a big smile on his face.

Bobby Ray had on a white sports coat with a pale yellow shirt, a black tie, black dress pants, and on his lapel, a yellow baby rosebud boutonniere. He looked Hollywood gorgeous, and in his hand he held a small white box with a corsage of tiny, yellow baby rosebuds with a ribbon the exact same shade as my dress.

"How did you know?" I asked.

"I came by one day and your grandma gave me a scrape from your dress so the florist could match it." I was so touched that Bobby Ray would go to all that trouble. "I guess we'd better go. Mama wants us to run by so she can see us together, if that's okay with you."

"Sure, that's fine." This would be my second visit to Bobby Ray's. We said our goodbyes and went out the door, and I stopped dead in my tracks. Sitting in our driveway was a brand new shiny, black and red 1958 Mercury. "Whose car is that?" I asked.

"It's mine," Bobby Ray said, and beamed with pride.

"Yours?" I looked at Bobby Ray questioningly.

"Yeah, Cole gave it to me for graduation." I didn't believe Cole had that kind of money, but I didn't say so. "Well, I have to work in his tobacco fields this summer, but it's mine."

Bobby Ray opened my door for me and I slid in. It had that wonderful new car smell. As we drove off I glanced across the road. Ross stood in his front door and I waved, but I'm not sure he saw me. He immediately turned and disappeared from sight. At Bobby Ray's his mama and daddy, Mary, and Henry Lee waited anxiously. Ms. Minnie had gone on and on about my dress and how pretty I looked. She had a new set of teeth and her hair freshly cut and permed. It was amazing at the difference it made in her appearance. Mr. Evans lay on the couch, his oxygen in his nose. He smiled at me, still without any teeth, and said in short, gasping, breaths, "Lookin' at you is like seein' a ghost of your mama. She was a beautiful woman too." Harlan Evans had just said I was beautiful.

"You'll be the best-lookin' couple at the prom," Mary said.

"You do clean up real nice little brother," Henry Lee spoke up. He didn't seem as full of himself as normal. "And Billie Jean, you look—like Billie Jean, fine as always."

"Why thank you, Henry Lee. I take that as high praise comin' from you." He grinned and inclined his head in a mock bow, but he didn't make any further comment.

Mary took a few pictures with her old Brownie camera and we left. Bobby Ray had made reservations at a nice restaurant in Big Town for supper. In the South, supper is your evening meal and dinner what you had at noon. I did worry about Bobby Ray spending money on me he needed for other things, but it wouldn't be polite to mention this. At the restaurant we saw several other couples already seated, also on their way to prom. We spoke and waved, but Bobby Ray declined their invitations to sit with any of them. "For once I want you all to myself," he said.

We had a really nice meal and talked about Bobby Ray's plans now that he was finished with school. I knew he didn't plan on going to college. "I'll work for Cole this summer. He's got near twenty areas of tobacco and several acres of corn, but I hope real soon to get a little place of my own."

"You want to farm, Bobby Ray?"

"Yeah, I love farmin'. Workin' the land and bein' outside and bein' my own boss."

"Really."

"What are you goin' to do when you get out of school?"

"I don't know. It really bothers me that I don't have a plan by now. I guess I'll stay at Mr. Utley's store until somethin' better comes along." I'd worked at the local grocery store for the past couple of summers. Mr. Utley had recently invested in gas pumps that greatly improved his business.

"You not goin' to do the college thing?" Bobby Ray asked.

"I don't know. Daddy wants me to, but I don't really like school all that much, and my grades sure aren't the best. Ross would like for me to go wherever he does."

"I'm sure he would."

I hadn't meant to say that out loud. "Henry Lee seems to be doin' well," I said, to change the subject.

"Yeah, Henry Lee will do okay no matter what he does. He's just that type of person."

I heard the love in Bobby Ray's voice. It seemed everyone found Henry Lee to be a very capable and reliable person, except me. Perhaps I didn't know him as well as I thought I did.

At school we posed for more pictures before we went into the dance. These we had to pay for. I had money in my bag for mine, but Bobby Ray wouldn't hear of it.

"It's my prom and you're my date. I'll pay for our pictures." I started to protest, but thought better of it. We talked, laughed, danced, and drank punch. Some of which I'm fairly sure was spiked. We had a wonderful time and time seemed to fly by. For me there is no music like the music of the fifties, and before I knew it, we had to leave. The dance would continue until midnight, but Bobby Ray knew my curfew. He assured my daddy he would have me home safe and sound and when he was supposed to. We pulled in the driveway with fifteen minutes to spare.

"I had a wonderful time, Bobby Ray," I said to him.

"Me too, the best time of my life," he replied, and leaned over and kissed me. A brief and tender kiss much like the ones we'd shared on the bus. Without saying a word, Bobby Ray reached for me and I went willingly into his arms, crushing my corsage between us. There was nothing brief or tender about this one. Bobby Ray's mouth was eager and firm, forcing mine open with his tongue. The kiss deepened and I surrendered to him, kissing him back with all my might. His arms tightened around me and I didn't want him to ever let me go. Bobby Ray was the first to break the embrace and gently ease me away.

"You've got to go in now. I don't want your daddy to shoot me." Bobby Ray inclined his head in the direction of my daddy's house.

I glanced toward Daddy's front porch and saw the lit end of a cigarette glowing in the darkness there. Bobby Ray grinned, but I knew he was as much affected by our kiss as me. I caught the husky tremor in his voice, and my heart beat a mile a minute. Bobby Ray walked me to my grandparents' and I heard a door close over at Daddy's house.

Bobby Ray gave me a light peck on the lips, "I'll talk to you later," he said, and left. I waited until he drove away before I turned to go inside. As I went to close the door behind me, I happened to glance across the road to the Williams's house. The windows were dark and I couldn't see any movement, but somehow I knew Ross was there, watching.

CHAPTER 11

I didn't see much of Bobby Ray that summer. Mary said he worked a lot of long hours in Cole's acres and acres of tobacco. Ugly rumors circulated that Bobby Ray might be running shine for Preacher, and that's how he got his new car. I planned to ask Henry Lee about this the next time he came to get Steve. The two were thick as thieves and together most weekends, Henry Lee being Steve's ticket to popularity. In Steve's eyes Henry Lee embodied the word "cool," and if you were his friend, then you must be cool too. The male bonding of the pair wasn't totally to the liking of Dora or my father. In actual years, Henry Lee was only a little over two years older than Steve, but in worldly experience, there a vast age difference. I believe this was Steve's main attraction to Henry Lee. There was nothing wrong with Steve's looks, but he lacked in confidence, especially where girls were concerned. And if there one thing Henry Lee had plenty of it was confidence, especially with members of the opposite sex. Oh my gracious, the women did love Henry Lee.

One Friday evening I stood in the doorway of our bathroom and watched Steve comb Brylcreem through his short-cropped, sandy blond hair. "Goin' out with Henry Lee tonight?" I asked.

"Yeah, we're gonna double date."

"Oh really? Who you goin' with?"

"I forget her name. It's a blind date. I think Henry Lee said it was Dolly, Lolly, or maybe it was Candy, somethin' like that."

"Huh, aren't they always?"

"What?"

"Nothin'. Where y'all goin'?"

"To the 'Hide-A-Way'," Steve whispered. "They've got a live band there tonight."

"Steve, you're not old enough to get in that place," I whispered back. "Neither is Henry Lee for that matter." The place in question was a honky-tonk on the river.

"I know, but Henry Lee nearly is. He says he can get us in with no sweat."

"Steve, if Daddy and your mama catch you, there will be hell to pay, you know that?"

"They won't, unless you rat me out." Steve looked at me with puppy dog eyes.

"You know I wouldn't do that, but what if they raid the place, or what if the police are in the parkin' lot checkin' ID's when you come out?"

"Billie Jean, honey, you worry too much. You're never goin' to have any fun if you keep that up. You have to take *some* chances in life." I could hear those words coming straight out of Henry Lee Evans's mouth.

"Please be careful," I said, "you're my favorite stepbrother."

"I'm your only stepbrother," Steve laughed.

"Well, if I had another one, you'd still be my favorite." I turned to leave, planning to go to my room.

"Billie Jean?"

I looked back at Steve. "Why don't you come with us tonight? You know Henry Lee has the hots for you. He says he has ever since y'all were kids, but he's always thought you were sweet on Bobby Ray. He wouldn't want to undercut his little brother, you see."

For a moment I couldn't think of a reply, partly because of the mental image of me and Henry Lee together. That was never going to happen, and I didn't want to share my feelings about Bobby Ray with anyone, not even Steve. At that instant a knock came at the front door and I followed Steve into the living room. Daddy opened the door and Henry Lee strolled in, all spit and polished with a big smile on his face. Hmm, he smelled so good, and there was no getting around the fact Henry Lee was a fine looking dude. It was uncanny how much he and Bobby Ray did resemble, but there I felt the similarity stopped. For me they were completely different, and for some unknown reason, I had never been enamored by Henry Lee charms. He now looked at me with raised eyebrows and I realized I had been staring at him. I felt my face flush. Good Lord, I hoped Henry Lee hadn't misinterpreted my stare and thought I returned his feelings.

"Where you kids goin' tonight?" Daddy asked.

"Probably just out to get a burger and to the drive-in, sir." The lie rolled off of Henry Lee's tongue as smooth as water off a duck's back.

"Y'all be careful, and Steve, you need to be home by twelve." Dora came in from the kitchen and looked pointedly at her only child.

Steve started to protest, but stopped. "Yes ma'am," he said, and I followed him and Henry from the house.

"Steve, I need to talk to Henry Lee for a minute. In private, you mind?"

"Sure, okay. I'll wait in the car." Steve had a big grin on his face. I knew what he was thinking.

I turned to Henry Lee. "I need to ask you somethin'," I began.

"Yes, the answer is yes."

"You don't know what I'm goin' to ask you yet, silly."

"It's not that you're dyin' to go out with me tonight? I saw the way you were lookin' at me in there."

"Don't you already have a date, Henry Lee?"

"Yeah, but I've always wanted to have me one of them, 'threesomes'." Henry Lee laughed robustly.

I know I had turned fire engine red, because my face felt like it was on fire. I glared at Henry Lee and started to walk away, but he caught my arm.

"I'm sorry, Billie Jean, but you look so durn cute when you blush like that." Henry Lee wiped the tears from his eyes with the back of his hand, and I continued to glare at him.

"I don't know why I even talk to you, Henry Lee Evans."

"Really? I'm sorry, what did you want to ask me?" At that second Steve honked the horn. "Keep your shirt on man, I'll be right there," Henry Lee hollered at him.

"It's about Bobby Ray—I heard he might..." I hesitated. Henry Lee might not be the best one to ask about this.

"You heard what 'bout lil' brother?" Henry Lee asked.

"I heard he might be runnin' moonshine for that man called Preacher. Is it true?"

Henry Lee's expression went blank, like a light turned off in his face, and he stared at me. I thought he wasn't going to answer.

"The only thing Bobby Ray's been haulin', is his butt back and forth to the backer patch." Henry Lee's voice was hard and cold, another side of him I had never seen, and I realized there many layers to this boy-man that stood before me.

"I didn't mean to make you mad, Henry Lee. I'm just concerned about Bobby Ray."

"I'm not mad at you, sugar, I could never be mad at you." Henry Lee raised his hand and gently slid his knuckles down my cheek. The old teasing grin came back. "You're all into the church goin' thing and havin' faith, ain't you? Maybe you could try and spread some of it in Bobby Ray's direction."

"Don't you believe in God, Henry Lee?" I asked. Henry Lee shrugged his shoulders. You could have taken it as a yes or a no.

"I don't think he hangs around our neck of the woods very much." The coldness was back in Henry Lee's voice.

"Maybe you're not lookin' in the right places for him, Henry Lee. I can promise you, he's always there."

"Maybe—but I can promise you somethin'. Preacher ain't gonna let any kid Bobby Ray's age haul any moonshine. He's not stupid."

Steve set down on the horn again.

"Come on, Henry Lee, the girls will be waitin'," he yelled out the car window.

"Then let 'em wait, and don't blow that horn again," Henry Lee yelled back.

"Okay, okay." Steve ducked back into the car.

"Look, Billie Jean, a lot of stuff you hear about Preacher is pure bullshit. He's really a good guy. You don't need to fear him. He'd never harm you or anyone else."

I heard the admiration in Henry Lee's voice. "But he's a bootlegger, Henry Lee, and that is illegal, and you of all people should be leery of messin' around with him after what happened to John Wesley."

"Things ain't always as cut and dried as you think, sugar."

"I don't know what you mean."

"I mean, you've never gone to bed at night with your belly gnawin' at your ribs 'cause it's empty, and you've never had to put cardboard in your shoes to cover the holes to keep out the snow. Folks will do a lot of things they never thought they would when their back's against the wall and they've got hungry mouths to feed."

Taken aback by Henry Lee's forthright disclosure of his up-bringing, I didn't know how to respond so I changed the subject. "Please, don't let Steve get into any trouble tonight, Henry Lee. You know if Daddy and Dora find out, you're both in really hot water."

"Yeah, I know, but he's got his mind set on goin', and I figure he's better off goin' with me than with someone else. I'll take good care of him, I promise." Henry Lee turned to go. "Oh, by the way," he said over his shoulder, "did you know Bobby Ray's lookin' at a place on the far side of Johnson's Bend? He's tryin' to work somethin' out with the owner. Maybe sharecrop for a couple of years with the option to buy. It's not a bad place at all. The lil' house ain't much, but it could be fixed up real purty, and it's got fifty acres of good bottom land and a big tobacco base on the ridge behind it."

"No, I hadn't heard. I hope it works out for him."

Henry Lee walked to the car, got in and he and Steve drove off. Steve waved to me from the car's side window, and I said a little prayer that nothing bad would happen to them at the roadhouse that night. If something did, I would feel guilty I hadn't tried to stop them from going—not that I could have. When Henry Lee opened up to me, I probably saw the real person on the *inside* for the first time. It nearly broke my heart when he spoke of having to go to bed hungry and wear shoes with holes in the soles. I was completely sincere when I said those things about God being there, but Henry Lee was right, what did I really know about living by faith. I had never been hungry or worn shoes with holes in the soles, and if Henry Lee suffered these things, I knew Mary and Bobby Ray did as well.

I suppose I felt a little cheated and sorry for myself on occasions, because I didn't have my mother. But it occurred to me, even without her, I had been a very lucky person, surrounded by love my entire life and in many ways, sheltered. Perhaps the gossip over the years I heard in regards to the man called Preacher, had been blown way out of proportion. Sometimes people have way too much time on their hands to speculate on what their neighbors might or might not be doing. The Bible says an idle tongue is the Devil's workshop. The gossip might not have been spread with malicious intent, but an unbridled, wagging tongue, can cause lots of damage.

Ross came over later that evening and I continued to fret over Steve and Henry Lee. I felt very fortunate to have a friend like him I could talk to.

"Steve's eighteen, Billie Jean, neither you nor his mama can protect him forever," Ross said. "He's got to learn to stand on his own two feet sometime. Besides, Henry Lee will look out for him."

"So, you think Henry Lee's a responsible person?" I asked.

"Henry Lee's basically—an okay guy. Really, he doesn't drink all that much. He would like for people to think he does, it goes with that bad boy image he's worked so hard to build."

"Why? Why would Henry Lee want people to think badly of him?"

"Because, Billie Jean, Henry Lee figured out years ago, if people think you're a bad ass, they'll leave you alone. Bobby Ray's the one who likes to 'pop the tops' pretty regularly."

"How do you know so much about what Henry Lee and Bobby Ray are doin'? I didn't know you were spendin' so much time with them these days."

"I'm not, but I hear other guys talkin'."

Ross knew he had said too much. I'm not saying there wasn't any truth in his words, but I knew Ross wanted me to think the worst of Bobby Ray. Putting one another down in front of me became another game to them.

"Don't be mad," Ross pleaded. "I'm just sayin,' you don't have to worry so much about Steve bein' out with Henry Lee. He'll look out for him just like he looks out for Bobby Ray."

Had I been so wrong about Henry Lee all those years? I knew he and Bobby Ray were really tight, but I never thought of it as anything more than the closeness between brothers. Did Bobby Ray look up to Henry Lee as a father figure the way he did Cole? Ross and I sat in the glider on

Daddy's front porch and he reached over and turned my face up to his.

"Please don't be mad at me, Billie Jean," he said gently. "You know I can't stand it when you're mad at me." Ross lips sought mine and I allowed myself to respond. It wasn't that I didn't have feelings for Ross, I did, but something held me back from saying the words he most wanted to hear, that I loved him. There were several kids in our senior class already engaged and making wedding plans for after graduation. Marrying young was very common in the South even if you were planning on going to college. Of course for many kids in rural areas like ours, college was out of the question. Their families simply couldn't afford the high cost. Ross planned to go to the University of Tennessee in Knoxville, most likely on a football scholarship. He was highly intelligent and advanced for his age, and made amazing grades all through school.

Daddy and my grandparents hoped Ross could persuade me to go to college, and that someday we might become a serious couple. I didn't know for sure what I wanted. Until I did, I couldn't say those three little words. Ross was so good and kind and dependable, I didn't want to hurt him, and it's not there wasn't any physical attraction between us. Ross had also been blessed with the good-looks gene, tall and broad shouldered with white blond hair women pay a fortune for in salons, and the most compelling blue eyes. But after Bobby Ray and I shared that passionate kiss on his prom night, I'd been restless, like I was waiting for something. Ross's kisses deepened and my thoughts were drawn back to the present. He pulled me closer and held me tightly, his hand sliding from my waist to my breast.

"Ross, stop. Someone will see."

"Like who? It's dark out here."

"Grandma might."

"She can't see through the walls, Billie Jean."

"Are you sure 'bout that?"

Ross laughed. "If anyone could, I guess it would be her. Don't you like for me to touch you, Billie Jean?" he asked.

The sound of an approaching car interrupted my response. Our embrace was captured in the glare of the headlights as it drove slowly by. The occupant of the vehicle honked the horn and we jerked apart. I recognized the truck with the make-shift tin cover over the back for his coon dogs—Bobby Ray. He had traded in the old Ford for the truck. I guess he didn't want to go back and forth to work and carry his dogs in his new car.

Steve did make it home that night unscathed, but his carefree days of running around and doing nothing had about come to an end. Daddy and Dora came down real hard on him. Either get a summer job or work on the farm. Those were his choices, and in a way I felt sorry for Steve. He had been as undecided about his future as I was about mine. The only thing he knew for sure he wanted to do, was hang out with Henry Lee, but Henry Lee had a steady job and from all accounts he never missed a day of work. My poor daddy must have thought he had a fine pair on his hands. With a few months left before our graduation, I hoped for some divine revelation, but I didn't hold my breath waiting for it to appear.

CHAPTER 12

Ross and I officially drifted into going steady that summer before our senior year. Like that was any big surprise to anyone, we were together all the time anyway. I allowed myself to be drawn into this because I didn't know how to let Ross down gently and not disappoint my family, and it's not like either of us had ever really gone with anyone else. Unless the few times we dated in a group with kids from our church counts, but even then Ross stayed glued to my side or hung over my shoulder, and of course there had been my date with Bobby Ray on his prom night.

Steve and I put our heads together and decided on a course of action. We would enroll in the local junior college after high school. We didn't have a clue what we would major in, but felt a sense of relief that at least we had a solid plan in place. Steve was just glad to have Daddy and Dora off his back somewhat. He still had to find a summer job. And isn't it amazing how one thing can lead to another? Steve complained to his paternal grandparents' that he expected to get a job but didn't have a car. How would he get back and forth to work? Being very doting grandparents, the only grandchild of their only *deceased* child, they decided to give Steve an early graduation present, and presented him with a classic 1956 light blue and white two door Chevy Bel Air. Steve promptly decked the car out with a full set of chrome pipes. It was sharp. He could afford this after his grandparents' passed along some more very vital information. A trust fund had been set up for Steve after his father passed away. He couldn't touch the principle until he turned twenty-five, but he could draw the interest if he so chose. He already received a monthly check from the government off his daddy. Until Steve became eighteen, Dora managed the money for him and placed it in a savings account with the expressed wish he would use it for college.

Daddy and Dora were rather exasperated at this turn of events. This totally defeated the whole purpose of the lesson they were trying to teach Steve—responsibility. Now that he had a regular income, or control of it, Steve couldn't see why he needed to get a job. On this point, our parents had stood firm. Henry Lee helped Steve get on at the grain elevators where he worked, but Steve didn't make it through the first week. He wasn't cut out for hard manual labor, he was more of the suit and tie banker-type, and it so happened he managed to land a job of this sort. He handled money anyway. He went to work for an amusement company, and all he had to do was go to the establishments with juke boxes and pin-ball machines and empty the money boxes. What a great, easy job, even though legally Steve probably wasn't old enough to go into some of those places. I guess it might have been okay, as long as he didn't sample any of the products they sold, but that didn't turn out to be the case. With money to burn and a new set of wheels, any kid can be led astray, and Steve was no exception. After only a couple of weeks I smelled the alcohol on him. I must have inherited my sensitive nose from Grandma. He tried to hide it when he came home. Making a beeline to the bathroom to shower and brush his teeth and using mouthwash, but the smell remained. I felt it my sisterly duty to try and talk to him.

"When did you become a beer drinker?" I asked from the doorway of Steve's room. He lay stretched out across his bed and I walked over and sat down beside him.

"What makes you think I have?" he answered.

"Because I can smell it, Steve. And if I can, so can everyone else in the house."

"I only had one, Billie Jean. It was hot and it was my last stop. The guy offered me one on the house, so I took it. It's no big deal."

"It'll be a big deal if Daddy and Dora get a whiff of it. Look, I'm not tryin' to be your mama or anythin', but I couldn't stand it, Steve, if anythin' happened to you."

"Nothin's goin' to happen to me, and I don't care for it all that much, but I don't want my customers thinkin' I'm a baby—and you worry too much, little Sis." Steve sat up and mussed my hair and then hit me with his pillow. I grabbed the other pillow from the bed and it was on. I loved having a brother.

Steve became quite the man about town that summer. No one could ever accuse him of being selfish or stingy. He was generous to a fault with his money. He wanted so badly to be liked and accepted that he tried to buy friendship. It hurt my heart to see this. I know there were many that took advantage of him. It was nothing for Steve to take a car load of kids to the drive-in on a Friday or Saturday night and pay their way in and buy their snacks. He should have known there are two things in life money can't buy, love and friends, at least not the kind that will last. There is one thing I can say for Henry Lee, he never took advantage of Steve.

Ross and I had sometimes double-dated with Steve and Mary. I really wanted that relationship to go somewhere, for both their sakes, but they were never more than good friends. Mary's feelings for Ross, which she adamantly denied, had made it a little awkward at first, but still we managed to have some great times together. Steve tried to pay mine and Ross's way the first time we went out, but Ross let Steve know real quick he was no freeloader and could pay his own way. Ross's football mentality had surfaced off the field on occasion. He was never aggressive with me, but I'd bet when he hit you, you knew you'd been hit. I think Ross's biggest problem, he tended to be a little on the controlling side. Steve offered to pay out of the goodness of his heart, but Ross really took offence to this, and if Steve suggested we go to a fast food place, Ross thought Steve implied we needed to go someplace cheap because he couldn't afford a nicer one. I think some alpha male thing might have been involved here too, but Steve never let it get to him, and after the first few times, we let Ross decide where we went and where we ate. It was much easier that way.

One afternoon as I came from Ross's, Bobby Ray drove up. "Hey, how you doin'?" he called, and got out of the car, leaned against the fender and lit a cigarette. I walked over to him. Bobby Ray now wore his hair in the Elvis style, long sideburns with a pompadour in front. His wasn't as big and full as Elvis's, he had too much curl in his, but it looked as good on him as it did Elvis, maybe better.

"I'm doin' just fine, how you doin'?" I asked in return.

"Can't complain. Here, I wanted to give you these."
Bobby Ray held out a brown manila envelope to me. I
took it and peeked inside. Our pictures from his prom.

"Oh, thanks, I wondered if you ever got them."

"Say, where've you been keepin' yourself. I never see
you anymore?"

"I've been right here," I replied sweetly. "I see you
passin' every now and then," and gave him a knowing
grin. He knew I referred to the times he passed the house
with some little hot tail girl sitting next to him. At least
that's the way I thought of them. He always made sure to
blow the horn so I would see them.

"Just passin' time darlin', just passin' time." Bobby
Ray had that wicked little half grin on his face and if eyes
could smolder, his did. *Damn!* I thought. Why does he
always make me feel like I can't breathe?

"So, I hear you and Ross are all hot and heavy now?"

"We're datin', if that's what you mean."

"What I mean darlin,' is if I asked you out, would you
go?"

"I went out with you before, didn't I?"

"Yeah, that night's burned into my memory." I could
have told him it was burned into mine as well, especially
the kiss at the end. "I'm no fool, Billie Jean. I know which
way the wind blows around here." Bobby Ray nodded
toward Ross's house. If Bobby Ray asked me out right at
that moment, I'm not sure what I would have said. Even
though Ross and I were supposed to be going steady, it
would have been very hard to say no to Bobby Ray. And to
tell you the honest truth, I hadn't been sure that I wanted
too. Thank goodness Daddy came across the yard right
about then.

"How you been doin', Bobby Ray?" Daddy asked. "Haven't seen much of you this summer. I hear you're sharecroppin' for Mr. James Henley."

"Yes sir, I am. He's fixin' up the little house for me. It's gonna be real nice." Bobby Ray spoke to Daddy, but he looked at me.

"That's a fine lookin' car you've got there. You buy it new?" Daddy ran his hand down the side of Bobby Ray's car.

"Yes sir, still as cherry as the day she came off the line." Bobby Ray realized what he said and blushed.

"Well, it's a mighty pretty car. I've been lookin' for a good used car for Billie Jean, and if you hear of one, would you let me know?" My ears perked up. I hadn't known Daddy planned to get me a car. Cool, my own wheels.

"I sure will, sir" Bobby Ray said. "Well, guess I'd better get goin'. Billie Jean, you think about what I said and get back to me." He gave me another little half grin and got into his car and left in the direction of his parents' house.

Daddy looked at me, curious I'm certain, about what Bobby Ray meant. He didn't ask and I didn't volunteer any information. He started to say something when we heard a car approaching from the direction of town. We could tell it was moving at a high rate of speed from the sound of the gravel being slung and scattered in its path. I heard the singing of the pipes, a sound I knew so well. Steve. He needed to be slowing down for the sharp curve right below our house. For some reason every teenage boy in the area had to find out how fast they could take this curve. The ditch on the right side of the road had been cleaned out more by them than it ever was by the county. We heard the rocks thumping and popping off the bottom of the car as it sped down the road.

"Daddy, that's Steve. Why isn't he slowin' down? There's no way he can make the curve goin' that fast."

"What the hell is that boy tryin' to prove?" Daddy said.

We started for the road about the time Grandpa walked from around the side of the house. We had a glance of Steve's car, a blur of blue and white, when it came into view and quickly vanished from sight. We heard the gravel being swept aside as the car went into the curve going wide open. I don't believe Steve ever geared down or hit his brakes. The awful sound of metal pushed beyond its endurance and breaking glass came next, followed by the boom, boom, boom, as the car rolled over and over. By then Daddy and I were in a dead run down the road and my grandpa not far behind. I don't know if I'd been screaming, or if it was the sound of the horrific crash, but by the time we three reached the corner, Dora, Grandma, Ross, and his parents were there too. Steve took out the entire ditch on the right side of the road along with a large portion of the barbed-wire fence around Mr. Williams's cow pasture. He then came back across the road and hit the small embankment on the left side that caused the car to become air-borne. It then flipped over and tore through our fence and rolled into the field and came to rest upside down.

From this point my memory is a little muddled. It was absolute pandemonium, and Dora, already hysterical, screamed Steve's name over and over as we climbed through the weeds and across the downed fence to get to the car. Once there we had to get down on our hands and knees to look inside. Steve's body had been tossed to the passenger's side and lay in a crumpled heap, wedged against the dashboard. Face down, his head and shoulders were in the floorboard, his legs dangling at an awkward angle toward the crushed roof. He hadn't moved and didn't have on one of the new-fangled seatbelts that car manufactures now placed in the newer cars. The men tried to open the driver's side door, but it wouldn't budge. The only other possibility was to try to get Steve out through the passenger side door. The door was cracked a fraction already, but wasn't nearly enough and it wouldn't budge either. There wasn't any way to get him out through the mangled window on that side, there wasn't enough room. In fact there hadn't been a great deal of space left available to navigate in, not in the front seat area.

The smell of gasoline filled the air along with Dora's frantic calls. "Steve, honey, can you hear me? It's Mama?" But no sound came from the interior of the car.

"Help me! God, please, somebody help me!"

The screams didn't come from inside the car, but from the field behind us. Mrs. Williams and I ran across the road to the other downed fence. Sweet Jesus. There tangled in the barbed-wire lay Henry Lee. He was a bloody mess, and from the looks of him, severely injured. I hurried to him. Blood gushed from his mouth and nose and his black T-shirt was in shreds and soaked with blood. In the middle of his chest, an open wound oozed a bloody fluid-like mixture and made a gurgling sound with his every breath. Henry Lee's right arm hung loosely at his side and when he made an attempt to lift it, screamed in pain. His right leg also twisted at an unnatural angle, but he hadn't made an attempt to move it.

"Help me, Billie Jean! I don't want to die. Oh, God, I hurt! Go get Bobby Ray." Henry Lee was nearly out of his mind with pain.

"Try not to move, Henry Lee. I'm goin' to try to get you out of this wire."

I kept telling myself to stay calm but never had I been more scared in my life. Mrs. Williams ran back to her house and called an ambulance. When she returned she brought towels and blankets and a pair of wire cutters. "I'll cut, Billie Jean, if you can hold the wire away from his body," she said. Together we managed to get Henry Lee untangled from the wire, but getting it from underneath him was the tricky part. I remembered hearing you shouldn't move an injured person, and Henry Lee screamed every time we barely touched him, but we couldn't leave him that way. By the time we finished, mine and Mrs. Williams's hands were torn and bloody from the pointed barbs and Henry Lee's numerous cuts and abrasions. We covered Henry Lee with a blanket and laid a folded towel under his head. Mrs. Williams went back to the other side to see if she could help there. Dora continued to call to Steve, still trapped inside the silent car.

"Am I gonna die, Billie Jean? Oh, God, I hurt!" Henry Lee tried to sit up—he in so much pain he couldn't lay still.

"No, Henry Lee, 'course you're not gonna to die. The ambulance will be here real soon and we'll get you and Steve to the hospital and get you all fixed up."

Henry Lee had a death grip on my arm with his good hand, and I ran my fingers across his forehead in an effort to calm him, dabbing the blood from his face with a towel. I prayed the ambulance would arrive before it was too late. The gurgling in Henry Lee's chest had become more pronounced and his breathing more labored. I glanced over to the other field and saw Ross try to wiggle through the car window, but his frame was much too large. Daddy was now giving it a go. He lay down on his belly and squeezed his upper torso through the broken window— and hopefully it would be far enough that he could reach Steve.

"Is Steve okay?" Henry Lee asked. "How bad is he hurt?"

"I don't know," I whispered. "They haven't been able to get him out yet."

"Billie Jean, I need to tell you somethin'—in case I don't make it."

"Stop sayin' that, Henry Lee, you're goin' to make it." I hoped with all my heart this was true.

"I love you, Billie Jean." I watched the situation across the road and only half listened to Henry Lee. I saw Ross and Mr. Williams pull my daddy from the car. It looked as though he had Steve in his grasp. Henry Lee's words caught my attention and I focused back on him.

"I love you too, Henry Lee."

"No, you don't understand. I really love you, Billie Jean. I always have." Henry Lee was so short of breath he hardly could get the words out. "You don't have to say anythin'. I just wanted you to know before I die."

"You're not goin' to die, Henry Lee. You're not goin' to die." My voice broke.

Henry Lee leaned up on his good arm and looked me square in the face, his demeanor completely serious. He opened his mouth to say something when a blood-chilling scream rent the air. Startled, we jumped, and it made Henry Lee wince in pain. Across the road, Daddy and Ross had pulled Steve's lifeless form from the car.

Dora was down on the ground cradling Steve in her arms rocking him back and forth and wailing, "My baby, my baby." Steve's broken and bruised body lay limp in his mother's arms.

Daddy knelt down beside Dora and put his arms around her, trying to comfort her, but there is no comfort for a mother who has lost the fruit of her womb, a part of herself. Everyone else stood with their heads bowed feeling helpless. There's not a thing in the world you can do at a moment like that, but turn it over to God. Henry Lee fell back to the ground, didn't move, and I said another prayer for him. This one for Henry Lee's life to be spared—he wasn't prepared to leave this world. And I prayed for strength for Dora and for guidance for each of us to help her get through this.

Mrs. Williams came back to where I sat with Henry Lee. He had closed his eyes but he hadn't lost consciousness. Huge tears seeped from beneath his lids and rolled down his cheeks, and I cried with him. Mrs. Williams shook her head, but I already knew Steve was gone. I think I had known from the second I looked through the car window at his poor battered body.

In the distance sirens blasted and a short time later the lights of a police car followed by the ambulance popped up on the horizon. It seemed hours had passed from the time Daddy and I heard Steve come barreling down the road until help arrived, but likely it was no more than forty-five minutes to an hour. Dora's wails turned into a keening moan that echoed up and down the lonely country road and across the dry pastures. She continued to rock Steve in her arms. It took Daddy and Grandma to pry her loose when the ambulance got there. It hadn't taken the EMS crew very long to determine nothing could be done for Steve, and they quickly turned their attention to Henry Lee. They immediately placed oxygen on him and started an IV in his left arm. His obviously deformed right arm and right leg they placed in immobilizers along with a cervical collar around his neck. He then was strapped to a backboard and placed into the ambulance. The county didn't have but one unit to service our remote area at the time, so Steve's body had to be placed in with Henry Lee. I can't even imagine what the ride to the hospital must have been like for him, to have to lie there next to his dead friend.

CHAPTER 13

After the doctors examined Steve's body, the cause of death was determined the results of a broken neck. Most likely Steve had been killed instantly on impact the first time the car rolled over. His blood alcohol level tested a fraction above the limit considered to be legally drunk. There wasn't any alcohol found in Henry Lee's system. His being thrown from the passenger's side door as the car made the wide swing into the curve probably saved his life. He suffered a puncture wound to the chest that caused his lung to collapse. He had several broken ribs, his right shoulder was broken and dislocated and his right knee was also fractured.

The gossip started as soon as the news of the wreck got around. "Had to be that Evans's boy's fault, everyone knows he's no good." When the doctors gave the police the okay to talk to Henry Lee, he refused to say anything. He let them think whatever they wanted and offered not a word in his own defense. Kind of like Jesus had done. I heard the truth of the matter later on at the hospital from Bobby Ray.

"Henry Lee was on his way home from work and his old truck broke down. He was standing on the side of the road when Steve happened along and offered him a ride. He didn't realize until he was already in the car that Steve was three sheets to the wind. Henry Lee says Steve couldn't hold his liquor and it wouldn't have taken much to put him on his butt."

"Why didn't Henry Lee make Steve let him drive?" I asked.

"He tried to, Billie Jean. Steve wouldn't pull over. What was he supposed to do, try to trade places with him goin' ninety miles an hour down the road?"

"No, of course not."

"Henry Lee said he knew the second they topped the hill what Steve had in mind, and he knew there was no way they could make it. He had already braced himself. He doesn't remember the exact moment he was thrown from the car, it all happened too fast, but he does remember the sensation of flyin' through the air. Then the awful pain hit him and I guess he must have blacked out, cause he says the next thing he remembers is openin' his eyes and lookin' up at the sky and thinkin' it had never looked so clear and blue. He wondered for a minute if he was dead, then the pain hit him again and that's when he called out for help. The next thing he remembers is you kneeling at his side. An angel come to rescue him." Here Bobby Ray pulled me into his arms and lightly touched his lips to mine. "You're always havin' to rescue one of us, ain't you, baby?" he whispered against my lips.

Bobby Ray's words were so sweet and tender. I slid my arms around him and held him close to my heart, right where he'd always been. "I know there's nothin' Henry Lee could have done, but he needs to tell Daddy and Dora the truth of what really happened," I said softly into Bobby Ray's chest.

"What good would it do, baby? Do you really think it would make Ms. Dora feel any better about losin' Steve? Besides, Henry Lee said if people need somebody to blame, let 'em blame him. He's used to it."

I never mentioned Henry Lee's declaration of love for me.

I couldn't tell Dora the truth, but I would tell Daddy after things settled down. It wasn't right to let people think the accident was Henry Lee's fault. His only mistake had been the misfortune of getting in a car unknowingly with a drunken person, and it nearly cost him his life. The entire Evans' family came to Steve's visitation and many to the funeral, except for Henry Lee and his daddy. Mr. Evans was pretty much bedfast by then. You could feel the tension in the air and hear the whispers each time one of them came in, but poor Dora was so distraught I doubt she remembered who came and went. The visitors fell silent when Cole led Mrs. Minnie in.

Ms. Evans walked up to Dora and took her by the hand. "I know the pain of losin' a child, a son. There's no other grief like it on earth," she said barely above a whisper.

I wondered if she realized how close she had come to losing another one. Dora embraced Ms. Minnie, tears streaming from their eyes, and thanked her for coming. I knew it had come from Dora's heart.

Henry Lee remained in the hospital for weeks and was unable to work for several months. Thankfully Steve's car insurance paid his medical bills. He required several surgeries on his right knee over a period of time, which left him with a slight limp that made him extremely self-conscious. Of his numerous injuries, the ensuing limp would be the one that bothered Henry Lee the most.

When I felt the time was right, I told Daddy what transpired prior to the wreck. I knew, he in return, would tell Dora when he felt the time right. Eventually Dora did concede the wreck wasn't Henry Lee's fault, but she still wasn't sure whether Henry Lee had been a bad influence on Steve. I didn't think so, but I kept it to myself. I believe in his own way Henry Lee had tried to shield and protect Steve. He knew there'd be many that would take advantage of Steve's goodness and innocence. Steve had searched for something, I'm not sure what—perhaps for that one thing that helps define who we are and where our place is in the world. Life is all about choices, the good and the bad, and these choices direct the path our life will take. Steve made the choice to drink and drive, and as Ross said, neither Henry Lee or Dora or anyone else, could be with Steve twenty-four seven. We all have to live, or in Steve's case, die, with the choices we make. I made choices at this time I would have to live with. But at seventeen, how could I have possibly known the choices I made then, would so greatly affect the lives of others on down the road?

Dora never fully recovered from Steve's death. Oh, she went on with her life, what else could she do? All her days she was a faithful and loving wife to my father, and so good to me and mine. In their declining years, she had been wonderful to my grandparents', but she was never the same. The light that once shined in her eyes was gone, for the joy of her life had been taken from her.

Bobby Ray didn't come around a lot after the accident. He didn't know for sure how he would be received. Instead, he would come to see me at Mr. Utley's store. I continued to work there three afternoons a week after school and on most Saturdays. We prearranged a time for me to come and see Bobby Ray's new place. On the days I worked, I drove Grandpa's old truck, that way no one had to come and pick me up. After Steve's death, finding me a car wasn't on the top of Daddy's priorities list. If I needed to go into Big Town for anything, Dora would loan me her car. She had on the day before Henry Lee's release from the hospital. I went to see him several times, but some of his family was always present and I needed to talk to him alone, even though I kind of hoped Bobby Ray might be there. Henry Lee was by himself when I went in and this was probably for the best. We really did need to talk in private.

"Hey, Henry Lee, how you feelin'?" Someone had recently washed his hair and it looked clean and shiny. I'm sure it took several washings to remove all the blood and dirt and glass. Dark circles lingered under Henry Lee's eyes. His right arm and right leg were heavily bandaged and propped up on pillows. His numerous cuts and abrasions showed signs of healing as much of the bruising turned that sickly shade of yellow. The chest tube had been removed days ago and the doctor said his lung should heal nicely without any further problems.

"Better, now that my angel's here," Henry Lee said.

"I hear you're gettin' sprung tomorrow."

"Yeah, the doctor says he's done all he can for now. I just have to be patient and let my body heal in its own time. How's Ms. Dora?"

"Day to day. It'll take time, like your body," I said and grinned. "Steve was pretty much the center of her universe."

"I guess she and the rest of your family hates my guts."

"No, Henry Lee, no one hates you. Dora knows the wreck wasn't your fault. She's glad you're goin' to be all right." And that wasn't a lie. I knew deep down inside Dora didn't bear Henry Lee any ill will.

"I feel like I should have done somethin', Billie Jean. I just don't know what." Henry Lee stared up at the ceiling, trying not to cry, and I walked to his beside and sat down in the chair and reached for his good hand.

"Henry Lee, what happened was not your fault. No one forced Steve to drink and drive. He made that choice on his own."

"I know, but he always seemed so—lost. He needed somethin', Billie Jean, or someone to do somethin'."

"I agree, but none of us knew what, or how."

Henry Lee looked down at me and squeezed my hand. "Do you remember tellin' me you loved me? Did you only say it 'cause you thought I was dyin'?"

"Yes, I remember, and no, I didn't say it because I thought you were dyin'. I do love you, Henry Lee, just not in the way you mean."

"Is it because I'm all busted up now?"

"No, of course not. Henry Lee, you're goin' to be fine. You've just got to give it time."

"Is it lil' brother?" I dropped my eyes. I didn't want to discuss Bobby Ray with Henry Lee. "Yeah, it is, that's okay. I kind of always knew it."

"Henry Lee, I'm datin' Ross."

"That's bull sh...do do. You're no more in love with Ross Williams than I am. I've seen the two of you together."

"It's—complicated."

"Ain't love always?"

I wanted to change the subject so I said, "I'm goin' to see Bobby Ray's new place real soon. He's so proud of it."

"It's a nice little place. The house needs more work, but it's a great place to start a family." Henry Lee grinnd and raised his eyebrows.

"Well, I need to go, Henry Lee. I'll come to see you at home in a couple of days and bring you a pie." I bent down to kiss Henry Lee on the cheek, and at the last second he turned his head and kissed me on the lips. I gently pulled back. I couldn't simply shrug his feelings off because they were an inconvenience for me.

"You sure you won't change your mind? I'm just a little older version of Bobby Ray."

"Henry Lee, you're hopeless," I laughed, and turned to go.

"You can't blame a guy for tryin'. Apple."

"What?"

"I like apple pie, or cherry, or banana." I waved my hand over my head and went out the door. As it closed behind me, I heard, "Or rhubarb."

In the hallway I met a pretty young nurse. "Are you Mr. Evans's girlfriend?" she asked.

"No, just a friend," I said.

"Oh. Well, have a good evenin'." She gave me a big smile and continued up the hall and entered Henry Lee's room. I surely had made her day. I, too, felt better after our little talk, more assured that he would be as good as new. It might take some time, but I was willing to bet, Henry Lee would live to love again.

A few days after my visit to Henry Lee, I made the trip to Bobby Ray's. I planned to leave right after work and stay for only a short time. That way I wouldn't be missed and have to explain to anyone where I'd been. The little farm was located on the opposite side of Johnson's Bend from where we lived. The narrow gravel road ran through a creek bottom of heavy dense woods, the same creek bottom that ran below our house. The road aptly named, Bobcat Creek Road, due to its inhabitants. The stealthy night prowlers were well known for voicing their presence in the dark with their high-pitched screams, especially in mating season. It would make the hair stand up on the back of your neck. Huge, thick tree branches overlapped and reached across the road with ghost-like appendages. It was as though they wanted to block out the light, but the sun was not to be outdone and managed to sneak through a few dappled spots that danced across my windshield as I drove.

When I exited the bottom, the road climbed a steep hill. Immediately at its crest and to my left, I noticed a dirt lane overgrown with weeds and briers. I would find out later the lane had been made by loggers going in and out to the ridge to cut timber but used mostly by hunters now. The ridge stood directly behind Bobby Ray's house and the obscure lane came out of the woods alongside his tobacco patch, and then wound its way to the path that lead down from the ridge to merge with the driveway beside his house. The little house sat at the bottom of the hill, right below the ridge on a small knoll, and the area behind the house was just large enough for a barn, a corncrib, and a small cow lot. On the far side of the house I could see a weathered outhouse and a dog pen. From there the yard sloped down into a huge, wide field. At the very back of the field I could see what I thought to be a tobacco barn. In the front of the house and near the road stood a stately maple and a row of tall pine trees flanked the drive. Henry Lee had spoken the truth. It really was a very pretty place.

I coasted slowly down the hill toward the house, suddenly a little nervous and uncertain of why I had come. I noticed the house was in bad need of a good coat of paint. As I neared the house, Bobby Ray walked out onto the porch. He must have been watching for me. He had on a clean pair of overalls without a shirt. He always wore them this way in the warmer months. Bobby Ray raised his tan muscular arms over his head and leaned against the low over-hang of the roof. He reminded me of a young Adonis standing there, the beautiful youth the Greek gods had fallen in love with. I parked the old truck and pulled on the emergency brake and got out.

"Hey, I was afraid you wouldn't show."

"I told you I would, didn't I?"

"Yeah, but people do change their minds. Well, this is it." Bobby Ray made a sweeping gesture with his arm toward the front door. My eyes had to adjust to the dim lighting inside. The walls and ceilings were made from a dark tongue and groove wood, and the old linoleum so worn, I'm not sure what color or pattern it originated with. The front room was mostly empty of furniture, other than a cane rocker with a cushion and a wooden straight-backed chair that stood beside a small table in front of the window. A lamp and a radio sat on the table, but there were no signs of a television anywhere. In the center of the kitchen sat a bare unfinished wooden table with another straight-backed chair that matched the one in the living room. Off the kitchen area was a partially enclosed back porch that featured a tiny sink, but no toilet.

"No indoor bathroom?" I asked

"Naw, but that's at the top of my list when I sell my first crop," Bobby Ray said.

The last room Bobby Ray showed me was his bedroom. A single metal framed bed resided there with a thin mattress thrown on top. A wire line had been strung across one end of the room for Bobby Ray to hang his clothes. An old army blanket had been nailed over the double windows to serve as curtains.

"No closets either?"

"Naw, that's on the list too. Look, Billie Jean, I know it's not much right now, but I think together we could make a real pretty place out of it."

"We?"

"Yeah, you and me, who else would I be talkin' about?"

"Why didn't you ask me out again after the prom? Until Steve's wreck, I hardly saw you the whole summer." I couldn't keep the hurt out of my voice. Still in the bedroom, Bobby Ray backed me against the wall and placed his arms on either side of me, holding me there. He leaned in and pressed his body up close to mine.

"Cause I didn't want to come to you with nothin' but holes in my pockets. With this here, I can make you a livin'. I can take care of you, Billie Jean." He kissed me. I felt there could never be another kiss like the one we shared on his prom night, but boy was I wrong. This was a kiss of a man staking his claim to what he believed belonged to him. The kiss deepened and went on and on until I thought I would lose my mind. I clung to Bobby Ray the way a drowning man clings to a rope, like I never wanted to let him go. I felt my whole life had been moving toward this moment. Bobby Ray's breathing quickened as did mine. We stood so close I could feel his need. I might have been young, but I wasn't totally naïve. Raised on a farm, I had known how the act of procreation worked, and I knew where this kind of kissing could lead. Bobby Ray had been the first to pull back, but only a little.

"Marry me, Billie Jean, tonight—you can still finish high school," Bobby Ray pleaded, his voice thick with unfulfilled passion.

"Bobby Ray, I'm only seventeen. Daddy would have to sign, and he won't do it, not right now."

"We could elope, go down to Mississippi."

"I want to have a church weddin', Bobby Ray, with our family's there."

"Don't you want to marry me? Maybe you don't love me the way I love you."

"That's not true. I do love you, Bobby Ray. I've loved you my whole life, and I want to marry you, but I want us to do it right. Please, for me, give me time to talk to Daddy, and Ross."

Bobby Ray bent his head and kissed me again. This one was long and slow, but as powerful as the one before, and for a moment I'd been tempted to say, "Okay, let's elope."

"Tell me you're mine, that you've always been mine," Bobby Ray whispered against my lips.

"I'm yours, I've always been yours," I whispered back, breathless, and we kissed again, and then again.

"I guess if Jacob could wait fourteen years for Rachel, I can wait a few months for you," Bobby Ray laughed.

"You know that Bible story?" I guess I sounded shocked.

"I've read the Bible, Billie Jean." Bobby Ray grinned. "And mama read Bible stories to us all the time when we were little."

"I didn't mean it that way, darlin'," I said, and happened to glance out the window. Pitch black outside. "Oh my gosh, I've got to go! Grandma will have the law out lookin' for me." I ran out the door and yelled over my shoulder, "I'm takin' a pie to Henry Lee on Sunday, will you be there?" But Bobby Ray was right behind me.

"You can count on it, babe, but listen. You talk to your Daddy and to Ross. I don't want to have to sneak around to see you, Billie Jean."

I drove home that night through those dark country back roads like a maniac. When I pulled into my grandparents' drive, I didn't see anyone, but the front porch light was on. I jumped out of the truck and raced toward the house.

"Billie Jean?" Daddy stepped from the shadows. He came out of my grandparents' back door. I stopped and tried not to look guilty.

"Yes sir."

"Where've you been, your Grandma was about to call the police."

"I went by a friend's house after work," I said, and sounded out of breath. It hadn't been a lie. Bobby Ray and I were friends, always. "The time kinda got away from me. I'm sorry. It won't happen again."

"It's all right for you to go to a friend's house, hon, only next time, call and let somebody know where you are and that you're goin' to be late."

"Okay, I will, I promise Daddy. Goodnight."

"Goodnight, darlin'." Daddy turned and walked toward his house.

This is where I should have said, "Daddy, wait, I need to talk to you." But I didn't, and procrastination is usually never a good thing, but we're all guilty of this. I believe it was Sir Walter Scott who penned, "Oh, what a tangled web we weave, when first we practice to deceive." No truer words were ever written. I trudged to my grandparents' house. When I turned to close the door and switch off the light, I looked across the road to the Williams's. Ross stood in his front door and watched me through the glass panel. I gave him a little wave and a small twinge of guilt pricked my conscience. But in my heart I knew, nothing short of death would keep me from marrying Bobby Ray.

CHAPTER 14

I dressed with care for my visit to Henry Lee to bring him the pie. Bobby Ray would be there. I slipped into my best pair of blue jeans and rolled the cuffs up to my calves. With these I wore a pale blue sweater that fit me just right and accentuated all of my womanly features. Since the days had gotten cooler, I added a matching long sleeve sweater and put on my new black and white bee-bop shoes with white bobby socks. My dark, waist length hair I pulled up into a ponytail and secured it with a rubber band and a blue scarf. I was now ready to go see my man. Bobby Ray came out of the house to greet me, and before I could get out of the car he stuck his head through the window and we shared a long, sweet kiss.

Henry Lee sat propped-up on their old couch and I handed him his pie. "Oh boy, lemon meringue, just what I wanted." I think Henry Lee would have been happy with any flavor as long as it was called pie. "I guess y'all will want me to share this?" he said, and looked up at us with a big grin.

"No big brother, you go right ahead and enjoy it. Billie Jean's goin' to make me one all my own, ain't ya, baby?" Bobby Ray slid his arms around me from behind and kissed my neck and I leaned back against him.

"Oh, really?" Henry Lee still had a grin on his face, but a flicker of something in his eyes caused me some concern. I didn't want to become a bone of contention for the brothers and drive a wedge between them. I didn't think I could live with that on my conscience. My decision would cause enough hurt already.

"Billie Jean and me are gonna get married when she gets out of school," Bobby Ray announced, and smiled from ear to ear, his chest swelled with pride. "Whata you think about that?"

"Well, I think that's great," Henry Lee said with barely a second's hesitation. "I always wanted her to be a part of our family." Only Henry Lee and I knew the true meaning behind his words, or so I thought. It needed to be our secret forever, and I certainly never intended to tell Bobby Ray.

"Congratulations, and I want some of that pie," Lester yelled from the kitchen. The bedroom door opened and Mary and Ms. Minnie came out. I could see Mr. Evans lying on the bed, freshly bathed and shaved, his thin gray hair neatly combed. Pitiful is the only word I can think of to describe him. His face was beet red and so swollen the oxygen tube appeared to be imbedded into the skin across his cheeks. He struggled for every breath, and his rounded barrel chest looked huge in comparison to the rest of him—nothing but skin and bone. I walked to the doorway of the bedroom and spoke to him.

"How you doin', Mr. Evans?" What a dumb question, I chastised myself. I could see how he was doing. He was dying, but one never knows what to say in those circumstances. He nodded his head up and down and smiled, but didn't have the air to speak. He tried to mumble something that sounded like, "Welcome."

"I'm so happy, happy," Mary sang, and skipped across the room, grabbing me in a bear hug.

Ms. Minnie came and hugged me too, and kissed me on the cheek. "There is no one I had rather have for a daughter-in-law than you, Billie Jean. I was hopin' one of my boys would have the good fortune to get you." Perhaps mothers always know, or had Henry Lee confided his feelings to his mother about me? Either way, I sure hoped I could live up to the high regard they seemed to have for me. Living up to other people's expectations can be a heavy burden to carry. I should know. I had done it for years. My family had high hopes I would go to college and that someday I would marry Ross. They had since the two of us were small, almost like an arranged marriage type thing. Not so much in what was said, but more in the way both families simply assuming it would happen. I knew I had to tell them soon. Bobby Ray wanted to talk to my daddy that very day, man to man, but I had begged him to wait. Yet I had known I couldn't put it off much longer. Now that his family knew, it wouldn't be any time until the news drifted back to my end of the road.

I needn't have worried about Henry Lee's discretion. From the moment Bobby Ray told of our impending nuptials, Henry Lee treated me like a sister. He not only became a brother-in-law, but one of my closest confidants. For some reason I felt I could tell Henry Lee anything and he would understand. Perhaps it was because we both loved Bobby Ray and had his best interest at heart.

The next morning as I was getting ready for school at my grandparents' house, I heard a knock at the front door. I looked out my bedroom window and saw Bobby Ray's car at my daddy's house and my heart sank. I figured Bobby Ray couldn't wait any longer and came to talk to him. I quickly ran down the stairs and was surprised to find Bobby Ray and Mary standing in the foyer. Maybe he planned to drive Mary and me to school as a way to spend time with me.

"I went to your daddy's, and he said you were here," Bobby Ray said. "We just come by to let you know Daddy passed last night."

The visitation couldn't be held for Mr. Evans until Margaret and her husband arrived. The family wanted her to be in on the final arrangements. I must admit, at the funeral home, I had been surprised not to see a single tear shed. Everyone behaved with the utmost respect, but I couldn't truthfully say I saw anyone that showed any real grief. Mary and I went back to the little room where they had coffee, soft drinks, and food if you wanted to bring it in.

Out of the blue Mary looked at me and said, "Once when I was little, I saw my mama out in the garden cryin' and wringin' her hands, prayin' to the Lord to let her die. It nearly broke my heart and I worried all the time. I couldn't figure out why my mama would want to die and leave me." Mary paused and looked down at her lap. She had never said a lot about her home life. She then looked up at me with a solemn face and said, "Maybe now Mama won't pray anymore to die."

I thought, how sad, to leave this world and there be no one to mourn your passing, but Grandma always said, we preach our own funeral while we're still alive.

During this time I should have made my intentions known to everyone, but still I waited. I'm not sure why. Maybe because I was young and afraid of upsetting so many people. I hated so badly to hurt Ross, but I knew there was no other way, and he was already suspicious. Every time he wanted to go somewhere or to be alone with me, I made some excuse not to. Bobby Ray and I set a time to meet each night at the corner below my house. Here a narrow dirt lane led from the road to our tobacco barn. Bobby Ray would back his car in and turn off the lights and wait until I could slip away. The car wasn't readily noticeable from the road unless you were expecting it to be there. It hadn't been a problem for me to get out of the house. If at Daddy's, I would say, I was going over to my grandparents' for a bit, and vice versa. We began this arrangement right after Mr. Evans' death, and Bobby Ray wasn't at all happy with the situation.

"Look, babe, I'm not tryin' to give you a hard time, but enough is enough. Let me come tomorrow and set down and talk to your daddy. You can talk to Ross at school."

"I can't talk to him at school, Bobby Ray. That would be awful."

"I don't care where you talk to him, babe, as long as you talk to him tomorrow," Bobby Ray said, and leaned down and kissed me. We had already steamed up the windows on the car. From outside the car I heard a twig snap.

"Did you hear that?" I whispered.

"Yeah, I did." Before I realized what he was about to do, Bobby Ray flung the car door open and jumped out. "What are you doin', you sick fuck, spyin' on us?" I heard scuffling and cursing coming from behind the car.

"Get your damn hands off of me."

Ross. I hopped out and ran around to the back of the car. I found Ross and Bobby Ray in a dead-lock like two grizzly bears. Ross was taller and heavier, but Bobby Ray was tough as a pine knot and neither gave an inch.

"Stop it, both of you," I screamed, and tried to break them apart, but they refused to back down. Somehow in the struggle I fell and hit my head on the bumper of the car.

"See what you did!"

"I didn't do it, you did."

They knelt down beside me and each attempted to assist me up. "You okay, baby? Are you hurt?" Bobby Ray put his arms around me and lifted me from the ground. Ross tried to help. "Get your damn hands off her. Don't you ever put your filthy hands on her again!" Bobby Ray yelled at Ross at the top of his lungs.

"She's my girlfriend," Ross shouted back.

"You don't get it, do you Williams? Billie Jean is mine, she's always been—mine."

Ross lunged at Bobby Ray, and Bobby Ray blocked him with his arm. At the same time he pushed me behind him and raised his fists, anger blazing in his eyes.

I hate to think what might have happened if we hadn't heard, "Billie Jean! Billie Jean!"

Daddy ran down the road and by the time he reached us, he was out of breath. I heard the fear in his voice and was ashamed to face him. That night couldn't have gotten much worse. If only I had been honest with everyone, maybe this whole ugly scene could have been avoided.

"Billie Jean, darlin', are you all right? I heard you screamin' and all that shoutin'." Daddy put his arms around me and looked from Bobby Ray to Ross.

"I can explain, sir," Bobby Ray spoke up.

"Oh, I know what you and Billie Jean are doin' here. I've known that from the first night you showed up. I'm not so old I don't remember how these things work. I suppose it's your presence here, Ross, I don't rightly comprehend." Daddy looked at Ross.

"I saw headlights and thought somebody was messin' around down here. So I come down to check it out."

I cringed at Ross's choice of words and was glad for the darkness, sure my face blood red.

"It appears everythin' is under control, Ross, best you get on back home. Bobby Ray, you probably need to get on home too. Why don't you give Ross a lift?"

"I'm not goin' home tonight. I'm stayin' at Mama's," Bobby Ray said in a sullen voice.

"Well, you need to be goin' then." Ross hadn't made a move to leave, and Daddy said a little stronger, "Ross?" With reluctance Ross turned and started up the road to his house. Bobby Ray got into his car, but I could tell he wanted to say more.

"Sir, if you'd just let me..."

"I'm sure we'll talk again, son. Tomorrow's another day."

After Bobby Ray drove away, Daddy and I waited until we felt Ross had plenty of time to get home and we started up the road. We didn't talk as we walked and I didn't know what to say to him anyway. At the edge of his yard Daddy paused. "You feel like talkin' a bit," he had asked.

"Okay." We walked to Daddy's porch and sat down. The night clear and crisp and the sky full of stars, and I began to cry.

"Why are you cryin' darlin'—are you hurt?" Daddy asked, and moved closer and put his arm around my shoulders.

"No, I did bump my head, but I'm all right."

Daddy opened his mouth to voice something, but I interrupted. "It was an accident. I stumbled and hit my head on the bumper of Bobby Ray's car. It wasn't anyone's fault."

Daddy gingerly felt the back of my head. "You sure did. You've got a huge goose egg back there. Maybe I need to take you to the hospital and have it checked out."

"No, please, don't. It'll be okay." And I started to cry again. "I'm sorry, Daddy, that I've let you and everybody else down."

"What? You haven't let anyone down, darlin', me least of all. Why would you think that?"

"You want me to marry Ross, don't you?"

"I want you to be happy and to have a good life. And I thought Ross could give you that, but if you don't love him—well?"

"I do love Ross, Daddy, like a friend, or a brother. But Bobby Ray—I don't know if I can put my feelin's for him into words. He's like the air I breathe, a part of me. I can't imagine my life without him."

"I know that feelin', darlin'. That's the way I felt about your mother. From the moment I first laid eyes on her, I knew I had to make her mine. They had just moved here from Louisiana. A man had threatened to kill your Poppaw. He thought Mr. Claudell stole a hog from him—turns out it was the man's own brother that took it. Your mama was no older than you are now, and she wasn't ready to get married. But I begged and begged until I wore her down. Nine months later, there you were. We might have made it if the war hadn't come along. But your mama wasn't the kind to do well on her own."

"Did she want me?"

"Yes. Oh yes, she was so proud of you. She used to dress you up and play with you like a baby doll, but she was so young, and you're so young, darlin'. I don't want to see you throw all your young life away on hard work and raisin' babies."

I chose to ignore the latter part. Now that Daddy was talking, I had so many questions I wanted to ask him. "Daddy, were you ever disappointed I wasn't a boy?"

"Heaven's no. Why would I have wanted a knuckle-headed boy when I had a tiny perfect little angel girl. You were, and are, so much like your mother, not only in your looks, but in your mannerisms. The way you smile and throw your hair back. The way you walk and sometimes the way you express yourself, but you're much more out goin' than she was. She was somewhat shy. I need you to know this, Billie Jean," Daddy said and took a deep breath. "I thank God every day that your grandmother didn't let her leave with you. If she had, you most likely would have been in the car when they wrecked and then my precious little angel would have been gone." Daddy's voice broke and he hung his head. "I was such a coward."

"Coward? Daddy, you fought in the war. You were discharged with honors. Why would you say you were a coward?" There a long pause before Daddy answered.

"I could have gotten leave to come home for your mama's funeral. But I'd rather face the Japanese than see the pity on everyone's faces here. 'There goes poor Will Carson, his wife ran off with another man while he was off fightin' in the War.' And I was a coward again when I did come home. I should have taken you and gotten out on my own, but I needed someone to see to you while I worked. I couldn't simply tie you up under a shade tree like a coon dog pup could I?" Daddy laughed. "Your grandma seemed to be the logical one, so we stayed put, and this was the only home you'd ever known. I truly believe your grandma would have grieved herself to death if I had taken you and left."

"Is that why you used to come into my room at night and cry?"

"Oh my lands, you remember that?" Daddy looked shocked.

"Yes, I had wanted to put my arms around you and tell you it would be all right, but I was afraid."

"Lord, I probably scared you to death. You were such an independent little thing, and I didn't know how in the world I was goin' to raise you on my own. So I took the easy way out and let your grandma do it. Hind sight is twenty-twenty, darlin'. I know Mama is bossy and pushy, but she loves you more than her own life, Billie Jean"

"I know that Daddy, and you're no coward. And deep in my heart, I've always known you'd be there for me if I really needed you, and I need you now. I need for you to understand how I feel about Bobby Ray. You do like Bobby Ray, don't you, Daddy?"

"Of course I like Bobby Ray. He's a heck of a good worker, and from all I've heard, he's a natural born farmer. It's the other part that bothers me."

"What other part?"

"Darlin', those kids weren't raised like you. Harlan was hard on them. I guess he believed in, 'spare the rod and spoil the child', and I'm sure that's the way he was raised. Then there's the drinkin', and that business back in Kentucky. Did you know Harlan was named after the town he was born in, Harlan, Kentucky?"

"No, but I know how Cole came by his name. What happened back in Kentucky?"

"After Harlan moved his family here, he quickly earned the reputation of bein' a man you didn't want to mess with. He had a few run-ins with some of his neighbors. They accused him of stealin' corn out of their fields to make moonshine, and likely he was guilty on both accounts. I never had any problems with Harlan, but some folks complained to the authorities, and after they did a background check on him, they found he had been arrested and charged with murder back where he come from. Supposedly he'd killed a man over a moonshine deal gone bad, but was acquitted for lack of evidence. Naturally there were many who were convinced he was guilty and from that time on people around here gave him a wide berth. I've always felt real sorry for Ms. Minnie and the children. She's a good, sweet, kindhearted woman, and I know she's done the best she could. The family has always been treated as outsiders, even though they have lived here for years."

"But what's any of this got to do with Bobby Ray? He's not his daddy."

"No, he's not, and I would never judge a person by their family, but it's somethin' you need to think about. Bobby Ray's had to live hard, and he's been exposed to a lot of things you haven't. And what about Ross, how are you goin' to handle that? Don't you think you owe him an explanation?"

"Yes, I should never have let it get this far. I feel terrible about hurtin' Ross, Daddy, but I love Bobby Ray with all my heart. I think I've loved him my whole life."

"Yeah, I guess I've always known this day would come. I think I've known it since the night I stood in our backdoor and watched the two of you together when Bennie was killed. All I'm askin', darlin', just please wait 'til you finish high school and turn eighteen. And if you still want to marry Bobby Ray, I promise I'll give you the biggest weddin' this county's ever seen."

"It don't have to be all that big, Daddy, but I do want a church weddin' and for you to walk me down the aisle with all of our family and friends there. I want to come back here and have the reception in the yard." We stood and Daddy placed his hands on my shoulders and looked deep into my eyes.

"You're the light of my life, Billie Jean. You always have been and you always will be, and if I ever made you feel otherwise, I'm so, so sorry. Please forgive me."

I threw my arms around his neck and hugged him tight and he hugged me back. "I love you, Daddy, and there's nothin' to forgive. Everythin' is good, so good."

CHAPTER 15

It hadn't been entirely true, that everything was good. I still had the unpleasant task of talking to Ross ahead of me, an encounter I didn't look forward to. The morning after the drama in the lane, Bobby Ray had stood at Daddy's front door before I even left for school. I stayed at Daddy's after our lengthy talk the night before. Bobby Ray wanted to drive me to school, but since it my afternoon to work at the store, I would drive Grandpa's old truck and make plans to meet Ross afterwards. As I drove away Daddy and Bobby Ray were about to sit down on the porch with a cup of coffee and a cigarette. I would have loved to hear that conversation, but it needed to be between the two of them.

School seemed to drag on forever that day. As had my time at the store, I couldn't keep my mind on my work. One customer asked for a pound of sliced bologna and I gave him two. Another bought a dollar and forty cents worth of coal oil and handed me a five and I gave him change for a ten. When it finally came time to leave I drove with a heavy heart to the meeting place with Ross. He was already there. I chose a small roadside park on the highway between Johnson's Bend and Big Town. Not many people stopped there unless they were having car trouble, so I didn't think we would be interrupted.

"Billie Jean, I want you to know I'm willin' to forget last night ever happened," Ross started in before I could get out of the truck. "We'll just go on like before, and I promise you that I will never mention it again."

"Ross, we can't go on like before. I love Bobby Ray, and I'm goin' to marry him."

"You don't mean that, Billie Jean. It's you and me. It's always been you and me. We're meant to be together."

"I think that might be the problem, Ross. We grew up together nearly like brother and sister. I do love you, but not in the way a woman needs to love a man and not in the way you deserve to be loved."

"I don't care if you don't love me that way. We're best friends, isn't that important in any relationship?"

"Sure it is, but it's not enough, Ross. Please, listen to me, I-love-Bobby Ray."

"Billie Jean, don't you see, Bobby Ray will never be more than a poor dirt farmer. I'm goin' to college, on a scholarship. When I get my engineerin' degree, I can get a good job most anywhere. We could move to east Tennessee, to the same place where I'm goin' to school. It's beautiful up there in the mountains. You'd like that wouldn't you?"

"Ross, my daddy and granddaddy, and your own father for that matter, are farmers, and they've done all right."

"They own their own land, Billie Jean. Bobby Ray's a—sharecropper." Ross made it sound like something dirty.

"You think you're better than him, don't you?"

"I am better than him, and so are you. I know what you want and need, Billie Jean. Does Bobby Ray?"

"I don't know if he does or not, but he would ask. When have you ever asked me what I wanted? It's always about you and what you want."

"That's not true, Billie Jean, and I thought we wanted the same things. We have the same goals and values in life. We go to the same church and believe alike."

Ross was so terribly hurt. Nothing I could do or say would change that, and it would have been better if I had left it there. "Ross, you'll find someone to love you the way you should be loved. Mary..."

"Billie Jean, please! You think you can fix me up with someone? Bobby Ray's sister and then we'll be one big happy family?"

"I meant there'll be someone to love you for you, Ross, but it's not me. I love Bobby Ray and I'm goin' to marry him. End of story, I'm sorry." I turned to leave but Ross wasn't finished.

"Please, please don't do this, Billie Jean. He's trash, poor white trash. The whole family is. Did you know Lester and Henry Lee were arrested the day *after* their daddy died for runnin' moonshine across the river?"

I paused in my retreat and turned to face Ross. "What? What are you talkin' about?"

"Yeah, you didn't know about that, did you? Ask your precious Bobby Ray about that."

I ran to the truck and jumped in. "That's the kind of family you're marryin' into, Billie Jean." I fired up the old truck and gunned it, but it didn't drown out Ross yelling at me, "You'll regret this, Billie Jean. I promise you, you'll regret this."

To label things strained between Ross and I after that would be a gross understatement, and a noticeable tension existed between our families. It made it very uncomfortable for everyone as we lived practically in one another's front door. Ross apologized to me a few days later and I accepted, but things never the same between us. Once angry words are out there you can't call them back. The Bible says in Matthew 15:18: "But those things which proceed out of the mouth come forth from the heart and so they defile the man."

I asked Bobby Ray about Henry Lee and Lester's, "fishing trip."

"Naw, they weren't arrested," he said. "The law was waitin' when they come back to shore, said they'd gotten an anonymous tip." I wondered where the tip came from. No one but the family would have known they were going fishing, and I knew it hadn't come from any of them, so the informant was a bit of a mystery. "The officers did search the boat, but all they found was fish, several empty crushed beer cans, and a pair of women's underpants."

"Women's underpants?" You mean like, panties?" I asked in disbelief.

"Yep. Everybody, includin' Lester, looked at Henry Lee. Lester said Henry Lee threw up his good arm and said, 'I swear, they ain't mine'." This cracked Bobby Ray up, and I have to admit, it was pretty funny. I could absolutely see Henry Lee doing that.

"What were they doin' out fishin' in the first place, Bobby Ray, the day after your daddy passed away? That's kinda cold, wouldn't you say?"

"No, you're lookin' at it from a recreational angle. Look at it as a necessity. We had a lot of mouths to feed at our house. We had the fish fry the day after the funeral before Margaret and Hugh and our kin from up in

Kentucky left. I wanted you to be there, but you needed time to 'talk' to everyone." Bobby Ray pulled me into his arms and kissed me.

"Where do you think the panties came from?" I asked.

"There's no tellin', and you have to remember, this boat is tied up in the back side of nowhere. We always empty the gas out of the tank, but it could be used for other purposes, if you're of a mind." Bobby Ray nuzzled my neck. "We could take it out for a moonlight ride down the river."

The object in question was an old, dented, flat-bottomed johnboat. "Yes, we could. I can ride and you can drive."

"We might run out of gas."

"We'd better not."

It would be a long few months until the wedding, and I didn't know how much longer I could hold Bobby Ray off. The natives were already pretty restless, and I had been taught the intimate relationship between a man and a woman was for the marriage bed only. I wanted to do everything by the Good Book, but Bobby Ray's desires weren't the only ones at a fever pitch. I couldn't sleep at night for wanting to be with him, to be in his arms and to feel him touching me. Only the fear of "Hell fire and damnation", and Grandma, had kept me from giving in.

On Christmas Eve, Bobby Ray presented me with a beautiful half karat, diamond solitaire on a gold band. He got down on one knee and officially asked me to marry him. Of course I said yes, and immediately began to worry he spent far too much on the ring. Where had he come by the money? It was like Bobby Ray could read my mind.

"Cole floated me a loan until I sell my crop at the first of the year. He knows I'm good for it. I wanted you to have somethin' beautiful, like you, and you can wear it with pride, Billie Jean, I give you my word."

When Bobby Ray gave his word, I would soon learn you could take it to the bank. That night in showing my appreciation, we almost let things go too far.

The next morning I don't know if I had a guilty look on my face or what, but at breakfast Grandma looked at me and said, "You tell Bobby Ray to keep his tallywacker in his pants. Just because a down payment's been made on the farm, the deed's not been signed yet."

My senior year crawled by at a snail's pace. I felt like I was only marking time until I could graduate, turn eighteen, and marry Bobby Ray. I did the cheerleader thing, only because Bobby Ray and Daddy wanted me too. They said I had the other three years and there no reason not to my senior year. The rule remained that we ride the bus to the away games but didn't have to on the way back. Daddy and Bobby Ray would take turns driving and I would ride home with them. It made me so happy to see how close Daddy and Bobby Ray became. In fact my entire family had embraced Bobby Ray with open arms. Daddy never got around to buying me a car and now it wouldn't be necessary. Bobby Ray had a good car and a pretty decent old truck. What we needed the most was furniture for the house. Daddy and Dora bought us a like-new used stove, refrigerator, and a brand new sofa with a matching chair. My grandparents' gave us a new dinette set and allowed us to raid the spare room in their upstairs where the unused furniture was stored. In the room was an antique, four-poster bed, the kind with the high back and footboard. Grandma knew I had always loved it, and with it came a chest and a dresser with a fancy mirror. The pieces were so large they filled Bobby Ray's tiny bedroom, and we had to place the armoire on the back porch to hang our clothes in.

Our landlord, Mr. Henley, bought the paint and Bobby Ray and his brothers painted our little house in two days. Henry Lee was getting around fairly well by then, but not allowed to get up on the ladder. He hadn't liked it, but when Cole said no, he listened. In fact, I noticed when Cole spoke, they all pretty much listened. I was hanging curtains inside the house and stopped to watch. The brothers worked together like a perfectly timed and oiled machine. I thought back to the anonymous and erroneous tip about Lester and Henry Lee planning to run moonshine across the river. Would they or any of the others have done that? Sure they would have, if it was necessary in order for them to provide for their families. Right or wrong, good or bad, does the end justify the means? I suppose at some point in everyone's life you must ask yourself this question.

After graduation, preparations for the wedding kicked into high gear. Aunt Grace, an amazing seamstress, and with the help of my grandmothers, made my wedding dress. It took yards and yards of ivory satin for the semi-full skirt and mock train and the bodice she covered in a candle light lace overlay. The dress featured a sweetheart neckline with thin, rounded shoulder straps, and my floor length veil was made from the same candle light lace and attached to a pearl and rhinestone tiara. A store bought gown from the finest salons in the world couldn't have been any more beautiful. Mamaw Chappell couldn't contribute anything money wise, but she had worked day and night sewing the numerous tiny simulated seed pearls to my dress and around the edges of the veil. This was what made the gown so very special. Every inch of it was made with love.

The weeks leading up to the wedding were happy and exciting and filled with activity, and more than a little stressful. The ladies from my church hosted a huge household shower for me and Bobby Ray. It looked as though the whole community, in addition to our families, turned out for the event. We received everything anyone could need to set up housekeeping, towels, sheets, dishes, cookware, pictures, lamps, and much, much more. Bobby Ray and I were overwhelmed and extremely grateful for people's generosity.

The only bad thing about this time was my numerous unanswered questions. You know those a girl might want to ask her mother. Like the more intimate details of married life and about birth control. Naturally, in school I had health education. I knew a little, and there were always a few high school girls that had been around and more than happy to share their experiences. The only problem, you couldn't tell the facts from the fiction. At various times my grandmothers had talked to me about certain things, but I felt some of their advice a little out-of-date. I could have, I suppose, talked to Dora, or to Ms. Minnie, although considering Ms. Minnie had eight children, I don't think she understood a great deal about birth control either. Once again my Aunt Grace came through for me. She sat me down in private and answered my questions and explained a lot of things that troubled me, and she gave me several pamphlets on various types of birth control. This way when I went for my physical for my marriage license, I at least could talk to the doctor with a little knowledge and choose the one I thought would be right for me.

The year 1959, Castro became the dictator of Cuba and *The Sound of Music* opened on Broadway. And in Tennessee, on August the seventh at four o'clock in the evening at the small Johnson's Bend Church of Christ, I married Robert Ray Evans. My Bobby Ray.

SUMMER

But thy eternal summer shall not fade
Nor lose possession of that fair thou owerst;
Nor shall Death brag thou wander'st in his shade,
When in eternal lines to time thou growest:
So long as men can breathe or eyes can see,
So long lives this and this gives life to thee.

From *Shall I Compare Thee to a Summer's Day*
Sonnet 18 by William Shakespeare

CHAPTER 16

My wedding day arrived sweltering hot with a clear blue sky, and humidity so thick it made it feel ten degrees warmer. August in Tennessee had a tendency to be this way, and I hoped by the late afternoon it would have cooled down a bit. I prepared for my big day at my grandparents' house. It just felt right. It was the house where I'd been born and spent most of my life. Daddy understood this and came to my room shortly before time to leave for the church. My grandma and Aunt Grace and cousin, Ruth, my Maid of Honor, were helping me put the finishing touches to my hair and make-up.

"Could you give me and Billie Jean a few minutes alone before we go?" Daddy asked.

"William, don't you make her cry and ruin all our hard work," Aunt Grace warned. After they left Daddy stood in front of me, unshed tears glistened in his eyes, and a lump formed in my throat.

"You look so much like your mother today, Billie Jean, an angel in white. You're the most beautiful bride I've ever seen. Course I could be a little prejudice," Daddy said, and laughed, his voice full of emotion.

"Thank you, Daddy." I could hardly hold back my own tears. Daddy took a small black box from his pocket and from it he removed a delicate gold locket and held it up in front of me.

"I bought this for your mother on my way overseas. My company had a brief layover in Hawaii. It took

139

everything I had in my pocket and a small loan from a couple of my buddies. I was goin' to send it to her on her birthday, but never got the chance, she was gone by then. I've kept it all these years to give to you on your most special day, on your weddin' day."

Daddy placed the locket around my neck and it looked perfect nestled there with the pearl drop necklace I wore. I'd borrowed the necklace from Aunt Grace in keeping with the wedding tradition. "It's beautiful, Daddy, I will cherish it forever." A single tear escaped from my eye and slid down my cheek. Later I would place a picture of my parents on their wedding day inside the locket.

"No cryin' now. This is a happy day, and your grandma and my sister will skin me if I cause you to mess up your face. Not that I could."

Daddy gently kissed me on the forehead and we left to meet my destiny. That's the way I thought of it, my marriage to Bobby Ray. It was meant to be, but my hands trembled so I feared I would shake the petals from the roses in my bouquet. I looked down the aisle and saw Bobby Ray there with a big smile on his face, his dark eyes shining, and my fears vanished. The ceremony was kind of a blur but I do remember looking into Bobby Ray's eyes and repeating our vows, "For better, for worse, in sickness and in health, until death doeth us part." Not even then for me, I thought.

It cooled down enough by the ceremony's end to be "tolable" outside. In our rural community, air-conditioning was nearly nonexistent. In fact, I hadn't known a soul with anything other than window fans in their homes. Somehow it didn't seem to bother us as much to be out in hot weather when you're not used to it being all that cool indoors. Henry Lee served as best man and he and Ruth drove Bobby Ray and me back to Daddy's in Bobby Ray's car. He then took the car to parts unknown, only to the far side of my grandparents' house, I'm sure. Bobby Ray warned Henry Lee when the car came back nothing better be on it that couldn't be washed off or removed. Henry Lee promised there wouldn't be, and then looked at Ruth, winked and gave her one of his famous, wicked, little grins. Ruth gazed back at him with stars in her eyes. Oh good Lord, I thought, that wouldn't be good. It would be like the lion and the lamb, and I said a little prayer that Henry Lee would realize that Ruth was a total innocent and would be a gentleman. That boy was such a charmer. Not many females of any age were immune to his charms, and Ruth, a natural beautiful in her own right could turn any man's head. I always envied her peaches and crème complexion, the way her light blond hair framed her face perfectly and brought out her deep blue, china-doll eyes. Yet it wasn't Ruth's beauty that made her special, but rather her sweet, gentle spirit. If one looked up the definition of a true Southern Belle, there would have to be a picture of Ruth beside it. But I couldn't worry about the two of them at that moment, not on my wedding day, and nature would run its course with or without my help. I'd simply hope for the best.

The wedding festivities were spread out across Daddy's yard from one side to the other. Never let it be said we Southerners don't know how to throw a wedding reception. We had borrowed tables and chairs from the local churches and a few from the funeral parlor. The churches also graciously loaned us their linen tablecloths also. Grandma and Dora begged and borrowed every lace tablecloth in a twenty mile radius. Vases of late summer flowers from the gardens of the ladies at our church and in the neighborhood adorned each table. My favorite Mrs. Williams's datura, also known as angle trumpets. It had a huge white blossom and silvery green leaves, and we used those for the centerpieces. In addition, there were smaller vases of mums in various colors and black-eyed susans. This was the perfect floral arrangements for an outdoor country wedding, and the flowers weren't the only thing the ladies helped with. They also brought food. Huge crystal bowls filled with potato salad, baked beans, cole slaw, and most anything else that would complement barbecued chicken and spare ribs. No hors d`oeuvres or finger foods for this crowd—there were farmers, working folks, and they expected real food. In small town communities like ours, weddings were a big deal, and people loved to help out and join in the fun and celebration.

Daddy and Grandpa built the wooden frames to cook the chicken and ribs. These were makeshift braziers, sat close to the ground and a little over half a yard wide and about four feet long. Across the top of the frames they stretched chicken wire and nailed it in place. This served as the grill. A fire was built underneath with hickory wood and allowed to burn down to glowing embers. Now it was ready for the meat to be placed onto the wire to slowly cook. It gave off the most wonderful aroma and sent the dogs into a wild frenzy. Daddy put them in their pen long before the reception began. Ross's dad came over to lend a hand in preparing the meat. This meant a lot to me and Dad. The Williams's were our closest friends and neighbors and it would have been a real shame to see this friendship come to an end. Ross came to the ceremony and through the receiving line. He hugged me and shook hands with Bobby Ray wishing us well. This, too, meant a lot to the both of us. I know it couldn't have been easy for him. I suppose we shouldn't have expected anymore from him. He didn't come to the reception, but I'm sure he could see and hear all of it since we lived so close.

My cake not only looked gorgeous but was delicious. You would have thought it came from some fancy bakery, but in fact had been made by a lady who did cakes for all occasions in her own kitchen. Daddy hired a local band, The River Road Boys, to play, a very talented bunch that sounded like fulltime professionals. The group performed all around the area for different events and could play and sing most anything—country, R&B, rock and gospel. Mine and Bobby Ray's first dance as husband and wife was to the beautiful and haunting melody, *The Tennessee Waltz*. As we twirled around the yard, I thought about the words to the song. To briefly paraphrase, the lyrics tell of two friends that meet up at a dance. One introduces his lady love to the other, and while they were dancing, the friend steals the other's true love away. It kind of reminded me of the situation between me, Ross and Bobby Ray. The only thing that kept my wedding day from being perfect, my childhood friend chose not to be a part.

"Hey, where did you go?" Bobby Ray asked, and pulled me closer and kissed my neck.

"Nowhere," I said. "I'm right here with you, where I'll always be. Tell me, Bobby Ray, that we'll always be this happy."

"We'll always be this happy, Mrs. Evans, and as long as we're together, there's nothin' else that matters."

Mrs. Evans. I couldn't believe it, married at last. I now belonged to this man and he belonged to me, until death do us part. I glanced around the yard at all the happy, smiling faces. I saw Ms. Minnie sitting in a lawn chair laughing and talking and having a wonderful time. She looked so pretty that day in her new lavender dress. Poor Mary ran back and forth to the house trying to keep the food tables replenished and bringing ice for the tea and lemonade. She had been my good right hand man, and I don't know what I would have done without her.

Mary received a very substantial scholarship to a prestigious school in Memphis. I was so proud of her and for her, but a little sad at the same time. Somehow I had known when Mary left, she would never again call Johnson's Bend home. I noticed something else while scanning the gathering. Both my grandpas and a few of the neighbor men going out behind the barn a time or two, or maybe three, but after all, it was a party and a very special occasion.

I threw my bouquet and my blue garter right before Bobby Ray and I left. The bouquet landed right in Ruth's hands and Henry Lee caught the garter after running over several other men. He then brought the car around and I can't begin to tell you everything that was either written on it or tied to it somewhere. One of the men from the church had his head bent to the side trying to read some of the *witty* little sayings. I suspected I'd never be able to look that man in the face again. Bobby Ray and I made a mad dash to the car in a shower of rice and tore out. He told everyone we planned to go to Nashville that night, but what we did was race through town with a trail of cars behind us blowing their horns and turned onto the main highway. Here our entourage stopped and went back. We continued on for a mile or so and then turned around and circled through the back roads and went to our place. At the house we removed empty tin cans and old shoes from the car's bumper and the condoms from the antenna that had been blown up like balloons and tied there. It took a while to wash off the drawings and the many colorful writings. I read the one the gentleman from the church had been reading. "She got him today, but he will get her tonight." No, I definitely wouldn't be able to ever face that man again.

After the car was washed and cleaned to Bobby Ray's satisfaction, we hid it in the barn. "If Henry Lee and them come snoopin' around tonight, we'll be okay as long as they don't find the car. If they do—well babe, you'll probably have company on your weddin' night." Bobby Ray laughed, and grabbed my hand as we ran to the house.

Once inside we lit only a small candle in the bedroom. My insides were quivering. Even though I knew I loved Bobby Ray, at that instant I felt I really didn't know him. I was scared and unsure of what came next. We changed out of our wedding garments at Daddy's but I still wore my locket. I fumbled with the small clasp trying to unfasten it and Bobby Ray came up behind me and put his arms around me. Without thinking, I flinched.

"Hey, why are you tremblin'? You're not afraid of me, are you?" Bobby Ray slowly turned me to face him. "This is Bobby Ray, sugar, you know me. You never have to be afraid of me, baby." He then kissed me tenderly and unfastened my locket and laid it on the dresser, then unzipped my dress and eased it over my hips. I stood before him in nothing but my bra and panties. Bobby Ray led me to the bed where I lay down and he quickly undressed to his under shorts and stretched out on his side next to me, his tanned skin warm and smooth as silk.

"You know when I first fell in love with you?" he asked while caressing my face and kissing my neck and shoulders.

"No. When?" I replied, beginning to feel warm and breathless.

"We drove past your house one day. I was real young. You and Ross were playin' in your yard at the edge of the road. You were sittin' in his little red wagon. Your hair was long and all tangled down your back and you smiled the sweetest little smile and waved. I think I fell in love with you right then and there. Kinda think Henry Lee did some too."

"I think I've always loved you, Bobby Ray. Even when we were little. I couldn't picture anyone with you but me."

Bobby Ray continued to kiss my neck and shoulders and on down my body. In the process he finished undressing me and slid out of his under pants. Good looks aren't the only similarity he and Henry Lee shared.

"I hope I don't disappoint you," I said. "I'm not sure what to do."

"There is no way you could ever disappoint me, baby. Just relax and do whatever comes natural. I won't hurt you, I promise, don't be scared."

"Blow out the candle."

"No, please, let it burn. I've waited so long for this. I want to look at you while we make love. I want to remember every moment of this night, Billie Jean. The night I truly make you mine."

Bobby Ray was a gentle and patient lover, but I couldn't truthfully say that first time I felt the earth shake or standstill, or whatever it was those *True Romance* books claim will happen, but I liked the closeness, the being as one. Early the next morning we fed the dogs and headed to Nashville. Daddy wondered when he came by later how the dogs had gotten food and water in their bowls. Eventually we told everyone what we did and Henry Lee had been so upset. "Dang," he said. "I knew we should have gone to the house."

CHAPTER 17

We didn't have a lot of time or money to spend on a honeymoon. It was nearly time to cut tobacco and Bobby Ray needed to get back and get things ready, but we tried to make the most of what we had. On our first day in town we had gone to the Ryman Auditorium for the afternoon matinee of the *Grand Ole Opry*. On the program that day had been Roy Acuff and the Smoky Mountain Boys, Billy Wayne Grammer and Wilma Lee and Stoney Cooper and The Clinch Mountain Clan, and of course, Ms. Minnie Pearl. The following day we visited the Belle Meade Plantation. What had started back in 1807 as a single, small log cabin would develop over the next hundred years into five thousand, four hundred acres and be the breeding place for world renowned thoroughbred horses.

While we toured the stables Bobby Ray leaned over and whispered in my ear, "This is nicer than our house," and I giggled. So sadly true.

The horses that lived on this plantation were treated mighty well. The next place we planned to visit was the Cheekwood Mansion, but we found it not yet opened to the public. It would be the following year before visitors could go inside. The house had been built by the Leslie Cheek family that owned and operated a wholesale grocery. Mr. Cheek and his partner was credited with having blended a wonderful tasting coffee that later became famous, and it was first marketed through one of the finest hotels in Nashville, The Maxwell House, thus the brand name, Maxwell House Coffee came to be.

Between our sightseeing adventures we would return to the hotel and make love. It hadn't taken me long to catch on to what all the fuss was about, like a, "aha" moment. Funny thing about it though; being intimate with someone you truly love can be a double-edged sword. The longing and yearning for that person makes you dependent on them, and very vulnerable. I didn't think I could ever be with another man the way I was with Bobby Ray.

Our last day in town we took a stroll down Broadway and happened into a small diner called Mom's. It wasn't much more than a hole in the wall at the time, but the very next year the small café would be bought by a lady by the name of Hattie Louise Bess, but everyone called her Tootsie. A hired workman, much to Tootsie's chagrin, painted the lounge a deep, dark orchid, and in the coming years the little place would become known as the world famous honky tonk; Tootsie's Orchid Lounge. Several country music stars got their start on her tiny stage, and even to the present day, the exterior of the old building remains an eye-popping orchid. Bobby Ray and I never dreamed the place would become a legend in its own time. There hadn't been much that memorable about it, other than the ladies of the night that loitered around out front, and pretty brazenly in the broad daylight as well. They let Bobby Ray know real quickly what they could do for him, and with me standing right there. It didn't make me mad. Instead I felt sorry for them, and wondered if they had ever loved someone, or been loved the way I loved Bobby

Ray. If so, I didn't think they could do that type of work on a daily basis. But that's only my opinion.

Our first day back from our honeymoon, the second Bobby Ray left the house I began planning our noonday meal. I wanted it to be something special. In the music city we had eaten a lot of greasy cheeseburgers and french-fries, but there's only so much of that a body can stand. I wanted to prepare Bobby Ray some of his favorite foods for our first meal in our home. I knew he loved fried chicken and mashed potatoes, two dishes I did well. The only problem was I had never actually killed a chicken. That privileged chore had fallen to Daddy and Grandpa.

Grandma had given us a few Dominecker hens and a rooster to get us started, along with a few Rhode Island Red fryers. How hard could it be I reasoned, as I walked out into the backyard with the unsuspecting victims? I had seen it done a few times, but I didn't like to watch and tried not to think about it while eating the end results. All I needed to do was pick the chicken up by its neck and give it a couple of good hard and quick swings around and the head would pop off. It was then ready to dress, or pluck, something else I'd never done. Grandma had always done that, but I figured now was a good time to learn. I crept up behind the first chicken and reached down to grab it, but at the last minute, I couldn't do it, I chickened out. No pun intended. I walked around the yard for a bit trying to muster up the courage to make another attempt. I could have gotten Bobby Ray to do it but I didn't want him to think he'd married a ninny. Finally with determination, I walked up to another young chicken and grabbed it by the neck and gave it my best shot, but I guess I didn't do it hard enough because the head didn't come off. The poor chicken let out a heart wrenching squawk and I dropped it to the ground. It ran off with its head twisted to the side carrying on something dreadful. I took off screaming up the path to the ridge to find Bobby Ray, and of course he'd heard me coming and met me halfway.

"What's wrong, baby, are you hurt?" he asked, anxiously looking me over.

"Come quick, it's terrible—you've got to do somethin'," I was crying and out of breath, but before he could say anything I turned and started back with him following behind. When we arrived in the yard I gestured toward the chickens. "Do somethin', Bobby Ray, its sufferin'!" It hadn't been any trouble for him to figure out which one I meant and what must have happened. I couldn't bear to watch and went inside the house. In a few minutes Bobby Ray came to the backdoor and laid the headless chicken on the bottom step.

"You want me to pluck it for you? I've got time."

I had my back to Bobby Ray pretending to be busy in the kitchen, but I didn't have to see his face to know he was about to bust a gut trying not to laugh.

"No, I can do it, but thanks anyway."

"You sure? I don't mind."

"No. No. You go on back to the field. Dinner will be ready at noon." I still hadn't turned around and looked at him and I heard him walk away. I peeked behind me through the open door and saw Bobby Ray's shoulders shaking with laughter. I probably wouldn't ever live this down, but I couldn't worry about it right then. I needed to get that chicken cleaned, cut up and fried.

For those of you who may not know, when you place a chicken with its feathers still on into a pot of scalding water, the odor is really bad. So much so it could put anyone off ever wanting to eat chicken again, but it does make it much easier to pull the feathers out afterwards. After plucking the chicken I poured a small amount of rubbing alcohol into a small saucer and lit it. I then held the bare chicken over the flame, rotating and passing it rapidly back and forth. This would singe off any tiny down feathers that remained. After this I cut the chicken into pieces, washed, salted, and rolled them in flour, and fried them in real butter in my cast iron skillet. Some people prefer oil over butter. I remember growing up when Grandma used lard rendered from our own hogs to fry everything. Anyway, ta-da, now you have real southern style country fried chicken. Of course, there are several variations to the process and many different seasonings and coatings, and most prefer to by-pass the first few steps and buy their chicken at the supermarket already cut up and ready to go—but you get the general idea.

I had dinner ready and on the table when Bobby Ray came in at noon. He washed his hands at the sink and sat down, never mentioning the fiasco from that morning. "It looks and smells wonderful, baby," he said.

"Thank you," I replied, rather proud of myself. After that one little incident of securing the chicken for the meal, everything else had gone perfectly. My mashed potatoes didn't have a single lump and neither did the gravy. My homemade peach cobbler was to die for. As the sweet and hot buttery culinary masterpiece slid down my throat, I silently thanked Grandma for taking the time and having the patience to teach me to cook. After we'd finished eating I went about clearing the table. Bobby Ray came up behind me and rubbed his pelvis against my back side. I could feel what was on his mind.

"Let's go into the bedroom and rest awhile," he said, and nuzzled my ear and ran kisses lightly down my neck.

"Right now?" I questioned. Bobby Ray led me into the dimly lit room. I kept the curtains drawn and the shade down to keep out the hot sun. We lay down on the big four poster bed, but we didn't rest. As we made love with our hands entwined I looked at our matching gold bands and smiled. Like our rings Bobby Ray and me were a perfect match. The old headboard beat a steady rhythm against the wall as the sounds of young love drifted through the quiet house and christened every corner. Bobby Ray didn't make it back to the field that day until mid-afternoon.

After Bobby Ray left I returned to the kitchen to finish the dishes. The phone rang. Daddy was on the line and the news wasn't good. Once more I ran up the path to the ridge to find my husband. Bobby Ray was unloading tobacco sticks along the side of the field and saw me coming, and a big grin had spread across his face. "Can't stay away from me, can you?" he teased.

"It's Poppaw, he's been gone since mornin' and they can't find him."

We dashed back to the house. Bobby Ray loaded Blue into the truck; our Blue a direct descendant from Daddy's Ol' Blue, my childhood companion. Young Blue could track anything when he got the scent. We always said he must have a little bloodhound in him. At Poppaw's what began with a few neighbors out looking for him soon turned into several. Daddy and Grandpa Carson and

Bobby Ray's brothers, Cole and John Wesley were already there and organizing the group into teams. They were about to go out again when we arrived. Mamaw was beside herself with worry and crying into the shoulder of a neighbor lady. I jumped out of the truck and ran to her.

"It's okay Mamaw, we'll find him," I tried to reassure her.

"He was so confused when he got up this mornin', more so than usual. He kept followin' me around sayin' he had to go to the river and get a big du poisson for you and William. He finally went out on the porch and sat down in the rocker. I got busy so I'm not sure when he left. I missed him about mid-mornin'." Mamaw broke down into tears. "I should have been watchin' him better," she sobbed.

"It's not your fault, Mamaw, we'll find him."

Bobby Ray led Blue to the porch and let him sniff Poppaw's rocker and a jacket Mamaw said he wore. Once Blue had the scent he took off baying into the woods behind their house. Bobby Ray said Blue had a "bawl mouth," his bark long and drawn out when tracking his prey. If Poppaw meant to go to the river, he'd headed in the wrong direction. The river was the opposite way, some five or six miles from their house. I wondered how far a sixty-seven-year-old man in poor health could go in that thick underbrush. I had realized that Poppaw's mind was getting worse. At mine and Bobby Ray's wedding he called me 'Tit Jean,' like always, but kept calling Bobby Ray, William. I really believe Poppaw thought Bobby Ray was my father and I my mother.

We followed Blue into the dense woods for over a mile as the evening shadows began to creep in. Soon it would be too dark to see anything in the heavy foliage. We called to Poppaw over and over as we walked. If he could hear us, I was sure he would answer or come to us. I had a really bad feeling this wouldn't end well; call it woman's intuition if you like. Blue came to a steep incline with a washed out crevice down the side and stopped. It was overgrown with briers and kudzu vines. Blue tried to go down but Bobby Ray held him back. He began to run back and forth on his lead barking. Bobby Ray looked down into the small ravine and I started to walk toward him.

"Stay there, Billie Jean, don't come any closer." He held fast to Blue's leash and looked from me to down into the ravine. "Stay there, baby."

Cole put his arms around me, and I knew we had found Poppaw.

Daddy and John Wesley and two of the other men made their way down into the narrow opening. We didn't need a coroner to tell us Poppaw's spirit had flown from this world. Someone had brought along a rope and a blanket and they wrapped Poppaw in the blanket and tied the rope around him and gently pulled him out.

One of the men helping search had been clearing the way for us with his machete He now cut down a small sapling and made a pole. The pole was long enough for two men to carry it on their shoulders, and a couple of the guys removed their belts, running them through the rope and then looped them over the pole. They would take turns carrying Poppaw. It wasn't an easy job in that terrain. I walked beside him with my hand on his arm. Even through the blanket I could feel the cold. I was so blinded by my tears I could hardly see. I would have fallen more than once if not for Bobby Ray on one side and Daddy on the other.

At the house Mamaw insisted we uncover Poppaw's face. "I need to see him to make it real, to be able to accept he's really gone," she said.

Poppaw's right eye and the right side of his mouth were drawn. He likely suffered a massive stroke the doctor would tell us later. Before we loaded Poppaw's body into the truck, Cole came and laid his hand on Mamaw's arm. "Don't you worry 'bout nothin', Ms. Andre Ann, we take care of our own."

"Thank you Cole, you have always been so good to me and Claudell."

I never realized—or thought about, for that matter, that Poppaw and Mamaw might know Bobby Ray's brother, but it stood to reason they would. The Evans family had lived in the area for as long as my Poppaw and Mamaw had.

When my Uncle Blanchard and Allain arrived, we decided to have a small service at the house. Poppaw then would be taken back to Louisiana for burial. Back to his beloved bayou where he'd always longed to be. Uncle Allain also wanted to take Mamaw there to live with him, and I knew that would be for the best. Daddy and I made the trip to Louisiana alone. Bobby Ray had to stay behind and cut our tobacco. He hated he couldn't come with us, but farmers are at the mercy of the seasons. It was time for the tobacco to come out of the field. This was our livelihood and there was no other choice to be made The big meal I had planned to impress the tobacco crew when they came to our place would be prepared by Dora and Grandma.

We laid Poppaw to rest in a small cemetery enclosed by tall cypress trees with their branches hanging full of Spanish moss. I could easily understand what my Cajun grandparents meant when they spoke of their former home and its beauty. Though fairly late in the season, the Louisiana irises still bloomed in an array of colors, whites, blues, and the deepest of purple. Some stood six feet tall. A few delicate leaves had fallen from the green Palmetto trees and lay scattered across the ground, but what I loved the most was the Bayou violets. I was reminded of the color of my mother's eyes, or so I'm told. This was a whole other world from my home in Tennessee, and I will never forget my reaction the first time I saw live alligators in the wild.

Daddy and I were driving around and crossed a small, narrow bridge. I happened to look down into the water below. I thought they were logs lying there, until one of them moved. They were sunning themselves on the creek bank, much like dogs would in the yard at home. Daddy laughed and said my eyes got as big as saucers.

My Louisiana kin, most of whom I'd never met, thought me pretty funny too. They tried their hardest to convince me to eat crawfish, but I never could get past their little beady black eyes. Uncle Allain's wife Rue had made a delicious seafood gumbo. I'm pretty sure it contained crawfish and several other things I wasn't familiar with, but I ate it anyway and tried not to think about the ingredients. The shrimp on the other hand, I couldn't get enough of. Daddy and I brought a huge ice chest full of big reds back to Tennessee with us.

It was a bitter-sweet moment when it came time to say goodbye to Mamaw. I felt I would never see her again this side of Heaven—and I didn't. She passed away a little over a year later and they placed her beside my poppaw; together again forever and always.

CHAPTER 18

Our lives had fallen into a routine like most people's do. The hard work was never ending and money was always in short supply. Many a night I stayed up late to can the fresh garden vegetables and Bobby Ray would come in from the field after dark, milking by the light of a lantern. In the fall we picked our corn by hand using the mules and a wagon. This life wouldn't have appealed to everyone, but it did to me and Bobby Ray; our idea of the American Dream. All I ever wanted was to be Bobby Ray's wife and take care of our home, and we knew what we were working toward. We shared the same hopes and dreams and the same goals—to own our home and the land we lived on. Shortly after we'd married the papers were drawn up and signed. At the beginning of each year after our crop sold, a payment would be made on the farm until the note was paid. The good Lord willing, the little place would be ours in no time. Bobby Ray and I would lie in bed at night wrapped in one another's arms and plan all the renovations we would make to our little house. Yoked as one in marriage and as long as we pulled together as a team we would do well.

Ross had once implied that Bobby Ray was a beer drinker, but that wasn't true. When Bobby Ray drank, he preferred the hard stuff, whiskey, the homemade kind to be exact. I always thought wherever he came by it he didn't have to pay for it. I figured it came from the bootlegger—Preacher. Sometimes when Bobby Ray drank it made him act crazy. Thank goodness he didn't drink on a daily basis, but he didn't miss many nights going coon hunting. After we were done with supper, Bobby Ray would take the dogs and walk up to the ridge behind our house and turn them loose. He would sit and listen to them run for a couple of hours before coming home. Most nights he'd be in the bed by midnight and up bright and early the next morning ready to go again. He would leave the gate open to the pen and when the dogs got tired they would come home on their own and go inside. Some evenings I would go with Bobby Ray and we would build a little fire and sit and talk. On clear nights the star filled sky would look like a huge dome over the ridge with millions of small, twinkling diamonds. It seemed like Bobby Ray and I were the only ones there, and when the big, yellow moon rose above the rim, it appeared to be so close that we could have reached out and touched its face. I cherished those moments. The times I had gone with Bobby Ray he never drank in front of me, but when I didn't go, I would smell the whiskey on his breath when he came home. He wouldn't be drunk, not even close. He never drank in excess during the week or any other time, except when he went to hunt at John Wesley's.

The first time this happened came about three months into our marriage. It was on a Saturday night and Bobby Ray loaded his dogs in his truck and went to John Wesley's to hunt with him and his friends, the Renfro boys. After Bobby Ray left I tried to occupy myself with household chores. I did some ironing and made a pie for Sunday dinner the next day—this was the first time Bobby Ray left me alone at night. I didn't count the times on the ridge right behind the house. By eleven o'clock I begun to get sleepy and I lay down on the couch. I knew I would only catnap until Bobby Ray came home. Midnight came and no sign of Bobby Ray. One o'clock rolled around and no Bobby Ray. Two o'clock and three o'clock came and went and still Bobby Ray didn't come home. When his old truck did come creeping into our drive around four-thirty, I'd been wide awake and loaded for bear. I heard his uneven footsteps on the porch and met him at the door.

"Where the hell have you been?" I yelled the second he opened the door.

"Huntin'," is all he said, and made to go around me, but I stayed right in his face.

"You're drunk—and who in their right mind stays out all night huntin'?"

Bobby Ray tried to push past me but I wouldn't budge. He finally placed his hands on my upper arms and lifted me to the side. Of course this served to only make me even madder.

"Don't you shove me, Bobby Ray Evans."

"I didn't shove you, Billie Jean, I just moved you out of my face, and stop yellin'."

"Don't you dare tell me what to do after you layin' out all night. Ross was right."

We all know the second we say something we shouldn't have and immediately we wish we could take it back. It may be something we never even realized we were about to say until it's out there. My words hung in the air and seemed to echo over and over in the small room. Bobby Ray stopped and turned slowly toward me. His eyes glassy with drink had suddenly turned black with anger. Before I could say I hadn't meant it he roughly grabbed my upper arms.

"What did you say?" he yelled into my face. At the same time he was half dragging, half walking me into the bedroom. Bobby Ray threw me down across the bed and straddled me. "I don't want to hear his damned name in my house ever again," he shouted at me, and raised his clenched fists above his head. I saw them coming toward me and covered my face with my hands. Grandma's words shot through my head, "If a man hits you once, he'll hit you again." Bobby Ray lowered his fists and struck the bed on each side of my head with such force, that I bounced forward. We would have smacked foreheads, but Bobby Ray was off me in a flash and out the door. The clock on the wall was jarred loose, fell to the floor and burst apart when he slammed the door.

I lay there several minutes, stunned, trying to figure out what just happened. I heard Bobby Ray crank his truck, slinging gravel as he left. We'd had our first big fight and I knew it was partly my fault, well, mostly my fault. Hot bitter tears poured from my eyes. I shouldn't have yelled at Bobby Ray the instant he got home, and I never should have mentioned Ross's name, the breech between the two still fresh. I would remember not to make that mistake again. I'd been glad Ross was at school in East Tennessee, for truthfully I felt the time and distance apart would be good for all of us.

I tried to stay busy until time to go to church. I certainly wasn't in the mood to go, but if I didn't, Daddy and Grandma would be calling me later to find out why not. I didn't want to have to lie to them, and there's no way I would tell them the truth. So I put on my best happy face and went, but I don't think I fooled Daddy.

"Everythin' okay?" he asked, after the service was over.

"Yeah, great," I said. "I didn't sleep very well last night. Bobby Ray went huntin' with John Wesley and didn't get in 'til real late. I never sleep very sound until he does." I didn't have to lie after all, every word of that had been the truth.

When I arrived home Bobby Ray's truck was parked in its usual place and I saw Blue, Little Jean, and Hank in their pen. They didn't look any worse for wear after their long night. Inside Bobby Ray sat on the couch trying to piece the clock back together.

He stood up when I came in. "I think that's pretty much a lost cause," he said, and placed the broken time piece on the sofa. "I'll get you another one first thing in the mornin' as soon as the store opens." Bobby Ray had freshly bathed and shaved, his hair still wet. I wanted to go to him and run my fingers through it where it tried to curl at his neck.

"It don't matter about the clock. It's not like it's a family heirloom or anythin'.

"I was afraid you wouldn't come back."

"Of course I came back. This is my home—and you're my husband, where else would I go?" I'm not sure which of us made the first move, but in an instant we were in one another's arms, kissing, hugging, and apologizing.

"I'm so sorry, baby. I didn't intend to stay out all night. We lost the dogs and one thing led to another, and before I knew it, the night was nearly gone."

"I'm sorry I yelled at you. I was so worried somethin' bad had happened to you."

"I'm sorry I worried you, and I'm sorriest most of all, about the other. I promise you, Billie Jean, I will never raise my hand to you again. You have my word."

After dinner we lay down on the bed, both of us feeling the effects of not having slept the night before. Not that we went to sleep right away. I always heard makeup sex is the best, and I couldn't argue with that. Afterwards we cuddled and Bobby Ray began to talk about his childhood. This was really the first time he talked to me about his father.

"Cole and John Wesley have said Daddy wasn't always as hard and unfeelin' as I remember him. They said it happened after they had to leave Kentucky. You know 'bout that I guess?"

"Only a little. Daddy told me some of how y'all come to be in Tennessee."

"Well, times were hard in Eastern Kentucky, even before the Depression, and they only got worse. People were poor there, Billie Jean, like you wouldn't believe. Daddy thought when he brought his family here, things would be better, but they weren't. Times here were just as hard, and people almost as poor as in Kentucky. Cole says folks didn't take to Daddy too well. Likely cause of the way he was brung up. That a man shouldn't show his true feelin's or it was a sign of weakness. My ol' grandpappy Evans was one ornery SOB I've been told. I couldn't say, he died a long time before I come along, but I figure Daddy came by it honest. Anyway, when he couldn't make a decent livin' here, I think he gave up. Cole and John Wesley said he started to drink, a lot, and got real mean, and I know he likely did a lot of things he shouldn't have tryin' to keep us from starvin'."

"Did he hit you?"

"Yeah, sometimes, you know me, can't keep my mouth shut. I'd piss 'im off about somethin' and he'd belt me, and Henry Lee, he was so stubborn. It didn't matter how much you beat 'im, if he didn't want to do somethin' you weren't gonna make him. But Henry Lee's the one who put a stop to it all. After Daddy got sick enough he had to have oxygen all the time, we would hide his tobacco and matches from him. He'd raise holy hell until we gave 'em back. He had a heavy hickrey walkin' stick that he kept beside him and he would try to hit us with it when we walked by. One day he swung at Mama, wantin' his smokes, and Henry Lee grabbed that walkin' stick and threw it clear across the room. He got down in Daddy's face and real quiet like told him, 'Ol' man, you ever try to hit one of us again, I'll put you in your grave right then.' He must have made a believer out of Daddy. He never tried it again, and he was always harder on us boys than he was the girls. I guess he was afraid one of us might turn out to be a sissy."

I could hear the bitterness in Bobby Ray's voice. "It doesn't make you any less a man to show your feelin's, you do know that, don't you?" I whispered, running my hand across his firm stomach and chest.

"I know, and do you know how much I love you?" Bobby Ray asked, and pulled me closer. "As long as I have you, I can do without anythin' else in the world, and when we have babies, I'm gonna hug 'em and kiss 'em and tell 'em every day how much I love them."

"I love you with all my heart, Bobby Ray, and I always will. Wherever you are is home, and that's where I'll be, and I know you'll be a wonderful father."

After Bobby Ray fell asleep I lay awake and thought about what he said. Had his father ever told him he loved him? Could anger be the only emotion Harlan Evans showed his family? Was that the best memory they had of him? I did believe those demons from his past was what plagued Bobby Ray and drove him to drink from time to time. I felt if I could love him strong enough and hold him tight enough, I could drive these demons from his mind.

Bobby Ray kept his word and never raised his hand to me again, but the drinking was a far different matter. About every three months, Bobby Ray would go to John Wesley's to hunt with him and the Renfro's and he would tie on a good one. But I learned my lesson the first time and handled it much differently after that. As a rule, Bobby Ray wouldn't stay out as late as that first time, and when he did come home, I left him alone. He would sleep it off, sometimes in the truck, and the next morning he'd be fine. Maybe a little grumpy and thick tongued for a while, but life would return to normal until the next time. Yet the alcohol was always there—in the shadows, on the fringe, biding its time and waiting to take over and destroy Bobby Ray. I was determined not to allow that to happen. Not without putting up one hell of a fight.

CHAPTER 19

I have often said I think of the fifties as some of the best years of my life, and for the most part they were. Even though I'd been born a few years before the Baby-Boomers generation, I, too, have a tendency to remember them with feelings of nostalgia and to view them through rose-tinted glasses. To do otherwise would be to spoil those *Happy Days* memories, but on occasion I do allow myself to think back on those things that weren't so pleasant. As a kid I often heard the word communism and the term Cold War, and I heard my daddy and grandpa speak of the Nuclear Arms Race, and of course, Bennie's death had brought home a lot of this and made it seem more real. So many troubling events were taking place. Most were in some distant part of the world, but it could happen right here in America—in my own state of Tennessee, the invasion by a foreign power. I sat and watched on TV the air raid drills at the big schools in the large cities. I don't remember ever having one of those at our small school in Johnson's Bend. The Government probably thought we lived so far back the Germans or Russians or whoever, couldn't have found us anyway. One thing I do remember well, people wanting to build bomb shelters and to stock-up on can goods and other nonperishables. Daddy said it was silly, and it would be like the Bible speaks of when Jerusalem fell—there would be no place to hide.

What I feared the most hadn't been the other countries coming into ours, but what they could do from their own backyard. When I lay down at night I worried one of those ballistic missiles might fly in and hit our house and we'd be gone in the blink of an eye like the Bible says it will be in the end. But my greatest fear was the menacing possibility the "Big Bomb" would be dropped on the U.S. the way it had on Hiroshima and Nagasaki. I watched the replays of the huge, ominous, mushroom cloud over and over and couldn't get the images of the massive devastation and destruction out of my head. If my father saw me watching this horror with fixed intensity, he would find any excuse for me to leave the room. I'd been old enough to know what he was trying to do. Shield and protect me from the ugliness that man can inflict upon his fellow man. The threat of a nuclear war and the takeover by communism in the 1950's was an ever present cross for Americans to bear. I'm sure at one time or another I'd heard the name Karl Marx, but it didn't make much of an impression on me nor did his communistic views. In our home, his beliefs and philosophies were not discussed as part of our mealtime conversation, but the increasing concerns over the fast growing influences of the German Nazis in Europe, would make the atmosphere of this decade one of fear and uncertainty.

The early stirrings of the Civil Rights movement in the 1950's was something I remember more than anything else, perhaps because it was much closer to home. In the South things really began to heat up, especially with the organizations of groups like the NAACP, The National Association for the Advancement of

Colored People. One name in particular associated with this movement had stuck in my mind. It was that of a young, black preacher from Atlanta, Georgia, Martin Luther King Jr. I would hear his name many times over in the years to come, and it would go down in history linked to the state of Tennessee. Another name from this era that stuck with me was that of a black lady from Montgomery, Alabama; Rosa Parks. She'd refused to give up her seat on the bus to a white person, and even in my early teens I remember thinking, why should she have to? I'd never been around colored folks or had any dealings with them at this point in my life. We didn't have black families in our community or black children at my school, and thus far there had been no reason to question this. To tell the honest truth, I'd never heard my daddy's or my grandparents' views on segregation—hate and racism wasn't taught in our home. Grandma said everyone's soul is precious in Jesus' sight, just like in the little song I learned in Sunday school, *Jesus Loves Me*. The only thing I do remember my daddy saying was "There's trouble comin'." How prophetic those words would come to be.

By 1955 two-thirds of the homes in America had a TV, but some still didn't have indoor plumbing. That just goes to show even then people had their priorities screwed up. They cared more about being entertained than their common sense needs. Television did make it easier to keep up with the news of our ever changing world, but I'm not sure that's always a good thing. The shows that aired in the fifties had greatly distorted reality to my way of thinking. People only lived in the suburbs of some big city in "cookie-cutter" houses just like their neighbors. The men went to work each day wearing a gray flannel suit and the little woman stayed home and did her housework in high heel shoes and pearls. This may have been someone's reality, but sure wasn't mine and Bobby Ray's.

Another movement that began to make its voice heard in the fifties was the Feminist Movement. What began in the 1800's as a campaign for Women's Rights had by the late fifties turned into an all-out battle of the sexes. I never thought it wise or necessary to conform to society's version of things. It's very simple, you only need to read your Bible. It speaks very clearly on individual roles. I was perfectly happy and more than satisfied with its explanation. I didn't need or want some robust old gal with a bad haircut whom I've never met speaking for me. If they didn't want men to open their door and preferred to use the same public conveniences, that's their prerogative, but don't be messing up my playhouse. Another thing that got my dander up were shows that featured some little "flibbertigibbet" running home to Mama and crying, "My man just don't understand me or appreciate me." The poor schmuck had the audacity to give her a home appliance as a gift. Let me tell you, those little gals had never washed on a ringer-washer.

Our first winter together Bobby Ray and I remained pretty much still wrapped up in only one another. We kept our little house warm and cozy with a wood stove that sat in the living room. We placed heavy plastic over the windows to keep out the cold wind, but continued to use the outhouse for a bathroom and I hated that. Bobby Ray promised me faithfully when our crop sold we would get a commode and he and Lester would install it at the first sign of pretty weather. At night we used the slop jar, or chamber pot. It's all the same, and we took turns emptying it in the mornings. Mostly Bobby Ray took it out when he went to milk.

Shortly after we'd married we brought an old used ringer washer and placed it on the back porch. That thing hated me. The porch was only partially enclosed and I nearly froze every time I did laundry. It wouldn't have been so bad, because the washer was electric, if not for that darn ringer. Every time I tried to run Bobby Ray's overalls through, it would pop off track. If I placed a short, thin, piece of cloth on there, it would grab it and wind it around and around the cylinder. Invariably I would get my fingers pinched trying to get it out. A job that should have taken me two hours max, often took me most of the day. Before long my hands were red and chapped to the point of breaking open and bleeding. One cold, blustery afternoon as I sat by the stove rubbing the good Watkins hand lotion on my sore hands, Bobby Ray came in from work.

"What you doin', babe?" he asked.

"Puttin' hand lotion on. Supper's 'bout done—by the time you get cleaned up the bread will be ready." Bobby Ray walked over and took my hands in his.

"I've seen my mama's hands look this way," he said, gently massaging my hands with his thumbs, "from scrubbin' our clothes on a washboard in the dead of winter on the back porch. There was no way to keep the water hot. I said then no woman of mine would ever have hands like that."

"It's okay, I don't mind," I lied. I didn't want Bobby Ray to think I didn't believe he was doing all he could. Until our crops sold we were strapped for money. I kept my job at Mr. Utley's store three afternoons a week. That provided us with groceries and we could charge anything else we had to have.

"Well, I mind, and tomorrow I'm gonna to do somethin' about it—should've done it already."

"What are you goin' to do?" I asked, but Bobby Ray only shook his head.

The next morning Bobby Ray loaded one of our biggest and finest fattening hogs into the bed of the truck and left. When he returned a new automatic washer had taken the pig's place. I ran around laughing and jumping up and down like a crazy woman. "Won't we need that meat this winter, baby?" I asked.

"Oh, we can eat a few more rabbits and squirrels, and maybe I'll get a deer or two if I can find time to go huntin'," Bobby Ray replied. "You wouldn't believe the prices on these things, babe. Some of them are over three hundred dollars. The hog sold well, but I thought I was goin' to have to make a down payment and put the rest on time, but a salesman come in from the back 'bout then and said, 'this is your lucky day.' Normally when a man tells me that, I immediately get suspicious, but he led me out back of the store and showed me this washer. They had just gone and picked it up—folks never made the first payment on it. Now I'm real sorry for their bad luck, but it ain't our fault, we might as well have it as the next person. You run inside, babe, and call Henry Lee. If he's not home, tell Lester to come if he ain't doin' nothin' else and help me get this thing off the truck."

I ran inside the house to make the call, glad we had a phone. Bobby Ray told me later he badly wanted to get the dryer that went with the washer. I told him, maybe next year, and assured him I liked hanging the clothes out on the line in the fresh air and sunshine.

Installing the washer turned out to be harder than we thought. Our little house wasn't modern appliance friendly. Holes had to be dug and lines run. Thankfully our former landlord had installed a fuse box large enough to accommodate a washer and a dryer. He'd done this back when Bobby Ray first began to farm for him. At the same time he put running water into the house. It had taken the guys a few days, but before long the washer was up and going.

Daddy brought a small heater to set on the porch when I washed, said it one he and Dora didn't use. I never saw the heater at their house but I didn't say so. Daddy was very careful never to say or do anything to make Bobby Ray feel that Daddy thought he wasn't taking good care of me.

Lester came up with the great idea to put shutters on the porch. He had designed them and installed them. You could leave them down in the winter and prop them open in summer, and Bobby Ray, he ran a clothes line across our spare bedroom for me to use when it was really cold or raining outside. I don't believe anyone in the world could have been more proud of a washing machine than I was of mine.

CHAPTER 20

In the winter Bobby Ray didn't go hunting as much and I liked having him home at night. He said he had to take the dogs out at least once or twice a week so they could get some exercise. Not that his hunting ever interfered with our love life. His favorite time to make love was after coming in around midnight. When he went to John Wesley's and stayed out longer than he should and drank more than he should, he didn't always sleep it off in the truck. I've heard women say that alcohol decreased their man's performance, but it sure never hindered Bobby Ray's. If anything it had made him more amorous. At first I didn't like making love when he had alcohol on his breath, but Bobby Ray didn't like to take no for an answer. Not in this area. Not that he was ever mean or rough, but the alcohol definitely made him a little more aggressive. Sometimes he drank only enough to be mellow and to have left all his inhibitions in the woods. He was pretty funny on these occasions, and others, he could take my breath away.

Our first Christmas together was such a happy time. We didn't have a lot to spend on gifts and decided to give one another only something small. We wanted to save every penny we could to put toward buying the farm. I gave Bobby Ray a pocket knife from the store. Mr. Utley had let me have it at cost. Bobby Ray had given me a bottle of wonderful smelling real perfume. He had gone into Big Town to purchase it and I knew he spent far more on me than I on him.

"I thought we weren't goin' to spend a lot on each other this year," I said.

"A woman needs pretty things more than a man. Besides, I like the way it makes you smell," Bobby Ray said, and leaned down and kissed my neck and my throat and on down to between my breasts. I guess the perfume was as much for him as for me.

On Christmas Eve we went to Ms. Minnie's and all of Bobby Ray's siblings were there, even Margaret and her husband. That's what I like the most about the holidays—spending time with family you otherwise rarely got to see. I'd never had the chance to be around Margaret very much. She was one of the older kids and gone from home before me and Bobby Ray got together. I had the impression she wasn't a very happy person. She had the saddest eyes and it was easy to see that none of her family cared much for her husband Hugh, either. He was a loud mouth know-it-all. He thought he knew everything and really didn't know much of anything, and was so lazy he wouldn't shake dead lice off himself. The couple didn't have any children and I felt that might be a good thing. Margaret likely had her hands full trying to raise him, but she sure did adore her nieces and nephews.

Cole and Ms. Minnie had driven to Memphis to get Mary and bring her home for the holidays. The family was shocked at how much weight she'd lost. She hadn't been very big to begin with.

Come to find out, Mary was trying to exist on a diet of pork-and-beans and crackers; more crackers than beans, I think. Her scholarship helped greatly toward her books and tuition, but it didn't pay much in the way of her personal needs. Mary worked part time at a drugstore, but most of that money went toward the rent on her little room. It was a good thing her boarding house was within walking distance of the college. Cole bought Mary some new clothes before she left, and given her a little money, as several had for her graduation. I knew Daddy and Dora and my grandparents' did. Mary tried her best to stretch the money as far as it would go, but apparently when it ran out, she quit buying hardly any food, and was too proud to tell anyone or ask for more.

When Mary returned to school, the family pitched in and made up boxes of food and sent with her. From that time on we took turns carrying food and other supplies to her on a regular basis, and continued to for as long as she needed. Mr. Utley always let me have any dented can goods from the store, as by law he wasn't allowed to sell them to the public, but there was certainly nothing wrong with them. Bobby Ray and I had eaten food from these barely damaged cans ever since we married, and it sure hadn't hurt us any, so I began to send Mary some of those. In her room she had a small hot plate and a tiny refrigerator. Mary called the food we sent, "her care packages," but you could tell she had been tickled to death to see each one arrive.

What a wonderful time we had that night. Everyone brought food and we ate and laughed and talked and played cards until way past midnight. It was their first Christmas since their daddy's passing, but no one mentioned his name. I couldn't help but wonder what their Christmas's had been like when he was alive. Would he get drunk and spoil it for everyone? John Wesley brought a bottle of whiskey for the homemade boiled custard his wife Queenie made. He didn't pour it into the whole bowl, but added a tad to your cup if you wanted. I allowed him to put a drop into mine, but I really didn't care for it all that much and made a face. Bobby Ray and his brothers had a big laugh out of it, but it was all in good fun. No one got drunk. Although, John Wesley had plenty by the time he arrived, thankfully he was very pleasant and held his liquor well. He and his wife had four girls and John Wesley was foolish over every one of them. Cole was the same with his and Sarah's four kids, two boys and two girls, and regardless of their upbringing, someone had taught them the love of family. I assumed their mother.

Another person present that night that tried a little whiskey in their boiled custard, was my cousin, Ruth. She didn't like it either. The attraction I witnessed between her and Henry Lee at my wedding, and had been so concerned about, gradually developed into a full-fledged romance. Oh, they'd denied it at first. Supposedly Ruth was only helping Henry Lee study to get his G.E.D. She had and he did, but they didn't fool anyone. I saw the moon-eyed looks Ruth gave Henry Lee, and Bobby Ray said he knew right off more was in the works than higher education.

On Christmas Day my family gathered at Daddy's and Dora's, and Ruth brought Henry Lee. The more I watched the two of them together, the more I realized they were perfect for one another. Ruth was patient, good, and loving, and Henry Lee needed to be somebody's hero. From the way Ruth looked at him, he fulfilled that role for her quite well. It was the same way I looked at Bobby Ray.

I was a little surprised at how quickly Aunt Grace and Uncle Ted had taken to Henry Lee and Bo was wild about him. Like two brothers they were planning a hunting trip for New Year's Day. Henry Lee had most assuredly been a diamond in the rough back then, but in time, Ruth polished him until he sparkled and shined.

After Christmas dinner at Daddy's we went to my grandparents' that evening for snacks. The whole reason Daddy and Dora had everyone at their house was to make it easier on Grandma, but she let it be known real quick she was far from too old to entertain. By the time we arrived home that night we'd been stuffed to the gills and really missing having an indoor bathroom. We turned on the lights on our little cedar tree and sat down on the couch. Bobby Ray was still admiring the new clothes he received from my family. Overalls and Levi's, flannel shirts and socks, and Henry Lee had gotten some of the same. They had thanked everyone profusely. Their family hadn't exchanged gifts between the adults, but only bought for the younger kids and Ms. Minnie. They had several small children in their family at the time and there was none in my immediate family.

I think you can always tell when a person hasn't had a lot in their lifetime. Not so much by what they say or the way they look, but by the way they perceive the little things that others might take for granted. Bobby Ray and Henry Lee were as proud of those new clothes as they would have been a big diamond ring, probably more so. I sure wasn't born with a silver spoon in my mouth, but I had what I needed and some of what I wanted.

As we sat quietly together in our little home on our first Christmas night as husband and wife, I looked down at my beautiful engagement ring. I knew in my heart Bobby Ray had gone without to buy it for me. He would never admit to it, but he had, and I made a silent New Year's resolution to myself right then and there. I would never allow Bobby Ray to do without again for me. From that time on I made it a habit to bring some little something home for him from the store each time I worked. It might be only a candy bar or a bag of peanuts, but I could see how much it pleased him, and I soon learned I'd better bring two of whatever it was. If I didn't, Bobby Ray wouldn't accept it unless I agreed to take half. I suppose when you come from a family as large as his, sharing was one of the first lessons you learn.

The day after Christmas the weather turned warm and a slow drizzle of rain set in. This made our tobacco come in order and we spent the rest of the week and New Year's Day stripping tobacco. Having a big family does have its advantages. Bobby Ray's brothers came and helped with ours and we in return helped with theirs. I had never stripped tobacco in my life. That was Daddy's and Grandpa's job. I did help, "book it", as it's called, into the small square boxes that are really only boards nailed together but don't have a bottom. There're used solely for the purpose of transporting the tobacco to the sale floor. I hadn't been real fast at the stripping, but Bobby Ray said I tied a mighty "perty hand."

That New Year's night Bobby Ray and I invited our families to our home for a meal. Everyone brought a dish and we furnished the country ham and biscuits. The one hog left after Bobby Ray sold the other to buy my washer, gave us plenty of meat, and Bobby Ray did a wonderful job curing the hams. Even if it hadn't, I wouldn't have cared. I would have done without pork for the rest of my life before I would have given up my new washer.

Ross came home from school for the holidays. I saw his car at his parents'. We didn't run into him, and I'm ashamed to admit it, but I was glad. The fifties came to an end and the missiles didn't fly, and the bombs didn't fall, and the Communists didn't invade. I suppose when things don't happen in your own front door you have a tendency to forget and to become complacent. Little did we know the sixties that loomed on the horizon would bring such turmoil and a whole new set of worries.

CHAPTER 21

Bobby Ray and I looked forward to the New Year and it rolled in with great promise. Our tobacco sold for a really good price. The man at the tobacco floor said it some of the best and prettiest he'd seen. They even gave Bobby Ray's name over the radio as having some of the top selling tobacco that year. With this money we made the first payment on our place. We paid our bill at Mr. Utley's store and Bobby Ray gave Cole the money he owed him for my ring. Cole told him there no hurry, but Bobby Ray had given his word. We bought a commode and the supplies to install it and put in a small shower. We did this by further expanding the enclosed area of the back porch. Not the bathroom of my dreams, but would suffice for the time. We again had Mr. Henley to thank. He had dug a septic tank at the same time he did the other improvements and this saved us a huge expense. It allowed us to put back a little to live on the coming year. He was a wonderful Christian man and there were not many landlords like him around. He figured Bobby Ray planned to bring a wife there and wanted to help him out. Most people in his position wouldn't have cared or wanted to spend their money. Of course it had increased the value of the property and the selling price. So I guess it all evened out in the long run. Some of the money we used to buy tobacco seeds and whatever else was needed to make another crop, and Bobby Ray gave me a nice contribution for the church. I was so proud of him. I hadn't said anything to him along those lines. I felt my life was good and I was happy and content.

On February 1, 1960, in Greensboro, North Carolina four black students from the Agricultural and Technical College had staged a sit-in at a segregated Woolworth's lunch counter. They were protesting their Civil Rights had been violated when they were denied service. This launched a national protest for Civil Rights and the action had been repeated across the nation with numerous sit-ins by thousands of students black and white. We had watched the events unfold on the television and read about them in the local paper but life in Johnson's Bend went on in much the same way as always.

In May of that year the Soviet Union shot down one of our U-2 reconnaissance planes and took the pilot, Gary Powers, hostage. Bobby Ray was highly upset by this. "We," meaning the United States military, "need to go after him," he said. "They shouldn't let them damn Commies get by with that shit." Bobby Ray felt we owed it to Bennie and to all the soldiers that died protecting our freedom. Daddy felt the same way but maybe a little more level-headed in his thinking. I know that freedom always comes with a price, but I didn't want Bobby Ray to have to go to war. The very thought of it struck fear into my heart.

By mid-July Bobby Ray had a good crop in the field, and our families were making plans for Ruth and Henry Lee's wedding in early September. The couple had announced their engagement at Grandpa Jack's birthday celebration in June. They would marry at Ruth's church in Big Town and the reception was to be held at the same restaurant Bobby Ray had taken me on his prom night. It had a large room in the back especially for such occasions.

One hot Saturday evening talking to Ruth on the phone, she told me how Henry Lee was now going to church with her regular. As I hung up the phone I saw Bobby Ray preparing to go hunting. It was barely seven o'clock and he never left the house before nine. He told me earlier in the day he was going to John Wesley's and might be out really late. That's the first thing that made me suspicious—it had been only a couple of weeks since his last hunting trip with John Wesley. In fact he acted strange all day, kind of nervous and restless. When I saw him put on a T-shirt under his overalls, I definitely knew something was up.

"Who you dressin' up for?" I asked.

"What're you talkin' about, I've got on overalls." Bobby Ray tried to act like he didn't know what I meant.

"You never wear a shirt under your overalls in this kind of weather when you go huntin'."

"Well, tonight I'm goin' to—look, I gotta go." Bobby Ray gave me a quick peck on the lips and hurried out the door. I stood at the window and watched him load the dogs into the truck and drive off. I thought to myself, she'd better be worth it, because it would be a cold day in you-know-where, before he got anymore in this house. I lay awake that night wondering what I would do if Bobby Ray truly was out with another woman. What if he had stopped loving me and wanted someone else? I suppose I was very naïve but the thought we might not be together forever had never crossed my mine. I'd still been awake at daybreak when I heard Bobby Ray's old truck pull into the drive and go behind the house. I slipped out the back door where I saw Bobby Ray taking the dogs to the pen and I walked quietly up behind him.

"Was she worth it?" I asked, my voice surprisingly calm. Bobby Ray hadn't heard me come up behind him and jumped.

"Damn, Billie Jean, don't sneak up on me like that."

Bobby Ray didn't seem drunk. In fact, I couldn't smell any alcohol about him. I repeated my question. "I said, was she worth it? Losin' your home and me and all that we've worked for? Cause I tell you right now, I'll burn it to the ground before I'll see another woman get her hands on it."

"Baby, what are you talkin' about? What other woman?" Bobby Ray slipped his arms around my waist. "There's never been any woman for me but you, don't you know that?" Bobby Ray's shirt was soaked through with sweat and stuck to his skin.

"Then where've you been all night...and don't tell me huntin'."

Bobby Ray hung his head, and he then looked at me with guilt on his face. "You're not gonna like the truth no better." I couldn't imagine anything that would upset me more than another woman.

"Well, try me." Already I could feel the knot in my chest starting to ease.

"I took a load of moonshine up to this side of Nashville for Preacher."

I don't know what I'd expected him to say, but surely not that. "You took a load of shine—in this old truck—to Nashville?" Bobby Ray nodded in the affirmative. "With the dogs in the back?" Bobby Ray nodded again. Dumbfounded, I couldn't think of a thing to say and I stood there staring at Bobby Ray with my mouth hanging open.

"I wouldn't have been gone so long, but I had a flat tire right before I got to where I was to meet up with the buyer. I was afraid he wouldn't wait—then this deputy sheriff pulled up beside me askin' if he could help. He was a real nice guy, and he wanted to see the dogs. So I let him. What else could I do?" Bobby Ray told this like it the most natural thing in the world for a person to do on a Saturday night, and all I did was stand there and stare at him. I heard what Bobby Ray was saying, but I couldn't wrap my mind around the reality of this. What I feared would happen, had. The homemade "hooch" had destroyed his brain.

"He never noticed the bales of straw," Bobby Ray continued, "or if he did, didn't think nothin' 'bout it, 'cause he never asked to look behind 'em. After he left I went on to the meetin' place and the guy was still there. I unloaded the goods and he handed me the money and I high-tailed it toward home. Say somethin', baby."

I was still standing there with my mouth open looking at him. What could I say—that this was the craziest thing I ever heard? I knew it had to be the truth. No one could make up a story like that. Without uttering a word I turned and walked back to the house.

After Bobby Ray fed the dogs he came inside. I stood at the kitchen sink watching the sky through the window turn from the purplish blue of early dawn to blush pink as the sun rose above the ridge. Bobby Ray came and placed one arm around my waist and with the other pulled my hair back and kissed my neck, but it wasn't going to be that easy. Not this time.

"How much trouble am I in?" he asked.

"Lots! Bobby Ray, why would you take a chance like that—gettin' caught—goin' to jail? We're not that hard up for money."

"I know, but I felt I had to, I owed it to Preacher. He needed to move the stuff last night. I don't mind tellin' you, I nearly peed my pants when that deputy sheriff rolled up beside me."

"Why do all of you feel such loyalty to that man? Who is he—and what kind of hold does he have on you?"

"I can't explain it, baby, or tell you who he is, he wouldn't want that. But I can tell you this, he never intended for it to go this far or get so out-of-hand. He just wanted to take care of his own."

"You can't be takin' them kind of chances anymore—you've got responsibilities now and people other than me dependin' on you."

"What other people?" Bobby Ray asked, and I placed his hand on my belly.

"The rabbit died," I laughed, "you're goin' to be a Daddy. I'm pregnant."

Bobby Ray didn't say anything for a moment and then it sunk in. "Baby, we're goin' to have a baby!" he shouted, and picked me up and swung me around and around.

"Put me down," I laughed, "you're makin' me dizzy."

"When, when will the baby be here?" he wanted to know, his voice filled with excitement.

"Not 'till next year around the last of April or thereabouts. I went to the doctor last Wednesday. You know the day I told you I was goin' into Big Town for material. I didn't want to tell you until I was sure. I meant to tell you last night with a special meal but then you told me you were goin' huntin' with John Wesley."

"I'm so sorry, baby. I didn't mean to hurt you, or to worry you in any way. You didn't really believe I was out with another woman, did you?"

"I didn't know. I'm not foolish enough to think there're not plenty of other women around who wouldn't love to have you."

"Well, I don't know 'bout that. Would you really burn the house down?"

"No, probably not. I'd just glue your pride to your hand some night while you were asleep."

Bobby Ray threw his head back and howled with laughter. "Woman—I believe there's a devious side to you I've never seen." Out of his pocket Bobby Ray took three, one hundred dollar bills and laid them on the counter beside me. "I promise you, baby, I'll never do anythin' like that again. You have my word."

Bobby Ray went to take a shower and I lay down on the bed exhausted. It seemed all I wanted to do those days was sleep. I thought about the money Bobby Ray gave me. I didn't have any idea what a case of bootlegged whiskey would be worth, but to me it seemed a lot for his part. No more than he could have hauled in his truck with the dogs in there. Maybe Preacher was trying to bait him, to show him what easy money it could be? I knew I should have burned the 'ill-gotten gain', as the Bible calls it, but that would have been foolish. What's done is done and we surely could use the money especially with the baby coming. I guess that's how sin sneaks into our life, a little at the time.

After his shower Bobby Ray slid in beside me smelling of Lifebuoy and his favorite cologne and I asked him, "Whiskey is legal now, why do people want the illegal stuff?"

"Some folks prefer the home brewed. There's still plenty of money to be made in the business. And Preacher's whiskey is so pure and tastes so good, it will make you..."

"I know, I've heard, 'see the light'," I said dryly, and Bobby Ray laughed.

"He truly never meant to keep doin' it for this long. He got started way back when times were so hard. He knew how to make good shine and could sell it for enough cash to keep body and soul together. He never did it with any expectations of gettin' rich, and he sure hasn't. Durin' and after prohibition, the price of whiskey went sky high, and many of the buyers were more concerned with the quantity than with the quality. Preacher was forced to deal with some of them and he didn't like it much. A lot of rot gut was turned out around then and it gave all moonshiners a bad name, but Preacher's stayed true to his craft. He would rather make less and it be good, than make lots and it taste like swamp water. He's been ready to get out of the business for a while, but his buyers don't want him to quit."

Bobby Ray fell asleep with his hand on my belly and I lay awake thinking. He knew making moonshine was illegal, and I think he knew it went against the teachings of God. Yet he talked about it like it was the only reasonable thing Preacher, and many others, could have done. I don't know what I would have done in their place, and I don't believe until faced with the situation, anyone can know for sure what they'd do.

We slept until noon and I missed church. When I thought Daddy would be home, I called. "I was just about to call you," he said. "Everythin' all right?"

"Yeah, I didn't feel too well this mornin' and stayed in bed. We'll be down later, around two or so. We have somethin' to tell you. Tell Grandpa and Grandma to be there too." It hadn't been a complete falsehood. I did feel queasy first thing in the morning.

I made us a bite of lunch while Bobby Ray went to milk. Ol' Bessie wasn't happy with the late start. I hoped my good news would help take Grandma's mind off the upcoming presidential race. She'd been all torn-up over the young Democratic candidate from Massachusetts, Senator John F. Kennedy, the first Irish-Catholic to run for the office. Grandma wasn't sure which might be worse to have in the White House, him or a Republican.

Everyone assembled at Daddy's by the time we arrived, even Ruth and Henry Lee. They'd been at Grandma's for dinner. She continued to cook huge meals on Sunday and expected us to be in attendance. Bobby Ray and I went sometimes, but we liked to have our Sunday's at home alone. Henry Lee grinned from ear to ear when we walked in as did everyone else. I'm sure they suspected the mainspring of the news, but I let Bobby Ray do the honors.

"I'm goin' to be a Daddy," he said with tons of pride in his voice, and I vow I saw his chest swell.

Never have I seen a man as excited about a baby. It was like he'd been the first man in the world to ever accomplish this feat. We received a lot of congratulations and many hugs and kisses and Bobby Ray was subjected to a lot of good-natured ribbing from Henry Lee, Bo, and

Uncle Ted. We stayed for a while and then went to tell Ms. Minnie and Lester. They had been overjoyed as well. Ms. Minnie said she could never have too many grandkids.

Bobby Ray went to church with me that evening without me asking. He got ready like he did it all the time. I hoped the baby would be a good thing in many ways. I tried to put Preacher and what happened the night before in the back of my mind. I prayed the worrisome bootlegger would stay there. Out of sight and out of mind and I would never have to deal with him again. I could never figure out how Bobby Ray rationalized all of it in his head. He knew the scriptures, could quote many of them from memory, and this amazed me. I am ashamed to admit with the exception of a few, I couldn't. Yet he could go for weeks or sometimes months and never set foot inside the church house door. I prayed every night that Bobby Ray would see that he needed the Lord in his life daily, not just when he was thankful or in dire need, but a realization he must come to on his own. I suppose we all use God as a convenience on occasion. We call on him in time of great sorrow and try to remember to give him thanks for our daily blessings, and we utter his name in public places when we think it is in our best interest, but who do we think we're fooling? The Lord knows the true intent of our hearts at all times.

CHAPTER 22

Bobby Ray and I celebrated our first wedding anniversary by going out to dinner in Big Town with Ruth and Henry Lee. We reminisced about our wedding day and talked about theirs coming up in little over a month. I wasn't showing yet, other than my breasts had gotten larger, but I worried by the wedding, I would be. Aunt Grace made allowances for possible weight gain when she fitted me for my matron-of-honor dress, and hopefully I wouldn't look too pregnant in it by then. Bobby Ray would be best man and planned to wear the black suit he bought especially for our wedding and hadn't worn since. He used to laugh and say, "Black suits are for 'gettin' hitched and gettin' buried'." I forgave him for the Nashville trip and really didn't think a whole lot more about it or Preacher.

Ruth and Henry Lee's wedding day would be as beautiful as mine and Bobby Ray's only cooler. Unseasonably cool for September in Tennessee. Bobby Ray and his brothers whispered amongst themselves for weeks before the wedding. I'd been pretty sure Henry Lee was about to get some payback, and I hoped poor Ruth would be okay with whatever they came up with. The day before the wedding I received a phone call from my Uncle Allain. Mamaw had passed away. I'd been torn between going to the funeral and Ruth's wedding, and Ruth won. I couldn't bring myself to abandon her on her big day. Plus I knew after the baby came I would want to take him or her to visit my Cajun relatives. It wouldn't be likely we could make two trips that far so close together. My uncle completely understood. He didn't want me to bail on Ruth at the last minute either, but it still was a very hard decision. Before hanging up Uncle Allain said he and everyone else would be looking forward to my coming with the baby. I didn't feel I had to be there in person anyway. I carried the memories of my Louisiana grandparents with me always locked away in my heart.

Ruth and Henry Lee's wedding ceremony was so beautiful and so touching. Ruth looked like a small, priceless porcelain doll in her Victorian white lace gown. They repeated the traditional wedding vows and then said a few of their own.

When Henry Lee looked down at Ruth and said, "You complete me. You're what I've been waitin' for my whole life." I knew it was meant to be, just as I knew Bobby Ray and I were meant to be. I glanced across at him and saw him brush a tear away and he looked at me and smiled. I felt my love for this man could transcend the bonds of time.

After the ceremony pictures were taken before we assembled at the restaurant for the reception, a formal sit down meal. Henry Lee had recently bought a new truck and he tried to make everyone believe they would be taking it on their honeymoon. You can bet his brothers and his cousins had done it up right, but we knew Ruth's car was back at her house locked in the garage. The new couple had left in a barrage of rice, a repeat of mine and Bobby Ray's get away. They raced through town with the lot of us following behind blowing our horns as they turned onto the highway to Memphis. After going a short distance they turned around and came back for Ruth's car. I wish you could have seen the look on Henry Lee's face when he raised the garage door and saw us there.

"Surprise," we yelled. We had decorated Ruth's car to the extent that the make or the model or the color could hardly be seen.

"I told you big brother—pay back's hell," Bobby Ray laughed. Henry Lee laughed too and so did Ruth. She really had been a good sport and I hoped she would stay that way. Henry Lee wiped off the car doors enough he could open them and cleaned the windshield so he could see before they headed out once again. The rest of us returned to the reception and settled down to eat wedding cake, but Bobby Ray and his brothers couldn't eat for laughing.

"Did you see Henry Lee's face when he raised that garage door?" Lester asked.

"Yeah," Bobby Ray laughed. "And that dead carp outta be kickin' in right about now."

"I wish you hadn't done that, Bobby Ray," I said. "Ruth may never forgive me."

"Yes she will, baby. And you know Henry Lee had it comin' for all the pranks he's pulled on us over the years."

After the guests left the immediate family stayed and helped Aunt Grace and Uncle Ted clean up. Ms. Minnie wanted to stay but we sent her home by way of my grandparents'. Plenty of us without them and they were getting tired even if Grandma adamantly denied the fact. I guess Bobby Ray and the others started to feel a little guilty. They cleaned the mess off Henry Lee's truck so it would be waiting for him spic and span when he arrived home from his honeymoon.

I spent the day after the wedding trying to catch up on housework as did Bobby Ray with his neglected work. By nightfall both of us were worn out and ready for bed by nine o'clock. It didn't take much to tire me out anyway. A little before midnight a loud, firm knock came at the front door.

"Bobby Ray, Bobby Ray, open the door." It sounded like Lester's voice. By the second knock Bobby Ray had jumped out of bed and headed to the door. I sat up in bed but didn't get up. Bobby Ray opened the door and I heard subdued hurried whispering. He then returned to the bedroom and quickly dressed.

"I've got to go out for a spell, babe, but I'll be back as soon as I can."

"Where're you goin' this time of night? Is that Lester at the door?"

Bobby Ray came and squatted down beside the bed and gently placed his hands on each side of my face. "Do you trust me, Billie Jean?" I nodded I did. "Then I need for you to trust me now, can you do that for me?"

"Of course I trust you Bobby Ray, but why can't you tell me where you're goin' and what's happenin'?"

"It's better you don't know, but please, please, don't worry. I'll be okay and I'll be back as soon as I can."

"Come on, Bobby Ray, we've gotta go," Lester called from the darkness.

Bobby Ray kissed me hard on the mouth and ran out the door. I heard the truck speed away. I crawled out of bed and sat in the chair by the front window. I wouldn't sleep anymore that night, not until Bobby Ray was home and safe. I don't know why men always tell women not to worry. The moment they say that, it's time to start. I didn't have to be told, I knew instinctively this had something to do with Preacher. I sat through the night gazing out the window. The whole universe centered on that one dark spot outside the small pane of glass it seemed. I strained my ears to hear the sound of the truck's return and my eyes burned from staring into the night for a glimpse of its headlights. The deafening silence closed in around me like a shroud. I don't remember what I'd been thinking, or if I thought anything of great importance. I sat without moving until daybreak and when the sun began to creep up over the top of the ridge, I pulled myself from my chair, stiff from sitting so long, and headed to the kitchen to make a pot of coffee and switched on the radio. The first thing I heard, "A daring before dawn raid was made by law enforcement officers on a large moonshine still that's believed to belong to the infamous bootlegger, Preacher."

My heart lunged in my chest. The news report went on to say the still was discovered earlier in the week by hunters. They accidently stumbled upon it after becoming lost in the thick foliage surrounding the lake area. Sources confirmed shots had been fired at the perpetrators as they fled just ahead of the law. It would appear someone had been hit as blood was found on the ground and the bushes where they entered the woods. All they left behind in the wake of their hasty departure had been the sour mash they poured onto the ground and the still warm embers of the fire.

My legs felt like they turned to water and I barely made it to the table where I sat down in the chair. I laid my head on my folded arms and breathed in slow, deep breaths. I really thought I would be sick or pass out. There was not a doubt in my mind this is where Bobby Ray had gone. Had he been shot? Was he lying dead in the woods? I knew Lester wouldn't leave him there, and I began to speculate on who else could have been involved. For some reason I always thought of the Renfro boys when I thought of Preacher. I don't know why, maybe because I didn't care for them. Every time Bobby Ray went to John Wesley's to hunt with them he had come home late and drunk, but it probably wasn't fair to lay the blame for that at their door. The Renfro's had never done anything to me and was always polite and friendly when they were around. Clayton, the youngest, was the one I really didn't like. He seemed sort of sneaky to me, but none of this made them Moonshiners, and not anymore their fault than John Wesley's about Bobby Ray's drinking. He was a grown man and should know when to stop and come home.

When my legs would support me I started for the phone to call Ms. Minnie, but stopped. She wouldn't know any of this was going on and I didn't want to run the risk of upsetting her. I sure couldn't call Daddy. That would be a betrayal of Bobby Ray. I would wait. The least I could do, and pray, the most. Around nine or so I heard the truck when it topped the hill and stood on the front porch when John Wesley, driving Lester's truck, pulled into our drive. He waved but hadn't killed the motor, and as soon as Bobby Ray climbed out, he put the truck in reverse and backed out and drove away. The look on his face was grave, much the same as the expression on Bobby Ray's, but right at the moment I hadn't given it much thought. I was too happy and relieved to have Bobby Ray home. I ran to him and he caught me close and held me tight, his face and arms covered in scratches.

"Thank God, thank God—you're home and okay," I cried into his chest, my arms locked around him.

"I'm fine, baby, don't cry, please don't cry."

"I heard it on the radio, the raid on the still, and I know you were there. They said someone had been shot, and I was so afraid it was you and I nearly died." Bobby Ray stiffened a little in my arms and I looked up at him. "Who got shot, Bobby Ray?"

"Lester." Bobby Ray hung his head.

"Oh my Lord!—Is he...?"

"No, he'll be okay. Mostly a flesh wound, but it bled like a son-of-gun. That's why I've been gone so long. We had to take him across the river to someone who takes care of people in these situations."

Takes care of bootleggers and people involved in things outside the law is what he meant. My daddy's words came back to me; that Bobby Ray was raised different and exposed to things I had only read about. It wouldn't have changed anything. I would have married Bobby Ray had I known it all. I loved him with all my heart and every fiber of my being, and nothing would ever change that. I knew there was no point in asking him why he felt the need to risk his life for this man I knew only as Preacher.

"It could have been you, Bobby Ray, and who's we? Who else was there? Lester, John Wesley—the Renfro's?"

"It don't matter, it's over. Preacher is officially retired. He got word the still had been found and the law was comin'. We had to dismantle it last night he didn't want nothin' left that might link it to him." Bobby Ray gently raised my head and looked deep into my eyes. "I give you my word, you never have to think on Preacher ever again, and I know it could have been me. All I could think about when we were runnin' and the bullets were flyin' that I might never see your beautiful face again or see my child born." Bobby Ray's voice broke and tears filled his eyes. I reached up and cradled his head in my arms, just as I had when we children.

"Are you sure Lester will be okay? Maybe you should've taken him to see a real doctor."

A hint of a smile played around Bobby Ray's mouth. "We did take him to a real doctor, babe. You'd be surprised how many people still hold with some of the old ways. And there's somethin' else I need to tell you. Mama thinks Lester has gone to stay with friends for a few days to hunt, and Ruth, I don't think she knows much about Preacher, other than the gossip she's heard. I'm pretty sure Henry Lee wants to keep it that way."

"Of course, I won't tell anyone, anythin'."

"I know you won't, and I wish you didn't have to know any of it, but it's over, done, finished. You never have to worry about it again." That hadn't been entirely true, I continued to worry about Bobby Ray's drinking every day.

CHAPTER 23

Our first child, Robert Ray Evans II, was born April 15, 1961, and we called him Robbie. His daddy didn't want him called Junior. Bobby Ray said we could shorten it to Rob when he was older. You have never seen a man so proud of a baby. From the moment we brought Robbie home, Bobby Ray took him with him nearly everywhere. When still an infant, Bobby Ray would place Robbie in his little carrier seat, and if the weather permitted, took the baby outside with him. If working around the house, Bobby Ray sat the carrier seat on the ground beside him and talked to Robbie while he worked. When he changed the oil in one of the vehicles, Bobby Ray would explain every step of the process to him.

"This is stuff you need to know son, so when you're older you can do it yourself and not have to pay someone to do it for you."

I would stand in the backdoor, listen, and smile. Robbie would seem to take in every word his daddy said before falling asleep. Bobby Ray would keep right on talking. Robbie couldn't understand a thing his daddy said, I'm sure, but I think the sound of his voice is what he liked. Bobby Ray came in from hunting one night right as Robbie woke for his twelve o'clock feeding.

"Here, baby, let me feed him and you go back to bed," he said.

"You sure?" I questioned. Not that I didn't trust him with the baby. He was wonderful with Robbie, but that's how new mothers are. I handed him the baby and saw them settled on the couch with the bottle and went back to bed. I didn't intend to fall asleep, but I was worn out, another characteristic of a new mother. About an hour later I awoke with a start, the house silent, and the bed empty beside me. I leaped up and dashed to the living room. Bobby Ray lay back against the arm of the sofa. His arms were around Robbie who lay on his chest and both were sound asleep. I tried to ease Robbie out of Bobby Ray's strong arms without waking either of them.

"Bobby Ray," I whispered. "Let me take the baby. You get in the bed." Bobby Ray opened his eyes but he wasn't really awake.

"Oh, okay," he mumbled, and released his hold on Robbie, got up and ambled toward the bedroom.

I placed Robbie in his crib at the foot of our bed and tucked him in. Bobby Ray took off his overalls leaving them where they fell, already in bed and back to sleep before I eased in bedside him and spooned up next to him. Automatically his arm slid around me and drew me closer. I could understand why Robbie liked to sleep in his dad's arms, there was no place on earth I'd rather be.

By a narrow margin, John F. Kennedy became the thirty-fifth president of the United States. And to his many critics disbelief, no one was forced to become Catholic, nor was the catechism being taught in our public schools. He appeared to be a man of great vision and sound judgment and he made a lot of brownie points with his inaugural address, "Ask not what your country can do for you; ask what you can do for your country." Bobby Ray and I voted for Kennedy, as did Daddy and Grandpa, but

Grandma, a diehard Democrat, wouldn't vote. She couldn't bring herself to cast her ballot for Kennedy on account of his religion, but she did begrudgingly admit, "He's doin' okay."

A lot went on in the world in 1961, at home and abroad. The Bay of Pigs in April was one of many efforts to overthrow the regime of Cuban leader, Fidel Castro. In May, the first U. S. manned sub-orbital space flight took place under the command of Alan B. Shepard, Jr. Twenty days later President Kennedy announced his intentions to put a man on the moon by the end of the decade. This caused more than a few eyebrows to be raised on both sides of the political arena. Some even questioned the President's sanity. Yet life in Johnson's Bend continued on much the same as always, and we liked it that way. But in late summer of that year something took place to open our eyes to the sad, real truth. Johnson's Bend wasn't immune to everything going on in the world around us.

"I think we've got new neighbors," Bobby Ray said one evening as he came in from milking. I had gone to my grandparents' house that afternoon to pick the late June apples, wonderful for canning and baking, and took longer than planned. I had just placed a fresh apple pie in the oven when Bobby Ray brought in the bucket of milk. His supper would be late, but Bobby Ray was not one of those men to get all bent out of shape if his meals weren't on the table the moment he stepped through the door.

"Oh, really? Where at?" I asked.

"The Ol' Brown place," Bobby said, while pouring the warm milk into the cream separator. I later would take the cream and churn it into butter and place the fresh milk in the refrigerator in a glass jug for drinking.

"The ol' Brown place? You're kiddin'? That dump's not fit for critters." The house in question was maybe half a mile down the road from us. In the winter without the leaves on the trees we could see a small portion of the rooftop, but if we were standing on the ridge, we could see a lot more of the place. It sat empty for years and was now overgrown with weeds and vines. The roof and the foundation sagged and the glass was knocked out of all the windows by kids throwing rocks at them as they passed by.

"Might not be, but I saw an old flatbed Ford in the yard this mornin'. That same truck just went by the house headed that way with a young colored boy drivin'."

"Colored boy? You think a colored family has moved in down there? I've never seen colored folks in Johnson's Bend."

"Me either. Have you ever wondered why?" Bobby Ray raised his eyebrows.

"No, I guess I haven't. Why aren't there?"

"It's always been told, colored folks know better than to be caught in Johnson's Bend after sundown." Bobby Ray gave me a knowing look.

"We don't have any Klan around these parts, do we?" I asked in disbelief.

"Not that I know of, but they don't always advertise their presence."

I finished up supper while contemplating the ramification of a Negro family in the neighborhood. I had never been around black people. Bobby Ray had played ball with them in Big Town. Several black families lived there. He said the black kids weren't any different than the white kids, they just wanted to play ball.

The next morning after Bobby Ray left for the field, I baked another fresh apple pie. When the pie was done, I loaded it and Robbie into the car and drove to the ol' Brown place. I noticed at once when I pulled into the yard someone had swept it clean and cut away some of the weeds. But the old house looked the same—as if a good puff of wind might finish it off. Bobby Ray said old man Brown was such a skin flint he wouldn't help his own mother. I supposed that spilled over to his tenants as well. I wondered what kind of rent he charged for this dump that needed to be condemned. It probably would have been if the right people had known humans were living there. To the right of the house I saw a black, cast iron kettle sitting on bricks with a low burning fire underneath. With Robbie on one arm, and balancing the pie with the other, I got out of the car and walked slowly toward the house. At the front steps, or what was left of them, I noticed a small, black face looking up at me from under the porch.

"Hi, how are you?" I asked softly, not wanting to frighten him. After all, he didn't know me from Adam. The tiny boy crawled out from underneath the porch where he'd been playing with a little truck. His diaper was covered in red clay dirt. He didn't look to be much over a year old, and had the most beautiful smile that lit up his dark brown eyes.

"Where's your mama, darlin'?" At that moment, a young black girl waddled around from the side of the house. She herself didn't look to be any older than sixteen, and had a belly full of another baby. "Hello, I'm Billie Jean Evans." I heard the nervousness in my voice. "I'm your neighbor from up the road. I wanted to bring you this pie and welcome you to the neighborhood." The whole time I'm walking toward the girl extending the pie. I thought she didn't mean to take it, but then she reached for it timidly.

"I thank ya' kindly, miz's. My name's Hope, that my boy, Isaac.

It didn't take a rocket scientist to figure out what Hope's mother was thinking when she named her, but I wondered what had been in Hope's mind when she picked a name for her child. The Biblical Isaac was a young boy nearly offered as a human sacrifice by his father, but saved at the last minute by the hand of God. In Hebrew the name means, "He will laugh." Maybe that would hold true for this Isaac.

"He's beautiful. This is Robbie," I said, and held Robbie out for her to see. "It's short for Robert, after his daddy."

"He pretty, how ol' is he?"

"A bit over three months—when you due?" I asked, and gestured toward her bulging stomach.

"Bout three weeks—I wants to be home with my mama 'fore then."

"Where's home?"

"Wes' Memphis, Arkinsaw."

"How'd you get here, if you don't mind me askin'?"

"My man Royal thought workin' the 'backer fields wouldn't be as hard as pickin' cotton, and maybe pay more. It don't. We tryin' to save enough money for gas back home."

I had never picked cotton, but I knew working in the tobacco field was no picnic by the lake. "How'd you end up workin' for Mr. Brown?" I glanced toward the run down shack. The little boy, Isaac, had gone back to playing with his truck in the dirt.

"He be the only one hire Royal, and he don' pay him hardl' nothin'. He say we's can lives here as part of his wages. Don' have no screens on the windows, no 'lectristy; not that we could afford it."

"No electricity," I exclaimed. That would explain the fire and kettle at the side of the house. "Where do you get water?" I asked, appalled that anyone would have to live in such primitive conditions in the sixties.

"There be a well out back. The water dirty, I's boil it fore we drink it."

"Well, I guess I'd better go and get my man's dinner ready. I'll pray that things work out for you, Hope."

"I sho' do 'preciate the pie, ma'am. It'll goes good with the beans I's got cookin'. Hope glanced toward the kettle.

I smiled at Isaac as I left, and he returned the smile, so sweet and innocent. On the way home and while I made dinner, I worried and fretted. People shouldn't have to live that way, not in that day and time. Old Man Brown ought to be strung up by his heels. He had plenty of money and could help those kids if he would. Bobby Ray and I were fortunate to have had a kind, generous landlord like Mr. Henley. I suddenly remembered I hadn't asked Hope to come and visit me, and that she could use my stove to cook or bake whatever she needed. When Bobby Ray came in for his noonday meal, I was still upset with myself over this.

"I went to see our new neighbors this mornin'," I said, matter-of-factly. "Do you know they don't even have electricity, or screens on the windows. We could put screens on the windows for them, couldn't we Bobby Ray?

We have all that extra left from our back porch." I hadn't given Bobby Ray time to catch his breath, or to get a word in edgewise. He held up his hand as he sat down at the table.

"Whoa, hold on a minute. You went to visit the colored people? We can't just go in and start making repairs on other people's houses, they might get mad."

"Bobby Ray, do you really think if you were livin' in a house with nothin' over the windows and with mosquitoes as bad as they are around here, you'd be offended if someone wanted to put screens on them for you?"

Bobby Ray surmised he wouldn't win this battle and changed his strategy. "No, but ol' man Brown might get real upset. I can't go on his property makin' a bunch of changes. After all, it is his place."

"Ol' man Brown be damned! They're just kids, Bobby Ray, with a baby, and another one on the way. They're tryin' to save enough money to get back home. They really need our help. Would you hesitate if they were white?" I asked in a lowered voice, and gave Bobby Ray my most pitiful look.

"Billie Jean, that's not fair, and don't look at me that way. You know I don't have anythin' against colored folks—but they're not like one of them stray cats and dogs your grandpa said you were always draggin' home. You can't save the whole world, baby."

"I know I can't, darlin', but we could help a little bit of it right here in our own front door."

Bobby Ray held up his hands in surrender. "Okay, okay—I'll see what I can do—maybe Lester will help me, he's better at that kind of thing than I am."

"Oh thank you, darlin'," I said. "I'll go tell Hope in the mornin'." And I threw my arms around Bobby Ray's neck and gave him a big kiss.

"Can I please eat my dinner in peace now?" he asked, but not really upset. Bobby Ray was a good man and loved doing anything he knew would make me proud of him.

The next morning I set out to tell my neighbors the good news. I saw Bobby Ray, true to his word, gathering up our left over screen wire along with everything else needed to do the job. Lester, now fully recovered from his "hunting trip", had agreed to help with the project that coming Saturday. I also saw Bobby Ray placing pieces of scrap lumber we had lying around in the truck alongside the wire. He probably figured while putting screens on the windows he might as well make a few other much needed repairs. Like the front door. It was barely hanging by its hinges. Maybe Bobby Ray could even put in a new front stoop. But one thing at a time, I cautioned myself.

When I arrived at the Brown place the following morning it looked deserted. The truck was gone and there wasn't a fire under the kettle in the yard. Hope and her little boy had likely gone with her husband to work in Mr. Brown's tobacco field. It wasn't nearby. The land around the decaying house wasn't in much better shape, mostly scrub brush and gullies. The rusted tin roof made a screeching sound when the dry, south wind blew underneath. The entire place was a tinder box just waiting for a spark. I cradled Robbie in my arms and stepped with care onto the porch and knocked on the precariously standing front door. No sound from within. I knocked again, but still no one came to the door. I started to open it but stopped. That wouldn't be right. Instead I eased with caution down the porch and tested each board before I placed my weight on it. The last thing I needed was to fall through the rotting wood and injure myself or Robbie.

I made it without incident to the end of the porch. An old tattered blanket had been nailed across the window there. The window didn't have glass in it and only part of the wooden frame remained. I realized Bobby Ray and Lester would have a much bigger job on their hands than I'd first thought. I gently pulled the blanket aside, enough to see into the room beyond, and it appeared to be empty of life. The fairly large room had a coal grate on the back wall, but the flue was likely too deteriorated to be used safely. An iron bedstead sat in one corner with a thin mattress laid on top and a patchwork quilt spread over it. On the other side of the room in another corner sat a small, and obviously homemade, unfinished wood table with two cane bottom chairs. A kerosene lamp sat in the center of the table, and nearby a few pasteboard boxes were neatly stacked one on top of the other. There something about the room that reminded me of my Poppaw and Mamaw's house. "Poor is poor," I said to the sleeping baby in my arms, "and it looks the same on everyone no matter the color of their skin."

I knew I should have left and was only being nosey, but I was curious to see what lay out back. I walked through the knee high grass praying I didn't step on a snake, and was kind of disappointed when I arrived at the rear of the house. There really wasn't much to see. A stone well stood at the end of a small back porch that had fallen in on one side, its wooden frame hanging by a prayer. Someone had placed a thin square of sheet metal over the well's opening and a new bucket and rope was placed there. The dilapidated porch roof sagged dangerously, and I feared any sudden movement might bring it down. For the life of me I couldn't see there was any way this young couple could bring a new baby into this mess. And where would Hope deliver, surely not here with no running water or electricity. And what if they were still there come winter. How would they stay warm? All these problems ran through my mind as I walked back to my car.

I found a piece of paper and a pencil and wrote Hope a note. As I walked back to the door to slip it underneath, it occurred to me that maybe neither Hope nor her husband could read and write. But I'd done the best I could. Slowly I drove home thinking about pioneer women, my own great-grandmothers. They had borne large families under similar trying conditions. Far worse I'm sure. Of course back then many babies didn't live to see their first birthdays, but they kept right on having them. I couldn't imagine the hardships they endured or the grief they must have gone through. And I couldn't help but worry about this little family and what would happen to them.

The next day was my Friday afternoon to work at the store and the weekends were always the busiest. I didn't have a chance to drop by and see if Hope had gotten my note. Dora kept Robbie for me as it was her turn. She and Grandma nearly fought over who would get to keep him when I worked, so I said they could take turns. By the time I arrived home with Robbie, Bobby Ray was coming in from the field.

"Baby, I hate to ask," he said, "but could you make the dogs some cornbread and gravy? I forgot to ask you to bring a bag of feed home from the store." He tacked on that little grin I could never say no to.

"Sure. I hope you don't mind leftovers."

"Naw, baloney and crackers will be okay."

"Bobby Ray Evans, when have I ever fed you baloney and crackers after you've worked hard all day in the field?" I tried to sound offended, but Bobby Ray knew better. He'd had my number from way back. "There's still a big pot of white beans from last night, and I'll make enough cornbread and gravy for us too. If the dogs can eat it, I guess it'll be good enough for us," I said with a laugh.

To make that much cornbread I had to use my long baking pan. If I only planned to feed it to the dogs, I wouldn't have used as many eggs, and in place of the milk, I would have substituted water. Coon dogs aren't all that picky. I made the gravy in my large cast-iron skillet. After the cornbread was done, I crumbled it into my metal dishpan and poured the hot gravy over it. When Bobby Ray finished bathing he took the pan to the pen and fed the dogs. They probably could have eaten twice as much, but it would hold them until the next day. Bobby Ray then came in and sat down to his meal. It's a good man that sees to the care of his animals before himself.

After supper Bobby Ray played with Robbie and gave him his bath. It was their special time together. After Robbie was asleep, Bobby Ray and I sat in the porch swing and talked a bit before he took the dogs and walked up to the ridge. I went to bed. I'd had a full day and would have another one the next day. It didn't seem I had been asleep anytime when I was awakened by heavy footsteps running across the backyard.

Bobby Ray stuck his head in the backdoor and said softly, "There's fire down at the ol' Brown place, I saw it from the ridge." With that he ran to his truck and took off in that direction.

I crawled out of bed and went out onto the front porch but I couldn't see anything. I walked out into the yard but it didn't help. I wasn't up high enough and the leaves were too thick, but I thought I smelled smoke.

"Dear Lord," I prayed. "Please let Hope and her little family be okay." I said that place was nothing but a fire hazard. I felt Bobby Ray had been gone a long time, but probably wasn't all that long. I was about to go in to get Robbie up and drive down myself, when I heard his truck coming up the road. Isn't it funny how you can tell one vehicle from another like that? He pulled slowly into our drive and went to the back of the house and parked in his usual spot by the dog pen.

"Are they okay—what happened, did their cookin' fire get out?"

Bobby Ray climbed out of the truck. The bitter acrid smell of charred wood and grass smoke assailed my nostrils. His face was smudged with black ashes and soot. "They're okay, physically—scared-to-death."

Bobby Ray looked down at the ground and wouldn't meet my eyes. I knew there something he didn't want to tell me. "What happened? Just tell me."

"Royal said there was three, maybe four men in a pick-up truck with white sheets over their heads and holes cut out for their eyes. They stuck a cross in the front yard and set it on fire, yellin', 'nigger, get out of town,' and drove off. The ground was so hard the cross fell over and set the grass on fire, but they'd got their point across.

Royal and Hope were tryin' to beat it out with burlap bags when I got there. I helped 'em finish puttin' it out."

I felt sick to my stomach. "Lord have mercy. I can't believe this kind of thing could happen here in Johnson's Bend. Do you think it was—Klan?"

"Naw, just some local crackers most likely. The cross looked like someone ripped the boards from their ol' chicken coop and nailed them together. I don't think they were tryin' to hurt Hope and Royal, just scare 'em off, and they succeeded. They're long gone by now."

"What do you mean? Hope said they didn't have enough money to go anywhere, not right yet."

"Well, they do now." Bobby Ray walked toward the house unfastening his dirty overalls as he went. "I had a five gallon can of gas near full in the truck. I poured that in their tank, and I had four dollars and thirty-two cents in my pocket. That should buy 'em enough gas, and maybe a baloney sandwich, to get 'em to West Memphis. That's if that old truck holds out."

CHAPTER 24

The following morning after Bobby Ray left the house, Robbie and I drove once more to the Brown place. Not that I doubted Bobby Ray's word that Hope and her family were gone, but for some reason I felt drawn to the place. When I pulled up in front of the house, it had that vacant look and the smell of burned wood and dry grass lingered in the air. What was left of the makeshift cross lay in the dirt. Bobby Ray had been accurate in his description. It did look like weathered boards from someone's old chicken coop, and I would bet there were some ticked off ladies somewhere in the vicinity that morning when they found holes in their good bed sheets. As I turned to leave, an object lying at the edge of the road caught my eye. I picked it up and studied it for a moment, and then stuck it in my pocket.

Sunday, in what had become a Sunday morning routine, Lester, John Wesley, and Cole, came by to visit with Bobby Ray. If he happened to be going to church with me, and most Sunday's he hadn't been, they would have a cup of coffee and be on their way. This particular Sunday he hadn't planned to go and the four brothers settled down on the front porch with a fresh pot of coffee and their smokes. This is the way I left them most Sundays, talking politics, the high cost of living, and who had the best coon dog in the county. As I went to leave, I stopped in front of John Wesley and held out my hand.

"I thought you might want this back," I said. "I laundered it for you."

John Wesley looked sheepish as he reached for the blue bandanna. "Thanks," he mumbled.

I could see from the looks on the other's faces they had no idea what this was about. I laughed as I drove off. I would have loved to hear the conversation that took place after I was gone. I knew the moment I saw the large handkerchief lying in the road it belonged to John Wesley, kind of his trade mark. John Wesley had gotten into the habit when in prison to keep the sweat out of his eyes. After coming home he wore one nearly all the time, whether working or not. Another reason I knew the bandanna belonged to him was another habit from his prison years. In one corner of the faded cloth written in permanent marker and still quite legible, were the initials, J.W.E., John Wesley Evans.

A little over a month later in the wee hours of the morning the ol' Brown house burned to the ground. Bobby Ray and a few of our neighbors stood by to make sure the fire didn't spread, but didn't try to put it out. It didn't take long for the old house to be nothing but a pile of smoking tin with a bare naked chimney sticking up. Bobby Ray said it would become an eyesore on the land that old man Brown would never clean up, and he didn't. In time weeds grew over the ruins and kudzu vines obscured the chimney.

John Wesley swore he didn't have anything to do with its burning. Maybe he didn't, but I would bet he knew who did. Every time I drove by the place I couldn't help but feel a little sad. I wondered if the house that once stood there had ever been a home. Did love and laughter ever live there? Or had it been simply a stopover for transients on their way to somewhere else?

In the years following Hope and her family's brief stay in our small community, many things took place in my South I never would have dreamt possible. It *was not* our finest hour. Every time I watched the news reports of black's being beaten with clubs and having water hoses turned on them for daring to stand up for their equal rights, I had thought of a tiny boy with dark eyes and a beautiful smile named, Isaac, and I prayed, like the Isaac of old, the Lord would again stretch out his hand of grace and mercy and protect this one from harm.

When Robbie was barely six months old I again became pregnant, and my family was greatly concerned for my health, having babies so close together. Bobby Ray had worried a little about his own health, afraid Daddy might want to castrate him the way they did the young pigs. Birth control only works when used. I'm not going to pretend it was easy, far from the truth. It seemed all I did for three years was change diapers and make bottles. Daddy and Dora and my grandparents' were a tremendous help, as well as other family members, but Bobby Ray and I felt the children were our responsibility. Unlike so many young people today we didn't feel it our parents' job to raise our kids. We had them and it was our duty to take care of them.

I continued to work at Mr. Utley's store three afternoons a week with the second pregnancy, up to nearly my sixth month. Even the meager amount I made helped greatly, and I was saving for Robbie's first birthday to buy him a tricycle. He wouldn't be big enough to ride it yet, but quickly would be. I looked huge to my way of thinkin, much more so than with my first pregnancy. I easily become fatigued and would cry at the drop of a hat, but was determined to tough it out at the store for as long as I could.

One afternoon right at closing two elderly ladies I had known my entire life came in. Ms. Vester and Ester Stillwater, twins, and neither had ever been married. The sisters lived alone in a big white house with tall columns and an open veranda on a bluff that overlooked the river. Supposedly their daddy and granddaddy had been some sort of well-to-do land barons. I always heard they were more in the class with, and no better than, the hated carpetbaggers that descended on the South after the Civil War. They would acquire their acres and acres of land and homes for a little of nothing when the owners couldn't pay their taxes. I don't know this for a fact, but that had been the scuttlebutt. The sisters came into the store once a month and looked at everything there, no matter how many times they had seen it before. Ours was a really small country store and not likely we would get a big variety of new things in from one month until the next.

"Billie Jean, you in the family way again?" Ms. Vester asked, and looked me over with an expression of disbelief on her face.

"Yes ma' am," I answered politely.

"Your other baby a year old yet?"

"Not hardly, real soon though."

Ms. Vester clucked her tongue with disapproval and walked off.

Ms. Ester, who was extremely hard of hearing said, "Who's that girl, I don't believe I've ever seen her before."

She thought she was talking in a whisper, but you could plainly hear her from anywhere in the store.

"Yes you have, Ester," Ms. Vester said with exasperation. "She's that Carson girl that married the Evans boy. You know, her mama's the one that run off with the neighbor man while her daddy was off in the war."

Isn't it strange how some people can't remember what they've done five minutes before, but can remember a good scandal from twenty years back? And like that should explain the reason for my growing abdomen. Mr. Utley watched and listened to this exchange and saw the color rise in my face.

"Billie Jean, hon, why don't you run on to the house, I can finish up here," he said.

Mr. Utley was a man that was never confrontational and probably never raised his voice in his life. I took his advice and left. Afraid if I didn't and the twins made anymore comments about my family, I might go over and snatch the blue right out of their hair. Chalk it up to changing hormones. I still boiled when I arrived home and Bobby Ray must have sensed I wasn't in a very good mood. He had already gotten Robbie from my dad's.

"Me and the baby are gonna ride to the back of the field and check on a fence I think might be down. Why don't you lie down and rest awhile—no hurry 'bout supper, I'm not real hungry anyway," he said.

I looked at this man I loved so much it scared me sometimes. He seemed to know what to say and when not to say too much. "Course you're hungry, I'll have your supper ready when y'all get back."

Bobby Ray smiled at me. "Bad day?" he asked.

"No, not really," I said. "I'll tell you about it later," and smiled back.

In February of 1962, the first signs of a looming Vietnam conflict reared its ugly head. President Kennedy had said if our military forces stationed in Vietnam as advisors were fired upon, they would fire back. February of '62 stood out for another reason. Lt. Colonel John Glenn made history when he became the first U.S. astronaut to orbit the earth three times in his *Friendship 7* Mercury capsule before landing.

So many changes taking place in the world, and I felt many of them hadn't been for the better. It made me apprehensive about the future, and the thought of Bobby Ray having to go to war if things escalated in Southeast Asia was nearly unbearable, but that's where faith comes in. The Lord has always been, and will always be, in control.

Our second son, William Carson had come along in late July of 1962. He looked so much like Robbie at birth I could hardly tell their baby pictures apart—and Bobby Ray was just as crazy about him. I now had two miniature Bobby Rays. It would have been nice had one of them looked a little like me. We didn't have health insurance when the boys were born, very few people we knew did. Country folks didn't go to the doctor without good cause, one foot nearly in the grave. Instead they used old time remedies to treat themselves, some of which really worked. That year after our crop sold and the mortgage payment made, we paid the hospital for two babies. It hadn't left much to put into savings for remodeling the house. Bobby Ray did buy me a second hand clothes dryer and we added a small tub to our already crowded minuscule bathroom. Still not the bathroom of my dreams, but I made do. It sure beat the old metal tub I bathed in as a child and anything was better than having to go to the outhouse. And we did obtain some health insurance. We thought we couldn't afford it, but with two small children, we figured that could add up to a lot of doctor visits.

In October of 1962 it took three thousand troops to quell riots in Mississippi, the results of James Meredith entering the University of Mississippi, the first black to ever attend classes there. Later that month the Cuban Missile Crisis occurred, thirty-eight days of a country holding its breath. Many believed this was the closest the Cold War had come to breaking into a full blown armed conflict. I often thought I was only raising my boys so they could go to war. Yet more often than not, the things we worry about never happen. It's the unexpected stuff that sneaks up and causes the most trouble.

The month of October arrived unseasonably warm and muggy for our region, storm weather. I'd been afraid of thunder and lightning my entire life, likely because of Grandma Carson. Every time a little rain cloud came up, she would take me to the storm cellar. One day in the first part of the month, it was exceptionally hot and humid with a warm, southwest wind blowing with showers off and on throughout the day. I had a very uneasy feeling. I went frequently to the door to gaze up at the dark clouds that gathered and scurried across the sky. Bobby Ray said it would have been perfect tobacco stripping weather if it was ready, but the fire hadn't been under the tobacco long enough for it to be completely cured.

Later that evening after helping me get the boys down, Bobby Ray took the dogs and walked up to the ridge.

"I wish you'd stay here," I said. "I'm afraid it's gonna storm. Maybe we should take the kids and go to my grandparents', to the storm cellar."

"Baby, if the storm's gonna get you, it don't matter where you are—besides I'm only up the hill behind the house."

After Bobby Ray left, I tried to stay busy to keep my mind off the weather. The wind picked up greatly and I heard thunder rumbling in the distance. I paced the floor back and forth wondering what to do. Should I put the boys in the car and go to my grandparents' without Bobby Ray? I couldn't bring myself to leave him behind, even if he wasn't scared of storms. The wind rattled the glass in our old windows and the wind chimes on the front porch clanged together in rapid succession. Around ten-thirty the noise from outside became a roar. I was about to take the boys from their beds and head to my grandparents' when suddenly it became very still. I started to the front door to have a look when Bobby Ray came barreling through the back door. "Tornado!" he yelled.

"Get the boys up against the wall," Bobby Ray said, and motioned to the wall between the living room and the bedrooms. At the same time he was running toward our room where he dragged the mattress from our bed and brought it to where I had placed the now awake and frightened little boys next to the wall. Bobby Ray pushed me down beside them and lay down next to me, pulling the mattress on the top of us. Within moments it seemed the world outside of our very vulnerable little house exploded. The roof heaved and groaned but mercifully remained on. The boys hadn't cried, it was more of a whimpering, and I tried to reassure them all would be well. Bobby Ray caressed my arm and patted the boys on the head.

"You're okay boys, we're gonna be okay," he said, trying to sooth them, and I prayed fervently it would be so.

Robbie managed to wiggle up into my arms leaving Will wedged between him and the wall. Bobby Ray placed his arm underneath of Will and tried to bounce him up and down in the confined space. We heard the sound of breaking glass and large objects striking the house like incoming missiles. It then appeared to be over and an eerie calm followed. We lay there for awhile longer to be sure.

When Bobby Ray felt the worst had passed, he shoved the mattress off and stood up. He reached for Robbie and helped me to my feet and I picked Will up from the floor and cradled him in my arms. It was pitch black inside and outside the house, the electricity was out, and Bobby Ray's big spotlight was in his truck. He said wished he had grabbed it on his way in. We kept a smaller flashlight in our bedside table as it was not uncommon for the power to go out once in awhile in the area, even when the weather was good. Bobby Ray had me sit on the mattress with the boys and he stumbled into the bedroom to retrieve the flashlight. He then went into the kitchen and got the coal oil lamp from under the cabinet and lit it, placing it on the kitchen table. It gave off a comforting light.

"You stay here with the boys," Bobby Ray said. "I'm goin' outside and survey the damage."

"Please be careful, Bobby Ray. I'm sure there're power lines down and loads of broken glass everywhere."

Bobby Ray made his way to the back porch. "Glass is gone from the back door," he hollered back, and I heard him open the door. "Blue, here boy. Little Jean, Hank, come on guys." Bobby Ray called to the dogs several times but they hadn't come in response to his calls. Likely they were hunkered down to ride out the storm and were hopefully safe and well. Bobby Ray took in a sharp breath.

"No! No! Please God, no!" he cried, and ran out the door. I jumped off the mattress to see what had upset Bobby Ray so, and the boys put up a fuss at my leaving them alone. The second I got to the back door I saw the cause of Bobby Ray's alarm. From down in the bottom in the midst of the darkness and the still heavy rain fall, yellow flames licked toward the heavens. They too wanted to join the lighting that continued to streak across the distant horizon.

Our tobacco barn was on fire. The rotating winds must have accelerated the smoldering embers and sent up a live spark that ignited the tobacco. I could only speculate until Bobby Ray returned.

Bobby Ray ran on foot to the barn and I wondered why he hadn't taken the truck. I didn't know until later a large cedar tree had fallen across the drive. Bobby Ray didn't come back for some time, and in the light from the fire, I could see him running back and forth. He was trying to pull as much of the fallen tobacco from the flames as he could. After an hour or so, it could have been longer; the flames died down and eventually went away.

The torrential rain was a blessing in many ways. It extinguished the fire. When Bobby Ray at last came back to the house, his hands were burned and scorched and discouragement was written all over his soot blackened face.

"We've lost about half of the barn," he said in a broken voice. "I'm always tryin' to save a buck and it ends up costin' us a lot more."

"That's not true, baby," I tried to reassure him. I knew he was referring to the crop insurance we hadn't taken out. It was a gamble that's for sure, but many of the local farmers, my daddy and grandpa included, didn't have the insurance, but this time we had lost. Thank goodness our entire tobacco crop wasn't in that one barn, but the majority of it had been. Bobby Ray said the storm tore the doors and the front half of the barn clean off, and guessed the high winds caused the smoldering sawdust to blaze-up into the rafters catching them and the tobacco on fire, which was what I figured.

I cleaned and dressed Bobby Ray's hands the best I could with what I had, but he would need to see a doctor the next day. But knowing him, he probably wouldn't. With the quilt and the pillows from our bed the four of us slept on the mattress where it lay on the floor.

"We're all okay, darlin', that's the most important thing," I whispered to Bobby Ray as we lay in the dark with our sleeping boys between us.

"I know, but there's so much I want to give you. It seems we're goin' backwards instead of forward." Bobby Ray was so down it nearly broke my heart.

"As long as we're together, Bobby Ray, that's all that matters. We'll be fine, hon, you'll see." And I truly believed that. As long as I had Bobby Ray and our boys, that's all that mattered to me in the world.

Some folks say everything looks better in the light of day, but that's not necessarily true, especially if it's the morning after a tornado. There were huge limbs and big trees down all over, and scattered debris everywhere. It's strange how one of these twisters can destroy one thing and leave something else beside it untouched. Our livestock barn suffered massive damages, every piece of tin ripped from its roof and flung across the ridge. One wall had totally collapsed. Our milk cow and the mules were in the barn when the storm hit, and not seriously hurt, but the cow had a large, wide, strip of hair literally sucked from her side. We doctored it for a few days and she didn't seem to have any lingering repercussions from the experience. However, the hair in that one spot never completely grew back.

Henry Lee, Daddy, and Grandpa came early that morning to check on us. They couldn't phone, the lines were down. They said it looked as though our side of the county had suffered the brunt of the storm. Limbs were down in their area and folk's lawn furniture tossed around, but no real property loss like we suffered. I still considered we'd been very lucky. An elderly couple less than two miles down the road from us had lost their lives. They found the woman's body in a tree at the back of their tiny mobile home and her husband's body was found in the creek at the end of their cow pasture.

"You have crop insurance on your tobacker?" Henry Lee asked.

"Naw, but I will have next year," Bobby Ray replied.

"What about the barn?"

"Yeah, only because I had to have it on the outside structures in order to get the loan. It's included in our mortgage payment."

"I've got room in my shed for the rest of your tobacker, son," Daddy told Bobby Ray. That afternoon Bobby Ray's brothers helped him move what remained of our storm ravaged tobacco over to Daddy's.

Daddy and Grandpa cut up the cedar tree across our drive and hauled it and several more broken limbs to the gulley. Our tobacco that year wouldn't be as pretty, or as much of it as other crops, but we would get by. People often ask why the Lord allows these kinds of things to happen. I don't have a clear cut answer to that, but I believe the Lord is often blamed for what's the Devil's doings. Where storms are concerned, I think it's the laws of nature. A natural progression of things set in motion at the beginning of time. But this I do know, the Lord giveth and the Lord taketh away, and blessed be the name of the Lord.

After the tornado I never had to beg Bobby Ray to go to the storm cellar if severe weather was predicted. I don't know that he became afraid of thunderstorms, but he gained a whole new respect for Mother Nature, and didn't want to take any chances ever again with his family. I, myself, am of the firm belief, if the good Lord has provided you with shelter from the storm, have the good sense to get inside.

CHAPTER 25

While Bobby Ray and his brothers moved the tobacco and Daddy and Grandpa cleaned up around the place, I took the boys and went looking for the dogs. We drove up and down and through the back roads surrounding our house and the creek. Every once in awhile I would stop, get out of the truck and call to them. "Blue, Hank, Little Jean, where are you?" About to give up on finding them, I made a turnaround at a dead end and heard a dog bark. I looked in the review mirror and saw Hank come loping out of the woods. I jumped out of the truck and ran to him.

"Hey boy, you okay—ready to go home?" I bent down and hugged and kissed Hank like a long lost friend. That's the way I felt about him. Our pets and farm animals are as much a part of our daily lives and families as our human relations. Hank had gladly jumped into the back of the truck and we drove home. When I pulled up beside their pen, Blue came out of his doghouse. He came home on his own and was ready to be fed. I hoped Little Jean would be with him, but she wasn't.

A few days went by and Little Jean didn't come home, and Bobby Ray feared the worst. That she'd been killed or injured in the storm and couldn't make it home. So he decided to take Hank and Blue and see if they could pick-up her scent. At the least find her body, but after the heavy rains Bobby Ray knew this might not be possible. Dogs can track up to the point the scent goes into the water but not in the water. The boys and I took Bobby Ray and the dogs in the truck and let them out. Bobby Ray planned to go for a couple of miles in one direction and if he didn't find Little Jean he would try somewhere else. I was to come back for him in a couple of hours.

I came back where I let Bobby Ray out but didn't see any sign of him or the dogs. I waited for a while and then honked the horn. The boys loved to ride but were not much on sitting still. After waiting another ten minutes or so, I honked the horn again, but there was still no sight of them. I started the truck and eased slowly up the road, thinking Bobby Ray may have come out at another location. I headed toward the main road but didn't see Bobby Ray. I thought maybe I should go back to the house and wait awhile and then come back, but something told me to go back to the spot where I first let Bobby Ray out. When I rounded the curve in the road, I saw him. He sat on the edge of the road and I could tell he was out of breath, and lying at his feet was Little Jean. Hank and Blue lounged on the ground beside them. My heart sank when Little Jean didn't move. I stopped the truck and Bobby Ray looked up at me and gave me his breathtaking smile and Little Jean tried to raise her head.

"We found her. She's hangin' on. She knew I'd come lookin' for her." Tears welled up in my eyes and the emotion in Bobby Ray's voice said it all.

Bobby Ray found Little Jean on the far side of the creek tangled up in an old rusty fence. Somehow she had gotten her left front paw through her collar in an effort to disentangle herself. After her paw was inside the collar, she couldn't get it out, and her head was drawn toward the ground. She probably pulled and tugged so long trying to get free that she wore herself out and lay down to wait for someone to rescue her.

A good thing Bobby Ray found Little Jean when he did. She was badly dehydrated and wouldn't have lasted much longer. We rushed her to the veterinary clinic in Big Town where she stayed for two days receiving IV fluids. It ran up a huge bill we really couldn't afford, but what else could we do? Little Jean was an important part of our family. Her first night home I slept more soundly and peacefully than I had since the storm. All my little chicks were once more home to roost. Little Jean made a full recovery other than a slight limp. Might have been a tiny injury to her leg or hip joint the doctor hadn't seen on the x-rays. Henry Lee said that it only added to her character and I laughed. That's what I always told him about his limp.

The decrease in our tobacco crop meant less money at the end of the year. It became necessary for Bobby Ray to take a second job in addition to his farming. He went to work with Lester part time driving nails, and I hate to admit it, but I kind of wished he would do the carpenter work full time. The money and the hours were very good and at the end of the week I knew what would be there, but still there's no way I would have asked Bobby Ray to give up his farming. He was never happier than when he out working the land.

With the extra income we could make minor improvements along on the house, but the big renovation remained somewhere in the future. At the beginning of 1963 we made our third mortgage payment. Only two more to go and the place would be ours.

We sacrificed and did without about everything but the barest necessities in order to pay the farm off in five years. It had given both of us a great sense of accomplishment, that we were this close, but Bobby Ray said he wouldn't be satisfied until we turned the place into our dream home. I felt my life close to being perfect, and Bobby Ray close to being the perfect husband.

If only it hadn't been for those darn hunting trips to John Wesley's every three months. I rarely smelled liquor on Bobby Ray's breath until he went hunting. And after staying out too late drinking, he would drag his butt home and slowly pull up to the dog pen. Sometimes he would take the dogs out of the truck and put them in their pen before staggering into the house and falling out on the couch. As though he thought this wouldn't wake me if he didn't get in the bed with me. At other times, if he was really wasted, he would leave the dogs in the truck and pass out on the front seat and remain there until daylight. I don't know how he did it, but when the sun came up, Bobby Ray was up. His eyes might be crossed and he hardly could speak, but he'd be up and going about his business.

I came to the realization early on that this was a part of our lives I must accept. I knew it could be a lot worse. Bobby Ray could have been one of those men who drank daily and chased after women. John Wesley drank every day and Queenie didn't seem to mind, but as far as I know, he never ran around on her. I think she would have drawn the line there, and Queenie was not a woman I would have wanted to mess with.

She'd had a very hard life growing up. Her father was a mean, abusive man that drank heavily and liked to take his woes out on his wife and kids. When Queenie was seven her father shot and killed her mother and then turned the gun on himself. Afterwards, she and her three siblings were farmed out to relatives. Queenie was brought up by her mother's sister. She said her aunt and uncle treated her well, but she always felt like a burden to them. They had four children of their own. Her uncle drank too, but was a happy drunk. The way Queenie described him made me think of Poppaw. I guess my problem was I couldn't figure out why, if Bobby Ray could go three months without drinking, he couldn't do without the stuff all together?

During the weeks leading up to Will's first birthday, the airwaves were filled with nothing but bad news, and racial tensions ran high throughout the South. On June 12th of 1963 thirty-one year old civil rights activist, Medgar Evers was shot and killed in the driveway of his home in Jackson, Mississippi. He left behind a wife and three small children, but no one had been arrested for the crime. Some people believe our frame of mind and our actions are influenced by what's going on around us. I have no doubt that is true, and I would like to blame my actions on this, but it's probably not the reason I did what I did.

It's not known what will be the straw that breaks the proverbial camel's back. Maybe it was that time of the month. Men love to blame everything on that, or maybe I'd simply been in a bad mood. Whatever the case, Will's birthday fell on a Friday that year. It so happened, it was also on one of Bobby Ray's scheduled hunting trips with J. W. We planned to celebrate Will's birthday the following day with a big party at the lake. Some of the old timers continued to refer to it as the river and could tell you where the original channels ran. Kentucky Lake was created during World War II and merged with the Tennessee River. All the same to me, it was a lot of water and meant to be enjoyed with all the associated outdoor activities.

Anyway, we invited our families to the picnic area on Saturday afternoon for a cookout and birthday cake, and I wanted Bobby Ray there, stone—cold—sober and in a good mood. As he made ready to leave that evening, I reminded him of the next day's special events.

"You do remember what tomorrow is, don't you?" I asked. Bobby Ray looked at me through narrowed lids but didn't say anything. "I wish you wouldn't stay out so late, and maybe you shouldn't drink so much tonight."

Now Bobby Ray was no different than any other man when it came to telling him what he should or shouldn't do. He didn't care for it much.

"Have I ever missed one of their birthdays?" he answered, and walked out.

I fussed and fumed and threatened what I would do if Bobby Ray ruined Will's party. I probably shouldn't have said anything. He stayed out later that night than any other since that first time right after we married. About two hours before daybreak when his old truck came creeping into the drive, a rage I had never experienced before came over me. I flung the bed sheet off and jumped out of bed and ran to the backdoor, grabbing my new straw broom on the way. I flew out of the house in my bare feet with my white, cotton nightgown flapping around my legs. I'm glad there wasn't a lot of traffic on our road especially at that early hour. It would have been a sight to behold.

Bobby Ray, intent on getting the dogs out of the truck and staying upright never heard me coming. I swung the broom with all my might and caught him square in the back, knocking him off balance. The dogs slunk back in the truck out of the line of fire. I hit him again and this time he fell to his knees, but I kept right on hitting him.

"I'm—gonna—beat—you to death, if you don't stop drinkin' and layin' out all night." I spat at Bobby Ray through clenched teeth and between swings. Of course, I wasn't really trying to hurt him. It was just a broom after all.

Bobby Ray managed to gather his wits enough to crawl under the truck. "Woman, have you lost your damn mind?" he yelled at me.

I couldn't reach him under the truck but it didn't matter anyway. I was out of breath by then. I likely could have done much more damage with the handle of the broom but that would have made it more difficult to swing, and Bobby Ray had gotten the message. I turned and went back into the house and locked the door behind me. He could sleep it off in the truck.

I went back to bed but couldn't sleep and about daylight got up and began preparing food for the party. I unlocked the back door and glanced out the window. I saw the dogs in their pen and Bobby Ray as he went into the barn to milk. Maybe he wouldn't remember the night before. I made breakfast and when the boys were up I placed them in their highchairs to eat.

Shortly thereafter Bobby Ray came in with the morning's milk and poured it into the cream separator.

He glared at me across the room as he went to put the milk bucket in the sink. I guess he remembered. Bobby Ray kissed the boys on the top of the head and we sat down to eat, but not a word passed between us. This went on for the rest of the day.

The party was a huge success, and everyone, especially Will, seemed to have a good time. No one appeared to notice the strain between me and Bobby Ray. That night when he crawled into bed, I saw the long, narrow bruise, like a broom handle on his shoulder. I guess I made contact with it after all, and a flash of shame shot through me, but I wasn't ready to make up yet. Bobby Ray laid down on his side with his back to me. He wasn't ready either it appeared.

The next morning I got the boys ready and we went to church. I certainly wasn't in the frame of mind to worship, but that's when you need it the most. Of all the sermons the minister could have chosen to preach that day, he chose to preach on anger, and I felt a bright light shone over my head, and it surely wasn't a halo. I felt the whole assemble knew what I done the night before. At the time I had thought I was filled with righteous anger. The plain truth being I was mad at Bobby Ray for going hunting and getting drunk and I struck out at him in my frustration. Not much different from what his daddy had done when he hit him as a little boy. I knew that I loved Bobby Ray, and a sudden realization came to me. His daddy had loved him too, but after life beat Harlan Evans down, his family became easy targets for his despair. I had been so filled with remorse I could hardly wait to get home and beg Bobby Ray for forgiveness.

When I pulled into our drive Bobby Ray came out of the house and helped me get the boys out of the car. He had set the table for dinner; a good sign he was ready to make up too. While I finished up our meal, Bobby Ray changed the boys out of their church clothes and put them in their highchairs. After their food was in front of them, I asked Bobby Ray to come into our room.

"Can I talk to you for a minute, please?" And he followed me silently out of the room. We left the door open so we could see and hear the boys. Bobby Ray watched me with apprehension. He may have thought I had another broom hidden in there.

"Forgive me?" I asked, in a low voice. Shock and surprise had spread over Bobby Ray's face.

"What?"

"Forgive me," I repeated. "I shouldn't have done that. It was wrong of me to hit you, Bobby Ray. Can you ever forgive me?"

"I already have." Bobby Ray gave a short laugh, but it lacked mirth.

"What? You have?"

"I thought you were gonna tell me you were takin' the boys and leavin'."

"Mama, Daddy," Robbie called to us from the kitchen. He and Will craned their necks to see what was happening. Children, even small ones, sense when things aren't right.

"No, you know I wouldn't do that Bobby Ray. Will, don't smear cream potatoes in your hair."

"I don't want you to, but this is who I am, baby, this is who you married. I guess all that's left is for you to ask yourself, do you want to live with me or not?"

Bobby Ray turned and left the room and sat down at the table with the boys. No anger or malaise in his voice, only very matter-of-fact. Of course I wanted to live with him. I loved him with everything in me, but I hadn't known how to go about it and keep our boys from following in his footsteps where the alcohol was concerned.

That night we officially made up. Bobby Ray didn't turn his back to me when he lay down. Instead he pulled me into his arms and held me tight and I began to cry. My hot, salty tears ran down Bobby Ray's smooth chest. "Don't cry, Billie Jean, you know I can't stand it when you cry."

"And...you...know, I would never leave you," I said between sobs.

"It wouldn't do you no good. I'd just follow you and lie around on your front porch cryin' and whinin' like an ol' hound dog." This time there was laughter in his voice, and I knew everything was all right between us once more.

A few weeks after the broom incident, Bobby Ray made a confession to me. He knew he shouldn't stay out so late and drink so much on his hunting trips, but found it hard to tell the others no when they encouraged him to stay. It was as I expected all along, "a man thing." Bobby Ray didn't want to lose face in front of the other men, to look hen-pecked. I could have told him that was the reason, but he needed to come to this bit of wisdom on his own.

Nothing more was said about it but Bobby Ray never went to John Wesley's again to hunt. Instead, about every three months, John Wesley and the Renfro's came to our house. They would go up on the ridge or down in the bottoms, and when Bobby Ray got tired, he would come home, usually a little after midnight. The others could stay as long as they wanted. For some reason it hadn't bothered Bobby Ray to leave when they were behind his own house. Men—go figure. This arrangement suited me just fine, except for the youngest Renfro, Clayton. He gave me the willies', and he stared at me like he knew what I looked like with my clothes off. When he came around, I made myself scarce.

CHAPTER 26

I always think of 1963 as being a very volatile year, one that ended with a bang. On August 28th in Washington, D. C. about 200,000 people would march to the Lincoln Memorial to hear Martin Luther King Jr. deliver his famous speech, "I Have a Dream." On September 15th in Birmingham, Alabama, a bomb exploded, killing four young black girls while attending Sunday school at the Sixteenth Street Baptist Church, the church a well-known location for civil rights meetings. After the bombing, riots erupted in Birmingham leading to the deaths of two more black youths. I remember wondering as I watched the bodies of the little girls being removed, how long the Lord would allow the world to stand if it continued in this way. Yet life in Johnson's Bend had gone on as usual, but no longer did we feel our small community an entity unto itself, nor separate and apart from the turmoil in the world around us.

On November the 22nd in Dallas, Texas, the events of that day would touch the lives of everyone in the United States and countless others around the globe. It for sure changed us as a nation as nothing else ever had. I worked around the house that morning and the kids watched cartoons off and on. Mostly they ran around and made racket. They got up when their daddy left for work at six, so I fed them an early lunch and put them down for a nap, leaving the television on low for background noise. I don't recall exactly what was said that caught my attention. The soap opera *As the World Turns* was on when a news flash interrupted the regular programming, and I stopped whatever I'd been doing and stood in front of the TV. On the screen, CBS news anchor, Walter Cronkite, was talking, and he said a report had just come in of three shots fired at President Kennedy's motorcade in downtown Dallas, and the President was seriously wounded; the time, 1:40 p.m. EST. I sat down on the couch, the wind knocked out of me. When the boys awoke from their naps, they climbed up on the couch beside me and Will crawled into my lap. It was unusual for them to see me sitting down in the middle of the day. At 2:37 p.m. another news person behind Mr. Cronkite handed him a piece of paper. He had quickly scanned it before he read it out loud:

"From Dallas, Texas, news flash, apparently President Kennedy died today at 1:00 p.m. CST, two o'clock EST." He then turned and looked at the clock on the studio wall. "Some thirty-eight minutes ago," he said, and momentarily lost his composure before resuming.

I'm not sure how long I sat and stared at the TV, tears streaming down my face as I listened over and over to the tragic news. I didn't want to believe it was true. Robbie and Will remained very still and quiet, and glanced between me and the TV. Even at their young age they understood something very sad had happened.

At five o'clock Bobby Ray came home from working with Lester and his crew out on the lake highway building a new house. I rushed to the door to tell him the awful news. When he opened the door I knew from the look on his face he already heard. That night we ate supper in our living room gathered in front of the TV, as would most of

America. Earlier that day Vice-President Lyndon B. Johnson was sworn in as the thirty-sixth president of the United States. Standing at his side, President Kennedy's widow, Jacqueline still wore the same clothes she'd worn earlier, covered with her slain husband's blood.

Over the next four days the United States seemed to come to a standstill while our country mourned its fallen leader. No matter your political or religious affiliations, you couldn't turn away from this untouched. Texas governor, John Connally, had ridden in the motorcade that day and he too was wounded. The networks gave periodic updates on his condition, but nothing overshadowed the assassination of an American President. Later we watched on life national television as the suspect arrested for the shootings had been shot and killed himself. Lee Harvey Oswald, an unknown that rose from the depths of obscurity to the realms of infamy. It happened while transferring him from the Dallas City Jail to the Dallas County Jail. Another unknown, Jack Ruby, was arrested on the scene and charged with the crime. It was an American tragedy that unfolded right before our very eyes. The best fiction writer in the world couldn't have come up with this plot.

The two most touching moments of this tragedy for me as a wife and a mother, came when Mrs. Kennedy knelt down beside her husband's flag draped coffin and her little daughter, Caroline, stood beside her. And later, when the coffin was placed on the horse drawn caisson for the procession to St. Matthews Cathedral, the President's small son, John F. Kennedy Jr., stood at attention and saluted. It was his third birthday, the same as Robbie at the time, and I thought, how sad, that these little children would have to grow up without their father.

From the announcement of his death outside of Parkland Hospital, to the final playing of Taps at the burial in Arlington Cemetery, I was struck by the poise and grace that Jacqueline Kennedy held herself. Partially hidden behind a black veil with her face edged in grief, she shared with the whole world looking on what had to be the most difficult time in her life. I couldn't have hidden my sorrow the way she did, but then we don't know what went on behind closed doors when the cameras couldn't see. In later years the Kennedy era would be referred to as the "Days of Camelot," but even this mythical, first century kingdom had known wars and death.

The year however, did have one redeeming grace. The day after Christmas, Ruth and Henry Lee's first child, Destiny Rose was born, and from the moment she entered the world, she had her daddy wrapped around her little finger.

The following spring our preacher, Brother Hicks, retired. He had been with our church for over twenty years, and I couldn't imagine it without him. He baptized me and performed mine and Bobby Ray's marriage ceremony and on numerous occasions talked to Bobby Ray about his soul, but to no avail. Bobby Ray wasn't ready to give up his old ways and obey the Gospel. That summer we took Robbie and Will for the long awaited and several times postponed visit to my Louisiana relatives. One night while we there my kin took Bobby Ray into the bayou on a gator hunt. His eyes must have gotten as big around as mine the first time I saw a live gator in the wild, and he must have been most entertaining. My cousins were laughing their heads off when they came back with a huge alligator. Bobby Ray was laughing too, but said he believed he would stick to coon hunting.

On our return from vacation we learned the elders at our church hired a new preacher, Nicholas Vee. He certainly wasn't what any of us expected, young, full of zeal, and a *Yankee*? Nicholas came south to attend seminary school at Harding University, fell in love with the place, and a young lady from Savannah, Tennessee. He met pretty Sandra Lane while doing his student preaching at her church. After his graduation he and Sandy married and wanting to remain in the area, Nicholas looked for a full time church, preferably in a small town, and Johnson's Bend fit the bill perfectly. He wasn't looking for a place where he could make the most money, but for a place where he could make the most difference.

To my great delight, and surprise, Bobby Ray and Nicholas hit it off from the moment they met. Nicholas insisted we drop the Brother and call him by his given name, Nick for short. After all, he and Sandy were about mine and Bobby Ray's age and had young children too, a boy and a girl.

Nick wanted to learn about being country, coon dogs, and raising tobacco, subjects Bobby Ray knew a lot about. Soon Bobby Ray had hooked Nick up with a couple of young dogs and they went hunting together. Several times Nick came to the tobacco patch and worked right alongside Bobby Ray. After the two of them had been together, often times Bobby Ray would tell me about some Bible trivia they discussed. I began to suspect Nick's intentions to be two fold, to make a new friend, and without Bobby Ray realizing, lead him to the truth.

Shortly after Nick and Sandy arrived, Bobby Ray began to attend church with me on a more regular basis, especially on Sunday mornings. The times I smelled alcohol on his breath became less and less, and then all of a sudden he stopped going. I could see he was deeply troubled about something, and I tried to talk to him about this, but Bobby Ray wasn't ready to share with me what was bothering him, but I thought I knew. A battle raged inside of Bobby Ray between God and the Devil, or you might say between good and evil for the rights to Bobby Ray's soul, and I prayed fervently for the good to win.

With Bobby Ray working nearly full time carpentering and farming, we were able to save quite a sum toward the renovations of our house. Bobby Ray didn't want to borrow any more money if we didn't have to. Our place was nearly paid for with only one more payment and it would be ours, so I had to be patient. I knew exactly how I wanted everything to be. I went over it in my head a million times. One Friday night in the early fall Bobby Ray took the dogs and walked up to the ridge. All day he had been quiet and withdrawn. When he didn't come home by one a.m., I began to become a little concerned. He normally didn't stay out very late when by himself and planned to work the next day. Around two, Bobby Ray came in and lay down beside me, the smell of alcohol overpowering, and my heart sank. It looked as though we were back to square one.

The next morning I was in the kitchen making breakfast and Bobby Ray came in and walked up behind me and kissed me on my neck.

"Good mornin', beautiful," he said, and flashed me his breath-taking smile. Bobby Ray's eyes were red and blood-shot and his lids drooped from the lack of sleep, but he was in a wonderful mood, like he was at last at peace with himself. "I think I'll cut some wood today," he said, "should be a perfect day for it Not too hot, not too cold."

I looked at his sleep deprived eyes. "Why don't you wait till another time—work around the house today, there's plenty to do here," I said.

"Oh, you won't be sayin' that come this winter when that cold north wind comes howlin' down the ridge."

"Daddy, can I go wive you?" Robbie stood in the doorway of the kitchen in his little Mickey Mouse underwear trying to rub the sleep from his eyes.

"Not this mornin', son, I'll be cuttin'. You can go with me after dinner and help me load."

"Okay." With that Robbie turned around and went back to bed.

"You know, babe, I've been thinkin'. We've got a little money saved and a good crop in the barn, and with what I'm makin' workin' with Lester, I think we can go ahead and start remodelin' the house. If we have to borrow a little money, well, I think that will be okay. That is the American way, ain't it?" Bobby Ray laughed.

"Are you sure Bobby Ray, we don't have to wait any longer?" It was all I could do to keep from squealing and jumping up and down.

"I'm sure. I'll get with Lester tomorrow and put some figures together—course I expect some good breaks where the labor is concerned," Bobby Ray laughed again, and I ran to him and threw my arms around his neck and kissed him. He held me tightly to him and kissed me back long and slow. "Hold that thought until tonight," he grinned.

Bobby Ray went to milk and I had breakfast ready and on the table when he came back. We ate and talked about the remodeling, mostly I talked, and after we finished and right before Bobby Ray went out the door, he asked, "My black dress pants clean?"

"Sure," I replied. "Why?"

"Well, I'll need 'em for church tomorrow," he said, and winked at me and left.

I watched him out the back window as he hitched the mules to the ground slide. We had a pretty decent second hand tractor, an Allis-Chalmers, but Bobby Ray said some jobs you just couldn't beat a good team of mules.

After I got the boys up, fed, and settled in front of the TV to watch Saturday morning cartoons, I started the wash. I could hear the power saw on the ridge as I went to and from the clothesline. Even with a clothes' drier there were some things I preferred to hang outside, like quilts, blankets, and throw rugs. Earlier that morning I put a pot roast with potatoes and carrots on to cook. All I needed to finish dinner was to make a pan of cornbread. By noon I had the table set and went to the backdoor to call the boys inside. Their cartoons held their attention for only a short time. They much preferred being outdoors. I looked up to the ridge to see if I could see Bobby Ray coming down. I didn't hear the saw anymore, but he was nowhere in sight. I washed the boy's faces and hands and set them down to eat, thinking Bobby Ray would be along shortly. At twelve-thirty when he still hadn't come home I went again to the backdoor and looked up to the ridge, but there no sign of him, so I walked out to the truck and blew the horn. We adopted this method through the years. If Bobby Ray was anywhere close to the house and heard the horn, he knew I needed him or it was meal time.

I went back to the house and sat down at the table with the boys, but I couldn't eat, a feeling of unease spread through me. Bobby Ray should have come home for dinner by then, especially after he heard the horn. I lifted Will from his chair and took Robbie by the hand and started up the path to the ridge, winded by the time I got there. I don't know why I didn't drive the truck, but by then I'd begun to panic and wasn't thinking straight. I put Will down and looked across the field to the woods. I could see the mules, Pete and Rowdy, standing at the tree line and still hooked up to the slide, but I couldn't see Bobby Ray anywhere.

I grabbed the boys by the hand to walk around the field. I wanted to cut straight across but I knew Robbie and Will couldn't easily maneuver the rough ground, and there was no way I could carry both of them. I tried to hurry but had to match my steps to their much shorter ones.

The mules turned their heads and watched our approach, and when within a few feet of them, I called out, "Bobby Ray? Bobby Ray, where are you?" But there was no answer. It was so still and quiet. The only sounds were the mules stamping and snorting, tired of standing in harness. I made Robbie and Will sit down on the ground well away from the mules and I told them to stay there. Hesitantly I walked toward the woods and with every step, an ever-increasing feeling of dread washed over me. When but a short distance away I saw the large tree on the ground and Bobby Ray's power saw sitting next to a rick of neatly stacked wood. I kept telling myself he only went into the woods. That perhaps something there had caught his attention. Yet deep down inside I knew what I was about to find when I pulled back the branches on the tree.

From that moment on time slowed to a crawl. My legs felt like they were made of lead and I had to force them to carry me the remaining distance to the tree. My hands trembled as I pushed aside the heavy limbs. There Bobby Ray's beautiful face stared up at me. His eyes partially open like squinting up at the sun through the leaves. I knew he was dead. The only mark on him that I could see was a deep, ugly gash on the side of his head where the tree struck him.

From what sounded like a long distance away and through the roaring in my ears I heard, "Mama, Mama?" I looked over my shoulder and saw Robbie and Will. They had gotten up and inched their way toward me.

"Stay there," I called. "Don't come any closer." I couldn't let the boys see their daddy this way. I stole one final look at my love, my heart, my life. I wanted nothing more than to throw myself down beside Bobby Ray and hold him in my arms forever, but I couldn't.

I turned and ran to our boys and placed them on the slide. I sat Will between Robbie's legs. "Hold him tight, Robbie," I said, and lifted the reins.

It was all the encouragement the mules needed. They headed for the barn in a fast trot and it was all I could do to keep them from breaking into a full run. I tried to stand up behind the boys but ended up having to sit down and wrap my legs around them in an effort to keep us from being thrown off. I held on to the reins for dear life.

At the gate that led into the barn lot the mules stopped, waiting for it to be opened. Instead, I grabbed a child under each arm and ran to the house and called Daddy.

"Come! Come! It's Bobby Ray!" I cried, and fainted dead away. When I came to, Robbie was patting my cheek and he and Will were crying. Huge tears streamed down their little faces. I heard the car when it arrived and soon Daddy was bending over me.

"What is it, Billie Jean, where's Bobby Ray?" Daddy asked.

"Up on the ridge." That's all I could say, and I motioned with my hand. Dora and my grandparents' came with Daddy and my grandpa ran out the door with him. Dora took the boys into their room and tried to comfort them. Grandma helped me to the couch where she sat down beside me and laid my head in her lap, stroking my hair. Great sobs burned in my chest but they wouldn't come out. I felt like I might suffocate from the pressure. Time for me had stopped the moment I looked into Bobby Ray's lifeless face.

That night I was aware of people coming and going, but I couldn't get off the couch, my legs simply wouldn't support me. Grandma and Dora took over the care of the boys. Lester brought Ms. Minnie and all the family came, but I remained frozen in place. Part of me died that day on the ridge. I felt the better part.

I could bear all their tears, everyone's, except Henry Lee's. When he knelt down beside me and held my hands in his, the tears that refused to be released earlier burst forth like a dam breaking. My entire body shook with racking sobs, and I thought I might never be able to stop.

Later that night Grandma spread a blanket over me where I lay on the couch. Around midnight, Bobby Ray's dogs began to howl and moan. It was like they knew he would never come home again.

The next day by sheer force of will I made myself get up and make the funeral arrangements. The money Bobby Ray and I worked and sweated for and laid aside to create our dream home, would now in part be used to bury him.

I didn't put Bobby Ray in his black suit. I remembered him laughing and saying, "Black suits for gettin' hitched and gettin' buried." The only times he'd worn it were on happy occasions. Our wedding day and Henry Lee's and Ruth's and I refused to put it on him now. I placed him instead in his black dress pants with a white, short sleeved shirt and a black tie, but before came time for the viewing I had the undertaker remove the tie. Bobby Ray hated ties.

I couldn't tell you a lot about the visitation or the funeral. That time is a void in my life. Maybe that's the body's way of coping.

One thing I do remember, even through the fog of my grief, was Cole coming to me and placing his arms around me and whispering in my ear, "Don't you worry 'bout nothin', darlin', we take care of our own," he said.

I looked up at the sweet, kind, sorrowful face of Cole Evans, and I knew beyond a shadow of a doubt, I looked into the face of Preacher. Why I hadn't figured it out before, I don't know. Who else would the Evans brothers feel such loyalty to but another brother?

Nicholas did the eulogy and I'm sure it had to be very hard for him. Bobby Ray and he had become so close. Not only was he Bobby Ray's minister, but his friend. We both had such high hopes he would soon bury Bobby Ray in the waters of baptism, but instead he stood beside me as we returned Bobby Ray to the earth he so loved.

I suppose that means the devil won and time ran out for Bobby Ray. Maybe we're only allotted so many chances and Bobby Ray used all of his. And according to the Bible, the great gulf is now fixed and hence forth Bobby Ray can't pass to the other side.

I lay Bobby Ray to rest beside Bennie. I know that's what he would have wanted. In the days following his death, the late afternoon often found me at the kitchen window staring up at the ridge, and I would recall a poem by Robert Frost that I'd read in school, *Nothing Gold Can Stay*. That's the way I remember Bobby Ray. Sometimes at twilight, right as the sun was about to go down and the sky turned that golden hue, that's when I would see him, there in the gloaming, walking down the path, coming home to me. But he would quickly vanish, and the world would become a dark and lonely place.

FALL

It is autumn; not without
But within me is the cold.
Youth and spring are all about;
It is I that have grown old.

From "Autumn Within" by Henry Wadsworth
Longfellow

CHAPTER 27

After Bobby Ray's death I couldn't seem to pull myself together, no matter how hard I tried. My grief and despair was so deep it became an actual physical pain. I was a widow at twenty-three with two small boys to rear and with only a high-school education. I gave serious thought to going back to school, isn't that what the heroine in a good fiction novel would do? But I still wouldn't know what I wanted to be. I had been what I truly always wanted to be, Bobby Ray's wife and the mother of his children. And I needed a job that paid better. Working three afternoons a week at the store wouldn't keep food on the table and a roof over our heads. I would have to make what little money I had left in our savings last for as long as possible. Naturally, I knew my family wouldn't let me and the boys go hungry, but I had too much pride to sit back on my laurels and let someone else take care of us. My biggest problem was I couldn't get beyond the moment I pulled back the branches on the tree and saw Bobby Ray's face. The scene was stamped into my mind and it was all I could see when I closed my eyes at night.

Some people don't believe in guardian angels, but I do. Without some type of divine intervention, I couldn't have left Bobby Ray's side and had the presence of mind to get the boys back to the house.

Within days of Bobby Ray's passing I found myself dividing my existence into two parts, B.B.R.D and

A.B.R.D, before Bobby Ray's death and after his death. And I started with the what ifs. What if I had insisted he not go cut wood that day? I knew he drank too much and didn't sleep near enough the night before, but he had done that sort of thing ever since we married and never suffered any bad repercussions. I suppose this time was the exception. His reflexes too slow for him to get out of the way of the falling tree. This scenario played over and over in my head like a broken record.

In the sixties not much was said about people's mental health. If you referred to a person as being depressed, it was just a polite way of saying either they were moody, or crazy as a Betsy bug. Because of this stereo-typing I didn't feel I could talk to anyone about this, not even Nicholas.

At Bobby Ray's funeral he said as humans, we often wonder why this sort of thing happens—a man out working and trying to provide for his family is taken away. A fellow preacher friend of his explained it this way. Bad things sometimes happen so a victory can be won in realms we cannot see or know about. I truly believed this, that there is a reason for everything and that often we suffer because of the choices we've made, and sometimes because of the choices of others. Bobby Ray chose to drink then cut wood that day.

I understood this, but at the same time my suffering was so great I questioned God, "Why, why have you taken Bobby Ray now?"

I realized I wasn't the only person to ever lose someone near and dear to them. I thought about poor Dora and what she'd been through, but knowing this didn't help. I had to go on with my life and take care of my boys, but I didn't see how I could manage without their father, and the fact that apparently my faith was not strong enough to sustain me in my darkest hour made me even more depressed. This was what I couldn't confess to Brother Nick. He would think me a terrible person, and this mad vicious cycle went around and around in my head. Recrimination, self-inflicted or otherwise can only go on for so long before there's a breaking point. Mine came shortly before Christmas, my first without Bobby Ray.

Mr. Utley allowed me to work nearly full time after Bobby Ray's death, until I could find additional work. He really hadn't needed me that many hours, but he knew I needed the money. If not for all the gasoline and kerosene we sold, he couldn't have kept the doors open. The big chain stores were popping up all over in the larger towns, and the days of the little country store were fast coming to an end. Our biggest sellers other than the petroleum products had been milk, bread, bologna, and cheese. The local folks were glad they didn't have to go into Big Town every time they needed a few items, but wouldn't fully realize how much they missed the little store until it was gone.

In the mornings I would take the boys with me to work where they played in the back of the store. On the weekends when school not in session, they played across the road on the school's playground. I could keep an eye on them through the windows. Back then we didn't worry about someone coming down the road and abducting them. Dora would get the boys in the early afternoon and take them home with her and I would pick them up after work. I don't know what I would have done without my family. This arrangement with the boys worked out really well, but I still had to make myself get out of bed every day. All I wanted to do after Bobby Ray's death was sleep. I then wouldn't have to think about the rest of my life without him. If not for the boys, I'm not sure I would have bothered to get up or ever leave the house, and it became harder and harder to answer their questions.

"Where's Daddy? When's he comin' home?" They asked. I didn't take them to the funeral or to the visitation. I didn't want their last image of their father to be of him lying in his coffin. I struggled greatly with this decision, and went back and forth several times, but in the end, I didn't take them. Maybe it wasn't the right decision, but it was the one I felt was right at the time. Instead, I wove a beautiful fairytale that their daddy had gone to Heaven and he waited for us there. I didn't believe this, but I couldn't bring myself to tell them any different, and I wanted so badly for it to be true. Someday when they were older and able to better understand, the boys could draw their own conclusions. I did tell them their daddy had been badly hurt when the tree struck him and that's why he went away. They'd heard, of course, other people talking and knew that day in the woods was a turning point in their lives, even if they didn't completely understand why.

About a week or so before Christmas, Daddy brought a cedar tree and set it up in the front window. Four days later it was still undecorated. One evening I came in from work really tired as was the boys. Dora said they didn't take much of a nap for her that day. They were too excited about Santa Clause coming. Dora wanted for me and the boys to stay for supper, but I made some excuse about having to get home and decorate the tree. I really didn't want to make small talk. I decided that night to have breakfast for supper, scrambled eggs, sausage, gravy and biscuits. Cooking for me and the boys had become a chore. Something I once loved to do. The boys normally liked this meal but on this night they were both whiney and ill-tempered and nothing pleased them.

Will took his sausage and threw it on the floor, "I don't want that," he said, and glared at me with defiance. Before I realized what I was doing, I snatched Will out of his chair and spanked him hard on his bottom and sat him firmly back. I don't know who was more shocked, me or the boys. Will began to scream and Robbie soon joined in. I felt I was the worst person in the world, or at least the worst mother and I didn't deserve to live. This was how bad my depression had gotten. I ran from the house and vaguely remembered hearing the phone ring. Shortly thereafter Daddy and Dora pulled into the drive, and they found me walking back and forth in the yard crying and wringing my hands. Dora rushed into the house to the boys and Daddy came to me and I fell into his arms.

"Help me, Daddy. Please help me," I pleaded. "I don't want to die, but I don't know how to live without him."

"I'm gonna help you, darlin'. Daddy's gonna help you," he said gently.

Dora quickly packed a few clothes for me and the boys and loaded us into the car and brought us home with them. At their house, Dora ushered the boys inside and Daddy took me to my sanctuary, my safe haven, to my greatest champion and protector. I came home to my Grandma Carson. She left my room the same and this was where I came to hide away from the world and lick my wounds.

Grandma might not have been the best person in the world to motivate me. She pretty much let me wallow in my self-pity and waited on me hand and foot. If I didn't feel I could get out of bed and come down for meals, Grandma or Grandpa would trudge up the stairs and bring it to my room. This went on for weeks.

Christmas and New Year's came and went. Daddy brought the boys to see me every day, and I looked forward to my time with them, I loved them so. Will seemed to have forgiven me for taking my misery out on him. I'm not saying at times a good old fashion spanking isn't warranted, but there is a difference. It soon became very difficult when it was time for Robbie and Will to leave. They would cling to me, but as much as I loved them, it was a relief. I wasn't ready mentally or physically to take care of them on my own.

The only person I allowed to visit me during this time outside of the immediate family was Henry Lee. For some reason I felt he understood more than anyone else. He would come by nearly every day after work and sit quietly in the room with me his arms resting on his knees and his head down. Sometimes we didn't talk, but shared a comfortable silence. I'd felt ashamed for others to see me this way, weak and broken. Grandma told folks I suffered a nervous breakdown. I suppose that's as good a way to describe it as any. I even refused to see Nick and Sandy, and I know it hurt them deeply. Nick came to the house often and called frequently, but he was the last person I wanted to see. After all, I couldn't even take care of my own children. I sent him word through Grandma to please pray for me and my boys.

I don't know how long this might have gone on, but one dark, cold, dreary day when Henry Lee came by, I was especially low. A fine mist fell all day threatening to turn into sleet. The depression bore down on me like a heavy weight, as it did every time it rained. There was a time when I loved rainy days and felt safe and cozy in my little home. That was back when things were right in my world. Once we'd said our initial hello, Henry Lee and I didn't speak.

After several minutes of this silence, Henry Lee raised his head and said to me, "You have to let him go, Billie Jean. You have to."

"I know," I said. "I know—but not today." I don't think that was the response Henry Lee wanted. Early the next morning Daddy came to my room. I suspect Henry Lee talked to him.

"Get up, get dressed, we're goin' for a drive."

"Where to?" I asked in a grumpy voice. Definitely not in the mood to go driving around the countryside, and certainly not the best weather for an outing.

"I've made an appointment for you to see a doctor in Nashville." I didn't need to ask what kind of doctor.

CHAPTER 28

The psychiatrist, Doctor Cromwell, an older gentleman wasn't very pretty, but had a kind and compassionate demeanor. So nervous at the start I could barely speak, he soon put me at ease.

"The first thing I want you to understand, Billie Jean, you're not crazy. You are severely depressed, it's not the same thing," he had said in a soothing voice, and looked at me over the top of his glasses perched on the end of his nose. It reminded me of Grandma, which normally meant she was displeased about something, but I think he did it in order to emphasize his point.

The visit didn't go at all the way I thought it would. He didn't make me lie down on a couch. Instead, I sat in a comfortable armchair in front of Dr. Cromwell's desk. "It's called reactive or normal depression," he explained, "and it's not uncommon in the least after suffering a sudden and tragic loss like you have. Your father filled me in on some of the details when he called for an appointment, but the problem is, many people ignore the signs and symptoms of depression, and left untreated, it can lead to much more serious problems, mentally and physically. You take care of your physical health don't you?" he asked with a smile.

"I try to," I said.

"Then why not your mental health as well, it's just as important."

At first Dr. Cromwell didn't plan to place me on an antidepressant, but since my depression had gone on for more than a few weeks, he was afraid it could have triggered a chemical reaction in the brain. "I'm going to place you on a very mild and low dose of this medication," he said. "I promise you won't need it for long, and I'm going to set you up with a counselor for talk therapy."

"Talk therapy?" I questioned.

"Yes, I think you will benefit from it greatly. It may be all you really need, and you won't have to see me again for a month," he said, and grinned at me again over the top of his glasses. "To make sure the medication is working properly. If so, I won't need to see you again until time to wean you off the medication. Unless of course you start to experience problems, and I have no reason to think you will, but if you do, you must call me immediately." And the visit over, Dr. Cromwell shook my hand and wished me well and that was that.

A change in my mood and my mental state hadn't come about as an instantaneous euphoria like the jokes about antidepressants imply. It was much more a gradual thing. I awoke one morning and it wasn't as hard to get out of bed. The day seemed to hold more promise, and the world in general didn't look as bleak, and Dr. Cromwell had been right, talking with the therapist helped tremendously, probably more than anything else. I really can't explain why talking to a complete stranger was beneficial, but it was. Maybe it was because George, a tall and slightly over-weight jovial guy, was a total stranger. He didn't have a dog in the race, so to speak. I found it difficult at first to open up to him, to reveal the innermost thoughts of my mind and the deepest emotions of my heart. George said in part I suffered from an identity crisis. Heretofore I had thought of myself as Bobby Ray's wife and the mother of his children. I knew what was expected of me and what I needed to do in order to accomplish that. I now must find Billie Jean, the woman, and I, too, soon discovered suppressed feelings about my mother I had never known were there. Not until they came tumbling out.

"I feel so guilty about dumpin' the boys off on my daddy and stepmother," I confessed. "It's the same thing my mom did to me—leavin' me with my grandparents'."

"It's not the same thing, Billie Jean, you see your little boys' every day, and you are smart enough to recognize, you can't take care of them right now. Not the way they need to be taken care of. This is only a temporary arrangement. As for your mother, she probably did regret leaving you behind and came back that day with every intention of taking you, but after your grandmother refused to let you go, she may've given it some more thought. If she had come back with the sheriff, he most likely would have made your grandparents' hand you over. Your mama loved you enough, Billie Jean, to realize she couldn't take care of you right then and you were far better off with your grandparents."

Another thing George helped me to see was that my feelings were not uncommon or unnatural. We are conditioned from early childhood to feel a certain way and to behave a certain way in order to be socially acceptable. Grief being one of these, but in fact, grief is a very personal thing. No two people will approach it in exactly the same way and there's no time limit attached to the process. Perhaps my mother had needed time to find herself. She'd been very young when I came along, and by my father's own admittance, far from ready to get married. I could now forgive her.

A few weeks after starting my counseling I called Nickolas to come and talk with me. He was so excited he came right over and we talked for a very long time. I quickly saw he understood far more than I gave him or my church family credit for.

"We try to pretend at times we don't have any troubles," he said, "because we are so afraid of what others will think. The truth is, we all have them, because we're human with human frailties and live in a world full of imperfections, and we need the prayers of the saints to get us through these trials. In Galatians 6:2 it says, 'Bear ye one another's burdens, and so fulfill the law of Christ.'" Nick expressed to me with a catch in his voice how much Bobby Ray's friendship meant to him. "I was like a stranger in a foreign land and he took me in," he laughed. We wept together, and we talked about Bobby Ray's soul. Nick felt as I did—that Bobby Ray on the verge of accepting Christ into his life when he died.

My talk therapy sessions started out at three times a week and tapered off to only once a month. Even after I stopped taking the antidepressant, I continued to talk with George. I know it was hard on Daddy, and after a while I could have driven myself, but he insisted on taking me. I greatly enjoyed our time together on the drive there and back and think he did as well. We talked as we never had before, and I told him a little about Bobby Ray's drinking. Not a lot, but somehow I think he knew, and I told him I believed the day Bobby Ray died, it had been his intentions to be baptized at church the next day.

"I think you could be right," Daddy said. "A few days before his death, he asked me, 'How do you ever live good enough to get to Heaven?' And I told him, you can't, all you can do is try your best everyday to follow God's word and grace will take care of the rest."

"I just can't bear the thought, Daddy, that I won't see him in Heaven."

"You can't dwell on that, Billie Jean. It's out of your hands, truth be, never was in your hands. God allows us to make our own choices, darlin', and he's a just and fair God. Leave the judgin' to him. Some things are not for us to know or to understand."

We also talked a lot about my mother, and the deep hurt remained in my daddy's voice after all these years. "I'm not sure your mama would have stayed if I hadn't gone off to war," he confessed. "She wasn't ready to settle down, but I loved her so."

"If you had it to do over, Daddy, and knowing what you know now, would you still have married her?" I asked.

Daddy had thought for a moment before replying. "Yes. Yes, I absolutely would have. Would you still have married Bobby Ray had you known how it would turn out?"

I didn't have to hesitate. "Yes, a thousand times yes."

The boys and I returned home in the early fall, a week after the first anniversary of Bobby Ray's death. Grandma and Grandpa begged me to move in with them with the boys, and I'd been tempted, but they weren't getting any younger. They dearly loved the boys with all their heart, but having two small, rambunctious young boys around all the time, might have gotten old. Besides, I wanted to go home to my own house, mine and Bobby Ray's.

Daddy was afraid this might cause another problem, and maybe I should sell and move somewhere else. I will admit that everywhere I looked reminded me of him. But for some strange reason, it now brought me comfort. Daddy took down the dog pen shortly after Bobby Ray died. I gave Hank and Blue to John Wesley, and Little Jean to Lester. Little Jean wouldn't be able to run as fast and keep up with the other dogs because of her limp, but Lester wouldn't push her. It was really hard to see the dogs go, but they were bred to hunt, and to keep them locked in a pen for sentimental reasons would have been ludicrous. When the boys were older and could take care of one, I planned to get them a puppy. No doubt their uncles would have been more than happy to give each a coon dog pup, but I was thinking more along the lines of a Collie or a German Shepard.

I made a point to stay away from the kitchen window at sunset and not look up at the ridge. In fact, I didn't go up there at all and rented the land to a neighbor. Ruth helped me secure a job three days a week at the bank in Big Town where she'd worked. She continued to work there fulltime after she and Henry Lee married until Destiny Rose born. She went to part time after becoming pregnant with their second child and quit all together after the baby's birth. Ruth loved being a stay at home mom and I completely understood. Being a mom for me was the most rewarding and full-filling job I could have, but at the moment, a luxury I could ill afford.

I don't mind telling you, I was scared to death to be entering the workforce in Big Town. After virtually being sheltered my entire life in our small town I knew it would be a big wake up call. A single unattached white female has always been easy prey, for even the more experienced in the ways of the world.

With my three days at the bank, and Mr. Utley letting me keep my Saturday's at the store, and by using my meager savings sparingly, I felt I could scrape by. Bobby Ray and I never got around to taking out life insurance, another of those "to do things" on our list. One Saturday at the store I glanced up when the bell over the door jingled and saw Ross enter.

While staying at my grandparents' I had seen him briefly in passing from time to time. He would wave and I would wave in return, but I wasn't ready to renew old acquaintances. I guess Ross sensed this as he never tried to push the encounter. Through Grandma I heard after college Ross accepted a job in East Tennessee in the same area where he went to school. He worked with a group of civil engineers that designed bridges and overpasses and the like. I immediately noticed that Ross's hair had grown longer and was very becoming to him. It made him look more grown-up and mature. Ross had been a big guy all his life and nice looking, but now a big and extremely good-looking man.

"Hi, Billie Jean," Ross said, with a big smile on his face. He seemed at ease, like we had talked only the day before.

"Hi Ross, good to see you."

"How you doin'? You look great."

"It's been rough, but I'm makin' it. I have my boys and they're the light of my life."

"Yeah, Mama and Daddy said you've had a real hard time of it. I'm surely sorry about Bobby Ray, Billie Jean, and that I couldn't make it to the funeral, but I was thinkin' about you."

"Thank you—and that's okay. I know it's a long way to drive from East Tennessee to Johnson's Bend just for a funeral."

"I'm home for a weekend visit before I leave for a job in North Carolina. I likely won't be home again until Christmas. Maybe when I do come back we could get together and catch up on things, and I sure would like to meet your boys. I hear they're great little guys."

"Yes, they are. And I'd like that too, to sit down and talk. I've missed our talks." And I had. I hated the breech between Ross and me. We grew up together and lived right across the road from one another since babes in rompers. I felt it a shame the way things ended between us, but Bobby Ray refused to ever talk about it and had never gotten over what happened in the lane that night.

"Great, we'll make a point to do that," Ross said. "Well, guess I'd better get what I come for and get back. Mama will be waitin' supper."

CHAPTER 29

It was a whole new way of life having to be a father and a mother, and things Bobby Ray used to do with the boys I now tried to do, but I loved spending time with them. A few days before Halloween we carved pumpkins and sat them on our front porch.

"They scary ain't they Mom?" Robbie proclaimed. "The little kids will be 'fraid to come here." He tickled me when he referred to other children, and Will, as little kids, Robbie was a very *grown-up* four year old.

"Don't say ain't, and yes, they're really scary, but the little kids will have their mama's and daddy's with them, so they'll be okay. Before I'd thought the *daddy* come out. Robbie hadn't seemed to notice. I tried to never bring attention to the fact their dad wasn't there.

"They scary, Mom," Will chimed in. "I gonna be scary monster. 'Gurrr'." He held up his little hands in claw like fashion. The Jack-O-Lantern's were more comical than scary. I didn't pretend to be a sculptor, but the boys were happy with them and that's all that mattered.

Will's costume wasn't very scary either. He would dress up as *Underdog* and he did look adorable. Robbie planned to be Eddie Munster but didn't want to wear a mask. He wanted me to paint his face. I enlisted the services of Ruth in this endeavor. She and Henry Lee would bring Destiny Rose to the house and we would go together in our neighborhood trick-or-treating. We would only take the kids to our families and people's houses in the area we knew. We figured that would give them plenty of candy, enough to rot their teeth out anyway. I likely wouldn't have but one or two of my closest neighbors kids come by the house, we lived so far out.

After going to bed that night I laid awake for a long time. Night time was always the hardest. That's when I missed Bobby Ray the most. For months after his death I did not wash his pillow case and his scent lingered there. I would hold the cloth to my face and breathe him in. In the years we were married I grew accustomed to only cat napping until I heard him come in from hunting. On this night a sound from the front of the house brought me fully awake. At first I thought I imagined the sound of someone stepping onto the porch. I lay very still listening, and after a bit I heard it again. Someone was moving slowly and quietly toward the front window, or the front door. I sat up in bed my heart pounding in my chest. I had only begun to lock my doors at night after Bobby Ray's death. I wasn't really all that afraid, but without the dogs there to alert me if someone came snooping around, I had thought it best. Not that we had much of that kind of thing going on in our neighborhood.

I heard the unknown visitor push on the window, but it was locked also. Bobby Ray's 12-gauge single barrel shotgun still hung in the rack on the bedroom wall. Holding my breath, I slipped silently out of bed and eased it down. In the top dresser drawer a few loose shells rolled around, birdshot I thought, but if someone was trying to break in, I guess it really didn't matter. I fumbled around in the drawer for what felt like forever and finally located a shell and slid it into the chamber. I never cared for hunting. I didn't want to shoot anything or anybody, but

Bobby Ray made me learn how to load the gun. Glad now he had, and without making a sound I tiptoed into the living room and stood in front of the door. When the door knob rattled, I raised the shotgun shoulder level and pulled the hammer back.

"I've got a loaded gun pointed at the door. If you try to come in, I will shoot." I'd been astonished at how calm my voice sounded.

From here things happened really quickly, a momentary silence from outside the door, then footsteps quickly leaving the porch and running through the mound of leaves from the maple near the road. I started to lower the gun when at that exact moment a small hand touched my leg and a little voice said, "Mama?"

Startled, I jerked the gun up and instinctively pulled the trigger and through the deafening explosion in the small room, I thought I heard someone scream from the outside. I blew a hole in the door large enough to toss a cat through. The kick from the gun threw me backwards and I fell across the couch knocking Robbie down in the process. Unbeknownst to me Robbie had come up behind me. The racket awakened Will, and terrified, he cried and called for me from his room. I retrieved him from his bed and with Robbie hanging onto my gown tail went to the phone and called Daddy.

Daddy in turn called the sheriff and before long my house was a three ring circus. They found blood in the yard near the road, leaving little doubt I hit someone. The fleeing, would-be intruder knocked the boys' pumpkins into my pink peony bush beside the steps and stomped through it. I worked so hard to get that darn bush to grow.

The sheriff immediately notified the surrounding hospitals to be on the lookout for any person coming in full of wood splinters and metal pellets.

Daddy tried to lighten up the situation. "Would you like a window placed where that hole is?" he asked, and grinned. I think the shells must have been buck shot instead of bird. Either one had the capability to seriously wound anyone standing on the other side of the door.

Early the next morning I had a return visit from the sheriff. Sure enough, a man covered in blood had showed up at the hospital ER in the adjoining county. The doctor told the sheriff from the looks of him he was lucky to be alive. I caught the guy in the lower back and buttock, and fortunately for him, he was far enough away when hit for the wounds not to be life threatening. The man was none other than, Clayton Renfro. The sheriff asked if I wanted to press charges and I didn't. I figured Clayton had been punished enough. I still was thankful I hadn't killed him. It would be hard to live with that. I guess I was lucky Clayton didn't want to press charges against me. Technically, I shot him while he was running away, but then he would have to explain the reason for being in my yard at two o'clock in the morning to begin with. I don't imagine Clayton wanted the law involved any more than necessary. He was already on the local law enforcement's top ten "pain in the butt" lists.

Clayton had a reputation for getting drunk, roaring up and down the roads and being involved in bar room brawls and busting up the places. He paid large fines and restitution and done time in the county jail on several occasions because of this.

He would be in and out of the hospital for several months with infections, and the doctors continued to get splinters and little metal balls out of his behind for quite some time. I bet he would think long and hard before making another late night *uninvited* visit to anyone.

Soon after this Lester came to replace my thin outside wood doors with heavier ones and put dead-bolts on, and checked the windows to make sure all their locks were secure. While he worked, Lester talked about his plans for his little campground on the river. A very private and reserved person, some of the local folks made fun of Lester and thought him slow, because he never married and continued to live at home and take care of his mama. But let me tell you, there was nothing slow about Lester.

When he returned from Korea in the early fifties, he bought twelve acres of land in the middle of nowhere, right at the river's edge for I think around thirty-five dollars an acre. At the time the land was mostly gravel washes and briers, but had a fair amount of good timber. Several folks laughed at Lester and called him crazy for throwing his money away, but he had big dreams for this small parcel of earth. Over the years he sold the timber and cleared the land a little at a time.

Since it was private property and located far from the main thoroughfare, the county refused to build a road to the area. Lester took a tractor with a blade attached and made his own. Only a dirt lane at the start, but it served the purpose intended. To connect his land with the main road, and eventually he did spread white gravel.

Lester started out real simple to begin with, renting camp sites to people. There wasn't any electricity or running water at the onset, but you wouldn't believe what folks will pay to come to the lake and pitch a tent and fish for a week. A few years later Lester placed his own tents with army cots on the sites, but he didn't plan to stop there. He told me about his dreams to turn his rustic little campground, which he named, "Whip-per-Will Retreat," into a real lake resort.

"I plan to run 'lectricity and water to each of the sites real soon," he said, "and build a bathhouse. First I need to improve the boat landing and build a better dock, but I'm gettin' there, slowly but surely." You could hear the excitement in Lester's voice.

"I think that's amazin', Lester," I told him.

Lester recognized from the start what a gold mine any property close to the water would become. When he bought the property the huge man-made Kentucky Lake that would join the Tennessee River hadn't been fully completed, but Lester was assured by the realtor that his land would be safe from the TVA. The agency had already relocated thousands of people and entire small communities in order to make way, not only for the lake, but for a huge 170,000 acre national wildlife and recreational area. You can believe it wouldn't take the state, or the county, very long to catch on to the potential wealth here and want to tap into their share of the cash cow.

"I hope in time to replace the tents with small cabins, and maybe dig an in-ground pool. What'a you think?" Lester asked, and looked at me expectedly.

"I think that would be great, Lester. You're really on to somethin' here."

"Well, after it's finished, I'll need someone to help me run it," Lester said, and he continued to stare at me with a rather strange expression on his face. At first I thought he wanted me to work for him, but when he looked away and his face turned red—I realized he was asking me to marry him. I didn't know what to say, and I guess Lester could tell.

"I mean, it wouldn't be, you know, like that. It's just people would likely talk if me and you were off down there alone." Lester's face became even redder if that was possible.

"I would love to work for you, Lester, but I don't think we would have to get married. I mean the boys would be there, and if it gets that big—you'll need lots of help."

"Yeah, I guess you're right, but the offer's there if you should ever want it." Lester gathered up his tools preparing to leave and I went and placed my arms around his neck. "Thank you, for everythin'," I said, and kissed him on the cheek.

Lester struggled for words. "I just wanted you to know, Billie Jean, you do have options. You don't have to settle for somethin' you don't really want to do." After some thought, Lester gave me a quick hug and left.

I pondered over what Lester meant—settle for something I really didn't want to do? What did he think I was about to do? I knew it took a lot of courage for Lester to propose to me. He had always been like a big brother and I didn't think there was any real interest there. Not that Lester was all that old and certainly not bad looking. He had the same good looks all the Evans men were blessed with, or in some of their cases, I think it may have been a curse. There some talk around Lester might be "funny", but it was only malicious gossip started by people who thought everyone had to fit into their idea of normal. I simply thought he hadn't found the right woman yet.

Sometime later, and rather by chance, I learned more interesting facts about Lester's property. This was where, Preacher/Cole's, moonshine still had been located, and nearby, hidden in the bushes, the Evans boys' old bass boat. I now understood how they managed to move the still that night and get away from the law.

CHAPTER 30

Mine and the boys second Christmas without Bobby Ray was better by far, but then anything would have been an improvement over the previous year. We went to Ms. Minnie's on Christmas Eve like we normally would and I couldn't help but notice how feeble she'd become.

Lester made several much needed improvements to the house. He wanted to build his mother a new one, but Ms. Minnie wouldn't hear of it. She said the old one had been good enough to raise her family in, and would be good enough for her to die in. By the time everyone assembled, children and grandchildren, spouses and boyfriends and girlfriends, the small house was full.

We did receive some really good news that Christmas, Mary was engaged. It helped take our minds off the war in Vietnam that cast its ugly dark shadow over the entire nation. It was all people could think about or talk about and certainly on the minds of the Evans' family.

Cole's youngest son, Clinton, was there, but due back in the states at any time. They hoped he would make it home by Christmas but he didn't. The announcement of Mary's upcoming wedding provided a happy diversion. She'd brought her young man, Ernest, home earlier in the year for the family to meet. He was fresh out of dental school. The two met and dated while attending their respective schools in Memphis, but said they hadn't wanted to get serious at the time, but kept in touch.

When Mary finished college, with a degree in elementary education, she accepted a position teaching first grade in a small town near Memphis. After Ernest completed his schooling, he went into practice with an established dentist in Memphis and the relationship resumed.

Ernest seemed to be a fine young man, and from all accounts came from a good family. Simple, hardworking country people like us. The wedding, set for the early part of spring, would be held at the little church where Mary attended, and the location chosen so that Ernest's family who lived in Rome, Georgia, wouldn't have as far to travel. This meant some of Mary's extended family and friends probably wouldn't make the long trip to Memphis for the wedding, but the young couple wanted to do what would be fair for both families.

When Ruth and Henry Lee arrived a lot of back-slapping and congratulations went on. Ruth was just beginning to show with their second child and Henry Lee was ecstatic. Though crazy about Destiny Rose, Henry Lee hoped for a boy this time around, and would get his wish.

"A little chip off the old block, hey little brother?" John Wesley ribbed, and punched Henry Lee playfully in the arm.

"Lord, I hope not," Henry Lee replied, and everyone laughed.

Margaret and Hugh were there too. They recently moved back to Johnson's Bend. Margaret was wild about all her brothers' kids but you could easily see who her favorite was at the moment—Destiny Rose. A beautiful child and sweet natured like her mother with Ruth's china doll complexion and a head full of the Evans's dark, curly hair. Margaret looked at her like she could have swallowed her whole. I brought Destiny home with me on occasion to play with Robbie and Will. They would fight like cats and dogs with each other, but with Destiny, they gave in to her every little whim. There was not a lot of doubt she'd been given the right name and destined to be a heart breaker with the opposite sex.

On Christmas Day at Daddy's I had a chance to visit with my cousin, Boaz. I'd hardly seen him in the last few years. He'd been away at school becoming a veterinarian. I didn't realize it takes nearly as long to become a doctor of animals as it does of humans. Otherwise, he likely would have been in Vietnam along with all the other young men.

"Now that you're, Dr. Taylor, when are you gonna make good on that garter you caught at your sister's weddin'?" I teased.

"I can't afford a woman now," Bo laughed. "I gotta pay off all them school loans."

"Well, sometimes these things happen whether you're ready or not," I grinned.

"Yeah, I know. If it does, it does. How you doin'?" He asked, on a more somber note.

"I'm doin' okay, one day at a time."

Bo went on to tell me his plans for the future. He hoped to one day open a small animal clinic in Johnson's Bend. I told him I thought that would be wonderful and felt sure it would do well. Folks had to take their animals into Big Town or call a vet to come out to their house. It would be nice to have our own Veterinary Clinic. It's funny, but some people will have a doctor see to their animals when they won't see one for themselves.

Before I left that afternoon I managed to get Daddy alone and told him about my proposal from Lester.

"Well, you wouldn't have to change your last name," he laughed.

"Daddy, be serious, have you ever seen Lester with a woman?"

"As a matter of fact, I have. Before Lester went to Korea he'd been quite the man-about-town."

"Really?"

"Yeah, the women loved Lester."

"Really? I've never seen him with anyone."

"Yes indeedy. It's only since he come back from the war he's become so standoffish. War has a way of changin' folks, and besides, you're not with him twenty-four seven are you?"

"No."

"Then you don't really know what he does in his spare time, do you? I'm sure if Lester wants female company, he can get it."

And I thought Lester would have fainted if I'd accepted his offer. I might have been the one in for a *big* surprise.

Ross arrived at his parents' house a few days before the holidays and called to wish me and the boys a Merry Christmas. He said he hoped we could get together, and that his plans were to remain in Johnson's Bend until after the first of the year and then return to North Carolina. He would remain there until the job was completed, probably in the late spring or early part of summer. We arranged for him to come to supper that Friday. It would be New Year's weekend. The bank would close at noon that day. This would give me plenty of time to get home and make sure the house was clean and to prepare a nice meal. Ross wanted to take me and the boys out to dinner, but for their first meeting I felt a home environment might be the best.

Ross showed on the appointed night bearing gifts. Green, metal Tonka trucks for the boys and flowers for me. The kids hadn't even played with all their toys from Christmas, but little boys can never have too many trucks and were delighted with their presents. I couldn't remember the last time someone brought me flowers. Quite the romantic in his way, Bobby Ray hadn't been much of a flower guy. While I finished the last minute details of supper, Ross got down in the floor with the boys to play with their trucks. He asked if he could help me but I told him to entertain the kids instead, and the squealing and laughter from the living room sounded so natural it conjured up so many old memories. For a moment I'd been transported back in time and Bobby Ray was the one down in the floor playing with his boys, but I quickly squelched that memory. It wasn't good to go there.

I'll admit I was surprised at how quickly Ross and the boys became acquainted, and how at ease he seemed with them. For some reason I never thought of Ross as particularly liking little kids all that much and I'm not sure why I felt that way. He was great with them and they took to him immediately. I worried what we would say to one another after so many years apart. It wasn't like we were children anymore and a lot had happened since our days as a couple back in high school. As it turned out, I had worried for nothing. The conversation flowed freely and wasn't a bit strained. It was as though nothing had ever happened between us.

"So, Ross, what do you think about the war in Vietnam? Now that you're out of school do you think you might have to go?"

We finished supper and settled down on the couch to talk. Not easy with the boys interrupting every few minutes. I told them they could stay up for a while if they would behave, and Ross didn't appear to mind their endless stream of questions. In fact, he seemed to welcome them.

"Well, it's possible. Right now they're takin' the younger ones right out of high school."

"Yeah, that's what happened to Cole's son. He graduated in May and by December he was in Vietnam. He's due home any time, then maybe Cole and Sarah can get a decent night's rest."

"If it keeps goin', they'll take anyone who can walk and tote a gun, just like they did in the two World Wars. I'm sure then Uncle Sam will be givin' me a call," Ross said, and grinned.

When it came the boys' bedtime Ross helped me get them into their pajamas and tucked into bed. Afterwards we walked back to the living room and sat down on the couch.

"Billie Jean," Ross began, and reached over and took my hand. "I can't tell you how sorry I am about Bobby Ray, and about everything else. I wish we could have made things right between us before..." His voice trailed off and a faraway look came into his eyes. Maybe he'd regretted the breech between the three of us as much as I.

I continued to allow Ross to hold my hand. "I know Ross, I understand. We were so young, and we all said and did things we wish we could take back. There are so many things I wish I had done differently."

"You mean you wish you hadn't married Bobby Ray?"

I jerked my hand away. "No! Lord no. I just mean I've often wished I had handled some things in a better way."

"Oh, yeah, I know what you're saying. We all would like to go back and change some things in our life." Ross gazed at me intently. "I guess it's a good thing I'm goin' to be in North Carolina for a while. I don't want to worry you to death, Billie Jean, and sure don't expect anything from you, but I'm not gonna lie about it either. My feelin's for you have never changed, but I promise, I'll never try to push them on you again. I just want to be a part of your life in any way you will let me."

I saw the sincerity in Ross's face and it melted my heart. Yet when he went to leave that night and asked if he could pick me and the boys up for church on Sunday, I hesitated. It would cause a lot of talk and I didn't know if I was ready for that. I didn't want to repeat the same mistake I had before, to lead him on. In the end I agreed and it did start the gossip tongue's a wagging.

After church that Sunday Ross's mom, Ms. Ellen, invited the boys and me to come home with them for Sunday dinner. I was so proud of my little guys that day. They were on their very best behavior. Of course they knew Ross's parents well, but when they saw their Grandpa William outside after lunch, they wanted to go to his house and I let them go. No one could ever take his place in their life. Ross returned to my house that evening following the church services. It was New Year's Eve. A young couple from the church invited us to their home for a party, but I declined saying the boys were tired, which was true. They'd had a long day and after a light supper they were soon down for the count. Ross stood in the doorway and watched as I kissed both of their peaceful, sleeping little faces.

"They're wonderful little boys, Billie Jean, and you're a wonderful mother, but then I always knew you would be."

"I try to be, but it isn't always easy. Unfortunately raisin' kids doesn't come with an instruction booklet."

Ross and I walked back to the living room and he turned on the radio really low. He found WLS out of Chicago and the song, *Can't Take My Eyes Off of You*, drifted softly through the room.

"Dance with me?" Ross asked, and held out his hand.

I stepped into his arms and somehow it felt right. We danced slowly and quietly around the tiny living room. Another song that used to play in this room had come to mind, that of a little 45 I would play over and over on my old turntable, *You Are My Special Angel*. Bobby Ray and I would hold one another tightly and sway around and around usually ending up in the bedroom. I quickly brushed the memory away right at the moment Ross placed his lips tenderly on mine, hesitant at first, waiting to see how I would react.

I started to pull away when I discovered I didn't want to. Ross's kiss deepened and I leaned into him and let my arms snake around his neck. Our breathing quickened and I felt myself being guided back toward the sofa, and I stopped.

"I can't do this Ross, not here, not with my boys sleeping in the next room."

"I'm sorry, Billie Jean. I told myself I wouldn't do this, but you're so beautiful, and I love you so much. I can't help it, I always have and I always will."

"Maybe you'd better go, Ross. I'm kinda tired myself."

"I have to leave in a couple of days. You think we could go out to dinner, maybe just the two of us before then?"

"Yes, I would like that very much," I said.

The night before Ross left we went out to dinner alone, Daddy and Dora more than happy to babysit. I was as nervous as a schoolgirl getting ready for her first date. I tried on everything in my closet before I settled on a black suede skirt and a red, long sleeved sweater with black trim. With each season the hem lines grew shorter, and my figure was still passable even after having two babies, but I felt a little above the knees quite short enough for me. Along with the sweater and skirt I wore patterned tights and my new, black, knee length boots Daddy and Dora had given me for Christmas. I never would have paid that much for boots for myself. A few months back I cut my waist length hair to my shoulders and styled it in the current fashion of smooth and straight and slightly flipped up on the ends. After I finished dressing I took one last look in the mirror and decided I wasn't too shabby for a mama.

Ross arrived in a snug fitting black turtle-neck with a waist length black leather jacket and black pants and black loafers. Rather breathtaking in contrast to his shockingly pale blond hair.

He took me to a new restaurant that recently opened on the lake highway, The Fisherman's Catch. It specialized in fresh Kentucky Lake catfish but had many other items on the menu. The food, the service, and the atmosphere was most excellent, and we tried to keep the conversation on a lighter note. We talked about Ross's college days and his playing football.

"Did you ever think you might want to do it professionally?" I asked.

"Naw, not really—I'm not sure I was that good anyway," he said. "And I could never really see myself spending the best years of my life tacklin' three hundred pound men over a little piece of pigskin." We both laughed.

Ross also told me he was about to finish his post graduate work. He had his degree in drafting but wanted an engineering degree to go with it, or maybe the other way around. It all sounded very technical to me but either way Ross had a lot of education.

We talked a little about Bobby Ray, nothing personal, and I wouldn't have told Ross intimate details even if he'd asked. My memories of mine and Bobby Ray's brief time together, belonged to me and me alone. I would never share those with anyone, not even his children—how my heart would sing and the blood coursing through my veins warmed at his very touch. Those memories were locked away in my heart and there they would remain forever.

"You remember when your dad remarried and built the new house?" Ross asked, and his question brought me back to the present. "And how upset you were over tryin' to decide who you should live with, him or your grandparents?" Ross laughed and reached for my hand.

"Yes, I definitely remember that, and Grandma was beside herself. And you came up with the perfect solution without even breakin' a sweat." I smiled at Ross and allowed him to hold my hand, and he began to rub his thumb over the back of it in a slow circular motion. I remembered something else about that incident also. The look on Bobby Ray's face, the way his dark eyes had smoldered when I laid my hand on Ross's arm.

When Ross brought me home later on I knew he wanted to come in, and I knew it wouldn't be a good idea. We weren't children anymore, and it would have been so easy to take Ross into my bed that night. The boys were away and no one would know, but it was the same bed where Bobby Ray and I had made love, and I couldn't do it, although I really wanted to. I was still a young, warm-blooded woman, with normal fleshly desires, and Ross was a very desirable man. I missed that part of being married, the human touch, but it needed to be about more than satisfying the lust and the passion of the moment. I still believed in what I'd been taught. The physical, intimate relationship between a man and a woman was for marriage partners only.

I feel sure Ross would have settled for anything on this occasion, but in my heart I knew he wanted more than a one night roll in the sheets. He wanted forever.

Ross leaned down and sweetly kissed me goodnight and whispered, "Will you think about us while I'm gone?"

I promised him I would. When Ross returned I needed to have made up my mind without any reservations, if I was ready to move forward in this area of my life, and did I want it to be with him?

CHAPTER 31

The top three songs on the pop charts at the start of 1968 were, *Hello, Goodbye* by the Beatles, *Judy in Disguise (With Glasses)* by John Fred and His Playboy Band, and *Green Tambourine* by Lemon Pipers, and the war in Vietnam raged on. I feared it would be Bobby Ray I would have to send off to war someday. Instead it would be Ross and my cousin Bo I worried about. They remained of draft age range, but I suppose Ross was still considered a student, employed, but going to school on the side. Bo said he thought of enlisting after finishing his veterinary training, but knew it would kill his mother. Ross said he would go if they called him, but didn't intend to volunteer. There were several casualties of this war from Tennessee already, some from families in the area that I knew. There were times I longed once more for that feeling of being exempt or isolated from the strife in the rest of the world. But life goes on, and I had a lot to do and a lot on my mind at the beginning of the New Year. Mary's wedding for one and the possibility of a future for me and Ross another.

One night as I lay in bed trying to read myself to sleep, I heard little feet hit the floor. I waited, and in a few moments Robbie appeared in the doorway of my bedroom.

"What's wrong, baby, can't you sleep?"

Robbie sidled into the room and crawled up on the bed beside me. My little man, I cried like a baby when he started school. He let me go with him the first day, but after that he insisted on riding the bus. Will and I would walk out with him. He had to cross the road and board from the far side. That first morning he turned and waved to us, all grown-up with his little backpack on. I knew I would bawl again when Will started. Bobby Ray would be so proud of his boys and the young men they much too quickly were becoming. I looked down at the serious expression on Robbie's little face and knew something pressing was on his mind.

"Mama, tell me 'bout Daddy, how he always took me everywhere with 'im."

A huge lump formed in my throat, but I managed to keep my composure. "That's right, he did. From the day we brought you home from the hospital, he'd put you in your little carrier and take you wherever he went. Sometimes he'd be talkin' to you and you'd fall asleep, and he'd just keep on talkin'. It would tickle me. And when Will came along, he did the same thing. He would put the both of you in the truck with him and off he would go."

"Mama, what did Daddy look like?" Robbie asked and looked up at me. I could tell how important this was to him.

"Darlin', you know what your daddy looked like. You've got all kinds of pictures of him."

"I know, but I don't remember what he looked like."

I then understood what Robbie meant. His mental images of his father had begun to fade. I knew it was bound to happen and would be the same with Will. In a very short time, neither of them would remember Bobby Ray. They were simply too young. It nearly broke my heart to have to accept this. Robbie said he remembered certain things, but I suspect it was more likely my memories I spoke about he truly remembered, and those of the rest of the family he heard over and over.

"Well, just remember this, Darlin'. Your daddy loved all of us and wanted to be with us more than anythin' else in the world, but sometimes things happens in life that's out of our hands, and we can't understand the why, and I don't think we're expected too."

"Mama, when's Ross comin' back?"

"In the spring or early summer. Why?"

"He said he knew Daddy. He said they used to play ball together."

"Yes, they did. You like Ross?"

"Yeah. He said he would take me to a real baseball game someday. Mama, you think Daddy would mind if I went to a ballgame with Ross?"

I looked at Robbie and struggled to keep the tears from my eyes. He put into words my thoughts and feelings. Would it be disloyal to Bobby Ray if we went on with our lives? I wrapped my arms around my little boy. "No Baby, I don't think your daddy would mind a bit. He would want you to go and to have a great time and to be happy."

"Mama, can I sleep with you tonight?

"Sure." Robbie snuggled down beside me and was soon asleep, but I lay awake for a long time. My boys needed a father. Not just a male figure in their life. They had plenty of those. No, they needed a real father to be there every day.

I really liked my job at the bank, but one thing that differed greatly from working at the store was my wardrobe. I hadn't been all that into the "hippie look." I could never really understand the attraction to that lifestyle, but I liked my bell bottom jeans and had a couple of tie-dyed shirts. This is what I usually wore to the store, but for the bank I had to come up with something a little dressier. I loved the dresses and the suits with the large buttons that Jackie Kennedy made so popular, but I felt for me, they looked a little too old. More to my taste were the simple A-line cotton shifts currently in style and so comfortable to wear. Put together with a nice pair of pumps and a necklace and earrings, made the perfect outfit for a young working woman. Grandma helped me out and made several of these for me in a variety of colors.

There something else that differed vastly about the job at the bank, and I quickly discovered this. Working with the public in Big Town was much more complicated than working with the local folks in Johnson's Bend. People would get downright mean when they overdrew their checking accounts and had to pay an over-draft fee. They first would insist the bank had made the mistake, and when I would show them that was not the case, they would get hateful with me, like I'd spent their money.

Once in a while the President of the bank, Mr. Fowler, came out and talked to these individuals. His quiet and soothing demeanor could smooth over their ruffled feathers. He looked every bit the part of a genteel, conservative Southern banker. Right down to his sensible leather brogan shoes. He normally wore suits in neutral tones, but now and then he would wear a black or a navy blue one, and he preferred the thin narrow ties to the wide ones in crazy prints. He probably thought they would be too risqué for the bank. I did see a thin red stripe in his tie once when he had on the navy blue suit. He must have felt frisky that day. He kind of reminded me of the Secret Service agents I saw on TV that guarded the president with his short haircut and black-rimmed glasses, but it only goes to show you can't judge a book by its cover.

As soon as Mary told me the date of her wedding I went to Mr. Fowler to ask if I could have that day off. I was a little hesitant about it as I hadn't worked there all that long. I gently knocked on his closed door.

"Come in," he called in response. I opened the door and tried to summon up my courage as I walked in and closed the door behind me. "Billie Jean, what a pleasant surprise. You look charmin' this mornin'. Sit down—what can I do for you?"

Mr. Fowler removed his glasses as he spoke and I realized he wasn't nearly as old as I thought. "I hate to ask you," I began, "but I need to be off Friday, March the 30th for an out-of- town weddin'."

"Uh-huh, I see. Well, I'm sure that can be arranged."

"Oh, thank you very much, Mr. Fowler," I said, and stood to leave.

"Sit down, sit down." Mr. Fowler indicated the chair behind me I'd just vacated. So I sat back down. "And when we're in private, you can call me, Marty. Mr. Fowler is my father."

"Marty" smiled at me with a peculiar expression on his face and it made me feel very uncomfortable. I wished I hadn't closed the door when I came in.

"Well, I need to get back to work," I said, and started to rise again.

"You can take another minute. After all, you're with the boss," Mr. Fowler laughed. "I've been meanin' to speak with you about somethin' else. You know a pretty girl like you could go far here at the bank. If you play your cards right, if you know what I mean?" Mr. Fowler leaned forward and winked and I swear leered at me from across his desk.

I might not be very wise in the ways of the world, but I knew exactly what he meant. I tried to think how I could get out of there without making a scene and was saved by a knock at the door. Before Mr. Fowler could respond, I jumped up and rushed to the door and jerked it opened.

His personal secretary, Ms. Claire, stood there, back from the post office with his mail. I rushed past her with barely a nod and went to my workstation. I trembled all over but tried my best to keep anyone from seeing. I didn't know what to do. Sexual harassment in the workplace was not a hot topic in those days, but always there. Most women if they wanted to keep their jobs had to put up with this humiliation. Other than find another job, they didn't know anything else they could do. I liked working at the bank and surely needed my job, but I wouldn't put up with it. Not for long.

After work that afternoon I ran by Ruth's and Henry Lee's. He was already home from work and mowing the yard. Our unusually warm March caused the new grass to really take off. Henry Lee wore his work overalls without a shirt and my heart leaped in my chest. As far as looks went, Henry Lee was right. He was a little older version of Bobby Ray. The smell of fresh mowed spring grass met me when I stepped from the car. I loved that smell. Henry Lee turned the mower off when I walked up.

"Hey, little sis, where you been keepin' yourself," he asked, and gave me a hug.

"Work, work, work," I replied. "Ruth home?"

"Yeah, go on in. Everythin' okay?"

"Oh, yeah, I just need to talk to her about weddin' stuff for a minute."

I found Ruth in the kitchen setting the table for supper. Six months pregnant, she looked picture perfect with not a hair out of place. I don't know how she managed to do this. Destiny Rose sat on the floor playing with paper dolls and jumped up when she saw me.

"Ainty Billie, Ainty Billie," she cried, "where's Robbie and Will?"

"They're still at their granddaddy's. I've got to go and get them in a minute, but I need to talk to your mama first."

"Sugar Pie, why don't you pick up your paper dolls and take them to your room. Suppers' 'bout ready."

Destiny gathered up her play things and without having to be told a second time, took them to her room. I wished the boys would listen that well, but maybe raising girls was easier. Ruth looked at me expectantly so I got right to the point.

"When you were at the bank, did you like Mr. Fowler?"

"Oh, yes, he was precious. Why, don't you like him?"

"Well, he's kinda creepy."

"Creepy? Mr. Fowler? He's one of the sweetest and kindest old gentlemen I've ever known."

"Old? I wouldn't exactly call him old. He's probably not that much older than me and you."

"Are you talkin' 'bout, Martin Jr.? Oh, that's right. Mr. Fowler Senior retired, I remember now. He was groomin' Junior to take over his job when I was there, and you're right, Jr. is kinda creepy." We both snickered.

"Did he ever make a pass at you when you worked there?"

"No, but I did catch him lookin' at me funny several times. Why, did he make a pass at you?" Ruth looked shocked.

"Yeah, I guess you could say that." And I told her what happened.

"What did you say? What did you do?"

"I didn't say or do anythin', yet. Maybe he won't pursue it and I won't have to."

"Well, he's married and a deacon in the church. I'd bet he wouldn't want it to get out that he's a sleaze bag."

Ruth tried to persuade me to stay for supper but I said I needed to go and get the boys. Dora normally had supper ready anyway by the time I got there. The boys and I would eat before we went home. It was her way of helping me out and I appreciated it so much.

The boys and I tried to eat at least once a week with my grandparents'. Grandma feelings were hurt if we didn't. I didn't say anything to anyone about the incident at the bank other than Ruth, and I prayed that Martin Fowler, Jr. wouldn't become an insurmountable problem. I hadn't wanted to quit my job at the bank, but I didn't know if I could ever feel totally comfortable there again.

CHAPTER 32

Shortly before Cole's son, Clinton, left for the army he married a little girl he began dating in high school. It was a hurried up affair. Not because he leaving, but because she was pregnant. Clinton's daughter Katie was two years old before he saw her in person. Sarah said Clinton was foolish about his little girl, and I hoped that was true, but after he came home he sure didn't spend much time with her and her mama. I don't think marriage is always the best answer in these cases. I know it's the honorable thing to do, and Cole told his son, that he would marry Barbara Gail, but teen marriages, especially ones due to an unexpected and often unwanted pregnancy is iffy at best. The child can have its daddy's name and he can be a part of the child's life, but the young couple must have something else working for them. I know you're thinking Bobby Ray and I were in our teens when we married, but I think we had been more mature back then, and a bond present between the two of us since childhood.

One Saturday afternoon while playing pool at his favorite hangout, Clinton and a guy got into an argument. I don't know if it was over the pool game or what. Clinton was never a trouble maker, actually he was pretty quiet, but not one to walk away either. Apparently the two yammered back and forth until Clinton had enough. The other patrons of the bar told the police Clinton grabbed the guy by the shirt and told him where he would put the pool stick if he didn't back off. The guy left the bar and

Clinton stayed for another hour or so. When he went out to his truck to leave, the guy walked up behind him and stabbed him in the back with a hunting knife. The razor sharp blade entered a little above his right kidney and severed his renal artery. Witnesses said the guy then withdrew the knife and calmly walked to his car, got in and drove off. Clinton bled out probably before the ambulance ever left Big Town.

Ruth called that evening and told me what had happened and it absolutely made me sick. It seemed to me the Evans family received more than their share of grief. I thought back to the day Clinton came to the house to give me a personal invitation to his going away party. His hair almost as long as mine was thick and wavy, not curly like his dad's and uncles, and he always kept it neat and clean. I remembered how it shined in the sunlight as he stood on my front porch.

"You know this will have to go?" I said, and reached up and tugged on a strand of his hair.

"Yeah, I know. They'll probably burn their shears up when they buzz my head," he laughed.

I went to Cole's and Sarah's as soon as Ruth called, but what can you say to someone at a time like this? The entire family was devastated.

"Made it through that Hell in Vietnam to only come home and get killed in his own backyard," Cole said, his voice filled with bitterness.

I'm sure there're folks who would say if Clinton had been at home with his wife and baby it wouldn't have happened. I guess that's so, but where and how he died didn't lessen the grief of his loss.

Later in the kitchen making coffee and setting out food for the quickly gathering family, Ruth leaned over and whispered in my ear, "Henry Lee said Cole talked to Clinton several times about his drinkin' and needin' to stay out of them honky-tonks."

I often wondered if Cole's children knew about his moonlighting job. Sarah had to know, as surely as did Queenie and Ms. Minnie. How can you tell your kids not to do something and expect them to listen, when you yourself have made and sold the stuff? But I don't think Cole and Sarah, or any of the Evans family for that matter, ever looked at it in the same light I did. To their way of thinking, making moonshine was a necessity for their survival.

At the visitation, Barbara Gail looked as I'm sure I had when Bobby Ray died. Like the world tilted to the side and you can't get your bearings.

"Me and the baby were sittin' in the porch swing watchin' for his truck," she said in a daze. "I had supper on the stove, and we waited and waited, but he didn't come. Then I saw Daddy Cole's truck comin' down the road, and somehow I knew, Clinton wasn't ever comin' home again."

How well I understood Barbara Gail's words. How many times had I sat and waited for Bobby Ray to come home? And when the realization finally hits that they're not, the pain is so deep it's nearly unbearable, and it can lay you low for a very, very, long time.

They buried Clinton with full military honors, and his funeral, as was Bennie's, was very sad, and very touching. Adding to the glum of the day, the sky was overcast, and right as Taps played; a fine mist began to fall. This was my fourth trip to this cemetery to bury a member of the Evans family. I glanced around at the stoic faces and I could sense the closeness that existed there. John Wesley's four girls, Reesa, Robin, Rachael, and Ramay, stood to one side with their husbands. I don't know what John Wesley and Queenie could have been thinking when they named them. Mary and Ernest came for the funeral. It sure had put a damper on their big event coming up, and Mary thought maybe she should postpone the wedding, but Cole wouldn't hear of it. We could have cancelled the flowers and the cake without any problems but the invitations had been sent weeks before.

Cole's oldest boy, Dwain took his baby brother's death really hard, and he and his brothers-in-law, Mike, Sharon's husband, and Kane, Tina's, were out for some good old redneck vigilante justice. Thank heavens the law found the guy first and took him into custody. The Evans family didn't need any more scandal and heartache in their lives. I'd heard rumors that Dwain was growing something other than corn and tobacco in the holler. I prayed that was not true. Marijuana was fast becoming the new cash crop in Tennessee. I thought back to our teen years and the time Henry Lee tried to outrun the law in that old Ford without a reverse. We thought that was a really big deal back then, but it was only child's play compared to this.

After the funeral the family gathered at Cole's and Sarah's and Ms. Minnie came up to me, her skin so thin and fragile she looked almost transparent.

"I can't understand why the Lord keeps takin' our young and leavin' me when I'm ready to go," she said.

"Don't say that, Ms. Minnie. We wouldn't know what to do without you," I said, and gave her a big hug.

"If Lester didn't have me to look after, he might get married. He's a fine, good man, Billie Jean. You could do worse." Ms. Minnie stared at me in earnest.

What is it with this family? I wondered. Taking the "we take care of our own," a bit too far. Of course the Bible does say when one brother dies that it's acceptable if the next brother takes his widow to wife and raise up seed to the other, but Bobby Ray had left his seed behind in his two sons, Robbie and Will, so that didn't apply in our case.

CHAPTER 33

We buried Clinton on Tuesday and on Thursday the ones of us in the wedding party drove to Mary's for the rehearsal that evening. Cole, as the oldest and acting head of the family, would walk Mary down the aisle. I'm not sure she would have wanted her father if he had been alive. I would be her bridesmaid and Margaret the Matron-of-Honor and Destiny the flower girl. One of Ernest's little cousins would be the ring bearer. Sarah, Lester, Ms. Minnie, and Hugh came with us. The remainder of the immediate family planned to come the next morning for the evening wedding.

The wedding was originally set to take place right after school was out in May. Ernest then learned he had to attend a dental seminar in Miami the first week in April and could bring a guest. Mary, out of school for a while had put back a little each payday into savings and accumulated a modest nest egg. Ernest was recently out of school and with his first paying job. Mary wanted to use her savings for the honeymoon, but Ernest didn't want her to do that, but when the Miami trip came up, it was too good to pass up. Their airfare and hotel room and part of their food would be paid for. It was basically a free honeymoon.

Mary's school was very good and understanding of the situation and willing to arrange for a substitute for the last few weeks of school.

Cole made it through the rehearsal fairly well but I worried he would be a mess at the wedding. Everyone tried to put on a happy face for Mary's sake even though it wasn't easy. After the rehearsal we did a little decorating and arranged the tables and chairs for the next day, but much of the decorating couldn't be done until the florist brought the flowers and the candelabras.

Mary and Ernest along with his parents' hosted the rehearsal supper at the small house the couple rented. Mary had already moved in and was staying there. Ernest moved most of his belongs in except for a few clothes and some personal items that he needed on a daily basis.

Ernest and his father had gone into Memphis to Beale Street and bought BBQ with all the trimmings. This cobblestone street is the most famous one in Memphis and known for its great food, especially barbecue and southern fried catfish. It once was an affluent suburb in the 1930's before it's decline after the Great Depression, but it never lost its mystique. Beale Street was a Mecca for musicians, most of them young and black. The music, a blend of Gospel spirituals and African rhythms brought over with the slaves. From every little juke joint and honky tonk a new sound had emerged, the Blues.

Beale Street was eventually declared the "Home of the Blues," and here many legendary Blues greats would perform—the likes of W. C. Handy, Muddy Waters, Rufus Thomas, and Robert Johnson. Folklore has it Robert sold his soul to the devil at the crossroads in return for the ability to play the guitar like no other. In the 1940's another Blues man had come on the scene, Riley "Blues Boy" King, later famous under his stage name, B.B. King.

In addition to the savory barbecue, Ernest's mom made lemon meringue pies and plenty of sweet tea. It was a wonderful supper and everyone seemed to enjoy it and relax a little. Mary's soon to be new in-laws appeared to be fine people and you could see they were crazy about Mary. I was so happy for her. I knew Mary deserved every ounce of happiness she got. After we finished eating, the kids wanted to go outside to play and Margaret volunteered to go and keep an eye on them. I followed her out. We really hadn't gotten the chance to get close. Margaret married and left long before Bobby Ray and me were together. Now that she back in Johnson's Bend, I hoped that would change.

"Mind if I sit here with you?" I asked, and dropped down beside Margaret on the steps before she could reply.

"No, of course not," she said, and reached into her pocket and pulled out a pack of cigarettes and lit one. "Cigarette?" she asked, and offered me the pack.

"No, thanks, I never developed the taste for them, but I think I easily could have. I didn't know you smoked," I said.

"Yeah, I guess you have to have some bad habits, and I figured smokin' is better than drinkin'," Margaret replied with a bitter laugh, and looked down at the ground. "The good ones do always die young, don't they?" she said, and pulled deeply on her cigarette and exhaled the smoke in a long, slow breath.

"It sure seems that way sometimes, Margaret."

"I miss them, Billie Jean." Margaret turned to me with tears glistening in her eyes. "Bennie, Bobby Ray, now Clinton."

"Yes, I know what you mean. I miss Bobby Ray every single day, and sometimes it gets so bad I think I can't stand it."

"But havin' the boys helps, don't it?"

"Oh sure, but it's not the same. It's kinda hard to explain. Bobby Ray was my soul mate, if there is such a thing."

"If Hugh and I split, I'd be alone. Sometimes I think that wouldn't be so bad, but if I had children it would be different. I'd have a reason to go on."

Margaret stared off into space and her demeanor worried me. She'd cut her dark curly hair short and styled it in finger waves, like back in the '20's, and it looked wonderful on her with her long slender neck and high cheekbones.

"I've been meanin' to tell you—I love your hair," I said, wanting to change the subject.

"Oh, thank you, do you really?" Margaret reached up and patted her hair. "I have always wanted to be a beautician. You know have a little shop, do people's hair and nails and listen to all the local gossip," Margaret laughed, but it was a hollow sound.

"Then why don't you?" I asked.

Margaret looked at me like the very idea of it was unimaginable. "I'm too old to think about that now."

"No you're not. What are you, thirty-eight—nine?"

"Try forty-one next month."

"Margaret, that's not too old to pursue your dreams. They have a Beauty School right there in Big Town."

"That costs money, Billie Jean, and the way we've moved around, Hugh's never worked in one place long. We ain't got a penny saved to our name."

Hugh went to work with Lester when they moved back and was making good money. As long as they lived close to Margaret's family, he would work and they would do all right, but the problem was, Hugh always thought he could get richer quicker somewhere else. He never figured out the only way to get ahead was to buckle down and stay with something. And speaking of the devil, Hugh came out the backdoor along about then and stood in front of me and Margaret.

"Hey, babe, Ernest says work is really good around Memphis. Maybe we should move up here," he said all excited.

"I'm not movin' again, Hugh. You do what you want." Margaret's voice was flat and left no room for discussion.

"Okay, babe, okay. I just thought it might be a great adventure for us."

"The first few times were an adventure, Hugh. The last ten have been a chore, and I'm stayin' put in Johnson's Bend."

Hugh looked embarrassed and glanced at me and grinned. "Well, I guess the boss has spoken," he said, and bent down and kissed Margaret on the cheek.

Good for you girl, I thought. Stick to your guns and don't let him pull you from pillar to post ever again.

Mary's wedding day was beautiful, if bitter-sweet, and Cole was so emotional I didn't know if he would make it down the aisle with her, but he did and the ceremony went fine. They held their reception in the Fellowship Hall of the church. It wasn't a sit down affair, but every finger food you could imagine, hot and cold, was provided.

Mary and Ernest catered part of the meal, but the ladies of the church prepared much of the food. The parishioners took the young couple in and really made them feel at home. Mary's brothers each gave a toast to the new couple, as did Ernest's brother, Lloyd. A hoot and a big cut-up and he reminded me a lot of Henry Lee in his younger days before Ruth smoothed out some of his rougher edges. While we sat around and socialized, Robbie and Will ran up to me all excited and out of breath.

"Guess what, Mama?" Robbie said, gasping for air. "Uncle Lester is gonna teach me and Will how to catfish wrestle."

"Yeah. Uncle Lester said Daddy was one of the best at it. Mama, did you know Daddy could wrestle catfish?" Will had asked.

"Yes, as a matter of fact, I did," I said, and glanced over their heads at a red faced Lester walking up behind them. He looked very uncomfortable, but very handsome in his silver gray suit and blue shirt, and he smelled so good, kind of woodsy like fresh pine and clean air and sunshine. I could see why women would like him.

"Did he also tell you when your daddy was about fourteen, his arm nearly rotted off when one of them big mud cats tore into him and wouldn't let go?"

"No. Did that really happen, Uncle Lester?" The boys asked, and gazed up at their highly embarrassed uncle wanting more of the story.

"Yes, that did really happen, and that's why I told the both of you, you have to be older, *much, much,* older, before I will teach you," Lester said, and looked at me when he emphasized the *much.*

I smiled at Lester and let him off the hook. "I guess that'll be okay, as long as you do wait until you're older, *much, much,* older."

Catfish wrestling is an insane redneck sport. Some places refer to it as noodling. No matter what you call it, it's very dangerous. The concept is to stick your arm into the underwater lair of one of these sometimes huge, bottom-feeders, and using your fingers as bait, try to get the fish to grab ahold. When it does, you then wrestle him out. Catfish date back to prehistoric times, and that should say right there, they're pretty resilient and probably don't like to be messed with.

We cleaned up after the reception, again grateful for a large family to help. We then left for the long drive home. Mary and Ernest planned to spend their wedding night in a hotel near the airport in Memphis, and fly out early the next morning. Several more cars returned to Johnson's Bend than had driven up with us. Lester drove my car with me and the boys, and Henry Lee, Ruth and Destiny, followed behind in their car. On the day we arrived the kids spotted a small Dairy Freeze on the outskirts of town. I promised on the way back, we would stop. Lester turned off at the ice cream place and Henry Lee pulled in behind us. I'm sure Destiny reminded him of my promise. The others went on ahead.

I got out of the car and walked to the closest window on the front of the building, and stood there for what seemed like several minutes. No one came to take my order. I could see the workers on the inside looking at me, and I wondered what was wrong with these people. Did they think I stood here for my health?

Finally a young wisp of a girl came to the window, opened it and politely asked me what I wanted. I gave her my order, which she quickly filled, and brought the ice cream cones back to me. I paid her and turned around and as I started back to the car I saw Henry Lee doubled over his steering wheel laughing his head off. Ruth with a big smile on her face gently patted his arm admonishing him to stop. I glanced over at Lester, he too had a big grin on his face and pointed behind me, I thought at the sky. I turned slightly and looked up. I didn't see anything, but sky. I walked on to the car and Lester rolled his window down and reached for the ice cream.

"You were standin' in the colored line," he whispered, and again pointed to the area behind me. I looked where he indicated and saw what he meant. A little sign over the window where I stood read, "Colored", and directly across from it, perhaps a distance of three feet, was another little sign above the other tiny window that read, "White." I never thought of such a thing, but this was Memphis and not Johnson's Bend. By law you could stand side by side and buy ice cream that looked the same, and tasted the same, and cost the same, but you couldn't stand in the same line together. Now how silly is that?

I must have caused a real conundrum for the employees. Maybe they thought I couldn't read and took pity on me. I walked over to the other car to give Destiny her ice cream and Henry Lee continued to grin from ear to ear. He took the cone and was about to say something, but I cut him off.

"I don't want to hear it," I said, and went back to my car and got in.

This hadn't been my first encounter with prejudice and racism. We had it at home as well, even if less obvious. Some of my coworkers at the bank would pretend they were busy or didn't see the colored people when they came in. Many of them were older folks and couldn't read or write. If they could, it was only a labored printed version of their name. It did take longer to wait on them, but I went out of my way to be patient and helpful. I truly wanted to make their banking experiences a pleasant one and most of them were so polite and appreciative of my help. I wondered if this was due in part to their fear of the repercussions if they weren't. Did I represent the oppressor to them because of the color of my skin? I truly hoped not. I didn't want them to think of me in any way as their enemy.

CHAPTER 34

On the Monday following Mary's wedding I was a little surprised to see Lester come into the bank shortly after we opened. He wore his work clothes and nodded to me but didn't stop to chat. I waved in return and watched him walk to Ms. Claire's desk and say something to her. She then picked up the phone and spoke into it and then showed Lester into Mr. Fowler's office. I assumed Lester came to ask for a loan to continue work on his resort. I knew he wanted to do even more improvement to his campground. I intended to speak with Lester when he came out of Mr. Fowler's office, but he was only in there very briefly. I was busy with a customer at the time. Lester left the bank without looking my way and from his body language it hadn't been a pleasant visit. I couldn't imagine that Mr. Fowler turned him down for a loan if he asked for one. I was extremely puzzled by Lester's presence in the bank that morning and his abrupt departure, but it wasn't really any of my business.

The remainder of the day remained uneventful, and as I made ready to leave that afternoon, Ms. Claire summoned me to Mr. Fowler's office. She said he needed to have a word with me and my heart began to pound. I hadn't been to his office since the day he made the inappropriate remarks to me. I walked with hesitation toward his opened door, and this time I didn't close it behind me. Ms. Claire picked up her purse and left as soon as she delivered the message and most of the other bank employees were leaving as well. I didn't relish the prospect of being alone with the bank's headman.

"Come on in, Ms. Evans and have a seat," Mr. Fowler said when he saw me in the doorway. Very businesslike he motioned for me to sit in the chair in front of him. He kept looking down at his desk and shuffling the papers around there, but didn't appear to be accomplishing much. I got the distinct impression he was as uncomfortable as me.

"You wanted to see me, Mr. Fowler?" I said, and wished my voice didn't sound so strained, but my throat was dry from anxiety.

"Yes I did, Ms. Evans." Mr. Fowler finally looked up but had trouble making eye contact with me. "I wanted to commend you on what a fine job you are doin', and I hope that you're happy here and will stay with us for a long time."

"Yes, I like my job here very much," I said.

"Good, good, glad to hear that." Mr. Fowler still only gave me a fleeting glance before looking back at the papers on his desk. "You know, Billie Jean, if I may call you by your given name?" I nodded my agreement. "You don't always have to be a teller. There are other positions available, if you would prefer one of them."

Mr. Fowler's words were courteous and professional, and I didn't detect anything suggestive in them. I couldn't be one hundred percent for certain, but thought he might be sucking up to me, and I felt sure it had something to do with Lester's visit that morning.

I didn't tell Lester about the previous incident, but that didn't mean it hadn't gotten back to him. I knew that

Ruth would tell Henry Lee, she told him everything, and he would likely pass this information on to Lester.

"No, thank you. I'm quite happy workin' the window, but if I change my mind, I'll let you know," I said, and heard the added confidence in my voice.

I guess Mr. Fowler heard it too. His head jerked up and he stared at me through his thick, black rimmed glasses. I think he suspected a hidden meaning in my words. I stared back at him with a little smile on my face, and it could have been interpreted as a tiny bit smug. There wasn't much doubt in my mind, that Lester had put the fear of God into Martin Fowler Jr., or to be more precise, the fear of Lester's retribution if Junior ever stepped out of line with me again. I spoke politely, but I feel sure we had understood one another, and besides, it wouldn't hurt to let him sweat just a little.

Ross called nearly every day he was away and some days he called twice. He planned to be home at the end of April or by the second week of May at the latest. I found myself looking forward to his return. One afternoon I stopped by to see Grandma and give her the details of Mary's wedding. She complained she never saw me anymore, but actually we saw one another in passing almost daily. I think what she meant was we never had our girl talks anymore. On this day I felt the need for some of Grandma's great words of wisdom. The house smelled of her fresh baked cornbread.

"Grandma, do you think it's possible to love two men in a lifetime? In different ways, but both of them still be good?"

Grandma looked at me over the top of her glasses. "Are we speakin' of someone in particular, or people in general?" she replied, and placed a slice of buttered cornbread in front of me.

"I'm talkin' 'bout me and Bobby Ray and Ross."

Grandma studied me for a moment before she answered, "Yes, I certainly do think it's possible, but you need to realize, it won't be the same. You and Ross aren't kids anymore, and you know what it's like to be with a man that makes you burn with desire. It might not be that way with Ross." Grandma placed a glass of milk at my elbow.

"Grandma!"

"I'm not so old I can't remember what it's like to be young—when me and your grandpa first married..." Grandma's voice trailed off, and I wasn't sure I wanted to hear the rest of that memory anyway. There's just something about picturing your parents and your grandparents having sex. "All I'm sayin', darlin', is the fire may not burn as high or as hot this time, but warm and steady can be good too. So, is this a done deal, you and Ross?"

"I don't know, maybe, but I know he's goin' to ask me when he gets back and I think I might say yes."

As I left I saw Grandpa Jack out by the barn. "Hey, Grandpa," I called out to him. "Where do baby mules come from?" Grandpa threw back his head and howled with laughter.

"You mean to tell me child that you've had two young'uns and not figured that out yet?" he yelled back.

I laughed too. "I love you, Grandpa."

"I love you, baby girl."

I lay in bed that night thinking about what Grandma said. That warm and steady could be good too. Everyone knows the fire that burns the hottest and the highest burns out the quickest. Yes, I believed that warm and steady might be the best.

On the Thursday following Mary's wedding, April 4, 1968, prominent civil rights leader Dr. Martin Luther King Jr. was shot and killed while he stood on the second floor balcony of the Lorraine Motel in downtown Memphis. This would spark an outrage across the land that would range from violent lootings and burnings to peaceful and silent prayer vigils. Someone even hurled a brick through the front window of Mr. Utley's little store, and he was the most non-racist person I ever knew. Very scary times with more of them to come, and I was so thankful Mary and Ernest were nowhere near Memphis when it happened. Two months after the shooting, James Earl Ray from Alton, Illinois, a person no one had ever heard of, was arrested and charged with the crime, and like with the Kennedy assassination, there would be years and years of speculation about who was involved.

Ross returned the first week in May with a beautiful diamond ring and as I expected, he asked me to marry him. I said yes. We set the date for the first weekend in July. There really wasn't any point in waiting. It wasn't like we hadn't known one another forever. And we needed to get settled in his home in East Tennessee before the new school year began. I asked Ross if he didn't want a church wedding with all the fuss and to do. After all, this was his first marriage. He said he really didn't. If it was all right with me he wanted for us to be married at his parent's house with only our immediate families present, and I was absolutely good with that.

Telling the Evans' family would be one of the most difficult things for me. Not that they didn't want me to remarry. Hard as it was to believe, Bobby Ray had been gone for nearly four years. At times it seemed like only yesterday. No, what bothered them was my moving so far away and taking his boys, and my family wasn't real keen on it either. In fact they weren't as excited about the marriage as I thought they would be.

Another difficult task came when I had to sell the farm. The day the realtor came and placed the "For Sale" sign in the yard I cried and cried, and thought back to the day I had gone to the bank and made the final payment on the place. It hadn't brought me the joy it once would have. Bobby Ray dreamed of the day he would own his own land. After leaving the bank I went to the cemetery and laid the note stamped, "Paid in Full," on his gravestone. "It's ours now, Bobby Ray, free and clear," I whispered.

I gave some thought to keeping the place and renting it out, but Ross said it would be more hassle than it was worth and he was probably right. We would be too far away to keep a check on it, and I didn't want to put it off on Daddy or someone else. One morning while alone at the house packing, a knock came at the front door. I opened it and Cole stood there.

"Good mornin', Billie Jean, can I come in and talk with you a minute," he asked. Cole had aged so much since Clinton's death and would still have to endure the approaching trial.

"Well of course you can," I said, and opened the door wide for him.

"You had any lookers yet?" he asked, glancing around the room.

"A few. There's one young couple who want it real bad, if they can come up with the money. I hope they can. I told them it's a great place to start a family."

Cole nodded his head in agreement. He was only making small talk. I could tell he had something else on his mind.

"I know you're busy, so I'll get right to the point. I want you to know, Billie Jean, no matter what your last name is, you'll always be a part of my family. If you get to East Tennessee and everythin's not like you hoped, you can call me day or night. There'll be no questions asked, and I'll come get you and the boys and bring you home."

I felt the tears well up in my eyes. "I know that Cole," I said, and put my arms around his neck and hugged him. "I love you, Cole, and I will miss all of you so much."

"I love you too, Billie Jean," Cole said, and hugged me back. "You were the best thing that ever happened to my baby brother." He then said goodbye and left, and I cried again.

CHAPTER 35

The young couple got their loan and we closed on the deal the week before the wedding. They reminded me of myself and Bobby Ray. So young, just starting out and filled with so many hopes and dreams. They would take possession of the house as soon as Ross and I returned from our honeymoon and moved my belongings out. In the weeks before our marriage Ross spent his time running between Knoxville and Johnson's Bend. He tried to be there as much as possible to help me pack and take care of the last minute details. I never dreamed how much there is to do when you moved. Thankfully, Ross's employer had been kind enough to give him two weeks off even with scarce advanced warning. In that time we had to get married, go on a honeymoon, and move the boys and me to his home in East Tennessee.

Ross persuaded me the smart thing to do was sell my car. It did have several miles on it but was still in excellent condition. Ross had a nearly new car and his company provided him with a work truck, so I suppose we really didn't need mine, but the car was my last material possession that linked me to Bobby Ray. He had loved that car, but I figured it better to make a clean break of it, and felt some better when one of John Wesley's sons-in-law wanted the car. At least it would remain in the family.

Ross's family and my Aunt Grace insisted on giving us a bridal shower, but neither of us really needed anything.

I had kept house for years and Ross's house came already furnished. Well, as much as most single men's houses are, but we didn't want to hurt their feelings and allowed them to go ahead. They said we needed all new things to begin our new life together, and I could see that.

On June 5, 1968 our nation was once more rocked by the assassination of a public figure. Robert F. Kennedy, brother of the late president, and winner of the Democratic presidential primary was shot at the Ambassador Hotel in Los Angeles, California and died shortly thereafter. I couldn't help but notice the similarities between the Kennedys and the Evans'. Oh, sure they were separated geographically and socially by light years, but the one thing they had in common was the tragic loss of their loved ones—especially their young. Death truly is the great equalizer, and it seemed to find these two families much too often.

A mixture of feelings and emotions flooded me as our wedding day approached. I looked forward to our wedding trip to Gulf Shores, Alabama and the boys were excited about having Ross as a stepfather and our move to the foothills of the Smokies.

I continued to be amazed at how well Ross and the boys got on, but I wasn't foolish enough to think there wouldn't be problems. When you see one another once in a while is one thing, but living together on a daily basis is another.

Late one afternoon a few days before the wedding, I dropped the boys off at Ms. Minnie's to spend some time with her and Lester. I avoided this visit for as long as I could. I knew Ms. Minnie was unhappy about me moving away with her grandsons, but until then she hadn't said anything.

"I know I'll never see them again, Billie Jean," she said, and her words tore at my heart. Lester had already wished me well, but I wondered, considering his proposal, what he really thought. While the boys were being entertained I walked the short distance to the cemetery. I brought fresh flowers to place on Bobby Ray's grave and I needed to tell him the news. Another job I avoided.

When I entered the cemetery I was again struck by the peaceful silence. The tall pines swayed overhead as the wind whispered through their branches. I always thought this the perfect place to be laid to rest. At the grave I knelt down to remove the old, dried flowers from the vases and replaced them with the fresh ones, and I noticed someone had recently placed flowers on Bennie's and Mr. Evans's graves. I would miss coming here, and I had made arrangements with Daddy to put flowers on Bobby Ray's grave at least every couple of months.

"I'm gettin' remarried Bobby Ray," I whispered. "To Ross—he's real good with the boys. We're gonna move up to East Tennessee." For an instant, I thought, I can't do this, and had to take a deep breath before I continued. "I love you Bobby Ray, and I always will, but I have to do what I think is best for me and the boys. They need a father."

The words were barely out of my mouth when from behind came a loud crash. I jumped frog-style across Bobby Ray's grave and cautiously looked over my shoulder. A huge old oak tree had fallen into the cemetery. If I was a superstitious person I might have thought that Bobby Ray was trying to tell me something, like he was less than happy about my news. When I could catch my breath and my heart stopped pounding, I went back to the house and told Lester about the tree. He said it had most likely been struck by lighting and died. He would go the next day, cut it up and haul it off.

Ross and I married on a beautiful hot July afternoon in the living room of his parents' house. We planned to have only cake, punch, nuts, and mints, but Ms. Ellen and Grandma thought we needed just a "little" more. No one went home hungry that evening. Everyone pretended not to notice Ross was in a tad hurry to leave. He said he wanted to make it to Nashville before nightfall, but there no way we could manage that in a car. We planned to spend the night there and continue on to Gulf Shores the next day. I knew why Ross was in such a rush and I'm sure everyone else did too. He had been patient for about as long as he could stand. If he could have been around a little more, I'm not sure we would have waited. I won't pretend I hadn't been a little anxious myself. I hadn't been with a man in a long, long time and it wasn't like I didn't know what it all about this time. I am glad, though, we did wait. It made it more special.

As we sped down the road it suddenly occurred to me. Bobby Ray had been my Summer. Ross would now be my Winter. Not because I was dead and barren. People have the wrong conception about winter. It's a time for the land to rest and renew so it can once more bring forth fruit.

And thus began a new season in my life.

WINTER

Thus in winter stands the lonely tree,
Nor known what birds have vanished one by one,
Yet knows its boughs more silent than before:
I cannot say what loves have come and gone,
I only know that summer sang in me
A little while, that in me sings no more.

"What lips my lips have kissed, and where, and why.
(Sonnet XLIII)

Edna St.Vincent Millay

CHAPTER 36

We made it to Nashville by ten o'clock and found a hotel for the night. I had no illusions about my wedding night, but I must admit I was pleasantly surprised. Grandma was right, warm and steady can be good. It made me look at Ross in a whole different light. He was no longer only the boy next door and my lifelong friend, but was now a man, my husband and my lover. I could tell it wasn't Ross's first time, and I wondered what else he'd been up to while getting an education, but after all, he was twenty-seven years old. It crossed my mind Ross might still feel he was in competition with Bobby Ray, but there no need for him to. I never compared the two of them in the bed or anywhere else. In my mind it had been two entirely separate lives.

As we lay in bed that first night Ross rose up on his elbow and looked down at me. "I've always felt we were meant to be together, Billie Jean," he said.

It then occurred to me Ross felt about us the way I had about Bobby Ray and me, it was meant to be.

"Wasn't there ever anyone else, Ross?"

"There was a girl once. I met her my second year at UT, but..." Ross shook his head and shrugged but never finished the sentence.

We continued our long drive to Gulf Shores the following day, my first trip to the ocean and I could hardly wait. When we arrived at last and I walked around the side of our condo, I was completely overwhelmed by the vastness of all that water. I immediately fell under the ocean's spell and all its charms. I loved the white sugar sand beaches, the waves crashing in, and the host of sea gulls that circled overhead. I thought I had landed in paradise. The first time I ran into the surf and felt the ocean floor shift under my feet, I marveled at its awesome power and it made me feel humble and very insignificant in comparison.

On the second day of our trip we went on a two hour boat tour to see the wild dolphins. I got some really great pictures and I couldn't believe how graceful and unafraid they were as they sliced through the water alongside the boat. At one point, one of them nearly jumped into the boat. I couldn't imagine why anyone would want to kill one of these marvelous creatures of the sea. I knew the boys would love it there and made Ross promise we would come back with them, and he promised we would.

During the day we ate at the condo and in the evening went out to a nice restaurant. If they had a porch or a pier we would ask to sit there, so we could eat under the stars and watch the moon rise over the ocean. I loved the tables with the palm trees. It was so easy being with Ross, childhood friends once more, but this time with benefits.

"You havin' a good time?" Ross asked one evening while we gorged ourselves on fresh king crab legs.

I'm havin' a fantastic time," I replied, with melted butter dripping down my chin. After eating we returned to the beach and walked hand in hand along the edge of the surf. I liked the feel of the sand cooling beneath my bare feet and watching the tide go out.

Later in our room we would make love to the sound of the waves in the background. Timeless and endless, the way love is supposed to be. I thought I could stay there forever if my boys were there. I missed them greatly. This was really the first time I'd ever been away from them. Even when I had the "nervous breakdown," as Grandma referred to it, I would see them every day. If not for the homesickness for Robbie and Will, I would have been sad to leave at the end of our week.

We arrived home in Johnson's Bend with suntans and a little something for everyone. T-shirts and shorts for the boys, along with plastic, inflatable dolphins to hang in their new rooms. For Dora and my grandma we selected beautiful seashell wind chimes, and for Ross's mom, a gold starfish necklace. The older guys got coffee mugs with ocean scenes and boxes of salt water taffy.

We didn't have very long to bask in the afterglow of our honeymoon. We had to move my belongings out of the house so the new owners could take over. I intended, for the most part, to take only mine and the boys' clothes and a few personal items. I would let the stove and the refrigerator and the washer and dryer go with the house. The young couple that bought the place needed all the help they could get. We did take the boys beds, the living room furniture, and my dinette set. Mine and Bobby Ray's bedroom furniture returned to the upstairs storage room at my grandparents' house along with the armoire. On the night before we left we had supper with Ross's parents. We stayed mostly at Daddy's and I felt we didn't spend as much time with his family as we should have.

"You won't know how to act, will you Billie Jean, when you get to that mansion in East Tennessee?" Ms. Ellen said.

I laughed it off, but didn't know how to reply. Ross did have a nice ranch style house. I had seen pictures of it, but would hardly call it a mansion. Ms. Ellen didn't mean any harm, but I felt she compared it to the house Bobby Ray and I had lived in. I told myself I was being overly sensitive. It was only natural for Ross's parents to be proud of him. At the same time, I was fairly certain they helped Ross finance his house. Bobby Ray and I worked for all of ours.

Early the next morning we pulled out, Ross driving the U-Haul truck and me following behind in his car. It was loaded down, so much so, one of the boys would have to ride with Ross. Of course they both wanted too, but two small kids in the same vehicle for a long trip is never a good idea and should be avoided if at all possible. Before Robbie and Will threw a fit, Ross stepped in with the perfect solution. He said they could flip a coin for who rode with him to start, and at our first rest stop, they could switch. Ross really was good with the boys and extremely patient with them. Robbie won the toss, but Will was not about to let him get the better of him.

"That's okay, me and mom need some alone time," he said like a grown-up. You never know what's going to come out of a kid's mouth.

I'm glad none of the Evans family showed up to see us off. I heard from each of Bobby Ray's siblings, Lester, and Ms. Minnie had dropped by the night before. As they left, Lester told me something rather puzzling. The tree that fell into the cemetery didn't appear to have been struck by lightning nor did it look to be dead. Instead it had been pulled from the ground by its roots. Lester had no clue as to the reason for this and neither of us remembered a recent strong wind.

It turned out to be more difficult to say good-bye to my family than I thought. I never lived away from them, and now I would be hours and miles away and wouldn't be able to run home every day or call them to come to the house, and we didn't plan on coming back until that Thanksgiving. After a lot of hugs, and more than a few tears, Ross managed to get everyone into their assigned vehicles and we were off. I really talked the move up to the boys and told them this would be a great new adventure and a whole different world for them to explore. They were nearly beside themselves with excitement as we drove away.

Normally it's a hard six hour drive from Johnson's Bend to the outskirts of Knoxville. It took us a little over eight—having to stop more because of the boys. I'm not too proud to admit I was overjoyed when I saw Ross's house. It was exactly what I always dreamed of, four large bedrooms with real walk-in closets, two and a half baths, a magnificent dining area, and a smaller room that could be used for a sewing room or a study. The huge kitchen was to die for. The very latest in modern home appliances with an island in the middle and a built-in stove top and a solid wood butcher's block. The laundry room, which Ross said the realtor referred to as the mud room, had its own sink and lots of cabinets. From there we could go out the back door into an enclosed two car garage. I could now pull right in and unload my groceries when it rained and never get wet. The living room, or as I was informed in the newer houses, was called the great room, had a real stone fireplace. I wondered why Ross would want such a large house. He was single when he purchased it, but I guessed he planned to marry someday. Perhaps the girl from college he had briefly mentioned. The house was truly beautiful, but other than the barest necessity had few furnishings.

"It was waitin' for you to pick out furniture for it," Ross had laughed, and kissed me on the mouth. He could be very charming with so little effort.

I figured Ross had waited for a wife, whoever she might be, to select what she wanted for the house, but on numerous occasions Ross would say he couldn't picture anyone there but me. I surmised from this, deep in his heart, he had never given up hope we might someday be together.

And so it was that I came to East Tennessee. To beautiful tree lined streets with perfectly coiffed lawns to become a suburban housewife. And I found I liked it.

CHAPTER 37

The boys settled into their new home without a moment's hesitation. They immediately chose their own rooms, but ended up in the same bed nearly every night. Robbie and Will had slept together for most of their lives. I knew sooner or later they'd want their own space, but for the time being they enjoyed the presence of the other at bedtime. I had one of the best times of my life buying new things for the house, but I did worry we might be spending way too much, but Ross thought anything the boys and I wanted, we should have. No one could have treated us any better than he did.

I tried to select furniture I thought could withstand two small boys on a regular basis, yet I didn't feel it had to be the most expensive—my conservative upbringing wouldn't allow me to do otherwise. For all practical purposes Ross was an only child. His sister had died when both of them were quite young, so to a certain extent, Ross pretty much got whatever he wanted growing up. Still, I felt we lived far above our means. Ross's job paid well but it took nearly all of his paycheck for the mortgage, the car payment, the new furniture, plus the daily living expenses for a family of four. We didn't put hardly anything back for a rainy day, and when I tried to talk to Ross about it, he would wave it off.

"I've got life insurance and a retirement plan through work, sugar," he said. "You and the boys will be well taken care of if somethin' happens to me."

"I'm not worried about that, Ross. I don't have to have all this stuff to make me happy," I told him.

"I know, but I want you to have everything you've ever dreamed of, Billie Jean." And he would smooth back my hair and gently kiss my lips. So I quit worrying over it. To the outside world looking in, we were the perfect all American, middle class family, and for the most part we were, but there was some little something not quite right, but I couldn't put my finger on exactly what.

One thing I did notice, and had caught it our first Sunday there. Ross no longer took part in the public worship service and it really bothered me. As soon as we arrived we began to attend a small church not far from Ross's house. He attended there from time to time, enough that people knew him by name. My first Sunday at church several people came up to me and said how glad they were to see Ross's family had finally arrived. I was drawn to the assembly on account of its size, a fairly small congregation that reminded me of my church back in Johnson's Bend. The people were friendly and for the most part country folks that had relocated due to their jobs. They made me feel most welcomed, so I knew the people and the size of the church wasn't the reason for Ross's non-participation. He wouldn't lead in prayer or serve at the communion table or lead singing. Even on singing nights when the men would take turns, Ross wouldn't. His voice was wonderful and he had done these things in church since his youth. Of course I couldn't let this go.

"Why aren't you takin' part in anythin' at church now?" I asked, and hoped it didn't sound like I was accusing him of something.

"I do," Ross replied. "When there's a grounds and building clean-up day, I'm the first one there and the last one to leave. And I'm the one that persuaded my company to design and install the new sign out front, free of charge, I might add. They donated it as a promotional type thing."

"You know what I mean, Ross. You never take part in the worship service, why? You always did back home."

"You know how it is, darlin', you get away from home, and you kinda fall away. I just don't feel worthy to serve right now. I'll do better soon, I promise."

And that ended that. Ross never wanted to discuss it any further and it ate at me. I wasn't used to not talking things out. Bobby Ray was probably better at that sort of thing than most men. Not that I compared the two, everyone is different. Ross would have to work this out between him and the Lord.

Our first really big disagreement came at the most unlikely time and in the most unlikely of places. At school the day we went to register the boys. I went with Will to his room since this his first year and it was a very emotional time for me. Both my babies would now be in school. Ross went with Robbie to his room and we planned to join up afterwards in the school cafeteria. The P.T.A, (Parents-Teachers Association), was hosting an informal get together so everyone could get acquainted. The second Robbie spotted me and Will, he ran up to us all smiles. "My name's the same as yours now, Mama," he beamed.

I didn't have a clue as to what he meant. "What do you mean, baby, your name's now the same as mine?"

"Williams—Ross put Robert Ray Williams on my papers—now my last name is the same as yours."

"You did what?" I spat at Ross, and he had the good grace to look ashamed and turned beet red. He probably forgot Robbie could read and write quite well.

"I want to be a Williams too," Will whined.

"Neither of you are a Williams. Your last name is Evans and will always be," I said, my voice louder than I intended and people turned to stare at us. I faced Ross. "How could you do somethin' like that without talkin' to me first?" I hissed at him under my breath.

"I'm sorry, darlin', don't be mad. I just thought it would be easier for the boys if we all had the same last name. You know, they wouldn't have to keep explainin' it to folks."

"I'm not just mad, Ross, I'm furious, but we'll talk about it later at home." And I spun around and went to Robbie's classroom to correct his paperwork. I found Robbie's teacher, Ms. Jenkins, a pretty, slim brunette, sitting behind her desk sorting through the stack of registrations forms. The room was empty of parents and kids except for one or two late stragglers' that wandered in.

I hurried to the desk and introduced myself. "Hi, I'm Robert Evans's mom, and my husband made a mistake on some of his paperwork and I need to correct it."

"Of course, Mrs. Evans," Ms. Jenkins said sweetly, stood and shook my hand before she began looking through the numerous papers.

"No, my name is Williams, that's the name my husband put on the paperwork but Robbie's last name should be Evans." For a moment the young teacher looked completely confused, but then brightened.

"Oh, I remember now. Your husband said he was in the process of adopting Robert and his younger brother. Is that correct? If so, we can just leave the paperwork like it is. That will be okay."

"No, that's not correct. My children's last name is Evans, and that's what should be on all their records."

I sounded a bit harsher than I meant to. I was past being polite and so upset with Ross the top of my head felt like it might blow off. Poor Ms. Jenkins looked confused again but at last found Robbie's paperwork. I quickly corrected it and made my hasty escape. What a way to begin a new school year in a new school I thought. Ross and the boys waited in the car for me. There was very little conversation between Ross and I on the drive home, but it didn't matter. Robbie and Will kept up an endless stream of chatter. I managed to calm down a little by the time we reached the house. I made lunch and after we ate I sent the boys outside. Ross intended to go to the office that afternoon but this couldn't wait, we needed to talk this through right then and there.

"I do understand, Ross that you were thinkin' of the boys, but you can't make those kinds of decisions without discussin' it with me first. And why did you tell Robbie's teacher you were adoptin' the boys. We've never talked about that."

"I'm sorry, I'm sorry, I'm sorry. I just thought it would be better if we all had the same last name. And I would like to adopt the boys. I know I should have talked to you about it first, but please, please, don't be mad at me, Billie Jean. You know I can't stand it when you're upset with me." Ross came and put his arms around me and rested his forehead on mine. "Forgive me, please?" he asked.

"Yes, I forgive you, but I will never, ever, take Bobby Ray's name away from his boys. Never. They're little now and don't understand, but they will someday. You're so good to them and with them, Ross and I can't tell you what that means to me. Robbie and Will love you, and their daddy loved them. He didn't leave us of his own free will."

Ross looked uncomfortable and leaned back a little and stared down into my eyes. "Was he really all that good to you and the boys, Billie Jean, really?" I could hear the skepticism in his voice.

"Yes Ross—he was. Bobby Ray loved me and our boys more than anythin' else in this world."

"But he wasn't perfect, he drank a lot." Ross looked away, his words more of a statement than a question.

"No, of course he wasn't perfect. I never said he was, and how do you know how much he drank?"

"I don't, just guessin' by what I saw when we were runnin' around. But he couldn't give you things like I can, darlin'." Ross glanced around at our beautiful home.

"He was workin' very hard tryin' to. We were about to begin remodelin' our house when he died." I tried not to think back to that beautiful, early fall morning when Bobby Ray left our home with my kiss on his lips and a heart full of promise. "Ross, you know that true happiness in life isn't found in material possessions."

Ross nodded his head that he did. He looked deeply into my eyes and said with such strong conviction, "Promise me one thing, Billie Jean. No matter what happens between us, you will always believe that I love you. I have loved you my whole life. I've always known there could never be anyone else for me but you." Ross bent down and kissed me long and deep and then left for work.

CHAPTER 38

In any marriage there's bound to be a few problems, especially ones that begin with a readymade family. Ours was no exception. We had words over the boys, but not for the reasons you might expect. Ross couldn't bring himself to discipline Robbie and Will. They were good kids but kids. If we gave them an inch they would take over the house, and I tried to explain this to Ross.

"You have got to be the grownup here, Ross. You have to make them mind."

"I don't want them to hate me, you know, be the 'big, bad, stepfather'."

"They're not goin' to hate you, I promise, but if you don't make them mind, everyone else will hate them and lock their doors when they see us comin'."

After our little talk, Ross did better, but was still a pushover where Robbie and Will were concerned. I think he played it down to them and used the old adage, "If Mama ain't happy ain't nobody happy."

When Ross came home from work, no matter how tired, or what he needed to do, if the boys wanted to play ball, he played ball. If they wanted to go for a bike ride, he would go for a bike ride. Many times I stood at the window or set on a park bench and watched Ross with Robbie and Will. Teaching them the correct way to hold a bat or to throw a football, and like so many other things in my life, so bittersweet. I couldn't help but think what Bobby Ray would give to be there. To be the one to show his boys the guy stuff, but in the same thought, thankful they had someone in their life that loved them enough to teach them these things. And it was obvious to anyone that Ross loved Robbie and Will.

I suppose my first reality check that my life was different now came that October. Living in the Smokies', fall comes early. The leaves began to turn all the glorious colors of the rainbow and soon thousands would flock to the area to view them. One afternoon while I prepared dinner, Robbie learned in school the evening meal is referred to as dinner, not supper. Whatever you call it, I was in the kitchen cooking when the phone rang. Ruth was on the other end of the line. She called to relay the news that Lester found Ms. Minnie that day when he came in from work in her flower garden. He didn't know how long she had lain there. She wouldn't have been easily seen from the road and there wasn't much traffic anyway. Ruth said she would get back with me with the funeral arrangements.

I called the boys in from outside and gave them the news. Robbie and Will felt sad and said they would miss her. They loved their grandmother Evans, but I wondered, if like with their daddy, they truly knew and understood the finality of death.

Sometimes it was very difficult to know what was really going on in their young minds, and I'd been thinking this when Robbie said, "Now Grandma can be with Daddy and Uncle Bennie and Clinton. She missed them a lot." He didn't mention his grandpa Evans whom he never knew and probably heard little about. When Ross came home from work I told him about Ms. Minnie.

"Oh, I'm sorry to hear that. She was a good woman, had a hard life."

"Yes, she was a good woman," I said. "I would like to go to the funeral, Ross."

"Oh, sugar, I don't think I can get away again this soon. I've been off so much already, you know, with the weddin' and the honeymoon and all."

"I know, but she's Robbie and Will's grandmother. Maybe I could take the boys and go by myself?"

"I wish you wouldn't, Billie Jean. That's a long drive, and what if you took a wrong turn and got lost?" Ross sounded a little frantic, and I hated to admit it, but he did have a point. I had never driven outside of Big Town unless following behind someone. When I first came to town, Ross was afraid for me to go alone the few blocks down the street to the local Piggly Wiggly. It irked me at the start, but Ross knew driving around Knoxville was a whole lot different than driving the back roads at home.

"Look, I'm not sayin' you can't go, sugar, I'm just askin' you not to." An unspoken plea was in his voice.

I pouted for a couple of days and reasoned that Ross could have taken off if he wanted to. I felt he wanted to sever all ties to Bobby Ray, but soon I conceded I wasn't being entirely fair to him. Ms. Minnie wasn't any relation to him and he had missed a lot of work, and this was when the reality set in.

For the first time in my life I was far away from family and friends. Ross was the only living soul the boys and I could depend on.

So I deferred to the wishes of my husband. It bothered me greatly not to be able to take the boys to their grandmother's funeral, but I was old enough and mature enough to know we don't always get to do everything in life that we would like to. Instead I wired flowers to the funeral home and called and sent sympathy cards to each of the children.

At this point Ross and I entered into what I think of as some of the happiest days of our marriage. There were times I felt I didn't tell Ross enough that I loved him. He had told me constantly. But I did love Ross. No, it wasn't the same as with Bobby Ray, and I never thought it would be, but I wasn't unhappy either, quite to the contrary. We had an active and satisfying love life, or at least I thought so and Ross certainly never complained. I didn't expect bells and whistles every time. I was nearly thirty years old and had given birth twice, but Ross was always eager to please, maybe a little too intense on occasion. Sometimes I wondered what he really thought. It was almost like he felt each time we made love it might be the last. Yet he made me feel loved, cherished, and like there could never be another. I had everything in life a woman could ask for.

Our preacher said the secret to true happiness was finding peace and contentment with what you have. In other words, make the most of the hand you've been dealt, and I thought mine had turned out pretty well. So well in fact, that sometimes it all seemed too good to be true, and normally when things feel that way, they are.

I enjoyed being a stay at home mom, but when an opening at the school for a teacher's assistant became available, I jumped at the chance. I guess I'd become more independent than I realized. I liked having my own money. Not because Ross didn't give generously of his. I wanted to feel that I too, was making a contribution to the financial stability of our family. The hours and the days were about perfect, Monday through Friday, with all weekends and holidays off. I would leave the house with the boys in the morning and come home in the afternoon when they did. I didn't know how Robbie and Will would feel about having their mother at school with them and I assured them I wouldn't embarrass them by hovering over them. I didn't, but you can bet if I saw one of them being mistreated or bullied I wouldn't have been in the mix of it in a New York minute.

The school the boys attended had a large number of black children. Many were bused in from great distances in an effort to ensure social, racial, and educational equality. The U.S. Supreme Court decision in 1954 that ruled racial segregation in public schools unconstitutional had met with great resistance in the South, and integration of the schools were slow to come about. The first public school to comply with the ruling in Tennessee was Clinton High School in Anderson County in 1956. The twelve black students that registered became known as the "Clinton 12." The first day had gone by without incident. The second day, several protestors and picketers showed up in front of the school and the Governor had to call in the National Guard and the highway patrol.

One of the first things I noticed after going to work at the school was that the black children kept mostly to themselves. And it was not uncommon for there to be a fight between the black and the white students, but mostly in the higher grades. As time went on this abated somewhat, especially after the black athletes were accepted on the sports teams. I'm sure the prejudice remained but they learned to work together and get along for a short period of time, and that was a beginning. Much of it had to do with what the children were being taught at home. Ross had been at the University of Tennessee in 1961 when the first black students, Charles Edgar Blair, and Theotis Robinson Jr., enrolled there, and his take on this, 'Who cared?' The university had thousands of students of all nationalities and races. You would have thought that would have been the case, but apparently there were many that did care considering the ruckus this caused.

We returned to Johnson's Bend for Thanksgiving as we had planned. Ross had a long weekend off as did the boys and I. We had a wonderful time and I'm sure my family drew a huge sigh of relief to see that everything was going so well. Before we left I took Robbie and Will by the cemetery. Ross asked to go along. It was my intent for me and the boys to go alone but what could I say? While the boys and I were at Bobby Ray's grave Ross kept his distance and gave us privacy and I appreciated this. We brought artificial flowers for the graves of Bobby Ray, his mom and dad, Bennie, and Clinton. It wasn't the best time of year for real flowers as they wouldn't last long. I noticed someone taking very good care of the cemetery. Especially the Evans' family plots. Lester, I felt sure, or a joint endeavor by all the family. I made a mental note to give Lester money for the upkeep if he would accept it from me. Thank heavens there were no falling trees on this visit.

We were a little sad when it came time to leave. We didn't know when we would make it home again. We already planned to spend Christmas in East Tennessee. The boys were older now and wanted to open their gifts

Christmas morning in their own home. We reminded our families the road did run both ways, and Daddy grinned and said he didn't know if he could make it that far. Mr. Williams spoke up and volunteered to pay for the gas if Daddy would do the driving. I felt certain we would have company in Knoxville sometime between Christmas and New Year's.

Sure enough, the day after Christmas, Daddy, Dora and Ross's parents came to visit. Actually it wasn't a surprise. They phoned ahead. I was so excited to have them but was disappointed my grandparents' didn't come with them. I'd called Grandma on Christmas Eve to wish her and Grandpa a Merry Christmas, and she became very emotional on the phone and we both ended up crying.

"Do you realize, Billie Jean, this will be the first Christmas since you've been born that I won't get to see you?" she sobbed.

"Yes Grandma, I do," I replied, and tried not to cry. "Why don't y'all come too? We have plenty of room."

"Oh, we'd just be in the way. You young folks need to be together, and besides, it would make it too crowded in the car for everyone."

"I promise you, Grandma. Next year if we don't come to Johnson's Bend for Christmas, I will bring you here somehow."

"Well, iffen me and your grandpa are still here. You know we ain't gettin' no younger and that's a long way off. You never know what might happen before then," Grandma finished on a long sigh. She'd predicted her and Grandpa's demise for years, and both of them were still as healthy as a horse and I laid odds they would still be around come next Christmas. At least I sure hoped they would be.

You've heard the old saying, "after three days fish and house guests begin to stink?" Not so with ours. Neither set of parents were the kind to come and stay and expect to be waited on hand and foot. Dora and Ms. Ellen took over the cooking for the most part and Mr. Frank and my daddy puttered around the house and yard like they were at home.

While they were there we wanted to show them around and took them to Gatlinburg, some thirty-eight to forty miles from where we lived, to see the Christmas lights and it was an amazing sight. If you have the opportunity to visit the Great Smoky Mountains during the Christmas season, I can assure you, it's a trip well worth making. Beginning in early November, thousands of twinkling lights that begin in Pigeon Forge and extend into Gatlinburg spread through the valley nestled between the huge mountains. The day we'd been there the weather was cold but the sun out and no snow to speak of. That's the one thing I hadn't liked about living in East Tennessee. It could be beautiful when it was coming down but slipping and sliding up and down a hill is not so bad, but on a mountain is a whole different story. On this particular day we could walk the strip in comfort.

Our guests left the day before New Year's and I hated to see them go. It was a wonderful visit and I looked forward to their coming back. The only thing to mar this near perfect memory was a comment made by Ross's mom right as they were about to get into the car.

"Billie Jean, did you ever dream you'd be livin' a life like this?" she asked, completely unaware of the implication of her words.

Everyone looked uncomfortable, even Ross. I never knew how Ms. Ellen expected me to reply to one of those comments. I don't think she did. They were rhetorical questions, it being a given with her and Mr. Frank that I was the happiest I'd ever been. I'm sure it was a subject my family tried to avoid with them. I only smiled and mumbled something under my breath. As difficult as it had been at times to be away from our families, it did have its advantages. Ross's mom doted on him and likely would have smothered us if she lived nearby. This way Ross and I needed to depend on one another and that brought us closer together and that was a good thing.

CHAPTER 39

Neither Ross nor my cousin Boaz ever received the "Your Country Needs You" letter from Uncle Sam. Perhaps the stars were in perfect alignment or maybe it was by the grace of God. It likely had something to do with them being in school during their peak draft years. It bothered Bo that he didn't have to go to Vietnam while so many others did. He often wondered aloud why he should be exempt. He probably would have enlisted if not for the pain it would have caused so many.

Richard M. Nixon became the 37th president of the United States in 1969, and the fifth president to have to deal with the war in Vietnam. On July 8th 1969 the first troops were withdrawn, but it had taken another four years before all the troops came out. By the end of 1969 over forty thousand Americans had been killed in Vietnam, and an estimated 50% of the troops stationed there experimented with drugs. A few years later some political guru labeled the war a tragic mistake. Isn't war always?

Ross signed the boys up for baseball and agreed to help coach their team. Robbie and Will showed a real knack for the sport, like their daddy before them. I knew Ross hoped one of them would become interested in football when a little older. On the weekends we would go into the city to shop and usually eat out and take in a movie. Ross insisted the boys and I buy our clothes at Miller's, a high-end department store that later became

Dillard's. He shopped for his clothes at the Toggery men's store on Cumberland Street. I told Ross we didn't need the best of everything, but he felt first impressions were made by the clothes you wore. I begged to differ with him on that assumption, but I didn't want to argue the point. Ross worried way too much, to my way of thinking, about what others thought and keeping up appearances. It got a little wearing at times. I truly believe he felt it would reflect badly on him as a provider if we didn't have the best money could buy.

Toward the end of the summer of 1969, a horrific event took place. So horrific, it replaced the war in Vietnam as the top news story: The Tate and LaBianca murders in California. My first thought was, what is this world coming to, my second, what else can people think of to do to one another'? Sharon Tate, a beautiful Hollywood actress, several months pregnant at the time, and four of her friends, had been shot and stabbed at her home in the Hollywood Hills. The following night not far from the scene of the first crime, Leno LaBianca and his wife, Rosemary were killed in their home. In mid-October of that year, Charles Manson, a hippie cult leader and self-proclaimed prophet, would be arrested and charged with being the mastermind behind these murders. This psycho managed to acquire a troop of dropouts and misfits that he called "The Family" and persuaded four of those zombielike minions to commit the senseless and atrocious acts. Helter-Skelter, he called it, the very name suggesting destruction and chaos. When asked why he had done this Mason replied that he hoped to instigate a racial war between the whites and blacks. Too bad someone hadn't told him this had already been done. Racial tensions continued to run high in the South and throughout most of the country—and riot activity was very common.

No one involved in this terrible crime received the death penalty, and I wondered how much worse it would have needed to be to warrant that. I hoped I never lived to find out. When we sat down in the evenings to watch the news, I found myself looking for reasons the boys should leave the room. Same as my daddy did with me. I wanted to shield my children from all the ugliness in the world, but that wasn't possible. Los Angeles might be on the other side of the country from us, but I wasn't so foolish as not to know it could happen on my quiet little street. I blamed the drugs. They seemed to be everywhere. For many, growing Marijuana had quickly become a lucrative pastime.

Ross would keep his promise and we took the boys to the ocean on summer vacation and they loved it every bit as much as I did. We bought them kites and in the late afternoon they flew them on the beach. We could see other kites in the sky up and down the long line of condos and hotels. It looked like a Norman Rockwell painting, but with sand and water instead of snow. At night, using flashlights, a little net, and a sand bucket we would capture the tiny ghost crabs as they scurried along the shoreline. We gave up on the white sand fleas, or mole crabs, they were too quick for us. I don't know who enjoyed this more, the boys or Ross. He got as excited as they did every time one of the tiny creatures was caught dashing across the sand. We would turn them loose before we went in for the night. I felt so fortunate to have someone who could love another man's children as his own and anyone could see that Robbie and Will were thriving.

On our way home, we swung by my Louisiana family for a quick visit. Ross got a real kick out of meeting them. I'd been a little surprised by this. Ross could be a tad *high-headed* at times and my Cajun relatives are about as down-to-earth as it gets. We didn't stay long enough for Ross to go on one of the famous, gator hunts, but he assured them, with a little trepidation, that on his next long weekend off we would most definitely come back. Before we left Uncle Allain and I had a moment to talk in private. He helped clear up a mystery I often wondered about. It started out by him asking me how Cole and John Wesley were doing.

"Okay, I guess," I replied. "They're about to begin the murder trial of the guy that killed Cole's son. You know how that goes. The hand of justice moves slowly. It seems it has taken forever for this thing to get to trial and it sure has aged Cole. I didn't know, Uncle Allain, that you knew Cole and John Wesley."

"Oh sure, we were great *amis* when we were kids. We used to drag race our cars on the back roads at night. They were at our house all la time."

On the drive home I thought about this, and it finally clicked in my head. I guess you could say I had an epiphany. Papaw had made moonshine with Harlan Evans, and that's why Mamaw knew Cole so well. Of course, it all made total sense now. After Uncle Allain and Uncle Blanchard left home, it was most likely Cole and John Wesley that had left the unexplained groceries on the front porch from time to time.

Living in town I really missed having a garden, and I broached the subject to Ross of the possibility of maybe having a small one. He was less than enthusiastic about the suggestion.

"Why do you want to do all that work, sugar? You can buy everything you need already canned or frozen at the store."

"I know, but I like growin' my own. I like fresh garden vegetables, and so do you, I've seen you eat. Lots of people at church have gardens in their back yards," I pointed out.

"Okay, if it will make you happy," he said, with a touch of exasperation in his voice.

I hated it when Ross made it sound like he only did stuff that he felt was "too country," in order to appease me. I was country and proud of it, and it wouldn't matter where I lived—in the back side of nowhere or in the big city, I would be the same. Soon after I arrived, I discovered there were two sides to Ross. He acted different in public than he did at home or when we visited in Johnson's Bend. I fully appreciated that Ross had a college education. His parents would never allow me to forget, it was an unwritten declaration of his superiority. I understood they were proud of him, and should be, but I got tired of hearing about it repeatedly. If Ross felt the need to put on airs, so be it, but it wouldn't change the person inside or where he came from. He was still a country boy from Johnson's Bend.

Ross bought a tiller and dug a small area behind our house near the fence for a garden. Not as large as I would have liked, but I didn't push my luck. Ross took great pride in his beautiful lawn and worked hard to keep it that way, but I think he enjoyed the garden a lot more than he let on. He helped plant it and hoed and tilled it faithfully, and when it came time to gather the fresh vegetables, he did the most of that. He and the boys helped me shell the peas and beans. One afternoon as Ross helped me can tomatoes and make juice, he suddenly threw up his hands. "I can't see. I've gone blind," he said, a serious note in his voice.

"What do you mean, you can't see?" I asked with some concern. I stood at the stove and laid down the wooden spoon I'd been using to stir the juice and walked over to him.

"I've peeled so many tomatoes, I've gone blind," he answered, and then looked at me and grinned. I nearly fell down laughing. This was the Ross I remembered from way back, and the Ross I loved. We still laughed when the boys came in from play and they joined in.

Ross felt much better about the garden after Mr. Rowland, an Elder at our church, complimented him on being so industrious. We became good friends with him and his wife, Ms. Margie. We invited them to dinner often and in turn went to their house.

During one of our visits, Ms. Margie told me something that puzzled me. She confirmed that Ross had attended their church for some time and that he always sat on the back seat and seemed to be very sad and troubled. After they became acquainted with him, they figured he was simply lonely and missed his family. Ross told them he recently moved there and that his family would soon join him. She was surprised to learn Ross was indeed a member of the church and that we were newlyweds. She didn't know I had been a widow with two small children. Ross led them to believe the boys were his. But what surprised me, or perhaps confused is a better word, as to when Ross told them this story. He purchased his house way before he and I were back together. I suspected Ms. Margie might be mistaken about the timing, and I never questioned Ross about this, it didn't matter either way. If Ross had fantasized about us getting back together, so what. There were much worse things he could have fantasized about. But a minuscule thought did pass through my head, perhaps the family Ross referred to wasn't me and the boys.

CHAPTER 40

Every parent knows there comes a time when you have to have "the talk" with your children. You hope it will be later than sooner, but when kids start to school, all bets are off. There's always someone in everyone's life that knows all about the birds and the bees.

Henry Lee was my first source of this well-kept, highly secretive information. Both him and the fact I grew up on a farm with livestock. They aren't known for being very discrete, and it hadn't been too difficult to put two and two together. Even if the finer points of the mating ritual remained an adolescence mystery waiting to be discovered. I always thought Bobby Ray would have the pleasure of this coming of age rite. Since that wouldn't be possible perhaps the privilege would fall to Ross. No such luck. Lord only knows how men explain it anyway, but I had been totally caught off guard when it came at the tender ages of 8 and 9. One Saturday morning I was in the kitchen making breakfast when Will came rushing in with Robbie close on his heels. Ross grabbed a bite earlier and left to meet some guys from work to go play golf.

"You'd better not," Robbie threatened, and glared at Will's back. Will glanced over his shoulder at his brother, hell bent on doing something his brother obviously didn't want him to do. Naturally this peaked my interest.

"Mama, do you have a virginia?" Will asked, and looked at me dead serious with that angelic expression on his face. It took me a few seconds to grasp what he meant.

"I'm never tellin' you nothin' else, blabber mouth!" Robbie shouted at Will, and stomped to the table and sat down. I could hardly keep a straight face.

"I think you mean, vagina, darlin', and yes, I do, why do you ask?"

Robbie glared a hole in Will's back. Disgust was evident on his face at his younger brother's inability to keep a secret. He huffed once and turned to stare out the window. I guess he figured there was no shutting Will up now.

"Fast Willy told Robbie, boys have penises and girls have va...va..."

"Vaginas'."

"Vaginas'—and that's why you go to the hospital and get a baby," Will finished in a rush.

I'm thinking, is this all that bad Fast Willy has told my precious little darlings? Nothing about what takes place between discovering men and women are different and going to the hospital to get a baby? At the same time I'm cataloging the faces of all the kids in Robbie's 4th grade class. None of them seemed to fit the picture that formed in my mind of Fast Willy. I kept waiting for the other shoe to drop, you know, the *BIG* question, how are babies made and where do they come from. It never came. I was saved by the appetites of two growing boys that still superseded their interest in the facts of life.

"Mama, are you makin' pancakes?" Will asked and stood on his tippy-toes to see into the frying pan.

"Yes, I am."

This caught Robbie's interest and he came to take a look. I stacked hot buttermilk pancakes onto their plates and they went to the table and sat down.

"The maple syrup and butter is on the table, help yourself," I said, and went to the refrigerator and poured two tall glasses of milk. I knew I should leave well enough alone. I'd been granted a temporary reprieve, but I just had to ask. "Why is he called Fast Willy?"

"Cause he's fast, real fast," Robbie responded around a mouthful of pancakes. "He can run faster than anyone in my class."

Well, the first thing I did Monday morning was to check out Fast Willy. I wanted to see the little monster that tried to steal my babies' innocence. Fast Willy materialized as a runt of a kid with a freckled face, an infectious gap-toothed grin and unruly red hair. I told myself that's all that saved him. Really, what could I do, give him a tongue lashing for doing what's as normal growing up as pimples? It turned out Fast Willy hadn't been all that fast. He was nearly eleven years old and still in the 4th grade. No wonder he could outrun the other boys. After taking a good look at him, I would have bet he knew very little more about the carnal side of procreation than my two did.

Ross worked for a really good company, Leland & Strauss Architectural and Design Engineers. It was a large consulting firm comprised of civil engineers that worked closely with state and county agencies. They had affiliate companies in Chicago and Philadelphia, and the main headquarters with the corporate offices located in Atlanta, Georgia. A family oriented company that highly promoted family values, and tried as much as possible to rotate the jobs that required an extended length of stay away from home. Like when Ross sent to North Carolina for that job that had taken over two years to complete. It could be for longer, depending on the size of the job.

Sometimes Ross would be gone for a week or two, then come home for a week and then go back. Fortunately much of his work could be done from his office with only an occasional on site visit. Ross hated being away from me and the boys, and I hated seeing our phone bill at the end of the month. Thankfully, his assignments fell mostly within a hundred mile radius of our house. He worked with the Tennessee Department of Transportation on several big projects. Ross's firm not only designed and built new structures, but helped to maintain and upgrade the existing ones.

Once a year on the anniversary of their hire date, every employee of the company had to go to Atlanta for a seminar with the Big Dogs. I think it was intended as a motivational type of thing. When it came time for Ross to go he asked his supervisor if he could bring the boys and me along. He explained he had promised to take the boys to a real pro baseball game. Not only did his boss say it would be okay but that we could fly on the corporate plane with Ross. He had season tickets to the Braves home games and was more than happy to let us use them. He said he rarely went anymore since his kids were grown and had other interests and his wife didn't care for baseball.

We flew out on a Thursday morning. I asked permission for me and the boys to miss two days of school. It wasn't a problem for me, but a little more complicated for them. Excused absences would normally only be given for sickness or a death in the immediate family. It turned out not to be an issue after all. Their principal was a huge Braves fan. He said an opportunity like this didn't come along very often. The boys' teachers were very understanding and excited for them too. Each gave me their homework assignments for the two days. Robbie and Will grumbled greatly about this.

"Gosh," Robbie said, "can't even go to a baseball game without havin' to do homework."

Their teachers also offered to give them extra credits if they would write a report about their trip. Naturally the boys were less than happy about this also, but I promised to help them with their stories.

The company plane turned out to be a small, sleek, Learjet with creamy white and pale blue interior. It was my first time to fly and I was scared to death. The boys were so excited we could hardly keep them in their seats. Ross tried to get me to take a Dramamine but I refused. I wanted my head to be clear so I could remember everything about the experience.

Ross placed me in the aisle seat directly across from the boys and made sure our seatbelts were on correctly before sitting down beside me and taking my hand. "Relax, sugar," he coaxed, "just sit back and enjoy the ride."

I don't care how big the plane was, when it left the ground, I could tell there was nothing beneath us. And I hadn't liked the climb up to get over the mountains, but once we leveled off, I did relax, a little. Thank the good Lord there little to no air disturbances. Ross tried to get me to look out the plane window, but I wasn't ready for that. The boys, on the other hand, looked down on the world below and "oohed" and "aahed" in amazement.

There several couples on the plane with us but Ross and I were the only ones with young children. Some of them I'd met but couldn't remember their names. There was one couple on board I'd become acquainted with and really took a liking to, Norm and Betty Lou Turner. They were a few years older than Ross and I and their children were already in high school. Betty Lou was my kind of woman, a country girl through and through. At first glance you might not realize this and think her uppity, with her perfectly cut, styled, and professionally dyed champagne blond hair and French, manicured nails. Betty Lou hailed from a small town in Alabama by the name of Sand Rock, with a population of less than a thousand. She met Norm when she was a freshman and he a senior at the University of Alabama. Betty Lou was loud and boisterous and didn't mind telling anyone her major in college had focused on obtaining her "MRS" degree. After Norm graduated, he proposed to Betty Lou and of course she accepted and had never gone back to school. Now it some twenty years later and Betty Lou said she'd never regretted a single day of it and would do it again.

The flight between Knoxville and Atlanta took a little over thirty minutes, so we didn't have long to entertain the boys and we talked back and forth over the seats to the Turner's. They sat in front of us.

"Darlin', are you really goin' to that awful doubleheader on Saturday?" Betty Lou asked in disbelief.

"Yes, I really am," I answered back, and laughed.

"Better you than me, honey," she said, "though it does seem a waste of good shoppin' time."

The company booked us into the new Hyatt Regency on Peachtree Street in downtown Atlanta. My way had been paid for, since Ross could bring his spouse, but we paid for the boys. John C. Portman Jr. designed the one of a kind hotel for that time, an open-air, twenty-two stories with a revolving rooftop restaurant. As patron's dined, they could gaze across Atlanta and sip the real mint juleps they served. When I looked at the hotel, I saw a beautiful building. When Ross looked at it he saw every angle and plane. "Man, what I'd give to design somethin' like this," he said.

"I thought bridges and dams were your thing," I teased.

"They are," he grinned. "But that doesn't mean I wouldn't like to have one of these babies on my resume."

The atrium was constructed and decorated to take your breath away when you entered, and it did. I guess the boys and I were the quintessential country bumpkins come to town. We stood with our mouths open and gazed up at the enormous glass chandelier, and stationed on each side of the lobby glass elevators. A huge brass and silver sculpture reached toward the skylights. I snuck a peek at Ross and saw that his eyes were round with admiration too. Our room was in the English Tudor décor and featured two king-size beds with a TV, a small refrigerator, a coffee maker and in the bathroom a hair dryer. Inside the closet I found a steam iron and an ironing board. It really could be a home away from home.

Ross and the other men had meetings on Thursday afternoon and all day on Friday. Betty Lou and I tried to entertain the boys with some sight-seeing and they swam in the hotel pool. The pool was located on the outside, but early September in Atlanta is still very warm and doesn't get much cooler after the sun goes down. The seminar finished on Saturday morning with plenty of time for Ross to get back for the game. The luxury hotel provided a shuttle bus that picked us up at the front door and delivered us right to the front gates of Fulton County Stadium, and the driver told us he would be there when the games was over to take us back to our hotel.

I learned to appreciate the game of baseball in my teens. I loved to watch Bobby Ray and Ross and Henry Lee play. I still enjoyed the game and occasionally, when not busy, would sit down and watch one on TV. Mostly though I only listened to it in passing through, but being at a real professional league ballpark for a game is completely different. From the moment we entered through the turnstyles and got our first whiff of the hot dogs and the peanuts and the popcorn, the atmosphere suddenly become electrified. The calliope played, the lights flashed, and the fans were hyped-up and loud. The boys were so excited they jumped up and down. I'm not sure they ever sat in their seats for more than five minutes at a time.

On this particular Saturday the Braves were playing the San Francisco Giants. We could see everything so well as our seats were ground level on the first base line. I worried we might get tired before it was over, but we didn't. There too much excitement going on around us. The Braves won both games and each time they hit a homerun, Chief Noc-A-Homa, come out of his teepee and did a little dance. The boys ate so much junk food, and I lost count of the sodas, that I nearly became sick watching them. Thank goodness I had the forethought to bring along a new bottle of Pepto-Bismol.

On the plane ride home the following day Ross and I helped the boys write their essays. All in all, it was one of the best times of my life, and I knew thus far, the highlight of the boys' young lives. I had felt very grateful to Ross for making it happen.

CHAPTER 41

I grew up knowing the church is to be the center of your life and around it everything else must revolve. I continued to follow this game plan with my own family, but there're always things along the way that try to entice you away from doing what's right. When Ross signed the boys up for baseball I told him no late Wednesday afternoon practices or Wednesday night games so that we might attend church, and we made this clear to their coaches from the start. They were in agreement, but of course they soon forgot this conversation and didn't pay any attention to the time or the day of the week. On this point I stood firm and thankfully Ross backed me up. I really expected the coaches to tell the boys they couldn't play, but they didn't. Robbie and Will were already showing signs of becoming outstanding young athletes. Their coaches wanted to cultivate this talent for when they were older. On several Wednesday nights the boys arrived at Bible study right from practice or a late afternoon game, still in their dirty uniforms, and smelling bad, but they were there. If the game was after Wednesday night service, they wore their uniforms and we left as soon as class ended. The games that were scheduled on Sundays usually began at one or two in the afternoon and we would have to rush out of church as soon as the last amen was said, so the boys could eat and change into their ball clothes.

Since the boys were involved in so many sports, I felt they needed a little culture in their lives; to balance things out and make them more well-rounded individuals. I signed them up to take piano lessons at school two afternoons a week. I waited until after baseball season was over so there wouldn't be any conflict. The boys were not old enough yet to play on the school's basketball team and piano lessons wouldn't interfere with their Pee Wee football. The music teacher purposely scheduled her lesson as much as possible around all the sports activities.

I didn't tell the boys beforehand that I signed them up. Again I hoped for Ross to back me up and help convince Robbie and Will they would enjoy piano. I broke the news to Ross one evening as we prepared for bed.

"I signed the boys up for piano lessons today," I said, and tried to make it sound like it no big deal.

Ross leaned out of the bathroom where he stood at the sink shaving and grinned at me. He had a towel draped loosely around his hips.

"Piano?" he questioned, and looked skeptical.

"Yes, piano. I think they need other interests in their lives besides sports."

"Yeah, but—piano? Robbie and Will just don't seem the piano type to me. Do they want to take lessons?"

"Well, they sort of don't know about it yet," I said, hedging, and Ross laughed. "I kind of hoped you would talk it up for me. I mean, you took piano when you were a kid."

"Yeah, only because Mama made me." Ross finished shaving, came out of the bathroom and walked over to where I sat at my vanity table rubbing body lotion on my arms and legs. He had a devilish gleam in his eyes.

"What'll you give me to smooth it over with the boys for you?" he asked, and bent down and kissed my neck and began to massage my shoulders. I knew where this was going but I played along.

"I don't know—what do you want?"

"Everythin,'" he replied, in a low husky voice. His hands slid down, cupped my thinly clad breast and his mouth found mine. I felt that familiar tingling in the pit of my stomach as the warmth spread over me. I relaxed and leaned back against Ross, allowing his hands to roam, and in one swift movement he pulled my gown over my head and dropped it to the floor. He then picked me up and carried me to the bed, his towel long since fallen off. As he hovered above me, I admired his firm, masculine body.

"Don't you know by now, there's nothin' I wouldn't do for you?" Ross whispered looking deep into my eyes.

Our lovemaking that night was like never before. Ross's every move, his every kiss and touch was slow and deliberate. Almost like we were making love for the very first time and Ross was laying claim to his prize and what he felt always rightfully belonged to him.

Grace Ellen was conceived that night.

I knew within a few days I was pregnant. I could just tell, but I waited until there wasn't any doubt before telling Ross.

"Are you sure?" he asked, thrilled at the news. "Are you absolutely sure?"

"Yes, I'm sure." I hadn't been to the doctor, but the only times my period was ever late, was when I was pregnant with Robbie and Will, and my breasts were already tender.

"The Lord is givin' me a second chance," Ross said with a catch in his voice, his eyes misty.

"What do you mean, second chance?" I teased. "I thought our life was pretty good now."

"It is, it is, but now it will be even better. You know how much I love Robbie and Will, Billie Jean. They're like my own, but this will be our baby, mine and yours."

I was as thrilled as Ross at having a new baby. Even if I did question the wisdom of this; bringing another child into this trouble riddled world. The long war in Vietnam dragged on and anti-war protests plagued the big cities across the land, especially on the East and West coasts college campuses. On May 4, 1970 at Kent State in Ohio, a peaceful demonstration turned into a blood bath when Ohio National Guardsmen shot and killed four students and wounded nine others. Things really got nasty after that, but this is where faith comes in, and I paused to remember who is in control and will always be. With this in mind I looked forward with great anticipation to the birth of my third child.

Ross was so excited about the baby that he could barely contain himself and became increasingly protective of me. He feared I might get sick or hurt, and I couldn't leave the house without letting him know where I would be and when I would be home. It became so bad I finally sat Ross down and talked to him before he wore me and himself out.

"Ross, hon, you've got to relax. I'm fine, the boys are fine, and the baby is fine. Everythin' is goin' to be okay."

"I know, but I'm so afraid God will..."

"God will what? What are you afraid of Ross—talk to me."

"I don't know. I guess I feel I don't deserve all this happiness and maybe He'll take it all away from me."

"Why would you feel that way, Ross? You've always been a good person."

He would never give me a straight answer. Something inside Ross tortured him, had for a while and it was the reason he wouldn't take a leading role in the church anymore. He wouldn't even pray in the assembly. Oh, he would say the blessing in our home before meals and did bedtime prayers with the boys, but he wouldn't pray out loud at church.

Even though Ross wouldn't pray in church and wouldn't serve at the communion table, he accepted the role of song leader after being asked numerous times. It came shortly after I announced I was pregnant, and I was a little surprised that the elders offered him the position, but hoped it was a step in the right direction.

Ross did have a wonderful voice and the church was badly in need of a song leader, someone who could actually sing and read music. Everyone encouraged Ross and complimented him on what a fine job he did. So much so, I was afraid the old song leader would get his feelings hurt, but that part of the worship service did greatly improve after Ross took over.

Robbie and Will began their piano lessons after Ross convinced them it would be "cool beans." I think what really convinced them was finding out Ross had taken lessons as a kid. The boys thought anything Ross did had to be okay. Robbie and Will loved and admired Ross and looked at him as a father, and for all practical purposes, he *was* their father, and they even began to call him

Daddy Ross. It bothered me at first but Bobby Ray couldn't be there and Ross could.

Robbie showed a real talent for the piano, but didn't enjoy taking lessons. Will, on the other hand, loved it, but showed only an average talent. I promised Robbie if he would stick with it long enough for me to go to one recital, he could quit. Will could continue for as long as it made him happy.

I kept my word to my grandparents and the next Christmas Ross went and got them and brought them to our house for a week. We had a wonderful time, and the smells that came out of my kitchen during their visit were simply amazing. Grandma baked everything she could think of, and then some, and brought a fresh coconut cake with her. I told her I didn't bring her there to cook, but she was the happiest when preparing good food for others.

Daddy and Dora came to take my grandparents home. They arrived on New Year's Eve and stayed for a couple of days. When it came time for them to leave, Grandma became very emotional. Upset that she wouldn't be present when the baby came.

"I was with you when the other two came into the world, and I feel I need to be here for this one too," she said.

"You will be, Grandma, maybe not right when it's born, but Daddy will bring you later."

"I just hope and pray me and your grandpa are still around," she sobbed. Grandma and her expectations of impending doom and gloom. I suspected she'd live to be a hundred or more.

Grandpa placed an arm around the both of us. "We'll see you come summer, darlin'—you take good care of yourself," he said, and gave me a kiss and a hug and lovingly helped Grandma into the car and off they went.

I felt great during this pregnancy and worked to the end of the school year. I missed not having a garden that summer, but Ross put his foot down this time. And he was right. With him away on a job for the bigger part of the summer and me several months along, taking care of a garden would have been difficult.

Ross worried the entire nine months that he might not be there when I went into labor, and the closer it came to my due date he would call several times a day to see if I having the least little pain. Thank goodness for everyone he was home when I did go into labor. He was off work for the 4th of July holiday, five days before I'd been due. I began having pains early that morning, and Ross and I joked how great it would be to celebrate Independence Day with the birth of our child. That would be the ultimate fireworks.

We'd made prior arrangements with Mr. Rowland and Ms. Margie to watch the boys and dropped them off on our way to the hospital.

My labor wouldn't be as easy with this baby as with my first two and lasted much longer, but I was older this go round. We said we didn't care what the sex of the baby was as long as it healthy, but I think we both secretly hoped for a girl. Grace Ellen made her appearance, however reluctantly, at two thirty-four p.m. July 4th, 1971. Beautiful and perfect from the top of her downy head of fine ash blond hair to her little pink toes, Gracie stole her daddy's heart from the moment her head crowned. After the nurse bathed, weighed, and measured, she wrapped Grace Ellen in a snuggly pink blanket and brought her to us. She had that wonderful newborn baby smell.

"She's perfect, just perfect," Ross cooed, kissing the top of her head. "Look how she can already wrap her little fingers around mine."

"I see, she knows you're her daddy," I said, with a big smile.

Watching Ross with Gracie brought back memories of how proud Bobby Ray had been when his babies were born. While Gracie slept in my arms, Ross knelt down and prayed the most beautiful prayer of thanksgiving. Toward the end of his prayer, he voiced words along the lines of something that he said before, "Thank you, Lord for givin' me another chance to make things right and good."

I couldn't for the life of me understand what Ross meant by this, or why he wouldn't share it with me. What could he have possibly done that would warrant the amount of guilt he seemed to carry? I did wonder if it had anything to do with the girl from college that he briefly mentioned.

CHAPTER 42

When I came home from the hospital Ross and the boys were under foot so much I could hardly breathe. They wanted to help and didn't want me to do anything. All things considered, I felt remarkably well. Ross took a week's vacation and Daddy and Dora came the following week, and brought my grandparents, still alive and kicking.

Ross's parents came within a few days of Gracie's birth—they couldn't wait to see their first grandchild. Ross's aunt and uncle brought them and they insisted on staying in a hotel even though we told them we could make room. Ross worried so much company so soon after my giving birth might upset me and make me nervous, but I totally understood. His mother wanted to see her namesake. We named Gracie after her and my Aunt Grace. Ms. Ellen had been a tremendous help to me and she and Mr. Frank were absolutely foolish over the baby, but like so many women of her generation, she was full of well-meaning advice about raising babies, some of it outdated. I listened respectfully and then did what I wanted. After all, this wasn't my first child but she did kind of rub me the wrong way about one thing. She kept insisting we shouldn't keep the baby in the room with us.

"You'll rest so much better, dear, if she's in her own room," Ms. Ellen said. We turned the small room next to ours into a nursery, but for the first few weeks, Gracie remained in her bassinette next to our bed. That's what I had done with Robbie and Will. When she was a little older I would move her into her room.

As much as I enjoyed the family coming to see the baby, it was a relief when everyone left. I was more than ready to settle back into a normal routine. My family brought good news to share. My cousin, Boaz was finally getting married. Although it wasn't too much of a surprise as Ruth had hinted at it when she called to congratulate me on the baby. The wedding was set to take place the first Saturday in October and Ross said he would ask to be off work the Thursday and Friday before. That way it wouldn't have to be such a whirlwind trip. I hoped the boy's teachers would understand again. It meant so much to me to get to go, and besides, Ross and I were anxious to show Grace Ellen off to everyone in Johnson's Bend. Aunt Grace was chomping at the bit to see her namesake. I had already sent her several pictures of Gracie.

After the baby came, I thought Ross would stop being so over-protective, but he didn't. He only got worse, and now there was one more for him to worry about. Ross began to worry over things he never had before, like the boys getting hurt playing ball. When I went anywhere in the car with Gracie, he couldn't relax until we were safely home. Every time the baby sneezed, he worried she was getting sick. When he went out of town he kept the phone lines hot calling home to check on us. I tried to convince myself this was only natural for a new father and eventually he would calm down.

Ross may have been a worry wart but he was a great dad. I had been a little concerned Ross wouldn't have as much time for Robbie and Will, but nothing changed in that department. I myself dreamed of all the things I could do with a little girl I couldn't with little boys, like dress her in frilly dresses with ribbons in her hair and fancy lace socks and patent leather shoes. Give her ballet lessons and piano lessons and maybe, just maybe, she might want to be a cheerleader. Shortly after Gracie's birth we posed for a family portrait at our church for the directory. It showed the smiling faces of a father and mother and three beautiful children. The perfect and complete family and I felt so blessed.

When Grace Ellen turned six weeks old I gave in and moved her into her nursery and we bought the best baby monitors we could find. We were surprised by how well they picked up the slightest sound. Gracie was such a good baby and mostly ate and slept. She'd developed her own schedule early on and it remained fairly regular. I would feed her at ten o'clock at night and she would sleep until about two, and after the two a.m. feeding, she normally slept until about six. If Ross was in town or working close by, he liked to do the six o'clock feeding before he left. I was happy for him to have the honors. It meant another hour's sleep for me before getting up with the boys.

Gracie loved her nursery and her crib, and not long after moving her, she began sleeping nearly through the entire night. I started adding a little cereal to her ten o'clock bottle. About the same time Gracie went into her nursery, Ross was assigned a job near Memphis. The job required he be on site most of the time. This would be the furthest he had worked away since we married. He really didn't want to take the job. He didn't want to be gone from home, but neither did the other men. When school started back I didn't return to my job. I felt with two young kids in school and a new baby at home that was enough of a job for me. One morning a little before six I awoke with a start. Gracie hadn't awakened me during the night to eat, and I smiled, thinking to myself, what a wonderful baby. She was barely six weeks old and already sleeping through the night. I lay there dosing, loving the early morning quiet of the house, and then my eyes flew open. It was too quiet.

I checked the baby monitor, and it switched on, but no sounds came from Gracie's room. No soft baby moans and sighs. No grunting and garbled noises that babies normally make in their sleep. I leaped from the bed and raced to the nursery, a terrible feeling of déjà vu washing over me. The mental image of a fallen tree and Bobby Ray's face flashed into my head. Out loud I prayed, "Please Lord! Please Lord, not again, not my baby girl."

I flipped on the light as I ran into the room and snatched Grace Ellen from her crib. She was still warm, but the delicate skin around her mouth was already a pale shade of purple. I couldn't feel any breath coming from between her sweet, rosebud lips. No life remained in her tiny body.

I must have been screaming without realizing it for Robbie and Will came running into the nursery. I hurriedly told them to call the new 911 emergency number. It had been in effect in our area for only a short while. I began CPR. At the school where I'd worked it was mandatory for all to take the classes in the emergency, life-saving techniques if you dealt directly with the children. I continued to press two fingers into Gracie's chest and blow air into her mouth until help arrived. The EMS had to coax Gracie from me and my arms immediately felt cold and empty and fell to my sides, useless. They continued CPR as they transported Gracie to the hospital, but I knew it was too late. Just as I had known before pulling the branches back on the tree and seeing Bobby Ray's lifeless face. Gracie, my precious, precious, baby girl, was now an angel in Heaven.

At the hospital the doctor pronounced Gracie D.O.A, dead on arrival, but used the term, expired. I suppose he thought it would sound less harsh, but the outcome was the same. The nurse asked if there was someone she could call for me. I couldn't call Ross. I couldn't bear to give him this kind of news over the phone, and a feeling of despair washed over me. For a moment I felt the boys and I were strangers in a foreign land. I looked at Robbie and Will's frightened and tear-streaked little faces; how they adored their baby sister, and I longed for the comfort and support from my family in Johnson's Bend.

I finally had the presence of mind to tell the nurse to call Mr. Rowland and Ms. Margie. They called our minister and within minutes the three of them arrived and took control of the situation. Mr. Rowland called Ross's boss, who said he would go personally to the job site and bring Ross home. I was so grateful to him. I knew Ross wouldn't be in any shape to get behind the wheel when he learned of his beloved baby girl's death.

As deep as my grief was, it couldn't compare to Ross's. He was inconsolable, and from the moment he arrived home, he kept repeating over and over, that all of this was his fault. He took me into his arms and sobbed uncontrollably, and begged me to forgive him.

"I'm so sorry, Billie Jean, I'm so sorry," he cried. "It's my fault, all my fault. God is punishing me, you know. I should have been here to watch over you and Gracie and Robbie and Will."

"It's no one's fault, Ross," I tried to reassure him. "It would have happened no matter who was here." SIDS, Sudden Infant Death Syndrome, is a silent killer. I slept through my baby's last moments here on earth and never suspected death hovered nearby.

Daddy, Dora and my grandparents came for the funeral. Ross's aunt and uncle came as well and brought Mr. Frank and Ms. Ellen. I felt so sorry for them. Gracie's birth had opened a whole new world for them. I thought someday Ross and I might give them another grandchild. Not that another baby could ever replace Grace Ellen. Ruth called upset she and Henry Lee couldn't come. It was a busy time at the grain elevators preparing for the upcoming harvest season. I told Ruth I understood and I did. Many times I had wanted to return to Johnson's Bend for things like Ms. Minnie's funeral, but it wasn't always feasible. As I became older I learned to accept these little disappointments in life.

My grief at the loss of Gracie was no less profound than when I lost Bobby Ray, but this time I didn't question God's wisdom. I knew it wasn't expected of me to understand. I was very young when Bobby Ray died, and for a time I took my eyes off the cross and my faith grew weak, but with the help of others and much prayer, I found my inner strength and my faith been renewed. This inner strength and my much stronger faith, was what enabled me to get through Grace Ellen's death.

After Gracie's death Ross became obsessed with the notion something would happen to me and the boys as well and it quickly reached epic proportions. Anytime I left the house I had to give Ross a detailed itinerary of where I planned to go, everything I intended to do and when I would return. He didn't even want the boys to ride their bikes up and down our street unless they stayed where he could see them. I hoped after Ross returned to work things would improve, but they didn't. He spent so much time on the phone trying to keep tabs on the boys and me that it began to affect his work. After a month or so of this, Ross's boss, a kind, compassionate man, suggested Ross take a leave of absence and seek counseling. I tried to convince Ross to do that very thing right after Gracie's passing. The boys and I began grief counseling provided through our church at once, but Ross refused to go, and every time I asked him to, he'd say the same thing.

"There's no one on earth who can help me, Billie Jean. God is punishin' me, why can't you see that?"

"Ross, what in the world do you think you have done that God would punish you in this way?" I asked him over and over, but never got an answer. He would only stare into space.

At times I felt Ross wanted to unburden himself to me, but something held him back. A dark, sinister force moved inside him, and he wouldn't allow me to help. I tried to think of every possible case scenario that could account for his strange behavior. Any past transgressions he might have committed and felt such remorse over it led to this blown out of proportion lingering guilt.

Maybe he had drank, partied, and smoked marijuana in college. He wasn't the first and surly wouldn't be the last. Or maybe he had a secret life—another family stashed away somewhere. I remembered thinking on our wedding night that Ross certainly was no rookie in the bedroom. Maybe he'd fathered a child out of wedlock, with that girl back in college? It was evident he didn't want to talk about her, or maybe he had been involved in a homosexual affair? I really hadn't placed much credence in any of this. Other than perhaps the illegitimate child part, but after seeing Ross with the boys and Gracie, I couldn't imagine he would stay away from the child and not be a part of its life. Yet that would kind of make sense considering his behavior. No matter the cause of his troubles, its unseen presence was destroying our home. Something had to give and soon.

One afternoon shortly after lunch, Mr. Rowland came by and managed to persuade Ross to go with him to look at some property, and I felt grateful to him. Maybe this would take Ross's mind off of things for a spell. When it was time for the boys to get out of school I went to pick them up. While I was out, I figured I might as well get a few groceries. I took my time and strolled leisurely up and down the aisles looking at stuff I knew I wouldn't buy, but allowed the boys to get some of their favorite junk foods, probably way more than I normally would have. It was so nice to be out of the house and the gloom hanging over it since Gracie's death. After we finished with the shopping and had the groceries in the car, we decided to go for ice cream. I hadn't seen Robbie and Will this happy in days, and I loved hearing their laughter once more. They felt the stress at home too and were glad for our brief fun time together. In the back of my mind I knew I was avoiding going home. Around five o'clock I pulled into our drive. I was gone much longer than I planned. Ross paced back and forth on our front porch, and came rushing to the car in a panic before I barely killed the motor.

"Where have you been, Billie Jean? I've been worried sick. I've called everyone we know and no one had seen you. I drove to the school, and you weren't there. I drove around town, and I couldn't find you. Why didn't you call me if you were goin' to stay out this late?"

"Ross, calm down, it's not that late. I picked the boys up from school, went grocery shoppin' and then went for ice cream. We're fine, everythin' is fine." Robbie and Will stared at Ross like they had never seen him before and was afraid to get out of the car.

After his tirade Ross seemed to run out of steam and his shoulders slumped. "I'm sorry. I just get so scared when I don't know where you are." He walked to the back of the car and began taking the groceries out of the trunk. I made my mind up right then and there to get to the bottom of this craziness that very night.

CHAPTER 43

Dinner that evening was a very silent and strained affair. Ross tried to make small talk with Robbie and Will, but they hadn't forgotten the scene in the driveway. They didn't know how to relate to this Jekyll and Hyde person.

As soon as we finished eating, I made the boys take their baths and go to bed. They weren't very happy at not having any television time. Ross kissed them goodnight and went to our room. I followed him shortly thereafter. I found him sitting on the bed with his arms resting on his thighs and his head down. I went in and closed the door behind me and leaned against it.

"I want to know what's wrong with you, Ross, and I want to know right now. No more bullshit and double talk. What are you hidin' from me?"

Ross dropped his head into his hands. "You have no idea what you're askin', Billie Jean. You don't want to know the truth."

Ross slowly shook his head from side to side and his words were muffled through his fingers.

"Yes, I do want to know, Ross. We can't go on this way. You know we can't."

Ross dropped his hands from his face but continued to stare down at the floor, and after several moments he raised his head and looked at me. A play of emotions crossed his face, one of which, anger. "Maybe I'm just tired of sleepin' three in a bed."

"I don't know what you're talkin' about."

"Sure you do, Billie Jean. I'm talkin' about me and you, and Saint Bobby."

"I've never said Bobby Ray was a saint. And what's he got to do with any of this?"

"Oh, he's got everythin' to do with it, sugar. He's always been there in the back of your mind. You thought I didn't know, but I did. You've put his memory up on a pedestal like he was some kind of god, or somethin'. Hell, Billie Jean, he was hungover the day he died."

I felt like I had been sucker punched. All the air rushed from my lungs. "How do you know what he was the day he died?" I asked, after I managed to catch my breath.

Ross stared at me with a startled expression on his face, realizing what he had said. "You...you...told me," he said, stumbling over his words, and another emotion settled on his face—fear.

"No, I didn't tell you, Ross." And I hadn't. I never told anyone about the hours prior to Bobby Ray's death. Ross once more dropped his head and stared at the floor. When he looked up again, I somehow knew the next words out of his mouth would change our lives forever.

"I...killed...Bobby Ray."

Shocked by his words, I shook my head no. I feared Ross had suffered a complete and total mental breakdown and was maybe delusional. "No, Ross. What are you talkin' about? A tree fell..."

Ross again slowly shook his head from side to side and his eyes never wavered from mine.

"I killed Bobby Ray, Billie Jean, but I didn't mean to. You've got to believe me, please, please, believe me, I never meant to. When I stopped that morning, I just wanted to talk to him. You know, make things right between us again, but you know how cocky Bobby Ray could be, sugar. He said somethin' like he said that night down in the lane, that you were his. That you had always been his and he turned his back on me like I'd been dismissed. I don't know what come over me, Billie Jean. Without thinkin' I reached down and picked up a piece of wood from the stack and called out to him. When he turned around, I hit him on the side of the head, and he went down like a rock and never moved again. I knew I had killed him."

This was where I suddenly saw the floor rising up to meet me. I crumpled in a heap at Ross's feet, like a rag doll discarded after play. But Ross kept on talking, no longer aware of my presences in the room, and the awful truth poured from him the way a mountain stream hurls over the precipice, unstoppable and with purpose. His soul was eager to be free of the terrible burden it harbored for so long.

"I dragged Bobby Ray over to the tree he'd just cut down and placed him under it. I then took a tree branch and wiped out my tracks and picked up the piece of wood I'd hit him with, and went to my car and went home."

Silent tears ran down my face and my throat felt so dry I thought it might close. I tried to swallow and wet my lips with my tongue, but I didn't have any spit. A hard knot formed in the middle of my chest. My mind couldn't grasp the totality of Ross's words. I then remembered something that at the time meant little. The chainsaw sat beside the stack of wood. If the tree had struck Bobby Ray when he cut it down, the saw would have been in his hand, or nearby. I knew then Ross's words were true.

When I could speak, I asked, "Why were you there, Ross, on the ridge that mornin'?"

"I made a quick trip home the day before for Daddy's birthday and left early the next mornin'. I thought I would swing by and see what y'all had done with the place, and that's when I saw Bobby Ray goin' up to the ridge with the mules and the slide. I drove on by and was already out on the highway when I turned around and went back. I really don't know why I turned around and went back." Ross paused before he said, "God, I wish I hadn't gone back," and took a deep breath. "I pulled into the old loggin' road and sat there for a good while, listenin' to the chainsaw rev up and slow down. I got out of the car and walked back to where Bobby Ray was."

Ross stopped and looked at me on the floor as though he'd just noticed me there. "I really didn't mean to kill him, Billie Jean, I swear to God I didn't." And Ross held out his hand to me pleading for me to understand. Never had I seen such torment in anyone's eyes.

After Ross finished, we sat in silence for I don't know how long, me on the floor and him on the edge of the bed. There was not a lot more to be said, but we both knew what had to be done. When I could find the strength to stand I went to the phone and called Daddy. I knew they would be in the bed, but it was either call then or early the next morning. Daddy answered on the second ring.

"Daddy."

"Billie Jean—what's wrong?"

"Oh Daddy, everythin' is wrong."

"Are you hurt, is the boys hurt?"

"Yes. No. I can't tell you over the phone, but we'll be home tomorrow and I'll explain all of it to you then."

"Where's Ross, is he there?"

"Yes."

"Did y'all have trouble—did he hurt you?"

"Oh, Daddy, I just can't tell you how much he's hurt me."

"I'll beat his ass! Put him on the phone!"

"No Daddy, it's not like that. I wish I could tell you, but I can't right now, the boys might hear. I'll tell you everythin' when we get home tomorrow, and please, try not to worry."

After I hung up I thought how pointless it was to tell Daddy not to worry. Of course he would worry. He would lie awake all night and continue to worry until we arrived and he saw that we were okay. I probably should have waited until the morning to call, but I needed to hear his voice.

Ross and I lay down on our bed side by side, but we didn't sleep, and as crazy as it may sound, it never crossed my mind that maybe I should take the boys and leave, after all Ross had told me. I never doubted for a second he wouldn't take care of me and the boys. Many thoughts and feelings swirled around inside me and my body felt cold and numb. I tried to hate Ross, but I couldn't. I kept seeing the little fair-haired boy that pulled me so many miles in his little red wagon. I couldn't accept Ross was evil, but he did an evil, evil thing, and that's what I hated. Not only had he taken Bobby Ray's earthly life, but his chance and his hope for eternal life.

Ross told me something else that night. I guess since he was clearing his conscience he wanted to make a clean sweep of it. He said he had been the one who called the law on Henry Lee and Lester. He overheard the fishing plans when bringing food to the house the day after their daddy died. He knew they didn't have any plans to haul moonshine. It was just another one of his attempts to try and discredit Bobby Ray and his family in my eyes.

My greatest fear had been that one day alcohol would take Bobby Ray away from me. Instead, it was something as simple and unobtrusive, but just as deadly; pride. Ross's pride had been hurt when I chose Bobby Ray over him. Throughout their lives they were in constant competition with one another, but Ross always felt he was the better man. I'm not saying he didn't really love me, I believe he did, but everyone faces disappointments in life. It's part of growing up, and we have to accept this and move on, but Ross couldn't let it go. He allowed envy and jealousy to dwell in his heart and to grow there and somewhere along the way, perhaps without him even realizing, it turned into hate, and that beautiful, early fall morning it consumed Ross's soul and sprang forth, robbing Bobby Ray of his life.

Before dawn we urged Robbie and Will out of their beds and still in their pajamas ushered them into the car. We placed blankets and pillows in the backseat with them so they could go back to sleep if they wanted. I threw as many clothes as I could get into our old suitcases, leaving out a set for each boy. They could change when we stopped. Neither had any idea what was going on. I told them we decided to go visit Grandpa William and Nana Dora. Will hadn't questioned this, but Robbie looked at me with suspicion in his eyes.

"What about school?" he asked.

I told him it would be okay if he missed a few days. He really gave me the eye then, staring at me in disbelief.

At times Robbie was way too smart for his own good. I often thought of him as an old spirit in a young body.

There wasn't much in the way of conversation on the long drive to Johnson's Bend. I wished I could turn my mind off as well. I kept thinking about me and Ross as children, and after we married. Night after night I lay beside this man, making love with him, making a baby with him, but had I ever really known him? I suppose the warning signs were there all along. Ross was always possessive of me even as kids and wanted to monopolize everything in my life. It seemed he felt entitled to know my whereabouts and what I was doing at all times, but what I will never be able to understand, was how Ross could look at Bobby Ray's little boys every day, the spitting images of him, knowing what he had done? And how could he look me in the face every day, knowing that we lived a lie. Mendacity is the word that comes to mind, a whole boat load of the stuff. It's funny what goes through your head when you're under great emotional duress.

The first time I heard the word mendacity I hadn't known what it meant. Bobby Ray and I were at the drive-in theater in Big Town watching a new film just released, *Cat On A Hot Tin Roof*, based on a screenplay by the great Tennessee Williams. In the movie, Brick, played by Paul Newman, said he was disgusted with all the mendacity, lies and liars that surrounded him. Little had I known that one day my entire existence would be nothing but mendacity in its purest form. Deceit and betrayal by someone I loved and trusted and thought I knew.

Somehow Ross convinced himself, if he could persuade me to marry him, and he loved and raised

Robbie and Will as his own, he could obtain redemption for his sins. He knew better. He was raised on the same gospel as I. When Grace Ellen was taken from us, I'm sure Ross did feel God was punishing him. Much as God punished King David for messing with Bathsheba and instigating the death of her husband. I think it was Ross's own guilt working on him. I can't even imagine what it must have been like to live every day waiting for the ax to fall. That's why Ross became so paranoid, afraid God was about to take away everyone and everything he loved. Deep down inside he had to know his life could never be right. Not until he openly confessed his sins before God and man, and willingly accepted his punishment.

CHAPTER 44

We arrived at Daddy's shortly after noon. He and Dora came out of the house when we drove up, likely watching for us. The boys immediately exited the car and ran to greet their grandparents. I followed, walking slowly, but Ross hung back by the car with his head down and his hands shoved into his pockets.

"Dora, could you take the boys in the house, please? I need to talk to Daddy alone for a minute," I asked.

"No, Mama, I want to stay with you," Robbie said, grabbing me around the waist.

"It's okay, baby—I'll be back in a little while. I need you and Will to stay here with Grandpa William and Nana."

"Is Ross comin' back?"

"No. No he's not, darlin'. I'll explain everythin' to you later. Right now, I need you to do what I asked. Please."

With reluctance Robbie returned to the porch. "Come on guys, I've got warm, chocolate chip cookies right out of the oven for you," Dora said, and led Robbie and Will into the house.

Daddy looked at me needing answers. Worry, concern, and the previous sleepless night were etched into his face.

"I need for you to watch the boys for a bit, Daddy. Ross and I have to go over and speak with his parents, and then we're goin' into Big Town to talk to the sheriff."

Daddy looked from me to Ross, but hesitated to ask questions. He knew I would tell him all of it in my own good time.

"I'll do whatever you need me to, darlin'. It's real bad, isn't it?"

"It's about as bad as it could ever get, Daddy."

I turned and walked back to Ross and together we crossed the road to his parents' house. My grandparents had come out onto their porch and I raised my hand in greeting but didn't stop to talk. I hated to keep everyone in the dark, but first things first. Ross wouldn't call his parents and tell them we were coming. I'm sure he wanted to postpone it for as long as he could. They were completely blindsided and my heart wept for them when Ross confessed what he had done. A look of shock and total disbelief settled on their faces. They couldn't believe their son, their golden boy, could do such a merciless thing, and to have kept it hidden for so long. I knew exactly how they felt. That it couldn't be real. It couldn't be true, but it was. There would be no winners in this game.

Ross's parents went with us into Big Town and on the way there they kept reassuring him everything would be okay. They would get him the best lawyer around and all of this could be worked out. I didn't think this would be the case but they needed some small measure of hope to hold on to.

When I returned from Big Town I told Daddy and Dora the sad truth but out of earshot of Robbie and Will. The only thing I told them was that Ross had done something very, very bad, and would have to stay in jail for now, but they could go and visit him in a few days. I then went and told my grandparents, and for the first time in my life Grandma didn't have any words of wisdom for me, and I sure could have used some.

After I left my grandparents, I returned to Daddy's and made one of the most difficult phone calls of my life. I called Cole and asked him to arrange a family meeting at his house for that evening. Without hesitation he agreed never asking why. After supper I drove to Cole's. Everyone had gathered, except Mary. I would have to call her another time and give her the grim news. I didn't beat around the bush. I came right out and told them that Bobby Ray's death hadn't been an accident, but murder, and who was responsible.

John Wesley immediately jumped up, going berserk, cursing a blue streak. He wanted to go that very minute and storm the jail and take Ross out and lynch him. Cole told him with kind authority to sit down and hush. Naturally, everyone was shocked and upset, and it brought back all the old painful memories. It was almost like losing Bobby Ray all over again. Henry Lee and Lester quickly assured me they in no way held me responsible. In many ways, I too, was a victim. Poor Ruth cried and cried and Margaret held me close and said she was glad the boys and I were safely home.

Before leaving, Cole gently placed his hands on my shoulders. "Don't you worry about nothin', darlin'," he said. "I've told you before, you'll always be a part of this family, and we take care of our own." For the first time I felt I truly understood what that meant.

Several days went by before I was allowed to bring the boys to see Ross. The jail had strict rules regarding visiting the inmates and apparently there are no exceptions. Ross was denied bail, not because he was a flight risk, he had turned himself in after all, but more for his own safety, and I agreed with the judge. I still hadn't told the boys the whole story, and maybe it was cruel of me, but I felt Ross should be the one to tell them the truth. Robbie and Will loved and trusted Ross and looked up to him as a father. They had started to call him Daddy, not just Daddy Ross, and he betrayed that love and trust.

Robbie remained quiet and sullen on the drive into Big Town, and I wondered if he had put two and two together. At the jail an officer led us into a small room with metal chairs and a metal table. One of our former classmates, Jamie Lee, had brought Ross in. He wore a bright orange jumpsuit and ankle chains and handcuffs attached to a chain around his waist. Jamie removed the cuffs and shackled Ross by the waist chain to some type of lock underneath the table.

"You can hold his hand across the table, but don't approach him," Jamie said. You could tell he wished he was anywhere but there. He wasn't the only one.

Ross looked as though he hadn't slept in days, but tried to put on a brave face for Robbie and Will. He reached across the table to take their hands, but Robbie kept his hands firmly in his lap. Ross looked at me and I shrugged. Will allowed Ross to hold his hand, and I saw Will's chin quiver.

"Boys, I did a terrible, terrible thing, and I hope someday you can find it in your hearts to forgive me—but I'll understand if you can't. But surely you know, please, please, you must know, how much I love you." This had to be very hard for Ross—I could see on his face and hear in his voice his deep remorse and regret. He knew the words he was about to say would change the way Robbie and Will looked at him for the rest of their lives.

"What did you do, Daddy?" Will asked. "When you comin' home?"

"He ain't your daddy, stupid," Robbie snapped at Will.

"Robbie! Don't call your brother stupid," I admonished, and began to think maybe this not such a good idea after all.

Ross dropped his head and his tears fell onto the metal table. He drew in a deep breath and looked across at Will. "I'm not comin' home, Will, not for a long, long time. I allowed my anger and jealousy and all that bad stuff to get the better of me. Don't ever do that. I picked up a piece of wood and struck your daddy, and he died. That was wrong of me, so very, very wrong, and now I have to pay for that."

Will sat silently in his chair and I could see the confusion on his face. He really didn't understand, but Robbie jumped up and ran from the room, and I let him go. "I'm so, so sorry, Will." Ross's voice broke and tears streamed down his face.

Will slid out of his chair and ran around the table and wrapped his arms around Ross's neck. Jamie made a move toward them but thought better of it and allowed them to embrace.

"I love you, Daddy," Will sobbed into Ross's shoulder, his little heart broken. That's when I lost it. No matter what Ross had done, Will loved him, and so did Robbie. That's why this was so hard on both of them. Ross was the only father either could remember and now they had lost him too.

I walked over to Will and gently took him by the arms. "I want you to go wait outside with your brother. I need to talk to Ross alone for a second."

Will didn't want to go but slowly released his hold on Ross. At the door he glanced back for one last look at the man he knew as Daddy.

"Are you okay?" I asked Ross, after Will was gone. "Are they treatin' you all right?" It felt so surreal, this man I had known my entire life, or at least thought I did, seemed like a total stranger to me now. I couldn't think of anything to say to him. "Do you need me to bring you anythin'?"

"No, I'm fine. Mama and Daddy brought me all I need for now."

"Well, I guess I'd better go then and check on the boys. This is so hard on them, Ross. For the second time in their young life they've had their world turned upside down." I couldn't keep the bitterness out of my voice.

"I know that, Billie Jean. I think about that every minute of every day. All I can say from the bottom of my heart is I'm sorry. I'm sorry. I'm sorry. I would give anything, even my own life, if I could go back and undo it, but I can't."

"I guess I'll see you next visitin' day." I said, and turned to go.

"No, I don't want you to come back, and don't bring the boys back either, and I'd rather you didn't come to the trial or visit me in prison. It's bad enough you've had to come here, but if you could find it in your heart, and I know I've no right to ask, could you send me some pictures of the boys, so I can watch them grow up?" I nodded, turned and left and never went back.

I found Robbie and Will standing by the car, Will was still crying. I put my arms around him and held him tight and reached for Robbie, but he pulled away, anger on his young face. Oh, my goodness, how much he looked like Bobby Ray, especially when he was upset.

"I hate him," Robbie said. "I hope they fry his ass."

"Robbie. Where in the world did you hear such a thing?" But I knew. The boys spent the afternoon before at their Uncle John Wesley's—I felt sure he said more in front of them than he should have. "You don't hate Ross, you love Ross, and he loves you. Yes, he has done a very bad and terrible thing, but we have to try and find it in our hearts to forgive him, because if we don't, we'll never really be able to move on with our lives."

"I'm never goin' to forgive him, he killed my daddy!" Robbie was unrelenting in his hurt and anger; a mixture of grief and sorrow and confusion. I could see a lot of counseling in our future. Thank heavens my friend, Sandy Vee, had a master's degree in child psychology.

"I'll forgive him, Mama," Will said hesitantly. Bless his little kind heart. He didn't and couldn't understand the magnitude of what Ross had done. Will had no memory of Bobby Ray, and this reality totally broke my heart. In Will's mind, Ross was his father.

Committing murder and trying to hide it is no new thing. It's been going on since the first family dwelt upon the earth. Cain slew his brother, Abel, in a fit of anger and resentment because Abel's offering was acceptable to God and his wasn't. And Cain sought to hide his sin from God, but the Bible says, Abel's blood cried out from the ground to the Lord. I can't help but wonder if the tree that fell into the cemetery that day was a sign. Had Bobby Ray's blood been crying out from his grave for justice? I suppose I'll never know.

Ross took so much more from me than he would ever realize. He took my happy childhood memories of spring, of our growing up together and being one another's best friend. He took away my summer, my one and only true love, Bobby Ray. And he nearly took my sanity, but Ross wasn't around in the early part of fall. He hadn't watched me struggle to get through the dark and lonely hours, through the days when the sun refused to shine and time ceased to matter from the moment I looked at Bobby Ray's lifeless face. This image was stamped into my mind and I hadn't known if I could ever get beyond that. But for a brief time in winter, Ross brought great joy into my life, Grace Ellen, and for that I will be forever grateful to him. I told the boys we must forgive Ross for our own peace of mind in order to move forward with our lives, but it wouldn't be easy. I would spend countless hours on my knees in prayer, but I would say again, "it is well, with my soul."

EPILOGUE

Ross never went to trial. After a year or more of legal wrangling, he accepted a plea deal, voluntary manslaughter. It really hadn't mattered. Nothing the criminal justice system could do to Ross would ever hurt him as much as having to face Robbie and Will. I signed the house over to Ross's parents. He hadn't wanted me to, but it was not mine to keep, and I wouldn't have felt right keeping it anyway. Maybe they can sell it and have a little left over after it was paid off. I know they have been out a bundle on Ross's legal fees. Cole and Lester came to East Tennessee in Lester's big work truck and moved my belongings home to Johnson's Bend. I left only with what I came with. Leaving Gracie behind was the hardest and I at once set about the legal process to have her brought back and Lester insisted on handling the financial part. Folks would be amazed if they knew what Lester was worth. Let's just say, between his construction business and the resort he did well for himself.

I placed Grace Ellen beside Bobby Ray. I know she's not his blood kin, but she's a part of me, so I think he would be okay with it. The war in Vietnam at last drew to an end, but racial tensions in the South continue to run high. Life goes on, and mine came full circle. I'm back where I began with my family and friends. By calendar years I'm still considered a young woman, but I thought I lived all the seasons of my life. Perhaps I'm wrong. Maybe I've only begun.

Lester moved me and the boys into a new house he'd recently completed at the resort and I went to work for him helping to manage the place. Lester and I get along well together, and I'm sure his offer of marriage still stands, but I can't see that far down the road at the present and besides, I'm still married to Ross. I haven't filed for a divorce yet, and I don't know that I would have any scriptural grounds for one. No adultery or fornication was involved, but of course, I wouldn't be married to him in the first place if he hadn't killed Bobby Ray. We are such creatures of habit, and it is only natural to be drawn to that which is familiar. Ross counted on that right down to the house he bought. He knew me well enough to know what I would like, but I will never live with him that way again. I guess we will cross that bridge when we come to it, but it'll be awhile.

They sent Ross to a prison in Georgia. He likely would have gone to Brushy Mountain here in Tennessee, but it closed down in 1972 before his sentencing. The distance makes it real hard for his parents to visit him on a regular basis. I have never been just as he asked but I do send pictures of the boys fairly often. I feel Ross's parents harbor some hard feelings toward me. They think I led Ross on when we were teenagers in high school and truthfully I do carry some guilt about this. I'm sure my former therapist would frown on that, but I do. If I could turn the clock back, I would tell everyone from the start, it was Bobby Ray, and it had always been Bobby Ray.

The boys and I are going to counseling at the church, and Robbie has begun to open up a little. If anything good can come out of any of this, it might be that Lester started to go with us to church. This happened after one Sunday morning Robbie was giving me lip over having to go and his uncle didn't. Lester hasn't missed a Sunday since, and he's teaching the boys the finer points of hunting. He had two coon dog pups waiting for them; after all hunting is in their blood. I love to listen to him explaining the differences in the sound of the dogs barking and what each one indicates.

"Most dogs run with a bawl mouth. That means their bark has a longer and more drawn out sound while they're trackin'. When they tree a coon, their bark is short and chopped."

I remember Bobby Ray trying to explain this to me. Lester is so good and patient with the boys and they hang on his every word.

There are times I look back on my marriage to Ross and it's like we were playing house, like we did as children. He would be the daddy and I the mommy and he rode off to work on his bicycle and I stayed home and rocked the baby dolls. Only pretend. I have a favorite place I like to go when I needed to be alone. It's a small rock ledge that hangs over the water. I can sit there in the early mornings, drink my coffee, watch the fish jump and the sun rise through the pines. In the evening I sit on my ledge and watch the sun go down and listen to the song of the river. I hope the Good Lord will allow me to live out my days here and to raise my boys here, teaching them not to follow after the ways of the world, but to follow after Jesus, the Truth and the Life, and to encourage them to never put off until tomorrow what they know they should do today. For we have no promise of tomorrow.

I may never know what really happened on the ridge that morning, but each of us has defining moments in our life, and the choices we make at these moments shape the rest of it. A defining moment in Ross's life came that morning, and so many choices he could have made. He could have chosen another route home. He could have chosen not to turn around. He could have chosen to stay in the car, and he could have chosen to simply walk away. I will never understand Ross's choices from that point on. Did he really think the end would justify the means? I've never believed that's possible, nor will that rationale hold water on the Day of Judgment, but that's only my opinion.

About the Author

D. R. Bucy began writing about "Her South" as a child. She is a short story author, novelist, and poet. Her genre, Southern Historical fiction and non-fiction. As a retired nurse, she feels her many years in healthcare has given her a much clearer insight into human nature and greatly helped her in her writing. *The Dark Side of Dixie* will be her debut novel and she has recently finished her second novel, *Arabella*. Ms. Bucy resides in Paris, Tennessee with her dog Ginger and her three cats, Critter, Shadow, and Callie. When she isn't writing, she enjoys spending time with her girls, grandchildren, and her many friends. You may visit her online at www.drbucy.wordpress.com.